MORE PRAISE FOR *SEXUAL HEALING*

"Jill Nelson takes on the world's oldest profession and sexual politics—not only flipping the script, but turning it inside out." — *Savoy*

"No voice could more effectively assert women's right to sexual equality than that of former *Washington Post* journalist Nelson (*Volunteer Slavery*). Her first novel, a fictional commentary on the sad state of our sexual mores and the collective frustration of half our citizens, is riotously funny."

— Jennifer Baker, *Library Journal*

"Beach reading at its finest: funny, lively and nasty enough that you'll want to keep it away from the young'uns. So scoop out a place back there in the lingerie drawer where you hide books like this and get a highlighter to mark the instructional segments for your partner."

— David Haynes, *Minneapolis Star Tribune*

"Yes, this is [Jill Nelson's] first novel, and thus she has no business stroking our mental erogenous zones with such cool confidence.... Despite all the racy scenes, *Sexual Healing* is also about the struggle to start a small business, the inner conflicts sparked by making money in the world's oldest profession and society's response to women who take charge of their sexuality."

— Tyrone Beason, *Seattle Times*

"A debut novel that is both funny and sensual....Nelson tackles the political, cultural, and sensual facets of female sexuality in an upbeat and funny tale."

— Lillian Lewis, *Booklist*

"This funny, carnal fiction debut from the author of *Volunteer Slavery* subverts traditional gender roles, challenging the notion that nice girls aren't interested in guilt-free fun. — Kelli Daley, *Book*

"Although humorous, *Sexual Healing* is biting social commentary about middle- and upper-class black America. It depicts the enmity between black men and black women, the competition, the mistrust, the recrimination, the incompatibility...a cast of Dostoevskian antagonists and sycophants...the plot is a patchwork quilt with logical design...a good read.

— Bill Maxwell, *St. Petersburg Times*

"Jill Nelson's first novel is sheer fun, a satirical tale of two best friends, successful professional women in their early 40s from Oakland, California, who decide to go into business together...Nelson's sharp portraits of an assortment of high-profile public figures is when she is at her savvy, satirical best." — Susan McHenry, *Black Issues Book Review*

"*Sexual Healing* is a wild, sexy ride, in which two inventive and hilarious sisters figure out a way to bring water into their sexual desert—and yours, too. It's a fearless look at what women want, and a fresh take on how they can get it. If you enter these pages lonely and wistful, you'll emerge refreshed and invigorated, in body, mind, and soul."
— E. Lynn Harris, *A Love of My Own* and *Any Way the Wind Blows*

"This is the novel her fans have been hoping Jill Nelson would have nerve enough to write! *Sexual Healing* is smart and sexy, funny and fabulous, jazzy and justified! Sister Jill isn't just a foot soldier in what passes for war between the sexes. She's our commander-in-chief and follow we must."
— Pearl Cleage, *What Looks Like Crazy On An Ordinary Day* and *I Wish I Had A Red Dress*

"In *Sexual Healing*, Jill Nelson brings her formidable wit to fiction. She pulls the covers off of American sex, demolishing hypocrisy and double standards with a pen wielded like a stiletto, drawing blood on every page."
— Ishmael Reed, *Another Day at the Front* and *From Totems to Hip-Hop*

"In a comic novel that is as insightful as it is irreverent, Jill Nelson takes a bold look at sexual mores and gender politics that will leave readers howling with laughter. Women have been waiting for this one!"
— Valerie Wilson Wesley, *Always True To You In My Fashion* and *Ain't Nobody's Business If I Do*

"Call it 'Black Women on the Verge of a Nervous Breakthrough.' In her stellar *Sexual Healing*, Jill Nelson shows the sexual revolution isn't over—it's just beginning."
— Farai Chideya, *Don't Believe the Hype* and *The Color of Our Future*

SEXUAL HEALING

JILL NELSON

AGATE

Agate Publishing, Inc.
Chicago

First paperback edition. Originally published in hardback in 2003 by Agate.
Copyright 2003 by Jill Nelson. All rights reserved.

Printed in Canada.

Library of Congress Cataloging-in-Publication Data

Nelson, Jill, 1952-
    Sexual healing / Jill Nelson.
        p. cm.
    ISBN 0-9724562-0-1
    1. African American business enterprises--Fiction. 2. African
American businesspeople--Fiction. 3. African American women--Fiction.
4. Male prostitutes--Fiction. I. Title.

PS3614.E4458S495 2003
813'.6—dc21

                                                2003004947

Paperback edition ISBN 0-9724562-5-2

*This novel is a work of fiction. Names, characters, incidents, and dialogue, except for
incidental references to public figures, products, or services, are imaginary and are not intended
to refer to any living persons or to disparage any company's products or services.*

Design by Al Brandtner
Cover photo by Kaz Chiba/Getty Images

Agate books are available in bulk at discount prices. Inquire via agatepublishing.com

Aishah Rahman,
Lynn Howell,
and Flores Forbes,
two queens and a king.
You each know why.

CONTRARY TO THOSE WHO THINK THAT WHAT HAPPENED WAS PART OF
a conspiracy of sexually insatiable black women bent on further dogging
the brothers, it wasn't. It also had nothing to do with confronting the system, celebrating decadence, or making a political statement. Really, all we
wanted was to find a way to give women more pleasure, without the pain it
often takes to get to it, and the way it all started was simple.

I was just sitting around catching some rays with my best friend Acey
on a Sunday afternoon. We always got together on Sundays, because just
about the time Acey got home from church and changed her clothes, I'd
have dragged myself up out of bed, thrown something on, and made myself ready to spend some time laughing and laying around with my best
friend. We were sprawled out on the deck of her house in Oakland drinking Taittinger, and—since we were alone—not having to worry about
spreading thighs or looking cute.

We're in our early 40s, still fly, and while we're not yet ready to call
ourselves middle aged, we're old enough to know it's gaining on us, although so far we've manage to keep a few yards ahead. Acey's my best
friend since forever, a semisweet chocolate-brown sister who's a perpet-
ual size six and always clean. Me, Lydia, I'm anywhere from a size eight to
a fourteen, depending on what's going on in my life and if I'm able to eat
just one bowl of Häagen-Dazs Dulce de Leche ice cream a day. What'd be
funny if it weren't so annoying is that just when you get to that age where
you start getting your head together, realizing that most of the stuff that
used to make you crazy isn't worth it, and that the really important battles
are few and far between, your body starts to turn on you. But me and Acey
were putting up a fierce resistance, which wasn't so hard since Acey owns
and runs a small spa in downtown Oakland. The massages and facials
were the easy part—the hard thing was forcing ourselves to go to the gym a
few times a week. The radio was playing softly in the background, and we
were talking in that lazy, few-words-needed, secret-code language that

old friends have, when the conversation, inevitably, came around to men.

Mostly Acey was doing the talking, giving me her post-Saturday night date debriefing. I've been in date recovery for six months, after being married to one of those men with "potential" for the ten years it took me to learn his would probably be permanently unrealized, and that if I stuck with him what was left of mine would erode. It didn't help that during the last two years we were together, both Lorenzo and sex had become as scarce as water in the Gobi Desert. I'd dated for awhile right after we separated, but soon got tired of all the work dating requires for the usually low returns. It doesn't help that I'm now in the middle of a nasty divorce suit—Lorenzo's suing *me* for alimony, if you can believe that!— and right through here a real relationship, the kind that requires work, commitment, and trust, is the farthest thing from my mind.

The truth is that when it comes to men, the only relating I'm interested in right now is sexual, and even that's not as easy to find as it used to be, what with AIDS, STDs, a plethora of closet switch-hitters, and that good old-fashioned male ego. I mean, damn, a lot has changed since I was last out there and single way back in my late twenties, but one thing that hasn't is men's need to feel they're the hunter and you're the game. Right now, I simply don't have the patience for it. So I'm on hiatus, although I do keep a friendly vibrator and an extra pack of C batteries in my bedside table.

Acey has been dating the same guy for a little over a year. Her father was a big muckety-muck in the Baptist church, and she was raised with a firm belief in God and family, if not country. (Since her dad had served in the segregated army during World War II and spent most of his time scrubbing the latrines of Caucasian soldiers, he wasn't strong on preaching patriotism.) The guy she's dating, Matthew, is a lawyer who's rich, intelligent, and profoundly self-important. Acey thinks he's distinguished looking, but to my mind he bears a distinct resemblance around the head to Homer Simpson. But she's hanging in there, hoping something will become of them, I'm not exactly sure what. Sometimes I think in the back of her mind she's praying she'll kiss him goodnight one evening and when she wakes up the next morning he won't be a middle-aged toad but will have miraculously morphed into an Afrocentric Prince Charming. Me, I'd rather have LL Cool J.

Anyway, last night Acey had planned a romantic evening with Matthew. She grilled red snapper, mashed potatoes with garlic and basil, spent an hour fixing *haricot verts* sautéed with mushrooms. She'd even stood me up for lunch in order to find a gorgeous black lace teddy at Victoria's Secret, and served raw oysters because she'd heard they were an aphrodisiac. So after dinner they went into the bedroom, where she'd lit a few pounds of mango-scented candles.

"We were kissing and that was nice, Matthew has those big pretty lips," Acey says. "I was really into it, because you know how these workaholic, successful men are, between the job and golf you're lucky to make love once a week, and my day of the week is Saturday night. Plus, ever since his triple bypass Matthew's been afraid to make love, even though his doctor told him it's not only medically safe but good for him. After a while I can feel him relax and I'm getting turned on, so I start trying to get him out of his clothes, which isn't easy, you know, he is a big man—"

"Kind of like undressing Godzilla, huh?" I interrupt with a snicker. Acey ignores me.

"I finally get his clothes off. We're lying front to front, getting that full body contact, you know that wonderful, warm, romantic feeling, still kissing, when he suddenly rolls on top of me. And I mean he's hard, but you know, not really hard-hard. It's as if he just wants to get it over with."

"Besides which, where is the foreplay? Excuse me," I say, squinching up my face and rolling my eyes. "Kissing is just not enough, there are many other uses for mouths, and this man is over fifty, he should know these things, am I right?" Acey doesn't respond but just continues her story.

"So I say, 'Honey, how about some oral loving?'" And really, I want to bust out laughing when she uses that quaint-ass phrase for what is more commonly know as head, but that's Acey. The sister can definitely be counted on to walk that walk, but most of the time she's way too ladylike to talk the talk, even with me, her best friend for more than thirty years.

"Well, Matthew gives one of those put-upon snorts like I've asked him to fix the water heater—which actually I did a week ago and he still hasn't, I'm stuck on lukewarm—and then he kinda scooches down my chest and belly and—"

"Eats that pie!" I yell.

Acey's perfectly shaped eyebrows furrow into a pained expression, then she tosses her hair. Or I should say her weave, all twelve inches of it, tosses her. Ever since we met in second grade, Acey has been hair obsessed, changing the style, length, color, even the texture, as casually, and maybe more frequently, as I change my bed linen. I used to wonder if this was because she was insecure, didn't give a damn, or had a great sense of humor. I've decided it's all the above.

"Not exactly," she continues. "Remember that show we saw on the Discovery Channel, the one about how they find truffles in France?" I guess I look blank, because Acey says, "Come on, Lyds, you remember, it was amazing. They take these enormous pigs into the forest, let them loose, and they just sense where the truffles are growing under the earth and go right to that spot . . ." Even though I want to scream, 'Forget the pigs and truffles, what about Matthew?' I don't. Instead I gently prompt, "And this story concerns Matthew in what way?" I ignore Acey when she rolls her eyes at me as if I'm an impatient child, which I sometimes am, only full grown.

"My point is that Matthew reminded me of that documentary. I mean, he slides down and snuffles and snorts around between my legs as if he's one of those truffle-hunting French porcines. Except, unlike them, he isn't finding my precious nugget of fungi! He is so far off the button, he might as well be on another continent," Acey sighs. I'm tempted to make that motion with both my hands that means speed it up, but manage to restrain myself. "So there I am, squirming around, trying to contort my pelvis in such a way that he'll accidentally hit the right spot. He's swinging his mouth back and forth so fast I'm afraid he's gonna give me razor burn with his five o'clock shadow, but he still isn't hitting it. I'm getting frustrated, so I take my hand and try and guide his head to my love spot, but he won't let me. You know how—"

"—men think when you're trying to show them how to eat you that you're trying to push them away because it's too good for you?" I interrupt sarcastically. I would toss my hair, but I've been wearing a short natural since 1985. The most loathsome position in the world to me is both hands above my head trying to extract a coiffure, so I don't have anything to throw. I don't even own a comb or brush. When my hair gets long enough to use either, I get it cut.

"Exactly," Acey nods. "I'm trying to show him, he's trying to tell me, and the next thing I know he's looking me in the face, full-lipped, panting, and fumbling around trying to stuff his semi-hard penis in. I want to scream, 'I'm not ready!' But it's too late. He's half in, half-hard, and, forgive me Lord, half-assed. Pounding away for all of two minutes like it's the greatest lay he's ever had—which it might have been—but the feeling is definitely not mutual. The next thing I know he grunts, howls, and falls on top of me. Girl, I swear, when I saw him coming, I wanted to holler, "Timber!" and run for cover. It took me hours to finally fall asleep, between being unsatisfied and his snoring . . ." Acey's voice fades away. She sounds disappointed, but me, I'm horrified at the thought of big tall Matthew crashing down on my five-foot-four homegirl, and relieved the only damage she suffered was compounded sexual frustration.

"You should cut his ass loose."

"Lyds, you're too hard," Acey says, shaking her head. "Matthew's a good man. He's hardworking, intelligent. He's not threatened by me. And the sex was good, before the bypass. He just needs a little work in the love-making department."

"A little work? Please. That's like being a little pregnant. Stories like that, my friend, are why I'm the founding and sole member of Dater's Anonymous, trying to avoid spending the next ten years dealing with too many Matthews," I say, and suck my teeth. "Plus recover from a decade of unholy matrimony with Lorenzo the Insane."

"Now, Matthew's not that bad," she says defensively.

"That's true. We've both had worse. But wouldn't it be nice to have better? I just don't have the energy to put into getting fly, going out, and not meeting anyone. Or meeting a marginal loser and hoping he'll magically turn into something. Girl, I've kissed so many toads my lips are slimy, and still no Prince Charming. Been there, done that. I'd rather stay home alone, eat cookies in my bathrobe, and break out Mr. V. if I'm desperate."

"Who?"

"My vibrator, girl." Acey manages to looks both disgusted and curious simultaneously.

"You named your vibrator?"

"Hell yeah. I gotta call someone's name when I'm coming. And better 'Mr. V' than that bullshit Lorenzo insisted on." Acey giggles.

"He was kinda strange, wasn't he? What was it he wanted you to say? Oh yeah, 'Take Daddy to the bank, take Daddy to the bank,' wasn't it?"

"Don't remind me, especially since that was the only bank that no-count Negro ever got close to on his own steam. Yuck. Ace, right through here it's me and Mr. V. I've been telling you to try it, but you're afraid you might like it."

"I'm not afraid, but I'd like a little romance, some tenderness, and I can't see how I'm gonna get that from six inches of plastic."

"Try ten."

"You are twisted, Lydia," Acey laughs and takes a sip of champagne.

"Anyway, about Matthew . . ."

"He's not all that bad, and besides, what's the alternative? I want sex, but I also want a gentle, loving man I can depend upon along with it. A relationship," Acey says wistfully. She holds up five fingers, the better to admire her nails (freshly painted in whatever the most popular shade of MAC red is at the moment) and avoid acknowledging the skeptical expression on my face, which is just as well. "Say what you will, but with a little tweaking, Matthew would be, well, not perfect, but—remember that Grace Jones song?—perfect for me."

"What Matthew needs is more like a major overhaul," I mutter, gnawing at an annoying hangnail. It's been so long since my nails have seen polish, they'd probably have an allergic reaction if I even walked too close to a salon.

"Now, you know you're exaggerating. All he needs is a little work, some TLC, a little training," Acey admonishes. Acey's spa is one of those places women go for a day of pampering: massage, wrap, facial, nails, hair, the works. She's a firm believer that anyone can be improved with the right amount of attention and money, and that if you look good, you feel good. Let's face it, beauty may only be skin deep, but most people really are superficial.

"What he needs is a training bra, and you know it," I tease. "His breasts are almost as big as yours, his hips are wider than mine, and he's got one of those big, squishy asses. If there's one thing I cannot tolerate, it's a man with a soft butt."

"It's not all that big," Acey protests, and even though we both know his ass is way wide, we also understand she has to protest. After all, Acey's been alone for almost twelve years, ever since Earl, who she married her first year in college, went sailboarding in San Francisco Bay one afternoon and never came back. Last we saw him he was skimming over the waves toward Alcatraz and waving back at us proudly. By the time they found his body two weeks later a closed casket funeral was mandatory. Acey'd used Earl's life insurance to buy this house and start the spa, and refused to date at all for seven years. I finally convinced her to start going out again with the argument that there were a few good men out there besides Earl, but they sure as hell weren't going to walk up to her door and ring the bell. Even so, she'd spent the last five years trying to recapture the past in every man she met, beginning again with where she was as opposed to where she is.

So I'm not surprised she's trying to talk herself into believing

Matthew is Him, whoever He is. You know, The One each of us is waiting for. Me, I'd been there, done that, and don't want to be there again. I'd partied hard until I was twenty-nine, then gone for the 'til-death-do-us-part bit and ended up with my soon-to-be-ex-husband Lorenzo. Fine as a he could be, but lazy and crazy as hell, too. I'm not interested in seriously hooking up again—though I would like to have fabulous, regular, safe sex with a man who doesn't hurt my eyes. But that's me, and being that Acey's my best friend, I love and support her unconditionally, even when we disagree. If she thought Matthew was a catch, well then, right on.

So I laughed and said, "Hey, sister, we both know big ain't all bad, especially not in the right places. What size is his dick?" Cutting to the chase. As I said, I'm not the patient one.

"Have I mentioned lately that you're crude?" Acey asks.

"I prefer to think of myself as direct. Now give up the goods." "Matthew's a nice size," Acey murmurs coyly. "Not that it's doing me any good." She sighs, reaches for her champagne flute, pushes the strawberry floating on top down with her finger, then takes a steady swig. I shake my head.

"Now that's a shame. And a waste," I snicker.

"I'm praying we can work it out," she says sincerely.

"Hey, if he's willing to do the work, anything's possible. But damn, he sounds so uptight since the surgery, and how long ago was that?"

"Seven long months," Acey sighs, "And that's how long it's been since I had an orgasm, too. The doctor's been telling Matthew for months it's okay to make love, it's even therapeutic, but he's afraid, I guess, since he won't talk about it, just keeps saying he doesn't feel like it. Given that, maybe I should consider myself lucky for last night's quickie. I suppose it beats a blank."

"Damn, a brother who doesn't feel like screwing? He must be terrified."

"Yeah, but I feel like I'm slowly petrifying, know what I mean?"

"Sister, you know I hear you," I say, reaching over to slap her high five.

"The truth is, we are not alone. Sisters come into the spa six days a week talking about their man troubles. I hear so many sad stories I might as well be a hairdresser—or a shrink. Sisters either don't have anything going on, or if they do, it ain't right. Their man's too busy, too brusque, or they've just been with him so long they're bored. Did I tell you about my regular who came in the other day? She's the manager of

the Ritz-Carlton in San Francisco. Told me this crazy story about her
man wanting her to dress up in raggedy clothes and pretend she was a
house slave cowering in her shack in the slave quarters and he was a
Mandingo field slave come to rape her?" We both fall back, laughing,
but it's that laughter that's funny and sad at the same time.

"We're laughing, but it's really pathetic," I say when the moment
passes. "I mean with men, it seems there's usually something missing.
The ones who are great in bed are broke; the ones who have money are either freaks, boring in bed, or too busy getting paid to take time out for
loving. The young ones are fun, great for sex, but don't have a dime or a
frame of reference. They look at you like you're Miss Jane Pittman when
you play the Temptations or Al Green—and don't even mention life before cell phones, they'll drive you straight to the retirement home. Then
if you do meet one who's easy on the eyes, has money, likes to go out, and
is good in bed, he's probably married, a player, secretly gay, or on drugs.
Anyway, to my mind they all need too much attention, take too much
time! Wouldn't it be great if we could just create our own man?" Under
the effects of the champagne I sway toward Acey, seize her upper arm, and
gaze at her intently, barely managing not to topple my chaise lounge and
spilling only a little bubbly. Acey's eyes have a glazed, faraway look; I'm
not sure if it's from thinking about Matthew or consuming nearly a bottle
of champagne, but I need her here, with me. I apply pressure to her arm.
"Wouldn't it?"

"You mean go to a store and buy bigger, better parts to replace the
ones men come with?" Acey asks. I nod. "Yeah, I guess it would," she
agrees. "Once you found a man you liked you could just improve him."

"Yep. Firmer abs, nicer buns, fuller lips, and the requisite bigger
penis."

"In Matthew's case lose twenty pounds," Acey adds.

"Make that thirty," I say, and this time Acey can't help but laugh with
me. Both fat as adolescents, we became friends by necessity when the
other kids in elementary school lumped us together as Roly and Poly.
Even though we were never sure who was which, we knew it didn't matter,
since we were both twenty pounds overweight and more often than not
thrown together by default. Last to be chosen for teams during gym, last
into the pool for swimming class because we were both so embarrassed to
wear bathing suits, last invited to the school dance, and then only because
Acey's dad forced or bribed two boys in the church choir to take us. I always suspected he did it more because he knew they were safe—he had

them so frightened of eternal damnation they wouldn't even think about laying a hand on us—than because he felt sorry for two adolescent social rejects. Together we suffered the thousand tortures of the fat preteen, and in the process discovered that we had a lot in common besides a love of food and too much adipose tissue. We read books and whispered secrets lying side by side on Acey's bed or mine, went fishing off the piers around Oakland, swam together in the YWCA pool during summer vacations, dreamed of growing up to be beautiful career women with nice husbands and happy lives.

And besides the husbands part—and the dependable sex that's supposed to come with them—both of us had pretty much realized our dreams, at least for now. The summer before we entered high school, sick and tired of being reassured by Acey's parents and my mom—my dad died when I was twelve—that it was just baby fat and would miraculously melt away like lard in a hot skillet when we got older, or that pretty is as pretty does, or that men liked women with some meat on their bones, we busted our asses and lost the weight. It didn't hurt that I suddenly shot up to my present five-eight. It was that summer, slim and suddenly desired, if not popular, that Acey later told me started her thinking about finding a career that made women look and feel good, if only for one day.

In college Acey majored in business, but me, I was too busy checking out the men and writing steamy love poems to think much about a career. Now I work as a copy editor at an advertising agency, writing catchy lines for generally unnecessary or useless products, most of which promise women they'll look or feel better but seldom live up to the sales pitch. After fifteen years, I'm bored, but not sure what to do next with the skills I have. What can you expect from someone who majored in poetry?

"I can see it now: The Male Replacement Parts Store," I continue. "Can you imagine how crowded that jammie would be? Sisters would be standing in line, shelling out big bucks to build their very own high-performance, low-maintenance bro." Acey drains her glass and reaches for a refill. Her eyes stare ahead, focused on a scene in her imagination. She looks blissfully happy. Do visions of firm buns dance in her head?

"We'd be rolling down the aisle with our shopping carts, stopping a clerk and asking, 'Can you direct me toward the penises?' 'Yes, ma'am. What are you looking for today, medium, large, or extra large? What ethnicity are you ladies looking for? Black, white, Latino, Native, Asian, or indeterminate? We have some lovely new arrivals in aisle four." Acey grasps her stomach. She's laughing so hard tears roll down her chocolate cheeks.

"Stop, you're going to make me wet my pants." She manages to choke the words out between guffaws. But I can't stop, I'm on a roll.

"Ladies! Ladies! Alert! Blue-light special in aisle seven. Firm, round, squeezable buns, two for 19.95! Thick full lips, soft and sweet as candy, complete with long agile tongues, 39.50 the pair, satisfaction guaranteed. Today only, aisle nine," I hawk, trying to make my voice sound like a carnival barker's. Acey stops laughing, wipes tears from her eyes, shakes her head.

"It'd be fun, but women would still be doing most of the work," she says, shaking herself out of the moment. "You know the men would resist accepting replacement parts, and even if they did, it'd be us who'd have to go to the store, wait on line, lug them home, install them, keep them tuned up." Acey shrugs and sighs. It sounds like she's already tired out from thinking about it. I'm whipped just listening to her.

"It'd be better if we could just go some place where the men were already equipped with the basics. By that I mean a great body, sexual stamina, nice teeth . . ."

"And a big Johnson, sister," I interject. "Because let's be real: It's the meat *and* the motion!"

"And they'd have to know how to be tender and romantic," Acey adds, ignoring my last comment.

"Fine, romantic, tender—and sexually expert. Forget building the man ourselves, it'd be too much work and they'd put up too much resistance. But what if there was a place sisters could go where there'd be all kinds of men available to fulfill their every fantasy, no questions asked? The only requirements would be they'd have to be committed and able to please women."

"Kind of a brothel for sisters. A place where you could fulfill your sexual fantasies without all the complications of a relationship," Acey says dreamily.

"We could call it a Bro-thell. A Bordello of Bloods." I laugh when I say this, and Acey laughs, too. We sit on the deck, sipping champagne, thinking lazy thoughts. I'm imagining myself in bed with a fine young blood, having hours of fabulous sex with an enthusiastic partner, then going on about my business. No emotional complications, no drama, no wondering if he'll call, no disappointments.

I sit bolt upright, spilling a little more of my champagne.

I put my glass down, reach over and lower the volume on the radio, and clutch Acey's forearm again. "Ow!" she squeals, sitting up and looking at me. Her eyes aren't glazed any more.

"Acey. This just might work." I look into her eyes and can almost hear that serious business mind of hers snap to attention. I sit up straighter and blink.

"Lyds, don't tell me you're serious?" she asks.

"As a heart attack," I chuckle. "Now, don't take that personally." She waves her hand casually, as if swatting away the whole Matthew dilemma. "Are you?" she repeats. Suddenly what had started out as a joke between two best friends on a lazy Sunday afternoon has turned into serious business.

"Bro-thell, Motel, Holiday Inn, whatever we call it, we'd get rich!" I hiss. "Can you imagine it? A place women can come, have their wildest sexual fantasies realized, have medically certified safe sex for a price? No more courtship, no risk of rejection, no games—just great sex, effortlessly. And no more of the dreaded AIDS conversation or arguments over using condoms," I add, warming to the subject. "If I hear one more man tell me, 'Baby, I know I'm clean, I haven't been fucking around,' I'm gonna go to the mountains and become a nun." Acey throws back her head and roars with laughter, as if the thought of me in a convent is about the funniest thing she's heard. I have to admit it is pretty farfetched.

"Wait, girl. My favorite is, 'It's not that I have anything against using a condom, they just don't make them big enough for me.' Have you noticed that the men running that line are usually the ones with the smallest endowment?"

"Amen to that. Now can you understand why I hang in there with Matthew?"

"Hell, yeah. Tired lines like that are why I'm on hiatus."

"A brothel for black women," Acey says thoughtfully. "We could sure use one. The situation out here is, unfortunately, pretty dry."

"Sister, it may be time to come out of the sexual desert. The drought is almost over, and we're the rainmakers." Acey laughs.

"Are you *serious*?" Acey looks at me hard. And while I'll admit I've got a buzz on, I'm not drunk and I'm definitely not just bullshitting. Even through the champagne and the heat, I know this idea's on a par with the invention of compact discs. At least.

"I don't know if it's legal or possible, but yeah, I'm serious," I say. "Think about it: How many women do we both know who are single and sexless with no prospects on the horizon? Or they're simply tired of the whole dating game, need a break from the complications, but aren't into celibacy? Sisters like us who work hard, are single, married, divorced, and maybe raising children. It'd definitely appeal to sisters without a man—and I think plenty of women with a man would go for it, too. Because even the best of relationships are work, and we'd be offering pure pleasure: plain, simple, and discreet. Fine sisters, plain sisters, plump, thin, smart, not too swift: quiet as it's kept, all kinds of women, of all ages, would love the opportunity to have fabulous, safe sex on demand. I mean, we'll be fulfilling a serious need."

Acey chuckles. "You're right, we both know more than a few married women whose husbands either aren't taking care of business or who just need a break, something new to spice things up. They'd be more than welcome as customers."

"Or women whose men have medical problems. Temporarily, of course," I add, hastily, winking at Acey, "And just need an occasional fling to take the edge off until he's back up to speed." She nods.

"You're right. We'd offer private, satisfying, safe sex at an affordable price, thoughtfully delivered. No need to prowl bars, engage in chitchat, or compete with other women."

"Exactly," I say, nodding. "Sex to order. Straight, no chaser."

"We'd advertise it as a deluxe, full-service spa, especially designed with the black woman in mind. Offer massages, herbal wraps, samba aerobics, Tae-Bo, facials, massage, hair, nails, same stuff I already do. The sex would be discreet, the most unique service we offer. That way, we take the edge off any embarrassment sisters associate with paying for sex," Acey adds. "Only our clients would know that our workout involves both losing pounds and gaining inches."

"Sisters need to get over it," I snort dismissively. "The truth is that everyone pays for sex, directly or indirectly. Men take us out to dinner, buy us nice things, and sometimes even marry us for sex. Women stroke men's egos, dumb themselves down, and fake orgasms for the same reasons, and none of that's going to change. What we're offering is a satisfying break from the rituals of male-female relations. A brief respite. I mean, let's face it, dealing with men is like being black. I don't want to not be black, but every now and then I sure could use a couple days vacation." Acey laughs.

"What we'd be selling is sex without stigma. Or a relationship. A revolutionary concept for women. The bottom line is every sister would arrive with great expectations and leave satisfied."

"Hey, if we planned this right we could even offer a money-back guarantee." I laugh when I say this, but I'm not kidding.

"Absolutely. There's one major problem, though," Acey says slowly, suddenly serious. I stop laughing. Acey's always been more methodical and careful about things than I am, the one who finds the tiny tear in the back of a great dress that's on sale before she buys it, or can tell by the way a car engine sounds if it needs just a simple tune-up or a new transmission. Me, I never see the rip until I'm dressed and about to walk out the door, and more than one car has, without my noticing the slightest warning sign, died in the middle of the road.

"Who would we get to work there?" she asks, and I let out my breath, because this time damned if the catch ain't a no-brainer. I'm so relieved I toss my natural, for what it's worth.

"Who wouldn't we? We're talking sex, not brain surgery. We'll go on scouting trips to find talent: attractive, highly sexed men who like women, are undiscriminating when it comes to fucking, know how to be seductive, and—here's the key—don't want to get emotionally involved. Face it, with that criteria, we'll have more applicants than we can handle." We laugh smugly, knowingly, thrilled by the prospect of using men's commitment-phobia, a characteristic that in the past had driven both of us damn near crazy, to our benefit.

"Mm-hm, we're talking some serious research," I giggle, reaching for my glass again. "We both know men are notorious about exaggerating their physical attributes. According to them, they're all at least six feet tall and have ten-inch penises. As founders and owners, it'd be our job to audition all applicants and make sure they are up to snuff," I giggle. "Or down to muff."

"Well, maybe that should be your area of expertise," Acey says, a bit primly. And that's my girl, able to soar right along with me for a while, but those feet always sink back into the earth.

"Excuse me, Miss Sunday-Go-To-Meeting, my bad," I laugh. "It'll be a serious sacrifice, but if I must go it alone, I shall." We sit there lightly buzzed, the smiles on our faces widening into great big grins as the idea of a brothel for women begins to become real in our minds.

"Is this legal?"

"In Nevada prostitution's legal for men, so I figure it'd have to be for women. But nobody's tried it. Plus, we'd keep it on the down low. As you said, we're starting a spa. It's nobody but our clients' business that we offer unique, in-depth services. "

"So, what's our first step? When do we start? What are we going to call the place?"

"I don't know what we're gonna call it, but we should definitely do this." I know, even if my sisters don't yet, that they are waiting for this. I'd spent my whole professional life selling women shit they didn't need; surely I could sell them something they did. "Sisters have a right to feel good too," I add, draining my glass.

We both chuckle. All at once my laughter stops and my lips turn up in the biggest smirk my face has felt since my last multiple orgasm. And just like then, I start hollering.

"That's it," I yell. "That's the name." Acey looks at me blankly.

"What? 'Sisters have a right to feel good, too?' I think we have to go for a little subtlety here," Acey suggests sarcastically.

"I was thinking 'Dr. Feelgood's,' from that Aretha song."

"Love the song, hate the name. Anyway, women twenty years younger or older than us might not get it."

"I guess you're right, we do want to appeal to horny women of all ages. Plus ReRe might not appreciate it," I laugh. We're both silent for a few moments, turning the name over in our heads. I'm visualizing a name that'll look good emblazoned on towels, condom wrappers, skimpy Speedo bathing trunks. Hey, it's all about branding.

"What about 'A Sister's Spa'?" I finally say. "It's simple, easy to remember, and to the point. It's also subtle."

"It just might work," Acey finally says as a smile slowly spreads across her face. "I like it."

"If *we* work it right, it's a sure thing, whatever we call it."

We sit silent for a few minutes, each of us spinning slightly tipsy plans for our ultimate full-service spa. The sun is almost gone and the light has turned that rosy-peach color of just before twilight, each particle of air becoming slowly distinct. In the years we have been friends we have become comfortable with each other's silences. It's a good thing we aren't running our mouths, too, because if we had been we might not have heard the DJ, one of those Barry White–sounding brothers who haunt the Quiet Storm, Kissing After Dark airwaves, murmur, "And now, for all you lovers and lonely women out there on this sultry evening, we give you Marvin Gaye and . . . 'Sexual Healing.'"

The insistent bedroom voice wraps itself around the two of us sitting in that particular air of twilight, that brief time between day and night when great plans are hatched and all things seem possible. For the first time, we know old Marvin is talking directly to us. After all those years of singing, dancing, and—let's be honest—more than a few times making love along with that song, we finally *hear* it. The wonder of it is that with our brainstorm, we've figured out a way to seize for ourselves and our sisters what Marvin has been singing about—and men have been getting—for all these years. Not love, but sexual healing.

2

I OFFER TO THROW TOGETHER A SALAD, BUT LYDIA DECLINES MY invitation and leaves to go home and get started on an advertising campaign she's scheduled to present on Friday. I suspect that even though it was true she had work to do, if I'd been offering a more appetizing and fattening meal, say fried fish, potato salad, and greens, she would have stayed for dinner.

Not that I don't love her dearly, but it was just as well she went on home. The sun and all that champagne had given me that drowsy, fogged-up feeling, but my brain was spilling over with thoughts and I wanted to clear my head with a hot cup of ginseng tea so I could think. As it was, my musings were a confused jumble of exhilaration about the idea of starting another (truly *full service*) spa, concern about Matthew, and memories of my dead Earl. Sunday nights are a difficult time for me. It's as if after the hopeful optimism of church and an afternoon spent with my wild best friend, the evening is empty. Earl and I used to cook a big Sunday dinner together, eat early, and spend the rest of the evening in bed, but I don't sleep all that well and bed's a place I mostly go when I'm falling out. But I'm a neatness freak—Lydia always calls me compulsive—and couldn't give myself permission to relax until I'd put the deck back in order. I wander around in the almost darkness, picking up glasses and brushing away crumbs, laughing when I step in a puddle of flat bubbly beside Lydia's chair, evidence of her animated gesticulating. I rinse out the few plates and glasses in the sink, not wanting to bother with the dishwasher. Lydia teases me that I'm country because I seldom use my dishwasher and refuse to hire a cleaning woman. Call me country, but the truth is I don't mind cleaning, and I get a lot of good thinking done when my hands are deep in soapy water or swinging a dust rag.

Ready for a long shower, I force myself to throw a salad together to eat later—not that I am looking forward to it any more than Lydia had been, but when you run a spa you're your own best advertising. Trying to build some enthusiasm for dinner, I walk into the pantry to see if I can find a jar of artichoke hearts marinated in Italian spices and oil, and walk smack into Earl.

He just stands there, leaning against one of the wide, open shelves that reach all the way to the ceiling that I've covered in midnight blue contact paper etched with silver stars. His deep brown elbow rests on an upper shelf, wedged between a bottle of ketchup and a jar of green olives. Six foot three, with broad shoulders, a slender waist, and uniform, sparkling white teeth; I almost gasp at the sight of him, pretty as ever. He has that dark skin that seems to absorb and refract light, almost creating an aura around him. He just stands there grinning at me, his brown eyes flecked with dancing gray, giving me that same look I'd first seen at the Black Student Union on campus more than twenty years ago, a look that says, "Woman, you do look delicious, and I intend to get myself a taste."

I'm so shocked to see him I don't even notice one of his hands is behind his back until he thrusts it toward me, extending the jar of artichokes, and asks, "Looking for these, baby darlin'?" which is what he always called me. In the moment before I reach for that jar, I realize that even though I'm shocked to see Earl, I'm not really surprised to find him standing in front of me in the pantry. He'd always been there to help me get something that I thought was out of my reach, even if it was just marinated artichokes. That was just the kind of man Earl was: helpful however I needed helping. It didn't matter whether it was passing trigonometry, finding pleasure in bed, or changing the oil in my car. Even Lydia the cynic had nothing but good things to say about Earl; it didn't hurt that because I loved her he did too, helped her out as willingly as he did me, never asking for anything in return.

Long before that day he went sailboarding, we used to lie in bed and dream about our future once he got out of dental school and I graduated from college. We thought we'd have four or six children and buy an old Victorian fixer-upper somewhere, one with lots of bay windows, great big old-fashioned claw-foot tubs, and a walk-in pantry. We both agreed that there was just something about a pantry, a whole room with shelves floor to ceiling filled with food, that made a house a home. But we never got past our little starter apartment with faux wood cabinets in the kitchen, and the first thing I did once I could get out of bed after Earl went away was to take his insurance money and buy this house. Before I even hung curtains, took the books out of boxes, or got a telephone, I found my neighbor Mr. Byrd, a retired master carpenter, and hired him to turn the enormous first-floor closet into the pantry of our dreams, a place I could fill with food and memories.

"Earl. I knew you'd come back," I say as he hands me the artichokes. His fingers, brushing past mine, feel chilly and I wonder if he's still wet from the cold waters of the Bay.

"Had to, baby darlin'," he says, grinning. "Wanted to see how you were doing."

"Honey, there's so much to tell. It's been so hard . . ."

Earl nods, his laughing eyes sad. "I know, I know, and I'm sorry I haven't been here to help out."

"Don't apologize, honey, the important thing is that you're here now. Come on into the kitchen, let me make you some herb tea and cinnamon toast with brown sugar, the way you like it, and we can talk." I'm already half turned around and headed toward the teapot and the stove, regretting I hadn't had my weave touched up Saturday instead of going to the office and doing the books. I smooth the back of my shorts with my other hand as I walk and pray Earl still finds me attractive.

"I'm not hungry, baby. Let's just talk right here."

"In the pantry?" I turn around and look into Earl's face. He grins.

"It's a lovely pantry, just like the one we talked about. You even got the light that goes on automatically when you step inside," he says. I laugh.

"Remember you used to tease me about not being able to see what I was reaching for after I seasoned the rice pudding with salt back in our first apartment? We vowed that when we got a house we'd have a pantry where you wouldn't even have to remember to turn on the light."

"And so you have. I'm gonna stand right here and enjoy it."

"But aren't you tired? You always were tired at the end of the day, just wanted to sit down in a comfortable chair and relax. Remember you used to say that the only energy you had was for eating and love-making, preferably at the same time." I can feel my face flush when I say this, from the words but more from the memory of Earl's gentle, insistent love-making, the way his hands and mouth could make me feel weightless and as heavy as the ocean at the same time. I can almost feel his hand sliding along my hip and it doesn't matter where he's standing, what I need to do is touch him, now. I walk back toward the pantry and reach for him, already feeling his smooth, always warmer than normal flesh beneath my hand.

"Don't!" Earl says, moving away.

"Don't? Earl, it's been so long! I need you."

"I know you do, baby darlin', but not like that. It's different now. I'm not what I used to be."

"What does that mean?" My mind is racing madly now, trying to overcome my joy over Earl's reappearance and figure out what he's talking about and how he could possibly be right here again, standing big as life in my pantry. My husband who I haven't laid eyes on in twelve years still looks like the twenty-eight-year-old almost-dentist who jumped on a sailboard and gallantly blew me a kiss goodbye. When I look into his eyes they've gone big and soft; I can see the same old crazy love we always had spilling out of them onto me. Then he clears his throat and says, "I'm still who I was, just not *what* I was."

"Which means?"

"That I'm no longer of this world—although sometimes, for a few seconds or minutes or hours, I can slip through and get in it. Like now. But most of the time I can't. I've passed." I stare at him incredulously. My eyes hurt from strain, as if I've been reading for hours in dim light without my glasses. I glance around the kitchen, doing a fast reality check. Microwave, refrigerator plastered with photographs, juicer, empty champagne bottles in the recycling basket, it's all here. Instead of being reassured, suddenly I'm more frightened.

"Passed what?"

"Passed *on*, baby darlin'. Remember, I died."

"Then in God's name, what the hell are you doing here?" I say angrily, without thinking. Because ever since he'd surprised me standing in the pantry I'd been trying to convince myself that all the years of being alone and missing Earl and trying to find him in someone else were the bad dream, and now that Earl is home I can finally wake up. Earl laughs.

"Started cursing since I been gone, huh?" Earl teases gently. "Your pompous daddy wouldn't approve. In addition to which, daughter of a preacher man, there is no hell as we think we know it, just somewhere else. Besides which, are you suggesting that if there were a hell that's where I'd be, hard as I tried to be a good man and husband?" His tone is playful, but I'm instantly embarrassed.

"Forgive me, Lord. And Earl, I didn't mean, it's just I'm so shocked, here you are but you're not here, really. How'd you get back, and what took you so long?"

"I don't really know. I was in that somewhere else place and without warning I could hear you and Lydia talking, clear as if I was sitting on that deck with you. Usually it's impossible to see or hear anything at all. Some of us spend eternity obsessed, futilely trying to make contact. No one ever has, at least not on purpose. I'd accepted early on that my time here, with you, sweet as it was, was over, that I was in a different place. Then, bam! I could see you and Lydia clearly, hear you as if I was sitting right there with you, soaking up that late winter sun. Woman, I could even smell you, and as always, you smelled good. I listened to y'all talking about this guy you're seeing, Michael—"

"Matthew," I correct. Earl shrugs.

"I laughed until I cried when Lydia was talking about the replacement parts store. I'd forgotten how funny she is," he says wistfully. "Or how sexy you are. The more I listened the more I kept thinking, 'My baby darlin' needs me to help her with this afraid-to-make-love man she's seeing, not to mention her new business venture."

"We were just kidding around about that," I interrupt, mortified that the love of my life heard me talking about sleeping with another man and plotting to open a . . . a whorehouse for women! "You know how Lydia is, wild and likes to talk stuff. We were just fooling." Earl makes a stroking motion in the air with his hand and I swear I can feel his hand along the length of my arm, cool but soothing.

"That's too bad. It sounded like a great idea from where I sit," he says. "You've got the business acumen, Lydia's got the vision, and sisters have the need. Even you, if I heard correctly?" His voice is light but full of challenge, as if he's daring me to either lie to his face or tell the truth. Either way, Earl always could get me to be honest with myself.

"I guess so, but—"

"But what, baby? I heard you talking, remember? I know Lydia's the one with the sharp tongue, but I could swear I heard you in her amen corner. Or was it those crossed wires?" Earl raises his eyebrows and smiles, staring into my eyes. I can glimpse his bright pink tongue between his parted lips, and just like that I feel myself begin to get wet.

"Earl, we were just talking, having fun. Lord knows, you're the only man I want."

"But the truth is, baby darlin', I'm the one man you can't have," Earl says softly. "And you deserve to have some sexual healing, isn't that what y'all called it?" He grins. "I can say with some authority that the Lord knows that while you're on this earth, you deserve to enjoy all of its fruits. It's all right with her."

"Her?" Earl waves his hand in the air dismissively, laughs.

"Just trying to be politically correct. Her. Him. It. They. You. The Lord is all those things and more."

I put my hand on my hip, glare into his eyes. "Are you saying the Lord wants us to fornicate? The Bible says . . ." Earl interrupts me.

"The Bible is a work in progress, as is the Talmud, the Koran, all the holy books. Unfortunately, the Lord is not alone in having some bad editors. That's the publishing business."

I lean one shoulder against the doorway of the pantry for support. I stand in my kitchen listening to my fine, long-dead husband's discourse on the Lord's will, way, and abuse by the publishing industry, and feel as if the ground below me has disappeared and I'm floating away. Is this how Earl felt that day when his sailboard swept him out to sea?

"Okay, you're right. I have needs. But I still feel as if I'm betraying you, being with someone else."

"Acey, darling, the only way you could ever betray me is by not making the most of your time on earth, because that would be betraying yourself. You know this. Remember the first time we made love, back when we were in college? You laid down on the bed, opened your legs, and shut your eyes like it was a sacrifice." I can feel myself begin to blush at the memory. "Remember? I stroked your arms, thighs, breasts, stomach, your face. Put my tongue in your ears, sucked your nipples, teased your navel. I'll never forget how you yelped in surprise when I slowly licked your vagina, or how you opened and got so wet when I licked and sucked your clitoris." Earl chuckles smugly. "As I recall, by morning you were wide open and calling for more, and my penis never left my pants." Listening to him with closed eyes I can feel my nipples harden, stomach clench, a thin sheen of wetness pooling in my panties.

"Oh, Earl," I hear myself moaning.

"I love you. I want what's best for you. Even if I can't give it to you myself," he says ruefully.

"So what should I do?"

"What you truly and honestly desire. What gives you pleasure and brings no pain."

"Is that possible?" Earl laughs so hard the china canisters of tea, coffee, and sugar lined up along the Mexican tile counter tremble. He may not be of this world any longer, but he can still rock it.

"Acey, have you forgotten what we had?" He asks when he finally stops laughing. I smile, nod no.

"Earl . . . are you going to be here in my pantry forever, now?"

"Who knows? According to the stories I've heard, we never know when this kind of contact will come or go."

"I need you." I can't keep the pleading out of my voice when I say this, don't even try.

"No, you don't need me. Not anymore. You just think you do," Earl whispers. "Baby darlin', I am always with you."

"Why are you whispering?"

"I'm not. I mean, I don't mean to. I think I'm going back," Earl's voice is so faint I have to lean forward to hear him. His image ripples slightly in front of my eyes, as if he is made of water and a pebble has been thrown into his center. He is fading fast.

"Honey, wait! I need you," I wail.

"What you need is to sit down with Lydia and figure out a business plan and strategy," he says faintly, his voice warping.

"Earl, do you really mean that?" I can hardly see him anymore. "Will you still love me if I do?" I can still hear his laughter, the kind that wraps around you like a thick comforter, even from halfway to somewhere else.

"Of course I will, baby. Forever. But I'm not there to take care of business. Life's too short not to get what you want and need, take it from me. And be sure to take all that money y'all are going to make to the bank," he adds. I think I can still hear him laughing, but maybe it's the cranky hum and sighs of my old refrigerator. Then he's gone and I'm alone, still leaning against the pantry door, feeling freaked, happy, and sexually roused, a jar of marinated artichokes from the highest shelf clutched in my fist, and not a footstool in sight.

3

I CLOSED MY EYES WHEN I FELT HIS TONGUE LEAVE MY NIPPLE AND begin sliding down my stomach, then squeezed them shut in anticipation when it acknowledged my navel with a quick flick and continued downward. I could feel his hot breath on my pubic hairs, sense his moist mouth hovering. Trying not to buck like a bronco, I shifted my hips slightly upward toward his lips and opened my thighs slightly, the better to eat me with, my dear. Then, having done all that I could, I held my breath, silently counting in my head, "Three, two, one . . . contact!" Hoping, just like the boys at NASA, for a perfect lift-off and not another aborted launch.

And honey, it was a good day at command central, this was a man who could take me where I wanted to go. With a few strategic swipes of his tongue he parted the hairs of my pussy, gently pushed back the hood around my clit and started nibbling, increasing and decreasing pressure, throwing in a little circular tongue action, but keeping the basic beat intact. He couldn't have been at it more than three minutes when I felt myself starting to climax. Right then I had to open my eyes, because there is nothing better than reaching orgasm while watching a fine man make love to you. And there he was, head between my legs, Denzel Washington, one of the finest brothers on the planet, and I was come, come, COOOOMMMMIIIING . . .

And then not only did the phone ring, but the alarm clock went off simultaneously, and I was wide awake, Denzel was gone, the radio was blasting the bad news of the day, someone was calling me at 6:30 in the morning, and my orgasm, just out of reach, was shrinking as fast as a piece of fatty bacon in a cast iron skillet. It is Friday morning and, not for the first time, I greet the day with a major attitude.

"Yeah?" I mutter into the phone. "Who dares call me so early?" This was purely a rhetorical question, since the only person I know who telephones me this early is my mother, oh she of the endless insomnia.

"Is anything the matter, Ma?" On the other end of the phone, I hear my mother take in so much air she sounds like a vacuum cleaner.

"Of course nothing's wrong honey, it's just I've been up for hours thinking. You know I don't really sleep much anymore. I had talk radio on, that's what I listen to all night long, and there was a sociologist or maybe she was a psychiatrist or a pathologist on. Anyway, whoever she was she sounded intelligent. She was talking about how a divorced black woman over thirty-five has a greater chance of being sentenced to life in prison for low-level drug dealing—and that can happen with these mandatory minimum sentences—and entering into a long-term lesbian marriage with her cellmate than getting remarried. So that got me to thinking that maybe you and Lorenzo might still be able to work things out. You know a good man is hard to find. That reminds me, the other morning I heard that creep Dick Dixmoor. Anyway, he was on one of those right-wing shows saying much of the crime committed is a result of displaced sexual tension."

I lie there staring at the Robert Colescott painting opposite my bed, the phone on the pillow next to my ear, as my mother continues her rant. I can't help thinking that if displaced sexual tension is a precipitating factor for homicide, I would have tried to kill her via the telephone for waking me up and scaring Denzel off before I reached my climax. But to be honest, in the last year I've had so much displaced sexual tension that if Dixmoor's theory were true, I'd have firmly established myself as America's first black female serial killer. It is some comfort that judging from what I hear from other sisters, I wouldn't be alone.

"Mom, haven't you always said Dixmoor and his ilk were responsible for Daddy having to work so hard and dropping dead of a heart attack when he was fifty? Didn't Daddy always used to say that a man who made his living off death couldn't have anything worthwhile to say about life? So why are you listening to that creep now, especially first thing in the morning?" My father, a longshoreman and head of his union local, was brave, outspoken, and politically astute, a fighting man in the best sense. I'd gotten my mouth from him, although the purposes for which I used it weren't nearly as righteous.

"Lydia are you listening? I know it's early but you should have been up. The world is going on without you. Why, I've already had my breakfast, walked three miles, and vacuumed the living room, or at least thought about it. Anyway, Lorenzo called last night and told me you won't take his calls. He says he's changed and wants another chance . . ." Since a lifetime has taught me that there is no point waiting for my mother to pause and take a breath, I simply interrupt.

"Mom. It's great to talk to you, but did you have a reason for calling? I need to get ready for work. Which is more than I can say for some people I know." My mother, a seventy-five-year-old former librarian, has been semiretired for years, so she knows I'm referring to her.

"Lorenzo. I told you he called last night and told me he had several important meetings set up. Things look good, his luck's changing and—"

"Mom! Hello! I was married to Lorenzo for ten years, during which time he barely worked twelve months. I'm not interested in his luck anymore. As far as I'm concerned it's too little, too late."

"Don't you think you're being a little harsh? Lorenzo's a good-looking man, he just had some bad luck."

"Mom. Lorenzo is suing me for alimony, do you understand? He wants me to pay to get away from him, even though he left me and I supported him while we were married." My ears are standing up, there's a throaty growl in my voice, and I can feel the beginnings of drool forming in the corners of my mouth, but there's nothing I can do about it. Lorenzo always brings out the dog in me.

"Lydia, the man's a creative soul searching for his muse. Did you know most millionaires don't make it until they're past forty? I just read a book by that Tropicana orange juice guy. He was a late bloomer, too." Sure it's early, but citing Reginald Lewis as justification for a loser like Lorenzo? Mom isn't up to her usual standards; maybe she's gone back on decaf. The truth is that Lorenzo was too self-involved, vain, and lazy to be successful at anything.

"A lot of good that does his soon-to-be ex-wife, huh, Mom?" I can't help snapping. Finally, she stops talking and gives a long sigh laden with concern, disapproval, and affection. It is the way many of our conversations end.

"All right, I've got to go weed before the sun gets too high. But think about what I told you about the likelihood of your ever getting married again before you rush into a divorce. Has it occurred to you that maybe one of the reasons you're so snippety is you're suffering from that displaced sexual tension Dixmoor was talking about?"

"Bye, Ma. Love you. Thanks for calling." I manage to actually place the receiver in the cradle, as opposed to slamming it down. Last time I'd done that my mother hadn't even noticed, and I'd ended up breaking my Panasonic cordless in half. I lie in bed on my Porthault sheets thinking that it isn't even seven o'clock yet and I'm sexually frustrated, pissed off, socially paranoid, and on my way to either committing homicide or enduring decades of celibacy.

The Bose radio beside the bed, permanently tuned to one of those news stations that endlessly loops the same bad information, tells me in ten minutes all I need to know. Today's temperature will be 41 degrees, unseasonably cold for San Francisco in early March, but welcome to global warming. The stock market had fallen 320 points the previous day, unemployment was up to 6.5 percent, and among black males it remained steady at 39 percent. The president was calling for an invasion of Iraq, ostensibly to make the world safe from terrorists, but more likely to distract attention from the failing economy and corporate corruption. Richard "Dick" Dixmoor, the conservative favorite my mother had quoted earlier, was supporting the invasion. Little wonder, since he manufactured weapons. Still, he had the nerve to try to spin his greed, suggesting that, "A war with Iraq would be good a way to get some of these black superpredators off the streets and into meaningful work." For balance, the news juxtaposed the mellifluous tones of the Reverend T. Terry Tiger, head preacher in charge and leader of the Black Baptist Brotherhood and Boulé, declaring that "Black men need a gig, not a MiG. Not a grenade to lob, but a job. Not a war, but a car."

The Black Baptist Brotherhood and Boulé, of which Acey's deceased father had been a staunch member, was once the largest organization of colored Christians in America, although over the past decade its membership had been shrinking steadily. Still, as its head, T. Terry is automatically a leader of the Negro people, although I'm not quite sure where he could be leading us. At sixty-seven, he is still a good-looking man, especially if you like them tall, dark, and with a full head of salt and pepper hair, which I do. Besides being a black preacher, it doesn't hurt that in his youth he'd been active in the civil rights movement, both prerequisites (along with a penis) for Negro leadership. Even though he was a chauvinist, a sexist, and a religious zealot who I wouldn't follow around any corner, I liked listening to T. Terry's weird cadences and marveled at his ability to rhyme damn near anything. I had cynical visions of him lying in bed at night muttering, "Now what rhymes with lob? Fob. Cob. Mob. Bob. Got it, job!" as he prepared for the next day's inevitable sound bite.

I lie in bed listening to Dixmoor ranting and T. Terry rhyming, thinking about Denzel, Lorenzo, and my mother's dire warning that it is my fate to spend the rest of my years unmarried. Frankly, although there's a lot to be said for the companionship and support of a good husband—but since Lorenzo was my only husband, this is pure theory, since I have no experience of the above—it isn't being husbandless that scares me. I'm terrified of spending my golden years—or any other years for that matter—sexless. The more I think about my rather tipsy conversation with Acey last Sunday, the better the idea seems. I lie in bed dreaming and scheming until the telephone rings again. I snatch that sucker out of the cradle and before she can take one of those signature long breaths, I snap, "Mother. I don't have time for this now. I'll be late to work. Can't we talk about Lorenzo later?" I am rewarded by a loud guffaw, then Acey's voice says, "Not unless that man is the last topic on earth, and even then, I think I'll pass, just end my days in silence." Good friend that she is, she just shushes me when I try to explain the context for my bitchy phone etiquette, and says, "Girl, I'm just calling to see what's up. And to ask you if we were drunk or serious about that idea we came up with last Sunday."

"Some of both. This proves once again that great minds think alike. I've been thinking about it, too."

"Good. And have I got something unbelievable to tell you!" I snuggle under my comforter, ready for a good story. I could use something juicy after my mother's "you're female, forty, and doomed" wake-up call.

"Tell it."

"Not now. I can't talk about it over the phone," Acey whispers.

"What is it, Matthew rose from the dead and he's lying there trying to sleep it off?" I tease.

"You're half right, but I'll explain everything when I see you. Can you meet me at Loehmann's later? I'm looking for something to wear when the National Bar Association comes to town. Matthew's giving a big-deal speech and wants me to go to the dinner with him."

"Today's my big presentation. Can it wait until tomorrow?"

"Okay. Around 4:00?"

"Perfect. See you there."

I hang up the phone and fly out of bed and into the shower, determined as I am to disprove single-handedly the truth in the expression Colored Peoples Time by always being not merely punctual, but early. I wrap myself in a thick terry cloth robe and step into what would have been the maid's room if Joyce Elaine, my housekeeper, lived in, but which I've converted into a luxurious walk-in closet. One wall is floor-to-ceiling shelves for sweaters, gym clothes, socks, and stockings. Another has three levels for hanging clothes—one for blouses, one for skirts, and another for slacks—and a revolving sixty-pair shoe rack. The third is for dresses, jackets, and coats, and the fourth wall is a fold-out mirror, so I can see all the angles. The whole thing is coordinated not only by garment but by color and size, from eight to fourteen. The way I see it, whatever size I am, I still deserve to look good—and anyway, what's the point of punishing myself for gaining a few pounds by wearing a skirt whose waistband spends the afternoon slowly and painfully eating through my flesh, not to mention leaving the impression of a button in my side? Even though I'm short on time, I can't resist spending a few moments standing in the middle of the closet, inhaling the scent of the cedar shelves and surveying the most orderly room in my apartment. I finally snap out of it and appraise the size twelves, choosing an Ann Taylor suit the color of a blood orange with a skirt so short and jacket so long you couldn't help wonder what, if anything, I have on underneath it. I call it my "making the big presentation to the client" outfit. I throw on a lacy taupe bra and matching panties, stockings, some eyeliner, shadow, and lip gloss, and slip into the perfect-fitting suit. As for my hair, all it takes is smoothing in some gel my stylist Dekar sold me that not only makes my afro shiny, but spreads tiny flecks of sparkly stuff throughout. I shove my feet into a pair of Joan and David pumps, burn my mouth gulping a cup of coffee, and forget to flick off the radio, which as I close the front door tells me that the temperature, instead of rising like it's supposed to, has fallen two degrees. Talk about bad omens.

I'm a copywriter, the person whose catchy (or annoying) phrases, if I've done my job right, you can't get out of your mind when you go shopping. I work for the fourth largest ad agency in the city, mostly on products designed for women: household cleansers, beauty aids, and lots of, as we euphemistically call them, feminine hygiene products. Generally speaking, it's my job to convince women that they're missing out on something crucial if they don't have what I'm selling. For years I loved doing this work, loved the good money I made doing it (filling that closet wasn't cheap), and loved working my way up in the city's ad scene. For the past few years, though, it's slowly been losing its appeal. My aggravation with Lorenzo, and my turning forty, certainly hasn't helped.

After a while it gets tired spending all day devising a reasonably subtle script to suggest that a woman will be unhappy if she doesn't use product X, Y, or Z, and following it up with a scenario demonstrating how much happier she'll be if she does. By now it's all pretty much a formula, most times: a woman's payoff for using a product is supposed to be true love, which of course is one of the few things money can't buy. I'm the one who created the image of the woman who washed her hair with Flounce shampoo and then flounced away with her new man to a Caribbean island; of the sister who boldly insists on paying for a romantic dinner with her new Empowered Woman credit card—as if picking up a tab spells real power, in the world or in a relationship; of the multicultural group of grown women rolling around in the grass for no apparent reason, legs spread, knowing they're "fresh" because they used Ripe and Ready feminine hygiene deodorant; of the mom-type standing at a sink of suds holding up a shiny plate and smiling smugly, knowing that her husband can safely eat off china that's "clean enough for the space shuttle," as if anyone knows how clean that is.

When I first started working in advertising, it was sort of a game to come up with words and images that would have women rushing to stores to buy something I'd convinced them they couldn't live without. But it's getting old. Or I am. I've begun to suspect that men and women aren't really so different after all. That underneath all the wining, dining, bikini-clad Caribbean vacations, deodorized vaginas, fluffy hair, Range Rovers, and gulped-down Diet Pepsis, women need good sex just as much as they need love. And that's something they *should* be able to buy.

I wheel my Saab into the garage under the office tower where I work at 8:01, with enough time to enjoy my latte before the presentation at nine. "Where's the fire, Mario Andretti?" Mr. Carter, the older black man who supervises the garage, teases as I screech to a halt. As he always does, he opens my door before I have a chance to, ushering me out with a sweep of his hand and a mischievous smile. I swing my legs out sideways; my skirt's too tight and short to do anything else. Mr. Carter watches me, but not like some elderly lecher, more like a concerned friend. Then he smiles approvingly. "Presentation day, huh?" he asks. I nod, hand him the keys. "Good luck, although I'm sure you won't need it."

"Some days I'm not so sure about that, Mr. Carter," I say, shaking my head.

"Well, that's good, girl. It's people who never think they need any help who gets into trouble."

"I'm definitely not one of them."

"Like I said, if you need something, you just give me a holler, Miss Beaucoup," he says.

"Thanks much," I call over my shoulder, rushing toward the bank of elevators and remembering with a pang in my stomach that my daddy used to tell me to "give him a holler" if I needed help.

I use the ride to the twenty-second floor offices of BTH, short for Believe the Hype, the firm I work for, to tug at the migrating waistband of my pantyhose. Blessedly, it's silent when the elevator doors open, and I slip into my office without having to engage in one of those early morning knife-fights disguised as friendly chit-chat with a colleague, especially Randolph Blagdon. Clutching my briefcase in one hand and the large latte in the other, I push the door to my office closed with my hip and lean against it. Opposite me, through the floor-to-ceiling window behind my desk, the city of San Francisco spreads out like a postcard, the bridge and the Bay sparkling around its edges, everything twinkling in the morning sunlight. I throw my briefcase on the leather sofa, sink into the matching chair, and sip my coffee, silently gearing up. I look at the framed Jonathan Greene prints on one wall, the Varnette Honeywood painting on another, the teeny-tiny but original Romare Bearden etching on my antique oak desk, slip off my heels, and feel the plush gray wool carpeting under my feet. I pick up the remote from the glass coffee table, press a button, and Missy Elliott's funky voice fills the room. I let my head fall back against cool leather and grin, feeling good and knowing that I've got it going on; for the moment, my increasing dissatisfaction with my work is temporarily overwhelmed by the perks. It would have been perfection to stay right there, but then a voice says, "Miss Beaucoup! Are you all right?" I open my eyes and Mi Lan, my assistant, looms over me, a worried expression on her face.

"Of course," I smile. "I was just trying to relax before the meeting."

"Oh. Sorry. I thought maybe something was wrong," she says.

"No, everything's all right. What are you doing here so early anyway?"

She looks embarrassed. "I know it sounds silly, but I couldn't sleep last night worrying about the account presentation today, the one for Craig's Cellulite Compactor, remember?"

"How can I forget, much as I'd like to." Craig's is one of our biggest clients, a manufacturer of dozens of products that are supposed to help women defy ugliness, age, and the ravages of real life. The latest of these, Cellulite Compactor, is a cream that promises to shrink cellulite until it disappears. The truth is that the only thing I can tell it does for the $48.95 it costs for a four-ounce jar is raise a stink like hard-boiled Easter eggs months after the resurrection.

I've been working on Craig's accounts for years. For their products,

BTH has developed a signature style of rhyming tag lines paired with gorgeous images depicting the products' supposed benefits. This one has me stumped. But it's D-Day, BTH's last chance to come up with a winning campaign to show to Ricky Craig himself, the kind of combustible petty tyrant who so often ends up running his own business, before he begins talking to other agencies. Rumor has it that he already has. "I was up most of the night too, to no avail. Did you come up with any brilliant ideas, Mi Lan? I could sure use one."

"Nope, but I'd love to hear yours."

"I hope Ricky Craig feel the same way," I say, rolling my eyes and reaching for my briefcase. I pull out a sheaf of papers and Mi Lan hovers eagerly above me. "Sit down and pretend to relax, you're making me nervous," I say, then clear my throat. "Okay. Picture two women walking on a gorgeous beach, maybe twins. Both slim, attractive, wearing bikinis, maybe thongs if we can get past the censors. Nice boobs, long hair, small waists, long legs, they're beautiful, right? Except one of them has thighs that look like the beach at Normandy after the invasion. The cellulite is so pronounced it's formed craters. The copy beneath the photo reads, 'Don't be a beach detractor, use Craig's Cellulite Compactor.'" I try to infuse my voice with enthusiasm, but I've never been good at faking it. Mi Lan's face looks blank.

"Interesting," she says, nodding, using one of the most meaningless, can't-stand-alone words in the English language. "What else have you got?"

"Picture a woman in a dressing room, surrounded by her girlfriends. She's wearing a wedding dress, her hands are above her head, and she's lowering her veil onto her hair. She looks blissfully happy. The copy reads, "For the moment that must be right, use Craig's Cellulite." Mi Lan looks puzzled.

"But that make's it sound as if we're selling cellulite, as opposed to a way to get rid of it."

"I know, I know. Why don't you try coming up with a word that rhymes with compactor," I snarl, wishing for a moment I knew T. Terry's number. If anyone could come up with a rhyme, he could. This has already been a long day, and it ain't even nine o'clock. Mi Lan, one of those gracious people who prefers to think of bitchiness as creative tension, cheerfully ignores me.

"What's next?"

"You mean last. It's curtain call at a hit play. Four women in can-can outfits, you know, the ones slit up the front to show a lot of leg, are taking a bow. There's a girl in every color, all different sizes. They're all gorgeous and have long, smooth, shapely legs. The audience is all men, and they're throwing flowers onto the stage and applauding. Underneath the picture are the words, 'You'll be the starring actor when you use Craig's Cellulite Compactor.' What do you think?" I ask, even though I can tell by her expression she's not impressed, nor is she planning to rush out and buy Craig's Cellulite Compactor. But why should she? She's twenty-three and a size four, damn her.

"I like the last one best," Mi Lan says diplomatically, glancing at her watch. "It's almost nine, you should start heading for the conference room, Miss Beaucoup." Do I hear relief in her voice?

I stuff papers into a folder, check my makeup, and head down the hallway to the conference room, trying to psyche myself up to sell! sell! sell! as I walk. The three white guys sitting around the oval conference table rise and smile with varying degrees of sincerity when I enter the room. My boss, Jason Hype, impeccable as ever, greets me in a warm voice, but I can tell by his slightly raised right eyebrow that he's nervous; he knows this project's been a tough one. Beside him, his deputy Randolph Blagdon, one of those early-bird-who-catches-the-worm types, purrs snidely, "Ah. Miss Beaucoup, at last," implying that I'm late, which I am not, and grinning smugly.

"Lydia!" Ricky Craig bounds from his seat, rushes around the table and hugs me as if I'm his long-lost best friend, which I am also not. What I am is the senior account executive whose campaigns have helped him make millions of dollars. Come to think of it, that might be the same thing as everlasting friendship in his world.

"What have you got for me? I cannot wait to see what you have in your bag of tricks," Craig says greedily as I settle myself in a chair. He rubs his hands together as if he's about to devour a fabulous gourmet meal, then runs one of them through the sparse hair on his head, in the process disturbing the comb-over and fully exposing his bald skull. At the same time, the index finger of his other hand unconsciously homes in on a nostril. This man is such a slob, I'd long ago convinced him I'm incapable of eating and thinking at the same time, so I wouldn't have to do lunch.

"Well, Mr. Craig, this was a tough one, primarily because of the product name—which, as you remember, you insisted could not be changed," I begin. He juts out his lower lip and nods, his imitation of thoughtfulness. "I've come up with a few ideas I think will work, but I still believe if we changed the name from 'Compactor' to 'Crème' or 'Gel,' we'd have more options."

"Forget it,' Craig barks, shaking his comb-over. "I like the sound of 'Craig's Cellulite Compactor,' it's got a nice ring to it. My wife came up with it, says it's poetic, alienation or some crap." Craig's wife, I know, has just returned to college at age fifty-six.

"Alliteration," Blagdon says pompously. Craig waves his hand in a gesture of dismissal.

"Like I told her, whatever, as long as it sells. Now, how're we gonna sell this baby, Lydia?"

I take a deep breath and explain my strategy, to make women feel not just beautiful but also unique if they use the product. Then I lay out my three campaigns, and with each one the silence grows more absolute. I'm either a genius or these are not happy campers.

"These suck," Craig breaks the silence with his usual diplomacy.

"Pardon me?"

"SUCK," he bellows, moving his mouth like an enormous guppy at feeding time. I stare at him blankly. "THESE." He points at the papers lying in front of me, mouth still contorting noisily. "You get it now? THESE SUCK."

I guess I'm not his long-lost best friend any more.

I sit there, my mind racing after some kind of appropriate response. Even though Jason Hype's face is expressionless, I know he's pissed, and trying to figure out a way to salvage the meeting. Beside him, Randolph looks downright smug. If he could do it without focusing negative attention on himself, I'm sure he'd turn toward me, stick out his tongue, and go nah-nah nah nah-nah.

"Ricky, it's not that bad," Jason offers in his best silky, soothing manner. "There're some good pieces here, and with a little reworking I'm sure Lydia could come up with . . ."

"More crap," Craig says as his chubby hands push his chair away from the table. He's breathing so hard the hairs in his nose flap below his nostrils like curtains in a breeze. "Here I've got a great fucking product, one every woman over forty with flabby thighs, marbled hips, and a goddamned fat wrinkled ass is gonna run to plunk down $48.95 to buy, and you idiots, with all the money I'm paying you, can't figure out a decent ad campaign. This isn't rocket science, folks! This shit just about sells itself."

"Shit," I say calmly, "is very difficult to sell."

"What?" Craig's head snaps up.

"What Lydia means is that writing copy is an art, not a science, one that may seem simple to lay people, but in fact . . ." Jason starts to say, but Craig interrupts him, turns to glare at me.

"Can it, Hype. Would you care to repeat that?"

"Shit is very difficult to sell."

"Are you calling Craig's Cellulite Compactor shit?"

"Ricky, Ricky. Of course she's not," Jason tries to placate, looks desperately at me. "That's not what you meant, is it, Lydia?" He gives me a look that's both plea and threat, telepathically communicating how important Craig's account is to the firm and my paycheck is to me, and it almost works.

But then, right as I'm formulating a phrase that'll turn the whole conversation into a joke, allow us to retreat and regroup, and allow Craig to save face after his blowup, Randolph says, "But Jason, Lydia's a woman who always says what she means. Haven't you always said that's one of the qualities that makes her such a valuable asset to the firm?" The nasty little backstabber is right. I can't sell my soul to Craig or the company store.

"Ricky, I hate to be blunt, but Craig's Cellulite Compactor is shit. S.H.I.T. It's got a smell like rotten boiled eggs and doesn't remove cellulite, in fact, it gave me a rash on my thighs and made the skin on my fingertips peel. You've made some good products, but this is not one of them. You're asking me to sell something that not only doesn't do what it's supposed to—which isn't too much of a problem, since most beauty products don't—but actually does harm, and stinks to high heaven." Jason's face is an expressionless mask composed, I know, to hide his emotions. He's too much of a veteran to show it, but I can sense a muted sob coming from his direction. Beside him, Randolph grins happily, Caesar watching a fallen gladiator about to be devoured by the lions. As for Craig, his eyes are red, narrow slits. I can actually see beads of sweat pop out on his forehead, and think to myself, now he's really about to blow.

"You know what's shit? Your campaign! If you knew what you were doing, and had gotten this job on merit instead of affirmative action," he sputters, his swollen, coated tongue tripping over itself, "if you were selling sweatshirts or sneakers to your homeys in the 'hood, that'd be a piece of cake! But give you a legitimate account and you don't know what the fuck to do with it! There's nothing wrong with my product. What's shit is that you got no ideas." Gone are all the years I spent working on campaigns to promote all the rest of his products.

I hiss back, "No? How about this one, Ricky: 'If you want skin like a

raptor, use Craig's Cellulite Compactor.' Or, 'For thighs red as a trac-
tor, just smooth on Craig's Compactor.' Too complex? How about a picture of the jar with the words, 'Wanna look like shit, just use it.' We could
even have an arrow aiming at the package, just to make sure no one missed
the point."

"How dare you?" Craig spits out.

"Don't like any of those?" I ask sweetly. "Relax, the good news is that
I've saved the best for last. Here's my very fave idea, a jingle, I know how
you do love jingles, Ricky: 'If you think you've got the blues/Craig's Cellulite Compactor's the thing to use/Accentuate your blues with an ugly
red rash/Be really depressed and out $48.95, cash.'"

I lean back in my chair and laugh so hard tears of mixed mirth,
rage, and sheer self-destructive grief roll down my cheeks. When I finally get it together and look up, Randolph has his arm around Ricky
Craig's shoulder and is ushering him out of the room, all the time whispering in his ear, the little Rasputin. Jason Hype sits across from me
looking like a once-impeccable designer dishtowel that's had to clean up
one mess too many.

"Lydia, I . . ." he begins, but I know he has no idea what to say, and
who can blame him? He's just watched one of his heretofore top employees lose it with a major account. This is a man I like and respect, who gave
me a shot; I owe him some explanation.

"Jason, I'm sorry, but it really is an awful product and . . ."

"Since when did that matter to us? We're an advertising agency," he
says, his tone soft and stern, as if he's talking to a precocious child following a particularly nasty tantrum. "Our job is to sell the client's product,
not judge it. Am I right?"

"I don't know."

"You don't know?"

"I used to know, but I don't anymore," I say, shrugging. "Jason, I
don't believe in the product . . ."

"Believe? Forget believe. If you want believe, go to church. This is
business, and we're not representing the Pope."

"I know. But it's hard to get behind a product I don't have any
faith in."

"Leave the faith to Billy Graham, T. Terry Tiger, or one of those
other professional Christians. We're selling Ricky Craig's cosmetics here,
not salvation." I nod, because he's right, but I just can't get with it at the
moment.

"I guess I'm tired, burnt out. I need a rest, a break, some . . ."

"Time off," Jason says crisply. "Take a few months off. That'll give you time to think about what you want to do." I breathe.

"And for BTH to think about what we want to do with you."

And just like that . . . Suddenly everything unfolding gets crisper, sharper. I can't believe what he just said, after all my years here. But what the fuck? It can't be worse than staying here, and I need a break.

"*With* pay?"

Jason looks startled, then stares at me thoughtfully. "Fine. With pay," he murmurs.

"Is a few still three?"

"Three? Fine," he says impatiently.

"What about Craig's Cellulite Compactor?" Jason looks alarmed. Maybe he thinks I have another jingle up my sleeve, but he can relax, I'm all jingled out.

"Don't worry about that. *If* I can smooth things over with Ricky, I'll give the account to Randolph. He's really in touch with the female consumer, got a real bead on what women want." Yeah, right, a traitorous, lecherous little devil—I think not. But what do I care? I'm free and paid for three months, plenty of time to work on exploring the idea Acey and I hatched on her deck. I'm already plotting how fast I can pack up my desk, make arrangements with human resources, and get the hell out of here.

"If we lose the account, so be it." Jason says, trying to sound nonchalant. "What's important is that you get some rest, and the help you need." He's speaking in that modulated monotone white people use to decline giving coins to a threatening-looking beggar or avoid having their windows soaped by a squeegee man. That, "Oh Lord, don't let the black person go crazy on my ass, if I can just keep her calm until the light changes I'm safe," voice.

Even though I understand where he's coming from, I'm more than a little offended by his suggestion that I need "help." I may be burnt out from all these years selling bullshit I don't believe in, but I'm not nuts. Still, if letting him think I'm a crazy, about-to-go-off colored girl is what it takes to get three months paid leave, so be it.

"Jason, thanks for your generosity. And understanding. I'll keep in touch." I stand, shake Jason's hand, exit the boardroom. Three months paid leave! More than enough time to convince Acey our plan is a winner and get the spa up and running. If I didn't know Jason Hype well enough to know he was watching my retreat, I'd kick up my heels.

4

"SO, WHAT'S THE UNBELIEVABLE THING YOU HAVE TO TELL ME?"

"Looking for something specific or just looking?" Acey asks, ignoring my question as we walk through the door of Loehmann's and join the line of a dozen women in front of the coat check room. You know you are in serious shopper's world when there's a coat check at a clothing warehouse. Inside, a wizened little lady with hair tinted the color of champagne struggles valiantly to hang coats that are taller than she is. No one complains, gets impatient, or walks away. Like Acey and me, the women who come to Loehmann's are deeply committed shoppers. Jews, Gentiles, Muslims, black, white, red, and yellow, we are united by our lust for shopping, our obsession with finding the ultimate bargain. Not only do we check our coats, we leave pocketbooks, scarves, and gloves secure in the trunks of our cars, and stuff our cash and credit cards in our pockets. We do not want our hands or shoulders encumbered by extraneous paraphernalia. A football field of clothing possibilities hangs on enormous racks before us: suits, pants, skirts, sweaters, dresses. There is even a section the size of a tennis court called "The Back Room," repository of higher-priced designer wear—Calvin, Donna, Eileen, Tahari, Ralph, Gianni, Giorgio—at discount prices. Forget about rapper's delight, this is shopper's delight. So many outfits, so little time. Every woman in the coat check line has the same breathless, vaguely frantic expression, as if we are horses at the gate waiting for the race to begin. We are, all of us, driven by the same fantasy; all that differs is the name of the specific designer. Mine is that I will find the perfect little Donna Karan dress; that it will fit perfectly even though it is tagged an eight and I actually (this month) wear a twelve; that there will be no buttons missing or rents in the fabric; and that it will be priced at $29.95. Such a find is what we road warriors of shopping dream of. If not, you go home exhausted, disgusted, and empty handed, unless you're a pudgy matron in her early sixties with either bleached blonde or rinsed blue hair looking for sequined sweat suits to wear on a cruise. These are the women who are always lucky at Loehmann's.

"Just looking," I answer Acey as I shrug out of my Perry Ellis coat and hand it to the frail attendant, who stumbles under its weight. "But I'll know it when I see it. Now, what's the news?"

"Let's start with dresses." Acey and I squeeze our way through racks stuffed with clothes until we get to the dresses, positioning ourselves on either side of the metal rack. We flip our way through the dresses rapidly, able to tell with a momentary glance at the neckline and shoulders if a color, fabric, pattern should be given more attention than just the finger flipping through the hangers. When something catches our fancy we stop, lean back for perspective, and use the flat of a hand to push the hanger on the rack severely to the right, thereby revealing the dress in its entirety. We work our way through hundreds of garments in minutes as around us dozens of women do the same. The only sounds are the screeching of plastic hangers against metal racks, an occasional squeal of triumph as someone finds her fantasy garment, and the familiar and pleasant sound of The Doobie Brothers singing "What a Fool Believes," piped in for the shoppers' pleasure.

"Okay, enough of the torture. What's the 411?"

"It's about Earl," Acey says, and pauses, forefinger suspended just above a hanger holding a hideous yellow and blue plaid number. Do my eyes deceive me, or is that really lace around the collar? It is seriously ugly. I know homegirl cannot be thinking about that dress.

"Yeah, what about Earl? Keep moving." I look down at the dress and roll my eyes. Acey follows my glance, shrugs.

"I wasn't thinking about that hideous dress," she says, grabbing my arm across the rack and pulling me almost on top of her. "It's Earl. I saw him last night."

"You mean you had a dream about him, right? So what's new?"

"No, not a dream. I saw him, I swear, I *talked* to him, right there in the pantry."

"Okay, if you say so."

"Lyds, I was not dreaming. It was Earl."

"So where's he been all these years—what'd he, have amnesia or some shit?" I chuckle, trying to lighten the mood, afraid Acey's traumatic episode with Matthew has knocked her back into mourning. Immediately after Earl died she refused to believe he was dead. She'd resurrected every B-movie scenario she could remember to explain Earl's disappearance and allow for him to miraculously reappear. He'd bumped his head and lost his memory, run away to die alone of a fatal disease, been kidnapped by the KKK—although I'd diplomatically told her if that were the case, he was definitely never coming back. It's taken a lot of years, but I thought she'd finally accepted Earl was gone and wasn't coming back. Matthew, tired as he was, was a step in the right direction, a man who was live and, if not exactly kicking, at least breathing. I turn to Acey and look her full in the face. "Ace, I agree Earl was a wonderful man, but you've got to let him go, get on with your life. That's what he'd want you to do. You have to accept the fact that Earl's . . ."

"DEAD!" Acey yells in my ear so loud it hurts. "I know he's dead, I'm not crazy," she snaps, "But he is back. I saw him right there in the pantry last night, talked to him. He hasn't aged either, Lyds, still as pretty a man as he always was." Her eyes are sparkling. I curse Matthew for his ineptitude, convinced that's what's pushed her over the edge, and wonder if I should suggest a few visits to Dr. Dolores Norris, Afrocentric feminist shrink, for a reality check.

"Don't you want to know what he said?" she hisses.

"Uh, sure. But let's keep moving."

"He said he thought the spa was a good idea, said he thought I should go for my heart's desire, and he thinks it'll work." She laughs and shakes her head.

"Really?" Well, at least Acey didn't bring Earl back from the dead as a member of the Moral Majority, preaching about the wages of sin and hell and damnation. Her dad, the right Reverend Esmont Allen, had done enough of that to last a lifetime, and then some, and apparently is still mindfucking her from the grave.

"Yep. Earl always was a surprising man," she says fondly.

"Is he still in the pantry?" I can't keep the skepticism out of my voice, hard as I try.

"No. He had to go, but he'll be back, I think."

"Call me. I'd love to say hello. But until then, I'm on a mission. Can we do some shopping?"

"Lydia, I know you think I'm crazy, but I'm not. It's okay if you don't want to talk about Earl coming back, but as God is my witness he did," Acey sighs. "Now, didn't you tell me you were supposed to hook up this weekend with that copywriter guy you met at the job?"

"You mean the kinda-sorta cute one with the teeth in need of dental work and nice buns?" I stop, looking at a blood red spandex Infiniti dress with long sleeves and an asymmetrical neckline, trying to visualize myself wearing it. The trouble is, I'm holding in my stomach and short on oxygen even in the vision. I move on.

"Yeah, him. He sounded like he had potential," Acey says.

"Potential," I sneer. "That word is the curse of all women. Shit, my first car had potential—remember that '72 Volkswagen I bought with a hundred thousand miles on it, so much rust it looked like it was painted in camouflage, and a hole in the floor underneath the clutch? And that was twenty years ago. I'm tired of men with potential. Can't I just once meet a goddamn man who's *there*? Is that asking too much?" I'm talking fast and going through dresses just as rapidly. When I look up, Acey is no longer directly across from me but a few feet back, trying to pretend we're not together. I suddenly realize my voice has risen. I'm not exactly screaming, but I'm not having a private conversation anymore, either.

"There's no need to use the Lord's name in vain," Acey admonishes. "Besides, no one's perfect," she adds, holding up a plain but classy navy blue knit sheath with gold buttons at the neck and cuffs. "What do you think about this dress for church?"

"Perfect. Can we talk about something else?" Acey looks at me hard, then shakes her head.

"He didn't call, right?"

"Tell me something I don't know."

"Maybe he got busy with work. Did you call him?" One of the many qualities I adore about Acey is that she's one of those rare people who manages to be almost perennially optimistic without being stupid, no easy feat. She's really good at giving people the benefit of the doubt, or a second chance, without being a doormat. Maybe it comes from her religious upbringing, but Acey has a genuine, tangible, everyday belief in forgiveness and transformation. Me, I am probably one of twelve black Americans who were raised by parents without religious affiliation. We only went to church when someone was getting married or buried, and said grace before eating only when company requested it. I'm still trying to figure out if I'm atheist, agnostic, or subconscious true believer.

"Yeah. I called him."

"And . . ."

"And some woman answered."

"Some woman? So what? Maybe it was his mother, sister, a friend," Acey starts in. "You know, we're in the twenty-first century. Just because a woman answers a man's phone doesn't mean he's in a relationship—" I interrupt.

"That's true."

"So, did you ask to speak to him?" Acey's talking to me in that same slow-motion tone of voice I last heard from Jason Hype.

"Yeah . . ." I know I'm drawing the exchange out, but I have a great punch line, and I want to give Little Miss Optimism enough rope to hang herself.

"And?" Acey holds both hands about chest height. Her fingers make flapping motions, sign language for come on with it.

"And I said, 'May I please speak to Kirk?' And she said, 'Bitch, don't you ever call my house again, enough is enough! How many times do I have to tell you Kirk is married, M-A-R-R-Y-E-D! Do you hear me? And another thing, loverboy's name ain't Kirk, it's plain old Ken. But get this straight, I ain't no skinny, plastic Barbie bitch. I will kick your motherfuckin' ass if you eva' call here again and one more thing, he may be cute, but the man cannot fuck, so consider yourself lucky!" Acey looks at me, her mouth open, eyes wide.

"What'd you say?" She whispers finally.

"Say? Say? Acey, what could I say? I didn't say shit. I put the receiver down as gently as I could and thanked my lucky stars I had star-69 blocked on my phone so she couldn't call back and dog me out some more."

Acey nods sympathetically. "How horrible."

"Yeah. The only saving grace was, you know that sister kicked Kirk's tight little ass big-time when he got home." We snicker and start moving down the rack again.

"That is truly pathetic." Acey shakes her head. "Clearly from what the woman said, this is a pattern with the man. One of those serial adulterers."

"And how about giving out his home phone number? Bad teeth, wannabe player, and stupid, too. He may be the only Negro in America without a beeper, a cell phone, or both. Damn."

"Women have got to do something."

"You're telling me? Acey, about the spa . . ."

"Um-hum. The spa." Acey nods. "What do you think?"

"Well, I've been thinking about it all day, and I'm with Earl. I really think we should do it."

"You're insane."

"Now, you know that's not true. Plus, it's a great idea."

"You think it's really possible?"

"Yep. And it's a fabulous idea. A sure thing, I'd say."

"Well then, why hasn't anyone done it already?"

"How the hell do I know? Why didn't anyone invent the electric light before Thomas Edison, peanut butter before George Washington Carver, Microsoft before Bill Gates? Because no one thought of it, pure and simple, or if they did, they didn't follow through. Besides, like James Brown says, it's a man's world. Do you really think men sit around thinking up ways for women to be independent of them, sexually or otherwise?" She shakes her head.

"Okay, let's say you're right. It takes time and costs money to start a business, and we don't have either one."

"We've got one of them—time. Or I do. I've got three months paid leave from Believe the Hype, starting today."

"How'd that happen?"

"It's a long, bizarre story, which I'll amuse you with later. The point is, I've got the time and together we've got the expertise . . ."

"What we don't have is money."

"We're gonna get some."

"From where?" Acey's truly skeptical.

"From whence all money comes: the bank. We're going to take out a business loan. If Donald Trump can leverage a few crappy buildings in Queens into a real estate empire in New York, surely we can borrow a few hundred thousand to open a business that's practically guaranteed to succeed."

"A few hundred thousand?" Acey raises a sculpted eyebrow, fingers one of her Coreen Simpson black cameo earrings, and looks at me as if I've lost my mind. "How many is a few? And have you ever heard of collateral?"

"$500,000 and yes, I've heard of collateral." I spit the words out in choppy little bites to let Acey know I don't appreciate her tone of voice. "Here's the deal: you own a house, I own an apartment. Combined we probably have a hundred thousand in cash. Then there's the spa. We put that and both houses up to secure the loan and pay it back when the dough starts rolling in."

"*If* it starts rolling in. If it doesn't, we'll lose everything," Acey corrects me. "I can just see myself broke, homeless, and jobless behind this mess . . ."

"Don't forget horny—not that that's anything new," I say, laughing. Acey glares at me. She is not amused. I wipe the grin off my face, reach across the rack of clothes, and grab my best friend's forearm. "Acey. Listen. I really think we can do this. Just work with me. Okay?"

"What do we tell the bank we want the money for? A whorehouse for women? I don't think so."

"A spa. We tell them we want to open a spa, a place where women can go for R&R. Secluded, good weather, that dry desert air, someplace the women can go while the men are gambling or attending some dull-ass convention. You know the drill. Meanwhile, we apply—quietly—for a license to operate a house of prostitution from the state of Nevada. Simple." I'm not sure who I'm trying to convince, Acey, myself, or both of us.

"Not to sound old fashioned, but there's a moral issue involved here, don't you think? Selling sex isn't exactly in the handbook of professional opportunities, is it?"

"No, but it should be. Isn't it the world's oldest profession?" I laugh.

"Lyds, I'm not kidding. What about thou shalt not commit adultery or covet thy neighbors wife, or husband?"

"First of all, most of our clients will probably be single, so that takes care of adultery. As for the married ones, aren't you the one who's always saying we shouldn't judge others? Nor should we deny them sexual satisfaction. And as for coveting thy neighbor's husband, that's easy—we'll only hire single men. Next objection?" Acey smiles.

"Okay, let's just say we get the money, we get the license, we resolve the moral issues. We'll need an application or questionnaire-type thing to help us find men who fit the profile we're after," she says. I can tell from her voice that she's getting into it. "It needs to be real specific, too. Looks alone are not enough."

"You're right. But we're not selling ugly, are we?"

"Lydia, be cool. Beauty is in the eye of the beholder. What we need is variety so that every woman finds a man to her liking."

"All right, once we find the men, how is it going to work? I mean the sex thing. Do we rent the brothers by fifteen-minute intervals, by the hour, by the day? Or by the orgasm? This much money for one, this much for two, what? Whose orgasms would we be counting, his or hers?" I'm laughing, but these are serious questions if we're actually trying to develop a business plan.

"Definitely not by orgasms," Acey says, frowning as she looks down at a gray herringbone coatdress, tilts her head to the side. "If our employees are doing their jobs right, there'd be no way of keeping track of how many times the sisters were coming. As for the men, even the young ones can only get it up so may times in a day. The last thing we need is guys who ejaculate, roll over, and pass out. If that's the case, what're our clients paying for?"

"Honey, have you heard of that new drug, ViriMax?" I ask.

"Yeah, I've heard of it, but I thought it wasn't on the market yet, and I don't have a brothel's worth in my medicine cabinet," Acey snaps.

"Getting it up will not be a problem."

"How you gonna work that?"

"Remember Reed, my gay friend who used to work for Otis Elevator out here before he got sick of all that up and down and moved to Rhode Island and opened a gay club? His former lover's a research chemist at Griff-Margetson Pharmaceuticals and supplies him with some little yellow pills. Sister, don't ask me what they're made of, but he tells me he puts bowls of them on the bar instead of mixed nuts and the girls stay hard for hours. You know those gay men are serious about their hard-ons. We could learn a lesson from them. I'm sure Reed will hook us up."

"Okay, so the men who work for us will have the stamina, if necessary chemically induced. They also have to be attractive to a broad spectrum of women. They have to be drug and disease free. They have to be able to make love. And . . ." I wait for Acey to add other elements to our composite man. I know she has thoughts on the subject because she's still staring at that tired gray Calvin Klein as though mesmerized, which I know couldn't be the case. Acey doesn't like the designer or the color.

"Romantic. They need to be romantic," she says.

"Romantic? Acey, we're selling sex, not relationships. Orgasm, not love and marriage. Truth, justice, and great head. The last thing we need is a bunch of studs running tired lines on sisters for a few bucks. Women can stay away if they're looking for love. Romance? No way. We're offering great sex that'll clear the sinuses. If you're looking for romance, stay the hell home!" I pause for effect. "Am I right?"

"I hear you. But get real. It's hard for most women to enjoy sex for sex's sake. We've all confused sex with love, and convinced ourselves that we don't have a right to the former without the latter. I know that's true, and so do you." As unhappy as I am with what Acey's saying, I can't argue with her. At forty, I might finally be able to distinguish, at least most of the time, between feelings of love and lust, but it hasn't always been that way. For most of my dating life the criteria I used to justifying jumping into bed with a man was to ask myself one simple question: Could I love him? Not did I, should I, or would I, but could I? That "could" gave me the broadest possible leeway. Since it's theoretically possible to love any-one, if the desire was there my answer was invariably a resounding yes. The "could" test allowed me to have sex with a wide spectrum of sexually attractive but otherwise unacceptable men. As much as I want to dismiss Acey's point and move on to more pleasant issues—say, holding auditions for prospective employees—I can't. Still, I can't keep the impatience out of my voice.

"Okay, okay, you're right. But what's your solution? Because we're not selling long-term relationships. That'd put us out of business. The truth is the sisters shouldn't be coming to hook up, either, but to relax, get laid, and have some fun. Not to feel guilty because they just had their brains fucked out by some man they didn't know, or like losers because they paid for it."

"Fine. My point is that women do not want to be *reminded* that this is strictly business."

"So what're we going to do?"

"Figure out how to blur the edges, how to create a kinder, gentler business transaction."

"We're talking window dressing here, right?" I ask.

"You got it. That should be right up your alley, oh queen of market-ing," Acey teases. I bow, acknowledging her compliment. My mind's rac-ing already, trying to come up with some ideas. Acey holds out a hand from which dangle a bunch of hangers holding dresses she'd picked up as we talked. Me, I've been so caught up in the conversation, I'm empty-handed.

"Okay, tell me which ones you like," she says, displaying the dresses one by one. "This one's for work or church: not too short, but not too long, not too bright, but not dull either." Acey holds up a purple dress of sheer wool with a boat neck and narrow belt. Nice. "And I thought about this for just kinda hanging out on weekends." She displays a short orange sheath with a zipper up the middle and what look like twelve zippers of varying sizes sprinkled across the front. What was she thinking? As far as I'm concerned all she needs is a pair of white Courreges go-go boots and she'd be ready for a role as a '60s throwback in a *Saturday Night Live* skit. "Then there's this. Something about it just grabbed my eye . . ." "This" is a purple knit jersey dress with a dropped waist and pleats. Not bad, but not good either. "Then there's this one." Acey holds out a black velour dress with long sleeves, short but not too short skirt, and a scooped neck. Very nice. "I figure I could wear this to work or church. Kind of an all-purpose garment I could dress up or down with jewelry, scarves, a jacket, you know, whatever. Just one of those little black dresses that looks different depending what you wear with it—"

"That's it!" I really can't help yelling. Acey looks startled.

"Glad you like it, Lyds, although it's not really all that—" I interrupt her.

"Not the dress. The spa! What we need are the right accessories, packaging. We both know what we're selling is great sex, plain and simple, just like we both know it's just one black dress, but what makes the dress seem different, or the sex special and romantic? The packaging! How we dress it up or down. We have to offer sisters packages! Something for everyone, with varying rates, from economy to super-deluxe. Fantasies! Complete sexual scenarios! A few hours, a night, a weekend of sexual fantasies—lascivious, romantic, acrobatic, risqué, you want it, we've got it—then it's back to home and reality, a little lighter in the pocketbook, sexually satiated, self-respect intact. The sex, like that dress, is the foundation, then we build the illusions around it. Women aren't just having sex, they're having a total encounter." I pause, breathless. "What do you think?" The grin on Acey's face is so wide I would have seen her tonsils if they hadn't been removed in seventh grade.

"Brilliant. Packages. Just like on those tours abroad. Customize your trip to fit your needs and desires."

"And wallet. After all, we want to make the spa accessible to working-class sisters, too, not just the bourgie divas. Everyone deserves the opportunity to avail themselves of some sexual healing."

"You know, if we can wrap the sex in romantic packaging, keep some of them economical so working women can come too, and make sure the men who work there know that tenderness is essential, this might actually work." She almost whispers these words, as if afraid that if she says them in her regular tone they'll blow away and escape us forever. Me, I have no such hesitation. Years in advertising have sharpened my ability to identify those few products that indeed offer women something they can use, few and far between as they are, and this is one of them. It doesn't hurt that it's something I can believe in, too.

"Hell yeah, it's gonna work! Think about it. We have a needy population, black women, and we're selling something that'll satisfy not only the need for sex, but, if they want, temporarily, the desire for romance. The only obstacle we have is how to overcome whatever stigma sisters might attach to paying for it."

"Well, weren't you just saying on Sunday how more than a few of us pay for relationships already, indirectly," says Acey. "I was thinking about it. How many women do you know who invite men to company banquets and spring for the tickets, go Dutch on dates, even give a brother a few dollars the next morning just to 'hold him over?' Several of my clients at the spa paid thousands of dollars to the same personal trainer, hoping he'd work out something other than their arms, then left in a huff and without a refund when he declined the opportunity. What about that fine specimen that sold you that life insurance policy a few months back? You know it wasn't all about having sufficient coverage, was it?" Acey may be teasing, but I give her a look to let her know I don't think it's funny.

"Actually, I did need the additional insurance," I say coldly. "In addition to which, me and Reynaldo did have a brief relationship."

"Why is it that women define a 'relationship' as sleeping with someone once? I don't care how good the sex was. It's me, Acey, you're talking to. You and Reynaldo had sex, not a relationship. Unless you've been holding out on me?"

"You're right, we had sex," I admit, laughing. "But damn, that sex was good. You remember he had the body of life; I don't think I'd ever seen a pec or an ab 'til that brother took off his shirt, and broad doesn't even begin to describe his shoulders. Let me break it down to you: those shoulders were wide enough for him to put me on them, walk around the room, and perform cunnilingus. Now *that* was a good man," I say with reverence. I guess she can tell I'm about to drift into sexual reverie and relive the highlights right there in the middle of Loehmann's, because she reaches out, puts a hand on my shoulder, squeezes hard.

"Lydia! There's a difference between a good man and good sex," she says. "And sometimes we get one without the other. Unfortunately, Matthew's a perfect example of that. The Earls of the world are few and far between. Don't forget: If the sex is good, women always want to rationalize it into a relationship." Although I'm not happy about being torn away from memories of riding high on Reynaldo's shoulders while he gave me head, I come back to the conversation.

"All right," I say bitchily, "I hear you. What's your point?"

"*Our* point is that what the spa will offer sisters is a positive, orgasmic, romantic-if-they-want-it-that-way sexual experience without trepidation or guilt. At a price they can afford. You know those sex surveys in *Cosmopolitan* and the other magazines? The ones that are always called 'How to Turn Your Man On,' or 'Are You Pleasuring Your Man?' or 'Test Your Sexual IQ?'" This was a rhetorical question. Over the years we'd taken plenty of these sex tests together. I usually "failed," revealing myself as a sexually selfish bitch primarily focused on my own satisfaction. Most of the time Acey "passed" with flying colors as a sexual giver of the highest order. Unfortunately, our grades didn't seem to have much impact on the trajectory of our relationships—more proof that test scores don't tell much about how you'll function in the real world.

"The trouble with them is that it's always about what men want. Our desires aren't even part of the equation. What we've got to do is devise a place where the emphasis is on men truly satisfying women. Then find men who can make women's fantasies reality. If we do that, we'll get paid at the same time."

"Not to mention the perks," I snigger.

Acey cuts me off. "What kind of packages are we going to offer?"

"How about The In and Out? That'll be for women who don't have much time, money, or both, the sexual equivalent of the lunch special. The In and Out'll be a half-hour massage and then an hour for a quickie with one of our studly employees. Kind of a long lunch without the food," I guffaw at my own cleverness. Acey grimaces.

"Okay. What about The Slow Jam? That'd be from Friday night to Sunday morning and include two massages, a body wrap, manicure and pedicure, a facial—"

"Hey! Where's the sex?"

"Be cool, I'm coming to that. And your choice of two different men for the weekend. What'd you think?"

"Nice, but we probably need something for sisters who want more than a quickie but less than a marathon."

"Definitely. A package where sisters spend a day and a night, get a massage, facial, a quick seaweed wrap, and of course, sex. What'll we call it?"

'The One-Night Stand?"

"Way too obvious. Remember, we're trying to be at least halfway subtle about this. Keep thinking, Miss Advertising Genius."

"Lust Weekend?" Acey doesn't even bother to respond, just arches those flawless eyebrows.

"What about Wrap and Roll? Wrap for that seaweed thingy and roll for the way that happy sister's gonna be rolling those hips." Acey grins.

"I like it. Not too obvious."

"Thanks. Now, Acey, you know we've gotta offer something 'deluxe,' like at restaurants where you can have a hamburger or a hamburger deluxe, and even though all the deluxe means is they throw in some French fries, folks are willing to pay more for it. Deluxe works, and we need a deluxe package. Say three nights and two days, your choice of as many men as you can handle, and, I don't know, something women want but usually can't get . . ." I twist the dangling earring in my ear, mentally flipping through more than two decades of sexual activity and trying to think of what I've always wanted to experience in bed and haven't.

"Two men at a time!" Acey and I say simultaneously, laughing.

"Yes, yes, yes." I say, slapping Acey's palm. "We are brilliant. What every woman wants and no self-respecting heterosexual man will give. You can't find a straight brother willing to be naked and in bed with another man, God forbid their penises might collide, and the gay ones don't want to be there with us. Girl, two men? That's about the only sexual fantasy I haven't been able to make a reality, and you know I have tried. Two men stroking, kissing, licking, and sucking while I just lie there and allow them to service me. Two hard penises at my disposal, to do with as I please? Now, that's heaven."

Acey shakes her head. "I'd be happy with just one man who was into me," she says wistfully.

"And you can have that at our spa, and more, if you want it. We're just giving women a chance to live out their fantasies for a few hours or days, then it's back to real life."

"What if the spa is better than real life?"

"That's why we're only going to offer these four packages, from The In and Out that's just a few hours of joy to, let's call it the Total Healing Deluxe, that's your choice of three men and a menage with two of them for a long weekend. We're trying to offer something for every taste and pocketbook, but when your package is up, you got to go. No rebooking on the spot, no extended stays, no attachments, but feel free to come back next week. As a matter of fact, please do."

"Come back to my house when we're done here," Acey suggests. "I'll throw together something to eat and we can sit down and start writing the employee questionnaires. Do you think they should be single answer or multiple choice?"

"You mean like: In foreplay, the first thing I do is a) kiss her neck, b) suck her nipples, c) stick it in, or d) none of the above?"

"Mmmmm . . . kissing," Acey says. "There's nothing better than being gently kissed by a man with soft full lips . . ."

"As opposed to the men who slam their chapped lips against yours, pry your mouth open with a stiff tongue, then almost suffocate you sticking it down your throat?" I ask.

"Definitely opposed to them. So, you ready to get to it?" We've worked our way through about a mile's worth of dresses to reach the end of the selection. Acey clutches the black velour, but I'm empty-handed.

"Nah. I need to find something to wear tonight," I say, looking back at the racks of dresses we've already mauled. "Now where the hell was that red spandex number?"

"Where are you going? I know you're not going any place with that Kirk—excuse me, Ken—fool."

"That's for damn sure. I'm going to dinner with Odell the UPS guy."

"Odell the who guy?"

"UPS. United Parcel Service," I explain.

"Lydia, don't be cute. You know I know what UPS stands for. This is the first I've heard of any Odell. When'd you meet him?" Acey's voice sounds a tad indignant. I sigh, acknowledging it's time for full disclosure.

"All right, let me tell you. My presentation didn't go over very well yesterday. I mean, I just lost it with Ricky Craig and his lousy Cellulite Compactor, and when the smoke cleared Jason had given me three months of paid leave, which may be a prerequisite to firing me, but once we get the spa up and running that won't matter. Anyway, walking back to my office, I was so busy scheming about our business I wasn't looking where I was going and—"

"Cut to the chase," Acey interrupts.

"I turned right toward the water cooler and the next thing I knew I crashed into someone so hard I fell down on my knees, and would have fallen on my face but some hands grabbed my arm. When I looked up it was into the face of one of the finest brothers I've seen in a while."

"And?" Acey sounds impatient.

"And he was wearing one of those weird-color brown UPS uniforms and since I was down on my knees and it's almost spring, he had

shorts on and some pretty legs. Keep your eye peeled for my dress: spandex, red, slanted neckline," I add as we retrace our steps.

"Yeah, sure," Acey responds. "The date? What about the date?"

"Anyway, I thanked him, got up, and he asked me where I was going
in such a hurry. I said to get a drink of water, and he made some joke
about how I musta recently returned from the desert and I said no, just
hot under the collar. I needed to vent, so I ended up telling him about
the meeting *and* that jiveass Kirk. Don't ask me why I was standing in the
hallway telling the UPS guy all my business, but he was so sweet and interested and—"

"The chase. Now."

"Odell Overton, that's his name, said something about how could
any man treat a fine sister like me that way, how he'd never treat any
woman like that. Acey, I don't know what came over me, but 'Prove it,'
just popped out of my mouth." My best friend actually laughs in my face.

"Just popped out? Lydia, please. Nothing's 'just popped out' of
your mouth since the last time you had the flu." I have to laugh, because
what're best friends for if not to call you on your shit?

"Okay, okay. He was great-looking, chivalrous, and obviously interested. What'd I have to lose? He's the UPS man, for god's sake. I know
where he works."

"So?" When she wants information, this woman is tenacious.

"So, I said prove it, and he said how about dinner Saturday night?
I'm meeting him at the Piranha Bar at eight," I say, glancing at my watch,
which reads 5:45. "*If* I can find something to wear." It's getting late and
I'm feeling tense, convinced that some other Loehmann's predator has
mistaken my dream garment for hers.

"What about this?" Acey says tentatively. I turn to see what she's
found, ready to compromise and consign the red dress to the lost opportunities file. What does my very best friend in the world hold out to me
on a clear plastic hanger? The red spandex. I laugh delightedly, as much
in celebration of my ace boon as the unearthed dress. How could I not
love this woman? I take it from her and hold it against the length of my
body, suck in my stomach.

"Acey, you are my girl!" I squeal. "Onward to the Piranha Bar."

"And to sexual healing," she responds as we head toward the cash
registers.

5

I WATCH LYDIA PULL OFF, SPEWING DUST AND GRAVEL AS SHE RUSHES home to get ready for her date. I feel vaguely jealous of her excitement; it's been a long time since I've felt that enthusiastic about a date. But Lydia is my girl, so I wish her well and hope she has a wonderful time. I know she'll call me as soon as it's over to give me all the details, so even if I'm not in on the action myself, at least I'll be able to live vicariously.

The fog is just beginning to roll in and the air is cool driving over the bridge back into Oakland. Underneath the lights twinkle on as people start dinner and call children in from playing in the yard. By the time I get home, it's turning into a beautiful evening. This is the time of day when I most miss having a family. A husband to greet me when I step in the door, children to clamor around me, thrusting test papers and paintings brought home from school in my face for approval, dinner for more than one to get started.

In the evenings, Earl and I used to stand hip against hip in our cramped apartment kitchen, slicing tomatoes and cucumbers for a salad, dicing mushrooms and zucchini for a stir fry and adding lot of noodles because they were cheap and filling, and we were poor students. Cooking together we'd plan our future in minute detail, picking out a house, furniture, fabrics for curtains, amicably disagreeing about whether to send our children to public or private school, weaving together a life for ourselves out of whole cloth. We'd eat our frugal dinner by candle light, our conversation skipping seamlessly between past, present, and future, then fall into bed and each others arms and continue the conversation wordlessly.

I turn into the driveway trying to remember if I have all the ingredients for pizza in hand, struggling unsuccessfully to visualize what's in the pantry. The pantry. Earl. I pull the key out of the ignition, grab my purse and Loehmann's bag, and vault up the two steps by the back door into the kitchen, banging my shin on the foot stool in the process. When I step into the pantry the light clicks on, revealing shelves of pasta, juices, and canned goods, but no Earl.

Suddenly grief mugs me, and without thinking I lay my head against one of those cool pantry shelves and sob. It doesn't matter that my mascara and eyeliner are running, or that the front of my cream silk blouse is covered with dirty tears, or that Earl's been gone for years. It feels like yesterday, and in a way it was, since that was the last time I saw, smelled, heard him. Missing Earl envelopes me like a fast rain cloud in the Caribbean, and I simply burst.

I stand there crying until the tears are almost gone and, seeing the ruined sleeve of my blouse, I come back to myself. By then the thought of cooking or eating or standing up much longer is absolutely unappealing.

I decide to take a bath in the old claw-footed iron tub I had refurbished when I bought the house. I pour some bath oil into the steaming water, fire up a stick of lavender incense, and light a mango-scented candle I'd bought for my unsatisfactory seduction of Matthew. The rattle of the water splashing into the tub is oddly comforting as the room fills with steam and the scent of mangoes and candlelight flickers against the tiled floor and walls, making the room seem to shimmer in welcome. I strip off my clothes and toss them on the rocking chair next to my king-size bed, pin my hair on top of my head with a big clip, then slip into the tub, letting myself sink down until the only part of my body not submerged is my face. Around me, the house creaks and groans softly, as is the way of old buildings; we're both settling ourselves after another day. Lying in the water, eyes closed, my body feels buoyant; I can feel the knots unfurling themselves in the warmth as relaxation floods through me. I spread my arms and open my legs so that the water can easily access those most closed places, feel warmth pass gently over and into me. Silently I repeat "Om," the universal mantra, in an effort to clear my head, with no luck. Earl's stuck in there, as big as if he were standing right here in the bathroom. The thing about really loving people is that even when they're gone they never really leave, but forever occupy that place in your mind and heart where the walls are made of love and desire.

Hard as I try, I can't get my conversation with Earl the night before to stop looping in my head. It's not just his words, though. It's his whole presence and what that made me feel. It's been a long time since I've felt the kind of love, desire, and plain need that Earl made me feel last night. It's as if he's reawakened a part of me that I thought, or convinced myself, had died with him.

I add some more hot water to the tub, grab a bar of mango-oatmeal soap, and with my loofah glove softly scrub the tight ball of tension I carry in my shoulders. I drop my head back and rotate my neck, hear the faint cracking as pockets of tension dissipate, wish for strong hands to knead the knots I seem to carry lower down and cannot reach. And then, just when I am no longer thinking about it, something I've heard Lydia say more than once pops into my head, "Life is short and you don't have forever to have a good time." What was it Earl said the other night in the pantry? "Life's too short not to get what you want and need."

I lie there in the hot, soapy water, watching my breasts bob up and down, thinking of Earl. I run the washcloth up my calf, along my thigh until it meets my vagina. My hand brushes against my hooded clitoris and a shock of yearning and arousal shoots through my body. I press the wet cloth against my hot spot, stroke it in gentle circular motions, and imagine that it's the talented tongue of Maxwell down there doing a little "sumpthin' sumpthin'." Under his serious ministrations it grows and swells, pushes itself erect past the flesh that covers it. I moan softly and slide down, feeling the warm water ease up and lap seductively against the hair at the back of my neck. I close my eyes, push upward to meet Maxwell's blessedly greedy mouth, grasp a soapy nipple, and imagine it's the mouth of that chocolate hottie Morris Chestnutt licking and sucking my tits hard enough to draw milk. Go, Morris, go!

Together Maxwell and Morris lick and suck, first gently, then, as my body opens and lubricates, harder. I can't help but bite my bottom lip as waves of sexual excitement flood through me as my vagina begins to spasm and I careen toward orgasm. But something is missing. Of course—the penis of whoever that well-hung brother in the locker room was in that football movie Lydia dragged me to, *Any Given Sunday*, and just as I identify him he's there, nude except for shoulder pads and football helmet, placing his muscular thighs on either side of my hips and sliding his fat, long dick in, in, in until I can feel it thrusting against my back. Reflexively, my body arches upward to pull these men, my own private sexual gang of three, deeper inside me as I come.

The water splashes, making little thrashing waves, my body suspended as my orgasm washes over, under, and through me. When I finally lower myself back down into the tub, and open my eyes, I'm alone. Maxwell, Morris, and the Football Brother are gone. I lie in the cooling water, satiated and slightly embarrassed by the boldness and greed of my own fantasy, confused and wondering if there's a conflict in simultaneously loving the dead Earl, being a good Christian, and wanting, really wanting, to get well fucked.

I shake my head, pull the stopper up, step out of the tub and wrap a fluffy bath sheet around me as I walk into the bedroom and toward the telephone to call Lydia, so we can continue talking about our spa idea. I'm suddenly wide awake, ideas tripping over themselves in my head. I slip on sweats and a T-shirt, grab a big pad from the table by the bed, and prop a mountain of pillows against the carved headboard. Then I climb onto the bed, cross my legs, and hit Lydia's number on speed dial. Before the phone even begins to ring I start making lists of what needs to be done to make A Sister's Spa a reality. Get money, find property, hire staff for massage, aerobics, and the more discreet services, get Lydia to come up with some catchy slogans and a logo. For the first time in years I'm on this bed neither missing Earl, wishing something about Matthew, or with my legs pulled up into a ball aching with loneliness. Even though she'd agreed, reluctantly, to join me for church tomorrow morning, I want to run my ideas by her while they're still fresh in my head. Lydia usually runs late, so I'm hoping to catch her before she leaves and tell her I personally know how much all of us can use some sexual healing.

6

I GIVE ACEY A QUICK HUG, PROMISE TO GIVE HER ALL THE DETAILS when we meet for church in the morning, and rush home to get ready to meet Odell, definitely in lingerie mode. Ronnie Isley, aka "Mr. Big," is on the stereo singing about "You're Contagious," and I'm hoping that after an evening with me, Odell agrees with him. I decide on the mono-chromatic look and slip into a red bra and panty set trimmed in pale gray lace, so sheer you can see my nipples and pubic hair through it. I pull on some Hanes super sheer thigh-high stockings with lace around the top, step into a pair of red three-inch Manolo Blahniks, and turn to check myself out in the mirror, happy with what I see. Thanks to exercise I still have a clearly defined waist and hips; genetics are to thank for the good legs. Acey and the women who work for her at her spa have a saying, "If you're over forty and not fat, you're fine," which I've taken to heart.

I spend a few minutes strutting around in front of the mirror in underwear and heels, admiring myself from various angles and sipping a glass of merlot. Occasionally, I break into a playful bump and grind, more funky than pornographic. This pre-date underwear ritual is the woman's equivalent of athletes getting psyched up in the locker room. While guys may butt helmets, pat each other on the backside, and cheer as their coach exhorts them to massacre the opposing team, women's psych-ing up, though quieter, is no less important. Come to think of it, the ob-jectives aren't that much different either: they're both about conquering and domination.

When I was a teenager and first started going out on dates, Acey would come over to my house in the late afternoon to help me choose my dress and earrings and decide how I should wear my hair. We'd speculate on what the date would bring and try to figure out if the boy "really liked me." In those days, underwear wasn't much of an issue. First, I didn't have enough money of my own to buy lingerie, so I usually wore standard mommy issue, plain and functional. Second, I wasn't interested in sexual activity that required disrobing, so most of what took place occurred fully clothed, confined to passionate rubbing through layers of fabric. Third, even after I became fully sexually active, it wasn't until I got a job and apartment and left my mother's house that I started having sex comfortably, and fully naked, for that matter. Up until then I screwed my boyfriends furtively, quickly, and truth be told, without much satisfaction. It didn't matter what type of underwear I was wearing, just that I could get it off, do the deed, and pull it back on before we were busted.

I put on an Al Green CD and flick on the ABC news, hoping to catch a weather report so I can decide whether to wear my Burberry trench or a new Jil Sander coat, and go into the bathroom for the makeup ritual. On the way there, I kick off my heels to give my feet a brief rest. Heels, whether they cost $30 or $300 a pair, are only comfortable for a few hours, and I didn't want to waste precious minutes. Cinderella should consider herself lucky she lost that slipper and had a midnight curfew. If she hadn't, those glass slippers would have eventually generated excruciating needles of pain from the tip of her toes to her eyeballs, the Prince would have been taken aback by her grimacing, and no one would have lived happily ever after.

I'm on my tippy toes in front of the mirror, surrounded by what looks like every cosmetic product MAC, Lancôme, and Clinique ever made, humming along with Al while he breaks it down about love and happiness, and keeping an ear open for the weather report. Then Peter Jennings—now he was a type to consider for the spa: older, distinguished, authoritative, and damn sexy—says sonorously, "We interrupt this program to go to breaking news from Dick Dixmoor's emergency press conference." If I weren't applying lip liner I would suck my teeth. I don't want to be late, I need that weather forecast, and I hate Dick Dixmoor. As far as I'm concerned his family's responsible for my father's death, which makes him responsible, too. Daddy died the summer I turned twelve. He was in the middle of a campaign organizing dock workers to refuse to load weapons bound for Vietnam, most of them manufactured by Dixmoor Munitions. I can still remember him coming home at night too late to read a chapter of *The Souls of Black Folk* to me before I went to sleep. Even so, he'd come into my room, kiss me goodnight, and sit on the side of the bed and stroke my hair. If I was lucky I'd wake up and find him there, smiling down on me, looking tired, worried, and happy all at the same time. Sometimes I'd convince him to tell me a story and he'd make one up on the spot. Daddy's stories were always about regular people taking

on a big fight and in the end they always won, just like I believed he would.
Then one morning I woke up and didn't smell coffee brewing or bacon
sizzling, couldn't hear the radio or Daddy's voice telling my mother what
the strategy of the day was going to be, and knew by the silence something
was wrong. When I ran downstairs only my mother, who seemed to have
shrunk overnight, was there, sitting at the kitchen table staring, and
Daddy was gone forever. They said his heart got so big it burst, but since
he'd always told me it was impossible to have too much heart, I held the
campaign against Dixmoor Munitions responsible. Rich Dixmoor died
in his sleep years later at 89 and passed the company torch on to his only
son, Dick, and I've passed my hatred of his father on to him. Over the
past twenty years, Dick Dixmoor has expanded the business into a diver-
sified conglomerate; today, the company makes most of its money in
pharmaceuticals.

From the television, I hear the voice of the correspondent whisper,
"No, Peter, none of us have a clue about the subject of this press conference. We were summoned an hour ago and told that Dixmoor had an an-
nouncement, and I quote here, of 'great national significance' to make."

"Herb, do you think he may finally announce his intention to run
for president? There's certainly been a lot of speculation about that,"
Jennings murmurs in response.

"That's not impossible—nothing is with Dixmoor," the correspondent says, "but I'd be surprised if that's today's agenda . . . Wait, Dixmoor's coming to the podium now," he says, just as my telephone rings.

"Hello?"

"It's Acey. You're not gone yet?"

"Almost. I just finished my face and I was trying to catch the weather
when they interrupted for some mess from Dick Dixmoor, goddamn
him," I growl. Acey sighs.

"Chill. I know you're ambivalent, but you still shouldn't take the
Lord's name in vain. What's that line your mom always uses?"

"Better safe than sorry," we say in unison, laugh.

"Lemme go turn this fool down. Hold on." I drop the receiver on
the bed, walk toward the television. Dick Dixmoor stands at a podium,
resplendent in a navy blue suit, red tie, and a lapel pin of the American
flag made of diamonds, rubies, and sapphires. He is balding, with a sharp
angular face, a nose like a beak, and skin the pinkish color of a newborn
mouse. He's also very short. At the edge of the podium I can see the sides

of the wooden steps he stands on to make himself appear taller. He's mid-harangue.

"All my grandson Little Dickie wanted was a custard from Dairy Queen. Instead what he saw was a man gunned down before his very eyes. This man approached my grandson and me as we were exiting the establishment, happily licking our cones. He was black, he was tall, his hair was riotous, and he was dressed in the style of those gangster rappers, the terror of so many Americans today. He was shouting something, advancing towards us, and waving his arms like a madman. Little Dickie clutched my hand and said, 'Grandpa, I'm scared. What does the bad man want?' Even though I am his grandfather, a man he looks up to, I could not answer him. All I knew was that this black superpredator was up to no good!" Dixmoor pauses dramatically, his voice defiant. I stand in front of the television, mesmerized.

"When he reached into his pocket, still yelling, still advancing toward us, I knew it was time to act. Not to save myself, but for Little Dickie, and for all America's children. So I pulled out my licensed handgun, which I have special legal dispensation to carry concealed on my person for purposes of self-defense, and shot him dead," Dixmoor says, mustering a tone of grave sobriety that's still got a note of triumph in it. I pick up the receiver, tell Acey to turn on ABC, and swing back to the television.

"Mercifully, some good citizen at Dairy Queen called the authorities. They arrived within minutes, we talked, and I will not be charged with any crime. Clearly it was a case of my trying to protect my grandson and myself. I am happy to say that today he seems to have forgotten the whole incident." Dixmoor says this proudly, as if the fact that his grandson can forget seeing a man killed before his eyes is a laudatory accomplishment. The kid, and gramps, definitely need psychiatric attention.

"But I have not forgotten! I will not forget!" Dixmoor roars. "I have called this press conference to tell America that I am sick and tired of being victimized by these black male superpredators. That I will stand for it no longer! Today, I instructed the leadership at Dixmoor International to take $100 million of my assets and create a foundation dedicated to the eradication of black superpredators through transformation or incarceration, employment or deployment. Send them to Yale or send them to jail, but by any means necessary! I hold this press conference to invite every American to offer suggestions and ideas, and submit proposals for funding that address this problem. We must all join together to stop the terror, so that no more innocent boys like my Little Dickie, who want nothing more than an ice cream cone and to be left alone, will ever again be victimized!" As he concludes, a ribbon begins to scroll along the bottom of the screen. It reads, "Join Dick Dixmoor and Stop the Superpredators! Call 1-800-HEP-BROS. Stop the madness, no more badness." Dixmoor stands proudly behind the podium as reporters begin to shout questions.

"Mr. Dixmoor, do you know the name of the assailant?"

"Is Little Dickie seeing a counselor?"

"What flavor cones were you and your grandson eating?"

"Do you always carry a gun?"

"What size grants are you planning to make?"

"Did your attacker have a criminal record?"

"Is it true he was carrying a semiautomatic weapon?"

"Have you talked with the president about your new initiative?"

"How does it feel to kill someone? Are you depressed?"

Each voice is raised a little louder, creating a cacophony of words. Then a very deep voice rises above the fray, yells, "HEP-BROS? What exactly does HEP mean?" Dixmoor grins smugly.

"Now Jacques, you know phone numbers have only seven digits, so we decided to spell 'Help' in the dialect your people use to say it. Thus HEP." He looks for another hand in the crowd.

"Sir, a follow-up," the same voice calls. "What caliber and make was your assailant's weapon?" The room goes silent as reporters wait for Dixmoor's response, pencils, cameras, and tape recorders at the ready.

"He had a knife," Dixmoor responds defensively.

"What size was the knife?"

"Not all that large, but large enough to do injury." Dixmoor's voice is downright snappish and his eyes shift back and forth in the crowd. "Next question," he demands, waving his index finger in front of him like a magic wand.

"Mr. Dixmoor, can you tell us the make of the knife?" the same voice booms. This reporter is tenacious. America's leading conservative looks vexed.

"Now, Jacques. We all know you work for a very important newspaper, but you don't want to monopolize this meeting and exclude your colleagues, do you?" Dixmoor uses the reporter's first name in that creepily cozy way politicians have, the one that makes the public feel dismally out of the loop. A soft wave of laughter sweeps through the crowd. I smile at the name. Jacques Westin of the *National Chronicle* is my favorite reporter. He's persistent, never accepts easy answers, doesn't perpetuate stereotypes, and always gets under the skin's skin of a story. The fact that he's a kinda cute, barrel-chested high-yellow brother who pumps iron doesn't hurt either.

"No, sir. I surely don't want to step on my fellow scribes' pens," Westin replies smoothly. I'd read in *Jet* that he's a native of Alabama, but wherever he's from, he has that good home training, knows how to be persistent without being rude. "I'd just like to know what make the knife was for my story. And if he had anything else in his pocket."

"Not that it matters, but it was a Boy Scout knife," Dixmoor spits out. "But a knife is a knife, and they can all cut you. He also had a small book of mostly blank pages, a few of which had unintelligible words scrawled on them. The police suspect it may well be the details of a larger conspiracy. They're trying to decipher it now, with the help of the FBI. Next question." The din of voices starts up. I pick up the receiver.

"You still there?"

"Yeah, that was a strange story, huh? Are we to believe some fool tried to mug Dick Dixmoor at the Dairy Queen?" I snort in disgust. "Sounds like bullshit to me. Everyone in America knows Dixmoor's face; it's like someone trying to mug the president. How about that foundation?"

"By any means necessary? Malcolm X must be twirling in his grave."

"I wish he'd rise up outta it. We need help."

"Don't you mean hep?" Acey giggles.

'Did you notice Dixmoor was rhyming like T. Terry?"

"Very odd."

"Yeah, he might as well have made the number 1-800-KILL-NIGGERS, but that's too many digits. I'm sure the crackers out there will get the message anyway. I'm glad that cute smartie Jacques Westin is on the case. Maybe we'll actually get the real story, eventually. So, what's up?"

"Girl, are you psyched, how does the dress look?" As Acey speaks, I pull the dress over my head, smooth it over my hips, step into my shoes, do an abbreviated pirouette, and can't help but grin.

"Fab," I laugh. "I am the bomb."

"Cool. Just don't blow up the brother," Acey cautions.

"Not until he blows me first," I retort. We snicker wickedly.

"Well, I was going to talk to you about some spa ideas," Acey says, "but I know you're probably in a rush. I'll be home. I'm just gonna chill and make notes, and I'll see you in the morning."

"You all right?"

"I'm great, but I'll tell you about that later."

"I'll see you in the morning, but if things go the way I plan, I may be a little tired," I joke, stepping into a short swing coat in sheer purple wool and giving my reflection a final confident smile in the mirror. Acey laughs.

"Have a good time. And don't do anything I wouldn't enjoy." I start to tell her I don't know of anything she wouldn't enjoy if she'd loosen up, but she'd probably be mortified, or pretend to be, and she's already hung up the phone. I rush out of the house to meet Odell, to the discordant accompaniment of Al Green asking how do you mend a broken heart while a hastily assembled gaggle of television pundits work themselves into a frenzy pontificating about violence in America.

I grab a taxi to the Piranha Bar and lean back in the seat, trying to focus my energy away from Dixmoor and onto Odell and the evening ahead. It isn't easy. Acey's always been the spiritual one, and not only because she grew up in the house of her father the reverend. Even when we were teenagers she'd had a spiritual bent. Me, I spent high school listening to Earth, Wind and Fire, Parliament/Funkadelic, and The Ohio Players, solely in pursuit of a good time. Acey was into Frankie Beverly and Maze, Najee, Phyllis Hyman, and the Coltranes, John and Alice. While I attributed my affection for an occasional joint to a simple desire to get high, feel good, and party, she insisted that drugs were a conduit to a higher spiritual plane. All that ended our junior year in high school, when we both realized that while we were taking ourselves higher, our grades were getting lower, and if we didn't buckle down and sober up we'd never get into college and escape the different, but no less oppressive, houses of our parents. What remains of those years are a wide and varied record collection, a lot of good memories, and a mantra bestowed on me for one hundred bucks by a teacher of transcendental meditation. I occasionally work that old mantra in times of stress, and this was one of them. During the fifteen-minute ride to the bar I sit back, eyes closed, palms open on my lap, and silently repeat my incantation.

The Piranha Bar is one of the city's hot spots, and from the several dozen mostly black people milling around in front dressed in their finest, cool down isn't anywhere in sight. There are women in skirts so short they make minis look matronly, heels that are either stiletto-thin or thick and clunky but invariably high, and dresses that are all a variation of your standard rubber band dress: very, very tight. The hairdos run the gamut, from dramatic upswept styles to beaded braids to long masses a la Diana Ross, in colors ranging from blonde to magenta to jet-black. Weaves and extensions definitely dominate, and there is more hair on that tiny patch of sidewalk than most sisters could actually grow in a lifetime. I see one or two women sporting close-shorn locks or cleanly shaven heads on long necks, but the dominant motif is hair, hair hair! Sleek, beautiful, in every imaginable shade, in constant motion, and tossing their manes, the women in front of the Piranha Bar resemble nothing so much as a corral of lively fillies.

If possible, the stallions are even more vain than the fillies. Brothers in casually elegant Armani and Hugo Boss, in collarless linen shirts or beautiful French cuffs, in FUBU, Phat Farm, Enyce, and the ubiquitous Tommy Hilfiger and Sean John, lounge on the street as if they own the sidewalk. They hold themselves with that casual, animal insouciance black men are masters of, simultaneously appearing both absolutely relaxed and coiled to spring. A pride of young lions on the urban Serengeti, their prey is neither antelope nor hyena but meat of another kind. The majority of the men's heads are smoothly shaven or close cropped. Their slick skulls give them a sleek, feral look. Those who aren't pushed right up to the bar's door stand beneath the narrow awning emblazoned with a painting of a seductive-looking piranha with thick, bright red lips, a row of outsize, jagged, wedge-shaped white teeth, and leering eyes.

I stand scanning the crowd for Odell and hoping that in this sea of people in their twenties and early thirties no one will come up and call me "ma'am," a term of respect that seems anything but when you've just recently hit forty. An arm slides around my waist, the warmth of another, lightly cologned body sweeps over me, and a deep voice says, "Hello, Lydia. You're here." Maybe it's wishful thinking, but I can swear I hear a touch of grateful surprise in his voice, as if it had occurred to him I might not show up, a thought that hadn't even crossed my mind. Still, just as no woman wants a wimp but most can appreciate a little begging, we all can get next to a little grateful, as long as it's coming from the right man. When we hear it, we hope it means he cares and is sincerely interested. On the flip side, it can mean he's a loser and you're just the first woman desperate or stupid enough to show up in a long, long time.

"Hi, Odell, I was looking for you," I say, turning to face him. Even though I'm not a religious woman, I have to stop myself from hollering "Thank you, Jesus!" The man is that fine. He's wearing a midnight blue jacket, chocolate pleated slacks, and a cream colored collarless linen shirt, open at the neck. His face is dark brown, smooth, hairless. The skin around his full lips is slightly darker than the rest of him, creating a natural outline that enhances their kissable shape. A small—not stingy but not ostentatious, because there's nothing worse than a man who wears more jewelry than you do—diamond stud twinkles from his right ear. Yum.

"Let's go in and have dinner," Odell says. "I hope you're hungry. I am." I nod agreeably and turn towards the door, thinking, yeah, I'm hungry, but not for anything that's served on a plate. Just like the wolf after the three little pigs, I'm ready to huff, puff, and blow your clothes off! But I don't say a word, just smile demurely, gesture toward the door, and say, "Let's hope we can get in." In the few minutes I've been here the crowd has swollen considerably.

"Sure we can. My friend works the door," he says confidently, grabs my hand and pulls me into the crowd. I'm not sure if it's simply luck, Odell's ability to be pushy in a charming way, or my advanced age, relatively speaking, but the crowd parts the same way that Red Sea made of Jell-O did for Charlton Heston in *The Ten Commandments*. Then we're inside and a beautiful young sister in a short, tailored black dress—the uniform for waitresses, while the waiters wear black slacks and tight t-shirts—is leading us to a table.

If the street outside the Piranha Bar was a circus, inside is like being part of a living organism, all pulsating to the beat of India.Arie wailing from invisible speakers, so loud I can feel my heart rate speed up, so funky my head can't help but move. The room is large, with an enormous mahogany bar at one end and circular banquets covered in red ultra-suede and piled high with an eclectic mix of pillows running along one wall. The twenty-foot-high ceiling is tin, and the room is broken by four columns. Enormous, slightly off-beat arrangements of irises, peonies, and lilies are strategically placed around the room. The bar and sitting area are on one side, and on the other, a few steps up, is the dining room. Both are packed. The young, restless, and predatory are bellied up three deep, laughing, talking, and sipping drinks from outsized martini glasses. The restaurant is nearly full, but the spacing of the tables is perfect. From the table the maitre'd leads us to we have a view of the whole room, alive with people enjoying good food, looking for a good time, digging the mating game at the bar: improvisational dinner theater at its finest.

I shrug my coat into Odell's waiting hands, stand poised for a moment before I sit down, sucking in my stomach and silently swearing to do more ab work at the gym, the better to give Odell a chance to admire my outfit. He does not disappoint.

"Wow, great dress. Red is definitely your color."

"Thanks. You look wonderful, too, even without shorts on. I like that earring." I imagine slowly running the tip of my tongue around it until a voice interrupts.

"Can I get you all something to drink?" I look up, and damned if Blair Underwood isn't our waiter, standing there in a black t-shirt and beautifully cut black linen slacks, smiling down at me like I'm a hot piece of cornbread waiting to be buttered and eaten. Well, not really Blair himself, but I'd swear it's his long-lost twin. Before I can order an apple martini, Odell says, "Tom L. Livingswell! What's up, my man?" and stands up and hugs our handsome host.

"Odell! How you doin'? I didn't see you, I was concentrating on this beautiful lady," he says, laughs, gives me a wink over Odell's shoulder.

"I'm good, man, real good. Let me introduce you to Lydia Beaucoup. Lydia, meet Tom L." I smile, extend my hand.

"Nice to meet you," I say. He takes my hand, lifts it toward his lips, and for a brief moment we stare into each other's eyes. They say you can read a man's soul through his eyes, and if that's true, this is one generous brother. His eyes are practically hollering sex, sex, sex! In any position imaginable, all night long! He kisses my hand, his lips just a touch moister than expected, but I'm not complaining.

Odell laughs and says, "Hey man, gimme my woman's hand back," and Tom L. gently places my hand on the tablecloth and says, "The pleasure's all mine. Can I get you folks a drink?"

Odell asks what kind of beers they have, opts for a Samuel Smith's Pale Ale. I give him a big gold mental star for choosing something only a discerning brother would drink. That's not to say if he'd asked for a Heineken he'd have lost points, but he wouldn't have gained any. I order an apple martini with Stoli, stirred, not shaken.

"Cool," Tom L. says, "I'll tell your waiter. Good to see you, man. Nice to meet you, Lydia. Hope I see you again," he says, emphasis on you. I watch his hard buns retreat as he saunters away, turn to Odell, and say, "Friend of yours?" Odell laughs, stretches out his long legs.

"Me and Tom L. go way back, we went to high school together. He's the one got me the job at UPS, then got bored and left to wait tables here, and now he's one of the hosts. Says he makes as much as at UPS and has a lot more fun, but he's restless. Last time we kicked it he told me he was getting bored, looking for the next challenge."

"What about you? Are you bored?" Odell shrugs, absentmindedly fingering the jewel in his ear.

"Yeah, kind of. I mean, driving a truck and delivering packages isn't exactly mentally stimulating, but the money and benefits are good. Would I do something else? Sure, if the money was better and the benefits right, I'd leave in a minute."

"Really?"

"Hell, yeah. I know I'm a young black man and supposed to be happy just to have a job and not be in prison, but hey, that's not enough. Right after high school I did four years in the Navy, but that was too rigid for me. After that, I worked whatever job I could find and went to San Francisco State, majoring in business and English lit, but got tired of being poor and left to take this gig when it fell in my lap. But my career goal isn't to work for UPS. I've been doing it for four years now, but I consider it an interim thing."

"Until what?"

"Until something better comes along." He chuckles, adds, "And I can see you like to ask questions, so before you say 'Better?' I'll tell you what I mean." I murmur a disclaimer, but the truth is I do ask a lot of questions, mostly because I'm curious and listening is the best way to get to know someone, but partly so I won't have to answer them. I remind myself that this is a date, not a product focus meeting. Odell waves my protestations aside.

"It's cool. I figure if you weren't interested, you wouldn't ask. What I mean by better isn't just about money. It's about work I look forward to doing every morning, that's challenging to me personally, and that ideally does something to improve the lot of the black man." Odell sighs. "Brothers got so many strikes against us, sometimes I wonder if we'll survive."

"Tell me about it. I was almost late watching a news conference on TV with that bastard Dick Dixmoor—"

Odell interrupts, "Yeah, I saw it, too. Why do you call him a bastard?" I look at him wide-eyed. Is this man stupid? Should I change the subject before he reveals some neo-con Negro politics and turns me off so bad that in spite of the straits I'm in I can't stomach seducing him? I take a breath and decide not to tell him about Daddy, that'd be revealing way more than necessary. Better to keep it light.

"1-800-HEP-BROS? That certainly doesn't make him seem like a good guy."

"Yeah," Odell says slowly, "That did sound pretty bad. But on the other hand, he's putting up a $100 million of his own money to try and make things better, inviting organizations to come up with ideas . . ."

Even though I know it's impolite, I can't keep from interrupting. "He could give up a trillion dollars. I don't trust him!"

"Hey, I didn't say anything about trust. But his money's green, spends like yours and mine, and he's got a lot more of it," Odell says calmly, blessedly oblivious to or unperturbed by the fact that my voice is getting a little loud.

"So what are you saying, that even Dixmoor's racist cloud has a silver lining?" I'm beginning to think I've made a mistake, that Acey, not me, should be out with this guy. After all, they're both optimists.

"Good can come of anything, depending on whose hands it's in." Odell smiles softly, sips his beer. I've been so busy being appalled I didn't even register that our drinks had arrived. I take a gulp. "Actually, I deliver to Dixmoor's office here, even met him once. I don't agree with most of what he says, but he seemed like an okay old guy, although I got a little tired of him patting me on the back and saying, 'Keep up the good work, son.' I mean, working for UPS isn't gonna change the world." Odell laughs, reaches for my hand, smoothly changes both mood and subject before I start foaming at the mouth. "So. How'd the rest of your day go? Didn't knock any people over in the hallway, did you?"

"Nope. The rest of the day was smooth," I chuckle, not bothering to tell him that I'm now on a mandatory leave of absence. I glance around the room. "This is a nice place. You come here often?"

"Yeah, about once a week."

"Must be a great place to meet women," I say, lightly fishing for a compliment. This is a date, and flirtation's part of the ritual. Odell licks those pretty lips and grins.

"Yeah, there are always lots of women. But I'm not looking at any of them tonight." I laugh.

"Glad to hear it. Now, what do you recommend?"

After so many years of dating, you'd have to be a moron or total social reject not to get it down to a science. Both the choice of topics and the depth of conversation about them progresses according to patterns set long ago. He asks about my job and I explain what it is I do, admit I'm getting tired of writing ad copy and thinking about starting a business with a friend, but don't go into specifics. I figure I'll get to the spa later, if ever, because I know if a man told me on the first date, or any date, that he was planning to open a whorehouse, I'd excuse myself as if I were going to the bathroom, surreptitiously get my coat, and be halfway home before he even wondered what was taking me so long. If he had my home number, I'd probably change it.

We talk briefly about our families, and it's clear that Odell has a close relationship with his mom, dad, and three younger brothers, twenty-one-year-old triplets his mother gave birth to late in life, all of them on partial basketball scholarships to the University of Nevada, Las Vegas. Without getting into specifics, I tell him that my dad died when I was twelve, that I'm an only child. I make him laugh over appetizers telling stories about my mother the librarian and how she has a quote or adage for every occasion. We both order another drink, and by the time we finish our entrees the conversation segues into each of us offering brief, edited, synopses of our most recent relationships, a crucial line of inquiry on first dates.

"So." Odell reaches over and takes my hand, looks at it hard. I am relieved I've taken Acey's advice and done my nails, short as they are from banging away all day at a computer keyboard, in the same color polish as my dress. When I look up into his eyes, it's an effort not to lick my lips in greedy anticipation, but I manage. "What's a fine woman like yourself doing available on a Saturday night?"

Now, I could tell him the truth: that for the past six months, since I'd stopped seeing Ray the Closet Crack Fiend (so named because he'd actually burnt up three of my silk blouses freebasing in my wardrobe while I was sleeping), my weekends have consisted of cleaning my apartment, eating Häagen-Dazs while watching HBO or *MAD TV*, and not answering the telephone when it did ring, unless it was Acey's secret signal, so no one knew I was home alone. The only evenings of lust I've had were spent with Mr. V.—although I shouldn't even call it that, since bringing myself to orgasm in five minutes and having no one to talk to afterward isn't really my idea of lust, more simply taking care of business. But of course I don't say all that. Instead, I do what any smart woman does: I lie.

"Well, I'm seeing a couple of people, but they're out of town on business," I say smoothly, adding quickly, "Nothing serious. I'm not looking for anything serious right through here." At least the last half of the sentence is true.

"Well, I guess both our timing's lucky," Odell smiles. "I'm coming out of a pretty intense relationship, just trying to chill right through here."

"Pretty intense?" I ask with a slight smile, tilting my head and fiddling with one of my clunky, Wake Up Little Suzie earrings. That phrase can mean anything from married and bored to currently being stalked by a former girlfriend, and a whole lot in between. Me, I'm not looking for complications and drama, just great sex with a nice man who isn't stupid, crazy, or broke. Odell laughs casually, and I can tell by the tenor of his laughter that we're on the same page.

"You know, we were together about a year, she's an attorney, twenty-seven, successful, smart, a great-looking woman. But after six months I realized we hadn't gone anywhere in the relationship except in bed. Not that the sex wasn't good, but that's not all there is to life."

"No? I bet they're a lot of people in this room who'd disagree with you."

Odell shrugs. "Don't get me wrong, I love sex, but I also like to go to museums, plays, galleries, read, or just stay home and talk. I even brought over my copy of *Their Eyes Were Watching God*, thinking we could read chapters aloud to each other, that it'd generate some conversation, and you know what happened? She fell asleep."

"You own a copy of *Their Eyes Were Watching God*?" I ask incredulously. Odell nods.

"Why should that be so surprising? Did you think women are the only ones who are sensitive?"

"Well . . ."

"Lots of women do, but you're wrong. I'm not asking for pity by any means, but there's a meat market out here for men, too, and it's not very pleasant to feel like just another piece of beef on the rack."

"So what happened?"

"A few months ago she started talking heavy about marriage, children, commitment, and I just couldn't see it: a marriage where the only thing we had in common was sex and children, that's not enough for me. When and if I settle down I want what my parents have, a partnership with common goals and interests, not just good sex and we go our separate ways as long as we come home at the end of the day," Odell says, shaking his head.

"It got to the point where we spent most of our time arguing about where the relationship was headed instead of actually having one. So we broke up six weeks ago." Odell concludes his summary with a sigh. I know it's time to refocus the conversation.

"Twenty-seven? So, how old are you?"

"I'll be thirty in a few months," Odell says, squeezing my hand. "Is that a problem? You don't have a problem with younger men, do you?" I smile demurely, but what I want to do is jump up on the table and do a rendition of the funga, African dance of welcome, lean over the table and kiss that little stud in his ear. Does it matter to me? Not one whit. I know that his skin will be taut, his waist absent even the hint of bulging love handles. It is reasonable to assume that his shoulder blades will be etched in sharp relief, his stomach smooth and hard, and that when he stands naked in silhouette he will evoke visions of Kunta Kinte, not Alfred Hitchcock. His is the body of a young man in great shape, the type of body a woman doesn't have to make any allowances for: a body made for love-making. Plus, he's intelligent. He can read me a story any time.

"Is it? A problem?" Odell's voice snaps me back to the Piranha Bar.

"Not at all," I purr. "As Satchel Paige once said, 'Age is a case of mind over matter: If you don't mind, it don't matter.'" Odell chuckles, flashes those pretty teeth, gently rubs his finger across that space on my hand between thumb and forefinger.

I smile at Odell, thinking to myself how even though the game of seduction is usually predictable, it's also great fun and a definite turn-on when the feelings are mutual. Odell's old enough to know the mating dance, and it's obvious that we both know not only the basic steps and more than a few variations, but can improvise. Since we're both focused on the same goal—having a nice dinner and ending up in bed—it's a game both of us are happy to participate in.

The odd thing is that in this case the roles of player and played are reversed. I mean, usually it's the woman who's busy trying to show she's more than just a pretty face and a one-night-stand piece of booty, trying to let the man know she has some value when she's other than prone. Yet tonight Odell's busy dropping Zora's iconographic-to-black-women's name and sharing career aspirations, letting me know he has some depth and isn't just a sex object to be used and thrown away. I'm the one sitting here having graphic sexual fantasies and, at least to some extent, feigning interest in what he's saying, and refraining from lunging across the table and jumping his bones.

"Would you like coffee, cognac, dessert?"

"Why don't we go to my house for dessert?" I suggest, letting the lust seep into my voice so he knows he's passed all the tests. Lickety-split we're wafting out the door, the sultry voice of Brian McKnight asking, "Do I ever cross your mind?" sending us on our merry way.

When we get to my house, I give Odell a fluffy Ralph Lauren towel and washcloth, point him toward the bathroom in case he wants to freshen up, and go into the living room to put on some music. I slip CDs by Babyface, Luther Vandross, Joe, and Heather Headley on my five-CD changer. After a moment of thought I put in a Cassandra Wilson disk and program her to play first. Her music is sexy, supple, and feminine, which sums up how I'm feeling and the mood I want to set.

When I walk into the bedroom, Odell is wearing nothing but a pair of navy blue silk boxer shorts. He stands before me, a magnificent specimen, and says, "Let me undress you." He carefully lifts the red spandex over my head. Then he steps back several paces and stares at me. I stand before him in my red lingerie and high heels and hope that all my quivering's on the inside. This is the moment of truth in the ritual of sex. Far more difficult than the fucking itself is revealing our bodies, obsessed as most of us are with their most minor imperfections. Even though I have never had a man run screaming from the boudoir after glimpsing me nude, the moment of disrobing still fills me with apprehension. I make a mental note to address this at the spa, instruct all employees to make women feel desirable and comfortable, whatever their size, shape, or age. Odell must be able to read my mind, because he says simply, "You're beautiful," as he reaches over and slides the straps of my bra off my shoulders, then adds, "You can breathe now." We both laugh.

He leans over, his body not touching mine, and kisses me, first on my jawbone, moves slowly upwards to my cheek, then down to the corner of my mouth, unhurriedly, until his full lips are on mine. He smells faintly of Polo, and his lips taste of licorice. He kisses me close-mouthed for a long time, then softly begins licking the place where my lips meet, until my mouth opens and he's inside. His tongue plays scales along my teeth, teases the roof of my mouth, his lips suck my eager and reaching tongue. His hands hang at his sides; the only parts of our bodies that touch are our lips. When I try to press myself against him, he does not move inward to meet me, but holds himself away, tantalizing the length of my body from that one small point of contact. I feel the place between my legs begin to pulsate and grow warm, my nipples grow hard and aching, my body temperature shoot up a few degrees. Just when I am about to turn into the female Jackie Chan and kick Odell's legs out from under him, he places his hands over my ears, runs them softly along my neck, down my collarbone, and across my breasts, until he holds my nipples between two fingers. I swear they feel as if they're dancing under his hands as Cassandra's sultry voice demands a little warm death. I make a note to tell Acey she's won the argument—warm death is orgasm, not oblivion, or maybe they're the same thing. He places his lips against my ear, murmurs, "May I kiss them?" It is all I can do to groan, "Yes."

There is an art to caressing a woman's nipples, and Odell has obviously studied with the right mistress. His tongue licks, first lightly, than harder around the aureole, causing my nipple to get so hard it occurs to me it might explode, but it feels so good, who cares? His tongue licks it gently, soothingly, before his lips close around it and he begins sucking. There are men who suck a woman's nipples (and other places on her body too) half-heartedly, a perfunctory act before moving on to the main event of insertion. Then there are men who clamp onto your breast like a baby calf on big mama's udder, and suck so hard you'd think their life depends on it for sustenance. Odell sucks my breasts gently yet firmly, using both his tongue and his lips, occasionally letting his teeth play lightly across my nipples. I step out of my shoes and place my feet solidly on terra firma, certain that I will lose my balance and keel over in ecstasy if I totter in those heels a moment longer.

"Lie down on the bed," he whispers, just when I know I can't stand anymore. He puts his hand against the flat of my back and lowers me onto the mattress, his mouth still on my nipple, pushing my legs up and apart with the other hand. Seamlessly, he snakes down, from breast to stomach to navel, until his head is positioned between my spread legs, kissing and licking all the way. He pushes my knees further apart, spreads my lips wide. I lie back, head on a pillow, and watch him, every nerve of my body on alert, my skin hot and covered with a thin sheen of sweat and saliva. Poised above my pussy, about to dive for and, I hope, find its buried treasure, Odell looks up at me and grins. All I can do is nod my head as if giving benediction: go forth, young man, and do good works. And he does. He must have clitoris radar built into his mouth because after a few seconds his tongue pushes back the hood to reveal the gem, his lips fasten on, and he begins licking and sucking, slowly increasing the pressure and intensity. Me? I place my hands on either side of his head and just lie there, enjoying ever minute of it. I can feel the waves of orgasm, first small ones, then bigger and bigger, building up from someplace in the core of my body. I will myself not to squirm away from his lips but to fall into the intensity of feeling, to get as far out as I can and wait for the tsunami to sweep me back to shore. I also make a mental note that giving great head is a must for the men who work at our spa.

There comes a time during great sex when control is no longer an option, when the body takes over absolutely and the mind has no choice but to go with it. Under the tender loving care of Odell's mouth, the waves build and build, me on top of them, until I am so high up I can't even recall what land felt like. My legs wrap around his head like a nutcracker attacking a Christmas walnut, my hands burrow into his skull, and I can feel the love juices drip slowly from between my legs. Every part of me is quivering now, but I'm neither holding anything in nor holding on. I let it all go, and that's when Odell slides two fingers inside me and I come, the muscles of my pussy clenching and releasing as wave after wave breaks and subsides until I am washed ashore, spent and happy, unable to speak in other than moans, cries, and gibberish. I'm not even worried that apparently I've been struck blind, because even though my eyes are open, I can't see a goddamn thing.

I lie there on my back, slowly pulling together the pieces of my self shattered in orgasm. I feel Odell lie down next to me on his side. Lazily, I slide my hand into the space between us, reach down, and wrap my fingers around his hard penis. Thumb does not meet forefinger. I rub my hand along its length, and can tell by feel that it is between seven and eight inches. It's the years of experience; I can size a man up the same way a woman who's worked selling clothes for years can tell what size you are at a glance, will peer over her glasses skeptically when you say you're a ten, because she knows damn well you're a fourteen, and who in the hell do you think you're fooling? Odell moans as I caress him. With my left hand I reach over to the night table, pull the drawer open, feel around until I find a condom, tear it open with my teeth. On the downstroke, I move my hand from his penis to his balls, squeezing gently, while I roll the condom down and over him with my other hand. When I finish I pull him on top of me, knit my legs around his sleek back. For a moment he is poised above me, the width of his shoulders tapering into a small waist, narrow hips, the bulge of muscular thighs, absolutely beautiful. Then I beckon him with my eyes and he slowly enters me. I can feel the hot rings of his penis as he eases inside, feel the interior of my vagina expand to make room for each inch and then close comfortably around it. Then he's in, our pubic hairs mingle, and I can't help hissing "Yes!" because Odell is all the way inside me and his shit feels *good*.

His fucking is just as methodical as the rest of his love-making, easy, unhurried, and thorough. He holds himself up on his arms and watches my face as he strokes, his expression happy and friendly as opposed to preening and self-involved, the way Lorenzo always was. He has a technique of kinda dragging his pelvis against mine when he moves into me that simultaneously draws out the stroke and directly stimulates my clit. I feel those waves building again. I tighten my legs around his back, put my arms around his shoulders, and prepare for a little more warm death. I guess he feels it too, because he asks politely, "Are you ready?" When I nod he speeds up his motion, pumping hard and steady. I can feel his balls slapping my ass, his dick stroking my insides, and his pelvic bone working my clit. As he comes he howls loud and I once again speak in tongues. I can't wait to tell Acey that I have found, if not the Holy Spirit, at least a reasonable facsimile.

7

MORE THAN A THOUSAND MILES AWAY, AT THE SAME TIME ODELL AND
Lydia are sprawled in post-coital bliss and resting up for the next round
in a bout of love-making that will end just before the sun comes up, the
Reverend T. Terry Tiger, chief and supreme leader of the Black Baptist
Brotherhood and Boulé, is pissed. He lies, eyes open, atop the custom-
made round bed that is the centerpiece of his bedroom in the tiny house
in Itta Bena, Mississippi, where he was born. It is where he returns in
times of crisis when he needs to do some serious soul-searching.

Even though it's three in the morning and his sixty-seven-year-old
body is dog-tired, his mind is wide awake. As much as he wants to rest, he
can neither quiet his thoughts nor keep his weary eyes closed. Instead,
they dart from ceiling to walls, resting momentarily on the sepia-tone
photograph of his mama that hangs opposite the bed. Everyone called her
Miss Net, not that it was short for anything fancy—her real name was
Emma—but because she always wore a hair net. Looking at her brown face
framed in thick, steel gray braids wrapped around her head like a crown,
her small, almond-shaped eyes that even in the darkened room seemed
to glitter, T. Terry sighs with longing. He may be a long-grown man,
head of the Brotherhood and Boulé, a prosperous, successful man, but
he still misses his mama. Maybe if he'd had children of his own it
wouldn't be so bad, but God hadn't so blessed him. In the more than
half-century he'd been lying with women, he'd always been shooting
blanks. Lying here, he can clearly remember his first time, with Aurora
Bonaventure when they were both twelve, making love in the tall grasses
in back of this very house. Aurora, so pretty and welcoming, Aurora who
loved him and who he loved. Lovely Aurora who he'd planned to marry
and have children with until Mama convinced him that she was black
trailer-trash, not fitting for the wife of an up and coming young minister. Still, he hadn't been able to resist bedding her in this very room the
night after his mother's funeral more than twenty years ago, and even

75

now when he thought about Aurora she seemed as vivid as if it had been yesterday. But the past was gone, and when he died, his name and his legacy would die with him.

He stares into that familiar face, the half-inch-long mole with a few hairs growing out of the end protruding above her left eyebrow, the slightly pursed heart-shaped lips ready to move into a sneer or a smile, and whimpers. He's certain that if she were here she would offer wise council, help him to find his way out of darkness, guide and inspire him with the strong Christian faith and shrewd sense of people that had dominated his life since he was a boy. Yet he is equally certain she would not approve of the turns his life had taken, would chide him for moving away from the pure Christian faith he'd been raised in and diversifying into business and industry, areas in which applications of genuine Christian doctrine were few and far between. He could imagine the passionate arguments they'd have as his mother held him to the word of the Bible, scoffed at his conveniently pragmatic interpretations, accused him of being seduced by worldly values. She'd always scorned that he'd tacked "boulé" on to the Baptist Brotherhood, dismissed his argument that black folks were more likely to join and contribute if there was an annual ball to attend where they could play Negro geography, style, and talk shit. He didn't even want to imagine what she'd have to say about his dyed hair, the corset he daily strapped around his midriff to tame a growing gut, the gold Rolex watch, and the ring encrusted with diamonds. He was seriously considering cutting off the shoulder-length process that she'd always hated, but he couldn't yet bring himself to do it. Those flowing tresses were his signature, same as the man upstairs. Dreading his mother's judgments, the honest and often cold eye she cast not only on others but herself too, still he knew her beliefs, harsh as they might be, would also guide and refocus him, and he missed that.

He shifts his eyes and turns over on his side, unable to bear looking at his mother's face a moment longer, his grief and her judgment both so keen it hurts. He doesn't mean to speak, isn't crazy enough to think he can communicate with his mother's photograph, but his need is so great that involuntarily he calls out in anguish, "Mama!"

The woman beside him stirs, wiggles her body closer to his, and lifts her head sleepily. "You all right, baby? You want to try again?" she asks. At the sound of her voice, he pulls away, startled. He'd forgotten she was there.

"No," he snaps, his deep voice thick and throaty. "Go back to sleep," he commands in his best orator's voice. It came up from his diaphragm, this voice that had moved people for nearly forty years, whether they were civil rights workers in Mississippi in the 1960s or members of his present congregation in New York City. Or it had worked up until a few years back, during the good old days, before too many people had started worshipping at the altar of free love, women's liberation, televised ministries, alternative spirituality, bling bling and rap music, before the world began to change and slip from his grasp.

It was no surprise that the woman did not obey, instead opening her eyes wide at the sound of his voice, suddenly awake. She points her feet and puts her hands over her head, stretching her petite, voluptuous body. Then she sits up, runs her hand through her disheveled shoulder-length hair, dyed chestnut brown with blonde highlights, and places a small but firm hand, each finger glistening with at least two rings, on his shoulder. "Look, don't get rude with me. These things happen to all men sometimes, Daddy. I'm willing to try again, if you want." She stretches again, this time rubbing up against him. She arches her body, runs her long nails up either side of his chest, and grins like a brown sable Cheshire cat. Even though he's a proponent of nonviolence, both politically and personally, for a second T. Terry wants to slap her upside her head. Then she purrs and he remembers a time, not too long ago, when he enjoyed her kittenish coquette act, actually encouraged her to dance and writhe around in an impressive imitation of Eartha Kitt, her hands held like claws, meowing in between verses of "I Want to Be Evil."

"Honey. Not now. I'm thinking," he says, the tone in his voice softer. Immediately, she shuts off the sex kitten act, sits up straight, crosses her legs underneath her, and gently rubs the sleep from the corners of her eyes. T. Terry lays back, arms folded behind his head, and looks up into her face. Her big round eyes are soft and shimmer with intelligence, her cheeks velvety and round. Even with lines from the starched white sheets temporarily molded into one side of her face, she's gorgeous, at forty-five still the smart, pretty new member of the church who'd volunteered to keep his books more than twenty years ago and been his unofficial second wife ever since. In the year since Connie, his wife of forty-one years, the good girl he'd married while at seminary, had passed on, Jeanette Howell had been agitating to make her status as wife official, but T. Terry wasn't sure. What was the point of getting married again? He couldn't have children, and there were plenty of women in his church who were happy to prepare his meals, type his sermons, maintain the church in his absence and, if he so desired, fulfill his less godly desires, too.

"Thinking is my second strongest point," she says, smirking lasciviously and wiggling her ass against the blanket. T. Terry dares to let his eyes drift across her full breasts, her stomach with only the slightest, cutest of bellies, down to the bushy forest between her crossed legs. Usually just the sight of her, even fully clothed, was enough to arouse him, but now, nothing. Involuntarily, he groans. He has enough problems without his main man Johnson letting him down. She reaches over, slips a hand around the back of his head, and gently massages the nape of his neck with her thumb.

"Come on, Terry. Enough of the lonely angst," she says. "Talk to me."

"I have lost my way," T. Terry murmurs. "I once was found, but now I'm lost, could see but now I'm blind." Jeanette smiles sympathetically, chuckles at his word play, and rubs his neck harder.

"Baby, I know you're worried about the Brotherhood and Boulé, how things are going," she says. "Talk to me. Maybe we can come up with some solutions, huh?" T. Terry looks up at her gratefully, shifts his body so his head lies in the warm cradle of her legs. The least he can do is smell her sex, maybe it will inspire him, fecund aromatherapy.

"Jeanette, you're my bookkeeper, you know as well as I do what's going on," he says impatiently. "Revenues have fallen dramatically, for both the Brotherhood and Boulé and the church itself. Collection after Sunday services used to be ten thousand a week, now we're lucky if we get three. Even that usually depends on whether we can rope in enough busloads of European tourists desperate to hear some authentic Negro spirituals." His voice is strained, bitter, and puzzled.

"Okay. What else?" Jeanette asks.

"Dues-paying members of the Brotherhood and Boulé have declined forty-two percent in the last three years, particularly among the young. They just don't seem to give a damn about civil rights, networking via social organizations, or hell and damnation. Meanwhile, our members are getting older and older and if we don't do something, the organization will die off with them."

"Got it. What else?" Jeanette says quickly, trying to break his train of thought. She can tell from his tone of voice that T. Terry is on the verge of ranting, going into his familiar soliloquy about the good old days, and she has no intention of going there. As far as she's concerned, every day could be the good old days, if they make it so. Why can't he keep his eyes on the prize and stay focused? But she's too late.

"I remember when the movement was at its height, back in the sixties, we had to turn people away—turn them away! Everyone wanted to come down here and get their head beat by some redneck crackers. The truth is we didn't have enough activist racists to go around; we had to stagger those freedom buses for maximum effect. Martin King, Hosea Williams, Ralph Abernathy, Fannie Lou Hamer, and me, we woke this nation up to the reality of racism and segregation, not just down South, but up North, too. When King came to Grenada, that's right down the road, you could damn near hear those peckerwoods shaking in their boots. 'Cause, see, they didn't want it and they sho' din't like it, but they knew a change was gonna come, and there was nothin' they could do 'bout it!" Jeanette listens, inhales and exhales deeply, an exercise she's learned in a church yoga class. T. Terry's eyes are glassy, a sign that he's off on a jag. Nothing will bring him back until he runs its course. Another telltale sign is that he's started speaking in southern vernacular, dropping those Gs and prepositions, a sure sign those dems and doses weren't far behind.

"Honey, you're too young to remember dem days, but those were some good times, everything was crystal clear, because we all knew who the enemy was, and that the Lord Jesus was on our side. Not like now. What it is, we've lost our sense of right from wrong, of mission, we have no moral authority!" He wisely pauses for breath, since he does have a tendency to hyperventilate and pass out, a weakness he'd learned to use to his advantage when preaching, appearing so possessed by the Holy Spirit he was about to faint just before the collection plate went around. She opens her mouth to refocus the conversation, but all she gets out is one word, "But," and he's off and raving again.

"But nothin', Jeanette, but nothin'! There are no buts about it. What we must do is rejuvenate that sense of righteousness, that sense of moral authority, become again the conscience of the nation, as Martin so eloquently put it, resurrect the spirit we had during the glorious days of the movement." He pauses. She can stand no more, has heard it all before. Much as she loves this man, she recognizes the smell of bullshit when she hears it.

"Now Terry, don't fool yourself, and you know damn well you can't fool me, I was a history major, remember? Aren't you the man who split with Dr. King when the chicken processing plant came to town and offered you a big job if you agreed to—now what did they call it?—oh yeah, their plan of 'gradual integration tailored to the mores of southern tradition.' What's that stupid acronym again?"

"GITTMOST," T. Terry snaps. "And I would not describe what happened between me and Martin as a split, simply a parting of ways at a fork in the road. Martin, bless his soul, went the way of integration, I went the way of integration with economic development."

Jeanette mutters, "Well, it's easy to see who was more threatening to the powers that be."

T. Terry's body stiffens as he bristles.

"Exactly what is that supposed to mean?"

"You're standing here, alive and well. King's been dead nearly forty years, am I right?"

T. Terry nods sadly.

"Still, even though we disagreed, I loved Martin like a brother. When we parted at that fork in the road, we did so as friends," he says self-righteously. Raised in New York and schooled with black folks, Puerto Ricans, and Jews, Jeanette wants to throw her hands up, put on her best Yiddish accent, and shout, "All right already! Enough! No mas!" but doesn't. Instead she simply inquires, "And did you ever speak to him again?"

"No. But, ah, we were both busy."

"And were you invited to his funeral?"

"As I've told you before, I am certain, considering the tragic circumstances of his death, my name was simply inadvertently left off the guest list," he snorts indignantly, but Jeanette will not let it rest, knows that nothing lies up this road of self-delusion but more anguish and impotence.

"Honey, this is *me* you're talking to. Did not the ushers, armed with a recent photograph for purposes of easy recognition, turn you away, on instructions from Coretta, when you tried to enter the church?"

T. Terry lies there limp, silent and hurt. "What's your point?" he mumbles, once again overcome by the knowledge that back in the 1960s he had blown the chance to take the moral high road in exchange for economic opportunity. Yet how was he to have known thirty years ago that Christian morality would sell? Not that he hadn't done all right for himself, he had. But as he got older without children to leave his worldly possessions, he found himself wishing for a moral legacy to leave the world.

"My point is that the good old days weren't all that good, and anyway, they're over. Let's talk about the here, now, and what we're going to do to rejuvenate the B&B and the church," she says kindly, stroking his rough cheeks.

"You tell me," says T. Terry, defeated.

"Now Daddy, don't give up on me," Jeanette whispers seductively. "Besides, you already told me what we need—to reawaken that sense of mission, of moral authority. We need an issue that will galvanize the people!"

He snorts dismissively. "And what would you suggest? Our people are too busy lying, cheating, and shopping to get involved. People just don't give a damn any more!"

"Everyone cares about something. It's your job to tell them what it is," she suggests gently.

"Well, what?" he asks sarcastically. "Children out of control, parents gone wild, hell, even some of the grandparents don't have no sense. The ones who manage to get two nickles to rub together don't want to do anything but listen to rap music, mimic white folks, and make it to Martha's Vineyard during the last two weeks in August."

"It's not that bad," Jeanette says impatiently. Really, enough of this whining, it just made him sound like a pitiful old man. Sometimes it seemed as if the vibrant, powerful, visionary man she'd fallen in love with had disappeared, consumed by the damn Brotherhood and trying to remain at the top of the heap in a changing world. True, he might be getting old, but who wasn't, and pathetic didn't necessarily have to come with it. Why was it, she wondered, that he was so afraid of change, wouldn't or couldn't let go of who he had been in the past and discover what was possible in the future?

"Not that bad?" he says derisively. "Shit. I'm afraid to call for a demonstration because nobody might come."

"They'll come if you make them feel the issue is important to their lives," she interjects, although she doubts he hears her. "T.D. Jakes, Iyanla Vanzant, even old Jerry Falwell are still packing them in. Why? Because they have a mission."

"Which is?"

"Family values. Putting fathers back at the heads of their families. Mothers back in the home where they should be. Advocating abstinence until marriage. Transcending organized religion for a deeper spirituality, whatever."

"Jeanette, do you have a point to make?" T. Terry snarls, sitting up, suddenly nauseated by the smell of her sex.

"T, don't get snippy with me, I'm trying to help. And yes, I have a point. You've got to find the issue that touches everyone sooner or later, right where they live. The point is that we need an issue, but an issue everyone can relate to. Something where there're no gray areas, just right and wrong."

"Do you have a specific suggestion?" T. Terry snaps impatiently.

"What about unemployment, crime, drugs, irresponsibility, you know, the crisis facing the black man? That whole endangered species thing usually works, doesn't it?"

"Jeanette, that issue's already been taken. Wasn't that you sitting beside me watching Dick Dixmoor at his press conference about black superpredators? Who's going to care what I say when Dixmoor's ready to give away all that money? Who?" T. Terry sounds as if he's about to cry.

"Let's get some sleep and talk about it tomorrow," Jeanette suggests gently.

"Be sure to wake me up when you come up with something. Let's hope I'm not as old as Rip Van Winkle by then," he says pathetically, but she doesn't rise to the bait.

"I'm not saying it'll be easy," Jeanette soothes. "But surely a man of your experience, oratorical skills, and brilliance can find an issue that will move the people. After all, baby, you helped do it once, you can do it again. The Lord will give us a sign. Close your eyes and let's pray on it."

T. Terry shuts his eyes and starts to begin a conversation with God, feels her hands slide down to caress his chest as her voice strokes his ego, and he relaxes under her touch. "I know you can do it. We just have to find the right issue," she whispers. He lies there and grows strong under the power of her hands, reminded again of why he loves her and has stuck with her all these years, even though she sometimes has a sharp tongue. Her hands and voice have the power not only to soothe away the hurt and anger, but to replace them with joy and a sense of possibility. He sighs as she touches him, breathes deeply. The scent of her womanhood, sharp, musty, smelling oddly of freshly turned earth, wafts into his nostrils. He feels his penis stir ever so slightly under her ministrations. Involuntarily, his eyes meet his mother's disapproving ones as they glare down at him. He can almost hear her voice admonishing him for the sin of fornication. And then it comes to him, a heavenly bolt of clarity and inspiration.

"Immorality!" he yells, sitting up in bed and inadvertently wrenching his penis from Jeanette's hands.

"It's a little late for guilt, isn't it?" she asks petulantly, licking her lips. T. Terry waves a hand for silence.

"Not us, them. That's my issue, immorality. Too much fucking and not enough responsibility. Teenage pregnancy, divorce, fornication, the death of the family. You name it, and if it's bad, black folks got it. Why? Because we have lost our moral compass, become sinners, sunk into the abyss of immoral behavior. What we need is a sexual counter-revolution, and I'm the one to lead it."

"You think people gonna stop making love because you say so?" Jeanette's voice is thick with skepticism.

"I'm not talking about making love, I'm talking about fornicating, sex purely for pleasure without responsibility or commitment."

She giggles. "You mean what we're trying to have?"

"Keep us out of it," T. Terry snaps. "This is business, and the business is the redemption of the black man. And unless things have changed in the last two thousand years, moral turpitude is a front-burner issue. This is the hot issue! Or it will be when I get through with it."

"What's your strategy?"

"I'm gonna preside at the funeral of morality. Declare morality dead on national Black Entertainment Television. Gonna put morality in a pretty silver coffin, lots of flowers on top, and preach over that baby as if there were a body inside. Decry morality's passing and what we have lost. I'm gonna preach up close and personal, so hard you'll think I'm talking about your mama or daddy. There won't be a dry eye anywhere in America."

"Sounds depressing," Jeanette murmurs, and T. Terry laughs loud and with delight.

"It will be, profoundly so. Just when they think there's no hope, that all is lost, when even the crackheads are clutching a tissue and sniffling, I'll call for the resurrection of morality. Challenge the people to raise him up!" T. Terry's preaching now, kneeling on the bed and holding his arms aloft, his face suffused with blood and raised to the ceiling. Watching him, Jeanette smiles. He's back, and she knows that whatever the issue is, if T. Terry believes, others will too. "Ask our people to spend time reflecting on the absence of morality in their lives and communities and pledge themselves to attack immorality wherever they find it, to take action, root out sinners wherever they may be."

"Brilliant, sugar, but you've got to give them the opportunity to

come together en masse, give them something to do," Jeanette suggests.
"You know how black folks love to get in a crowd and get loud."

"That'll come, don't worry. Fortunately for us, we won't have any
problem finding sin," T. Terry chuckles. "I might even call for a National
Day of Abstinence. A Million Monogamy March. The possibilities are
endless."

Jeanette smiles.

"Terry sugar, you're on fire. You're back, baby. I'm getting hot just
sitting here listening to you talk about it."

"Baby, Little T's feeling the heat, too. Go on down there and cool
him off," he whispers. She stands up, her bright pink tongue darting cat-
like as she licks her lips. Kneeling by the side of the bed, she takes the
head of a flaccid and rather forlorn looking Little T into her mouth. She
holds it in her hand. It feels like a fat slug or earthworm, as if it has no
muscle, no substance. She wills herself to think of better, harder days.
Slowly, she lets her mouth travel down the length, licking its diameter in a
circular motion as she goes and gently sucking. She works her mouth over
his penis patiently and lovingly. After a few minutes she feels Little T start
to stiffen and fill with blood. Flat on his back, dreams of future glory
dancing in his head, T. Terry feels it too as she lowers her mouth that last
inch and engulfs the length of his hardening penis. He speaks, and his
voice is no longer that of a frustrated old man, but of T. Terry Tiger,
man of the cloth and orator, chief and supreme leader of the Black Baptist Brotherhood and Boulé. "Thank you, Jesus," he cries out. "He rises!
He rises! He is arisen!"

8

"ARE YOU REALLY SERIOUS ABOUT LEAVING UPS?" I ASK ODELL.
We're sitting in my kitchen the morning after, drinking Jamaican Blue
Mountain coffee and scarfing down eggs, turkey bacon, fried apples, and
biscuits. After the previous night's sexathon, I'm confident we can both
use the calories. Odell grins lazily.

"Why? Are you making me an offer?" he asks in a voice laden with
innuendo. I can tell he's teasing, but he's not far from the truth.

"I might be. Are you?" Hey, two can play this game. Odell stops
smiling, looks serious.

"Sure, if the right job comes along."

"What would you think about working for women?"

"No problem. I love women. Can't you tell?" He reaches over and
playfully runs his hand up my thigh, stopping just short of the danger
zone.

"What about doing work that's, er, unorthodox, shall we say?" I
smile seductively.

"Actually, this gig with UPS is the blip on my screen. I've never
thought of myself as the traditional type. Do you?" He grins when he says
this, shovels in a mouthful of apples. I don't know if he's thinking about
when I pushed him onto his back, held his hands over his head, and
mounted him, or the moment I knelt on all fours and we did it doggy-style,
him slapping my ass playfully. Either way, traditional is not a word I'd use to
describe him, even after one night together.

"You wouldn't have any problems taking orders from two sisters?"

"Now what do you think?" Odell smirks, and I grin, remembering
how quickly he responded to my commands last night: harder, softer,
stop, don't stop. "What's your proposition?"

"Me and my best friend Acey, we're going to open a full-service spa
for sisters, and we're looking for people to work there," I say tentatively.
Odell raises his eyebrows, the same ones I kissed the night before.

"I work out, but I'm not an aerobics instructor or anything like that," he laughs. "I know you told me last night I had great hands, but I'm not a certified masseuse either." Now it's my turn to laugh.

"Not a spa like that. I mean, yes, a spa like that, but much more. In addition to exercise, massage, herbal wraps, and yoga, we plan to offer other, more personalized services."

"Oh, you mean like personal training?" And because there is no delicate way to say it, and because after last night there surely shouldn't be anything sexual I couldn't say to this man, 'cause there sure ain't nothing sexual I wouldn't do with him, I cut the coy bullshit.

"No. I mean like sex."

"Sex?"

"You remember, S-E-X?" I spell it out. "What we've been doing for the last eight hours?" Odell's smile fades and he looks at me intently. "We plan to open a spa in Nevada, a deluxe retreat where sisters can avail themselves of the whole gamut of customary spa services, with one important addition: fantastic, orgasmic, safe sex. What I'm looking for are sex workers, men who enjoy giving women pleasure and can deliver that sexual healing to the needy masses." I spit this all out in a rush, before I can get embarrassed or intimidated and cop out.

Sex?" Odell repeats. He says it as if he's never heard the word before, I guess because the context is so new. I laugh.

"In all its variations. Soft sex, wild sex, family style—as they say in the joint—doggy style, cunnilingus, fellatio, sex standing up, sitting down, sex in water, sex on dry land, sex with one man, two, maybe even three if a sister wants to go there. Sex with two women and a man. Whatever a woman's fantasy, as long as it's about pleasure, A Sister's Spa guarantees to make it her reality. And for a reasonable price, too."

"You're serious," he says incredulously. It is both a question and a statement. I laugh again.

"Hell, yeah, and why not? Quiet as it's kept, women are as much into pure sex as you guys, we've just been conditioned to believe that if we get it without love we're bad girls, doomed to a pathetic, lonely life, not to mention hellfire and eternal damnation."

"What about love?" Mention women and sexual freedom in the same breath and you're almost guaranteed to bring out the traditionalist in every man, even a reasonably liberated bro like Odell.

"As Tina Turner put it so well, 'What's love got to do with it?' We're selling sex with a little romance to make it go down more easily. Not love.

You know as well as I do, if you're honest, that the two don't always go together. Come on, Odell, pitch me another softball." Now it's my turn to
smirk. Odell looks both startled and puzzled.

"You mean sometimes women are dogging, just like men?" I can
tell by the tone of his voice he wants me to say no, but as Moms always says,
honesty is the best policy. I laugh.

"Absolutely. The difference is that in the everyday world, sisters
have to pretend we're not just after the booty. If we don't, the odds are
most men will think we're skeezers or hard-up or get turned off and run
away. I mean, do you really think every woman who's interested in you is
looking for a meaningful relationship? Come on. We're offering the
same phat fuck without the mind games, plain and simple."

Odell looks slightly offended.

"Are you saying nice sisters, sisters like you, would pay for sex without any other involvement?" He sounds indignant. If he thinks rephras-
ing the same tired query is going to change my response, he's way off base.

"Hello? Odell, are you the same man I spent last night doing exactly
that with? Let's break it down. You're a nice man, I'm a nice woman.
We're physically attracted to each other, have a lovely dinner, laugh and
talk, then come home and fuck until we pass out. Am I in love with you?
No, and you're not in love with me, either." He opens his mouth as if to
protest, and before he can utter a word I hold up one hand like a school
crossing guard when she means stop. "Let's be honest. If I never saw you
again, I wouldn't sweat it. I'd remember a fabulous sexual interlude and
keep on getting up, and the same's true for you. Come on, brother, open
your mind."

Odell sits there chewing, not looking at me or anything else, just
staring. I can almost see his brain work as he tries to wrap his mind
around what I've said, as though he's flipping through his file of what he
heretofore considered sexual conquests, reevaluating them in light of the
stunning new information I've just laid out. It's finally dawning on him
that maybe the apparent conqueror is sometimes the conquered. I concentrate on my breakfast in order to give him time to make peace with this
new reality. I understand it may not be easy: revelation usually isn't. Especially when it involves letting men know that often they don't know
doodleysquat about women when it comes to the game.

It isn't until I've almost finished my food and am loading that last
half biscuit with apples that Odell finally says, "Lydia, let me get this
straight. You're saying that all women, not just tramps, hard-ups, and

nymphomaniacs, are into sex for sex's sake. Sex without dating, commitment, a future, love, and marriage?" I start to laugh, but Odell's face looks stricken.

"Look, I can't speak for all women. But I'd definitely say, at some time in their life, most. That's not to say a lot of women don't want all those other things too—love, marriage, the horse and carriage—but most of us have those in-between times."

"In-between times?"

"Yeah. When we're in-between relationships. Or when the relationship we're in isn't going well and the crisis extends to the bedroom. Hell, maybe we're just too busy at the job and don't have time for a relationship, or we're just too tired. Whatever. Most of us still would like to be able to have great sex without the drama." Odell looks at me expectantly, so I continue.

"My point is simply this: It's a sure bet that whether a sister's happily single or married, unhappily single or married, if her biological clock's ticking loudly or long since worn out, if she's divorced, or bisexual, whatever her age, whoever or whatever she is, she's into sex. And she's probably not getting enough of it. Or if she is, it may not be the way she wants it. And even if it is, she might just want to do it with someone new, no strings attached."

"Even my Moms?" Odell's voice is plaintive. Before I open my mouth, I take note of the mental signpost up ahead that reads, "Tread lightly! You are entering the familiar yet always dangerous territory of Men and their Mothers."

"Odell, I never met your mother, so I can't speak specifically about her sexual needs." Odell looks relieved. Until, that is, I say, "However," then he again tenses up. "I can say that all research indicates that both women and men want, and are capable of having, active sex lives into their geriatric years. Women, because they don't have to tackle issues of impotence as men sometimes do, are often able to be sexually active longer, since the major physiological impact of aging on women is vaginal dryness, a condition that can be addressed using a number of lubricating products on the market." I pause for breath. "So yes, older women, while maybe not *your* mother, still want and need sex."

I finish my spiel, and while Odell's digesting, send silent thanks to my mother, since that's actually her rap, not mine, which she delivered sternly to me in 1993, her sixty-fifth year. That's when I ran by her house one afternoon on the way home from work to borrow her cast-iron collard green pot, let myself in with my key, and busted her doing the nasty with Mr. Blanchard, her neighbor from three houses down. My father had been dead for eighteen years from a heart attack, but I was still surprised and angry. I'd thought that when she buried her husband, my mother buried her sexuality with him and glided into the cold sexlessness of widowhood, after which came the grave. Boy, was I wrong.

When my mother saw me standing in the doorway of her bedroom, mouth hanging open as I watched Mr. Blanchard's slow, careful strokes, she didn't jump up guiltily or even look embarrassed, just snapped, "Lydia, didn't I always tell you to knock at a closed door? Go into the parlor and wait for me."

The wait wasn't all that short, either. I'll never know if it took that long for the two of them to disentangle and put their clothes on, or if my ornery mother simply finished what she'd started. I sat on the hard, green velvet horsehair sofa in that parlor for more than a few minutes. The more time passed, the more stupid, guilty, and embarrassed I felt, the way I did when I had messed up as a little girl and was sent to the parlor to await my parents' decision on exactly what punishment to inflict. When my mother finally arrived, neatly dressed, hair tidy and unmussed, she lit into me like a whip into a runaway slave's back. "Girl, haven't I told you to call, or at least ring the doorbell, when you decide to drop by? Well, you didn't listen, and now you've got an eyeful, haven't you, and embarrassed poor Mr. Blanchard besides. Next time, knock."

"But Mama, I didn't think—" I started to say, but my mother didn't want to hear it.

"Didn't think I was alive since your daddy died? Didn't think I have the same needs as other women, including yourself?" She peered at me hard, daring me to respond. What could I say? Even if I had thought my mother entered the land of celibacy the day Daddy died, I was clearly way off base. I didn't say a word. My mother's voice softened.

"Baby, your father was the love of my life, always will be. But that doesn't mean I don't have physical needs and desires. Your father and me made love several times a week until the day he died, had an active, healthy sex life . . ."

I groan as a deeply disturbing vision of my parents doing the 69 tries to unfurl in my head, mutter, "Spare me the details, mother. Please." Does my mother take me into her arms, apologize for revealing to her daughter what would better remain hidden? Not my Mama. After all, this is the woman who brought an obstetrics textbook home from the library, complete with illustrated diagrams, when I asked her where babies came from. While other children still thought it was the magic of the stork, me, I knew the graphic, bloody truth. I think I was five at the time. My mother laughs in my face and shakes her silver bouffant.

"All right, Ms. Liberated Woman, I'll spare you the details. However, let me make this point . . ." That's when she launches into the speech about sexuality among senior citizens, the same one I just gave Odell.

"Let me be sure I have this straight," Odell finally says. "You and your friend . . ."

"Acey," I interject. "Best friend."

"You plan to open a whorehouse . . ."

"We prefer to call it a spa," I interject.

"Where women can come and buy the sexual services of men. Women of all sizes, shapes, age, and colors . . ."

"Only women of color."

"No white women?"

"Nope."

"Why? Your research has found they're getting enough sex, not into sex, what?"

"We haven't studied white women, because they're not our target audience," I say snippily.

"Still, from the number of hits I get from white women, I'm sure they'd be happy to be paying customers. I mean, if sisters are gonna pay for some black dick, I'm sure white girls will, too."

"I don't doubt it," I say, unable to keep a tad of huffiness out of my voice. "But A Sister's Spa is for sisters, black women. Exclusively."

"Isn't that discrimination?" Odell's teasing, but there are few, if any jokes in this territory.

"Listen, Odell. Black folks spend most of our lives in circumstances where white people have most of the power, economic and otherwise. When it comes to white women, our history until recently—and actually, I have my questions about how much that stereotype's changed in America—has been black men as rapists and black women as mammies, although now we call them "lovers" and "au pairs." Our spa is going to be a safe space for sisters. A place for black women to be pampered, to relax, and to be adored in all our beautiful, brown diversity. A refuge. For the duration of a sister's stay, black women represent the pinnacle of desirability, the ultimate standard of beauty, the be-all and end-all. Get it?

An escape from the so-called real world of white women tossing their hair, taking our men—in short, ruling the game." I don't say this, I practically spit it. Black men and white women are another sensitive subject.

"Still, a lotta those white women got cash, and I can tell you, they're horny."

"Enough," I say, and do that black people's hand-waving thing, like I'm doing air karate on a fat, slow-flying insect. "A Sister's Spa will not accept money from white women who want to come and act out their I-was-raped-by-a-big-black-buck-with-an-enormous-dick fantasies."

Sensitive black man that he is, Odell picks up on my ire, reaches over, and playfully tweaks my nipple.

"All right, cool, it's your world—and your spa. Let me say for the record that while I've slept with a few white women myself, I'm into sisters."

"Good. Because if you're not, I'm rescinding my job offer."

"You haven't made one yet," he says, pulling me back to the business at hand. "But if you want me to come work as a male ho, forget it. I'm not like that."

"Like what? Sexual? I beg to differ," I say, trying to lighten the tone, but Odell ain't having it.

"Listen, last night was great, but I don't want to screw women for a living. Maybe I come off to you as just a dumb guy who works for UPS who can fuck, but don't assume that's all there is—any more than you'd want me to clock you as just another high-siddity professional sister who can't get a man and has to pick up guys at the water cooler."

"Whoa, chill. No reason to get hostile."

"Just trying to be clear," Odell says. "Sure, I like sex, but if that's all I wanted I would have married my girlfriend. I want to start a business, work for myself, make some cash, and eventually get married and have some kids, in that order. This UPS gig is just something to keep me going until I figure out how to do that."

"Odell, I'm sorry if I insulted you, really. You know you don't have to get hostile."

"I'm not hostile, just trying to be straight-up about what's going on with me. Hey, I'm a man, I like sex, but I like lots of other things, too. Contrary to the stereotype you and most sisters seem to have about us, most brothers are about something besides just getting the pussy."

"Okay, point well taken. But if you'd let me finish, you'd know I wasn't offering you a job as a 'ho,' as you put it."

"So what are you offering?"

"A career opportunity. What I want you to do is help Acey and me find brothers to work at the spa. The requirements are simple. They need to be in great physical shape, reasonably intelligent, in good health—and by that I mean disease and drug free. The majority need to be under thirty-five. We're looking for men who get off on getting a woman off. And they have to be capable of tenderness and committed to pleasuring women. Men like yourself."

"I know a lot of men who fit that bill, though I can't testify about their sexual appetites or stamina. That's not my area," he says in the voice of a proud heterosexual.

"Don't worry, me and Acey will have that area more than covered. What we can't do is find the forty men we need to hire as sex workers— that'd take too much time, energy, and beating around the bush, so to speak. That's where you come in. You're a man, you know lots of other men, and you can cut straight to the chase about exactly what the gig entails."

"So, I'd be sort of a director of recruitment?"

"And more. We'd need you to move to Nevada once we're open for business, live on site, and help make sure everything runs smoothly. I guess we could say you'd be our director of human resources."

"Which means?"

"You'd be in charge of all the male employees. Acey and I will help you identify them, but you'll train them on procedures, arrange schedules, iron out whatever problems arise, and generally ensure that this aspect of the business runs smoothly. What do you think?"

"I'd have to move to Nevada?" Odell shakes his head. "I don't know, I like the Bay Area, and my family's here."

"Odell, live a little. Nevada's kinda cool, once you get outside Vegas, and right now we're thinking the spa will be closer to Reno, anyway. Didn't you say your brothers are in school out there, too? They're making it, aren't they?" Odell sucks his teeth.

"Barely. Those three knuckleheads are always in some kind of trouble, worrying my parents half to death. Now they're on academic probation. If they flunk a course, they lose their scholarships, and there's no way Moms and Pops can afford to pay full tuition," Odell shakes his head sadly. "They're not stupid, just immature, misguided, and arrogant on top, like so many young brothers. Think they can party, never crack a book, act simple, fuck women, and still get a degree. As far as the basketball team goes, they're hatchet men, plain and simple. Expendable, but they don't get it. Fools think they're gonna make the NBA, when the best they can do is get a damn degree and a life. DeJuan, DeQuan, and DeMon can't really play no ball, they're just big as hell and most players are afraid to even try to get past them," Odell laughs.

"Sounds like they could benefit from their big brother being close by."

"Yeah. I guess they could . . ."

"So, we've got a deal?"

"Slow down, Lydia. What about salary and benefits?" Smart man, he goes right for the money—a sensitive area since at the moment we don't have any, won't start talking to banks until we finish our business plan in a few weeks, and haven't even discussed it. I don't want to hesitate or appear unknowledgeable, since if he takes the job I'll be his boss, and it's important that even in the beginning I know, or at least make him think I know, all the answers. Keep that upper hand. I think fast.

"During the recruitment phase, we'll pay you $100 for every man you bring to our attention and who we subsequently employ." For a moment I feel like a bidder at a twenty-first century slave auction, placing a price on the heads of black bucks, but only for a moment. It's more accurate to think of Odell as a headhunter and myself as the CEO, paying him to identify talent, whom we plan to pay very well for their services.

"To help us get the spa up and running, you'll move to Nevada. We'll give you room, board, and pay you $10,000 more than you're making now, and provide full health coverage. There'll be a doctor on site, since a major element of our sales pitch is being clean and *safe*."

Odell listens, rubs the place where his beard would be if he had one, and finally says, "I want a percentage."

"Excuse me?"

"A per-cen-tage. You know. Of the profits. A piece of the action, so to speak," Odell says, and rears back on the legs of my kitchen chair, hands folded behind his head.

All I can think is, well goddamn, brother, five minutes ago you were acting like the idea was crazy and I was a high sexual deviant, now you want a percentage. Shit, I guess the idea ain't so farfetched after all, huh? But I don't say that. I don't kick over his chair, either. All's fair in sex and money.

"How much?"

"Twenty-five percent."

I roll my eyes, do my best imitation of a Bette Davis scoff, and say, "Too much. Forget it."

"Fifteen."

"I hope that's not your best offer."

"Okay, ten."

"How about five percent, and a bonus for every hundred women we satisfactorily service? Kind of a management by incentive program."

"Seven and a half percent, and a bonus for every fifty women and another one if I bring in conventions."

"Six." Cute and sexy as he is, the brother's shrewd. Frankly, Acey and me hadn't even thought of convention business. I can see vans packed with Deltas, AKAs, and union members pulling up to the spa. If Odell works as hard for us as he does negotiating for himself, we can't lose.

"Cool," Odell says.

"Welcome to A Sister's Spa," I say, smile, and extend my hand. I look into his eyes as we shake. Now that breakfast's eaten and the deal is done, I'm getting that early Sunday morning, sleepy, let's go back to bed feeling. I'm just about to suggest it when the doorbell rings. Before I can even wonder who it can be, I remember: Acey. Sunday. I finally got tired of her nagging and told her I'd go to church with her. I whisper to Odell to put on some clothes and hurry to buzz her up, coming up with excuses as I go.

9

THE EXPRESSION ON ACEY'S FACE WHEN I OPEN THE DOOR AND SHE sees me standing in the bright red foyer of my apartment in a robe and nothing else, grinning, my hair uncombed and wild, is a familiar one. It's not the first time I've blown or partially blown some plans we had made, and it probably won't be the last. I start talking fast and friendly.

"Girl, am I glad you're here, you have got to meet Odell, the brother is slamming. Smart, smooth, sexy as hell, and did I mention fantastic in bed?" Acey jerks her wrist in front of her to pull the sleeve back, glances dramatically at her Movado watch. Her hair's done and she's wearing the black dress from Loehmann's, matching pumps, some bad silver earrings, and a disapproving expression.

"We're supposed to go to nine o'clock service."

"Did you hear what I said? I have found our first employee, and he's right inside waiting to meet you."

"I hope he's dressed."

"Yeah, yeah, he's dressed," I say, pulling her inside. "He's in the kitchen, and he's definitely The One." I lower my voice, tilt my head in that direction. "You're gonna love him." Acey follows me inside, obediently slips off her shoes. I've got five rooms in my apartment, each painted a different bold color to match my many moods—the bedroom's terra cotta, den's hunter green, kitchen's purple, living room's teal blue—and decorated in entirely different styles. So when it came to the floors, the easy thing to do was cover the whole place in cream wool carpeting and ask people to take their shoes off upon entering.

"The One what?" Acey asks crabbily, pausing to check her hair in the antique beveled mirror over the hall table. She manages to look both righteous and sensual at the same time, a look I've never been able to achieve. "I thought you were looking for great sex, not The One."

"I am, I am. Sex with Odell was great, but that's not why he's The One. What I mean is he's the perfect man to work at the spa, so I offered him a job with us and he accepted." Acey stops walking and clutches my arm, squeezes so tight I can feel her long fingernails digging into my flesh through my chenille robe.

"You told him?" she hisses. "About the spa?" I wrench my arm from her grasp and rub the sore spot with one hand.

"Damn! What's the big deal? Yeah, I told him. It took some convincing, but he loves the idea and wants to work with us."

"Oh he does, does he? Doing what? Screwing?" Her voice is heavy with sarcasm.

"No, not screwing," I snap back. "Although he's highly competent in that area, if you haven't forgotten what that means since you've been hooked up with Matthew. Odell's ambitious and serious, so I offered him a job helping us recruit men to work at the spa, and once we get started as sort of a director of human resources." Acey looks mortified.

"Have you lost your mind?"

"Not at all."

"And he accepted?"

"After we did a little bargaining."

"What kind of bargaining?" Now she sounds alarmed.

"No biggie. I agreed to give him six percent plus a few bonuses if he does good work."

Acey looks incredulous. "Let me get this straight. You told some man you just met about our idea for the spa and then you not only hired him, but for two jobs and a percentage of the profits?" She shakes her head. "You know, you are truly pitiful. The sex *must* have been fabulous, since the man apparently fucked what little sense you have out of your head."

"I beg your pardon?"

"Lydia, you know you heard me. What've you got to say for yourself?" I wrap my robe tightly around me, smooth my hair, trying to look as serious as I feel, not like some sexed-out sister recently released from a night of passion. Which I am, but that doesn't mean I've suddenly gone stupid.

"Acey, I have not lost my mind. I have found a good man to work for us. Think about it: he's almost thirty, in the middle, so he's in contact with men of all ages. He's cute, and he's confident, which is a good indicator that his friends are at least cute, if not fine, since it's only the insecure fineys who have unattractive friends. He's intelligent and has a good sense of humor. And of course, he's open-minded and creative in bed, which means he'll be able to train any employees who need a little fine-tuning." I finish on a triumphant note, but from the look on Acey's face, she's not convinced.

"Tell me you didn't sign a contract."

"Of course not. I wanted you to meet him first." She looks relieved.

"Okay, so take me to the wonderful Odell." I can tell by her voice and expression that she's not optimistic.

When we enter the kitchen Odell's fully dressed, his jacket slung over the back of a chair, his sleeves rolled up, standing at the kitchen sink busting suds. He's wearing a silly bib apron with the words "Preserve Wildlife: Party" written on it that my mother gave me years ago. On him, it looks good.

"Odell, this is my best friend, Alice Clothilda Allen, also known as Acey." He turns from the sink, wipes his hand on the dish towel draped over his shoulder, grins, and extends his hand.

"Acey. I'm glad to meet you. Lydia has told me about you."

"Nice to meet you, Odell. Your reputation precedes you." Odell looks a little taken aback, but only for a moment. The brother's smooth.

"All good things, I hope."

"So far. But then you haven't known each other long," she says pointedly. Odell picks up a plate from the drain board and begins drying it.

"That's true. But haven't you ever met someone and it just clicks?"

"Depends what you mean by 'click,'" Acey says guardedly.

"That depends on who you meet and what you're looking for," he says, letting a hint of that bedroom voice escape, but not enough to offend, maybe not even enough for the average person to recognize—but then, Acey's not your average person.

"And you were looking for . . ."

"Actually, I wasn't looking for anything, which is what makes meeting a cool sister like Lydia so special." He says this with a disarming, boyish smile, and what can Acey say? She knows I'll be deeply offended and mad as hell if she follows up with "And what's so special about her?" so she turns to me and changes the subject.

"Remember church? Are we going?" Both arms above my head, I stand on my toes and stretch lazily, try run a hand through my hair, but its sleep-matted self is having none of that.

"Isn't there an eleven o'clock service we can make?" Acey sucks her teeth.

"You can make the eleven o'clock. I'm going to the nine in twenty minutes."

"Look at me. There's no way I can get myself together that fast." She looks me up and down, nods agreement.

"Guess I'm going alone then."

"If you wouldn't mind some company, I'd love to go. And I'm already dressed," Odell says. Acey turns to look at him.

"You want to go to church?"

"I may look like a heathen, but I assure you I'm not." Of course he doesn't look anything like a heathen, whatever one looks like, and he is ready to go.

"Are you certain you want to?"

"Sure. I was raised going to church every Sunday. These days I don't always make it, but I'm always ready to hear what the Lord's got to say. Might help."

"No might about it, as some of us know." This last comment is for me, but I ignore it. Right now my priority is getting back in bed, alone. I'm exhausted from the night before.

"Amen," Odell says. "Are we ready?" Would you like me to drive?"

"Let's just meet at Last Shall Be First Baptist on Nineteenth Street. That way we can go our separate ways after the service." It's obvious Acey has other plans, and taking Odell along for the ride isn't among them.

Odell doesn't miss a beat. "Cool. I'll meet you over there. Lydia, thanks for a great evening," he says, putting his arms around me and giving me a hug. Still holding on, he leans back until he can clearly see my face. "I'll talk to you soon, partner," he winks. Over his shoulder, I see Acey roll her eyes right before her face disappears as Odell bends over and gives me a big, warm kiss.

"I'll come back by or call you after church. We've got a lot to talk about," Acey calls over her shoulder as she walks toward the door.

"See ya." Almost asleep on my feet, I mumble good-byes, wave weakly, and I am already on my bed underneath my fluffy L.L. Bean down comforter, face down on sheets aromatic with the faint smell of cologne and the unmistakable odor of sex, when I hear the front door click shut.

10

LAST SHALL BE FIRST BAPTIST, MY DADDY'S CHURCH UNTIL HE DIED, is an enormous stone edifice that takes up nearly half of Nineteenth Street. It crouches on the block like some gigantic stone gargoyle waiting to pounce on the unsaved. Situated smack dab in the middle of Oakland's black community, it has remained vibrant through the ebb and flow of political chaos, economic decline, and America's ever-changing attitudes about its black citizens. The programs offered at First Baptist are an important element in its longevity. Along with the standard choir practice, deacon board, usher services, and men's and women's committees, my father understood that it is more than a spiritual institution. As conditions changed, so did the church, without ever losing sight of its fundamental spiritual mission. In response to increased unemployment, crime, hopelessness, and despair, particularly among young blacks but affecting all segments of the community, First Baptist initiated programs and activities to respond to the crisis at hand. The church offered midnight basketball to keep young men off the streets, job training programs to prepare them for employment opportunities, rites of passage programs to offer both girls and boys definitions of self other than those portrayed on television, and substance abuse counseling. Not long before he died, my father started a housing reclamation program in partnership with city government, and it was now thriving. The church purchased abandoned city-owned housing for a few dollars, renovated it, and offered apartments at rents well below fair market value to its members. This project was more than a little responsible for a steady increase in church membership, as citizens desperate for decent housing found the Lord and an apartment at the same time.

But the truth is that wonderful services and responsive programming accounted for only a part of First Baptist's prosperity, and would not have been implemented at all had it not been for the vision and savvy of my father and his youthful successor, the Reverend Doctor Herman P.

Rutledge V. Since taking over the church, where he'd been my father's assistant pastor, Rutledge has used his youth to disarm and disguise, and his tremendous energy to build the church into one my father, his mentor, would have been proud to see.

As the bells of the carillon ring out in welcome, Odell and I mount the stairs leading into the sanctuary, joining hundreds of parishioners as they make their way to seats in the already-packed pews. Unlike most Baptist churches, in which seventy percent of the parishioners are women, First Baptist boasts nearly an equal number of men, thanks to its emphasis on outreach programs for black youth. We find a seat as the deacons and Reverend Rutledge walk to the altar. I shrug out of my coat and Odell reaches over to help, smoothly slides it down over my arms, and thoughtfully places it around my shoulders. As the choir begins singing "How I Got Over," I can feel the warm pressure of Odell's thigh beside mine, discern the faint scent of Polo mixed with the intriguing odor of smoldering wood. I sniff gently, wondering if I can pick up the scent of Lydia on him, too. Next to me, Odell shifts, leaning down so his lips almost touch my ear, whispers, "You all right? Comfortable?" as if he has heard me thinking about him.

"Fine, thank you." I close my eyes, let the soaring voice of the soprano soloist and choir wash over and soothe me, and feel myself relax. Since I was a little girl, I've loved going to church, never had to be forced like my brothers. Even before I was old enough to understand the message of the sermon, I'd delighted in all aspects of Sunday. Waking up early to a warm bath as my mother ironed and starched a dressy dress. Sitting still in a hard-backed chair a few feet from the kitchen stove while Mommy first oiled and then pressed my thick hair with a hot comb, pulling it back so tight my eyes slanted upward, the smell of hair that close to burning (but not quite) wafting into my nostrils. Once dressed, I'd sit in the parlor in one of the enormous wingback chairs, waiting for my four older brothers to finish dressing and tumble downstairs full of argument and complaint. The slow ride to church in my father's big old Buick, rolling past sidewalks filled with parishioners hurrying to Sunday service, the women in gay dresses, high heels, and stockings, the men in somber suits, the children in miniature replicas of their parents' clothes. From the pew I was surrounded by a sea of women's hats. Dark hats, light hats, hats of pink and purple with brims stingy and wide. Hats with flowers, fruits, short and long veils. Once I even saw a wide-brimmed hat crowned by a miniature nest, complete with a tiny stuffed mama bird with three open-mouthed babies. I'd sit in this ocean of chapeaus as the music rose around me and my father's voice preached the gospel, and feel safe and content, believing that for this time, in this place, all was right with the world.

Sitting beside Odell in First Baptist all these years later, I try to recapture some bit of that childhood feeling of peace. Knowing as I do now that no place is absolutely safe, and that more often than not evil receives its rewards on earth and only the good die young, still church always offers a brief respite, solace, and some measure of spiritual renewal. I work at holding on to my faith, hold onto the word as I know and interpret it, try to believe that the Bible is a book of guidance, not judgment, that sin and missteps are part of being human, that actions speak louder than words. I take what I can use from church and leave the rest, gambling that the Lord—and my father—will understand.

This morning I can't help wondering if God understands the physical needs I have, that most women have, and what he would think about A Sister's Spa. Was Earl right that God is a God who understands and encourages pleasure? Or is it the Lord of my father who rules, a God who judges, condemns, and offers sacrifice? Had Earl been sent to my pantry to deliver a message, to help me, or did I simply conjure him up to justify my base feelings and perverse fantasies? Involuntarily, a sigh of frustration gusts softly from between my lips.

"Nice sermon. I've heard about Rutledge, but never heard him preach. He's good," Odell whispers, pulling me back into the present, abruptly aware of Odell's corporeal presence. I can feel the warmth and energy of blood and muscle emanating from him in waves. I turn to catch his eye, but Odell stares straight ahead, watching and listening to the soaring voice of Reverend Rutledge, whose topic that morning is "Judge Not Lest You Be Judged." Squirming slightly, I try to concentrate on the sermon as a sudden wave of raw desire washes over me like a hot flash.

"Yes and some of us, some of us, we don't know what we're looking for. We think what we want is a better job, when what we really need is a better way. We say we are tired of the life we live, that what we want is a new day. When what we really need is a new way. We look at our lives and we are angry and discontent. Then we look around for someone to blame. We say we are bored and point the finger at others. Our spouse. Our boss. The government. The children. We rush around searching outside ourselves for the cause of our discontent, when all we need do is look two places: In the mirror and to the Lord!" Choruses of "Amen" greet Rutledge's words, sighs of agreement escape the pursed lips of his congregation.

"We are, every last one of us, responsible for ourselves. Owed nothing by anyone. But we are not in the wilderness. No. The Lord has left us this book." He pauses, raises his thick, ornate Bible above his head, waves it so that all can see. "This good book. To succor us in time of crisis. To guide us in time of need. To show us a way!"

Rutledge's next pause is even longer, more theatrical.

"I said *a* way. Not *the* way. Because there are many paths to choose from when we choose to serve the Lord. The Lord wants us to make choices. The Lord wants us to take responsibility for ourselves. What the Lord does not want us to do is judge others. That is his job. Beware any man or woman who dares to judge others. Judge not lest you be judged.

"Now. I hear too many of you passing judgment on others. This one's business isn't straight, that one thinks she's cute, the other one doesn't meet your standard for righteousness. I say stop it! You are not doing the work the Lord wants you to do. If you think you are, you're mistaken. You've overstepped your bounds. You are trying to take the Lord's job from him, and none of us takes kindly to being downsized. He will not be pleased!" Laughter and scattered applause rises from the assembled, and the ladies' hats nod in agreement.

"Many of you justify your bitter judgment of others by saying you are doing God's will. You are not. Our God is a God of love, not censure. He is a God of joy, not pain. Our God wants you to live life righteously and to its fullest, and finds no contradiction there. The Lord tells us, set your house in order. He doesn't say his house, their house, or her house. He says *your* house. He reserves the judgment of others for himself. And have no doubt we will each be judged at the end of this earthly life when we go to meet our maker.

"Look in the mirror. Don't involve yourself in judging others, judge yourself. Don't try to change others, change yourself. Don't look to the Bible for words to justify your judgments, but for words of guidance. It is all there for us. Right under our noses. In our hands. In the mirror. Right there inside us. Judge not lest you be judged! Amen. Let us pray."

Herman Rutledge bows his head, the bells high in the bell tower peal, and the organist begins softly playing "Jesus Walked That Lonesome Valley" as ushers pass the collection plate.

I fumble to open the clasp on my purse on the bench beside me, then feel Odell's hand on mine. "Don't worry. I've got it," he says as he pulls a ten from his pocket and drops it into a collection plate already overflowing with bills, few of them ones. "That sermon was certainly worth it. Sometimes what you're looking for *is* right under your nose." Slipping my coat around me, I nod absentmindedly, wonder if Odell is thinking solely of spiritual enlightenment and guidance or, like me, of more worldly gratifications.

"Those bells sound beautiful," Odell says as we walk toward the doorway. "I've heard them before, but never knew which church they came from."

"First Baptist's bells are famous. Tourists from all over the world come to hear them," I say, then add without thinking, "Would you like to see them?" Odell nods and grabs my hand, we make a hard left through a doorway leading to a twisting, narrow staircase. "The view from the bell tower is gorgeous; you can see almost the whole city," I say as we squeeze up the steps, pausing to greet Mrs. Hutchinson, the elderly sister who's been ringing the bells since my father was pastor, on her way down.

When we climb the final step we are in the small hexagonal room that houses the carillon. Its walls are made of rough, thick, gray stones the size of cinderblocks, fitted together tightly without benefit of mortar. On each of the six walls the stone has been cut to create an arching window, offering a 360-degree view of the city and outlying suburbs. In the center hang the ornate brass bells with their hammers, silent now but still vibrating slightly. Odell pauses at the top of the stairs, turning full circle to admire the surrounding view.

I stand at the window facing east, squinting toward San Francisco Bay, pierced with the wish that Earl had never taken that sailboard out and left me alone. I rest my hands on the cold stone sill, bend forward slightly as I stare at the water, another in a long line of women waiting for their long-lost men to return from sea. A chilly breeze sweeps over me, blowing tendrils of hair across my face, reminding me of Earl's appearance in the pantry and his strange words of love and support. I close my eyes and lean into the breeze, my mind confused with thoughts of the meaning of Rutledge's sermon and Earl's words, and of Earl, Earl's body, Earl and me together . . .

As much as I hear his approach, I smell the scent of the cologne he always wears, feel the air thicken with sexual desire, and suddenly, urgently taste the piquancy of copper pennies on my tongue, their metallic sweetness. I do not turn around, but am not surprised when two sure hands touch my hips, cupping that place between waist and thighs that women too often think of as saddlebags to be exercised away, but are really grips for a man's tender hands. As he softly eases his body along mine, I can feel his hard chest along my back, his pelvis against my ass. He leans over and licks the rim of my ear, lets his mouth drift down until he is kissing behind it, his lips descending the nape of my neck. Slow as the movement of molasses on a cold day, he lets one hand slide from my hip to the hem of my skirt, softly teases his long fingers up the inside of my thigh, gently works his fingers underneath the leg of my panties, two fingers lingering softly but insistently, gently stroking the hairs there back and forth. His thumb travels cautiously upward to my honey pot, gently peels back the surrounding skin. My flower jumps out to meet and welcome his finger as he strokes the delta between my legs.

His other hand drifts down to rub and trace the curvature of my ass, and slowly pushes the skirt up around my waist. His two fingers dip in and out of my now-dripping pussy as his thumb caresses my love mound with a steady, circular motion. His hands work me slowly, his lips lingering in the nape of my neck, grazing and gently nibbling with kisses. I moan as his fingers unhurriedly explore and tantalize this aching body, so slow it is almost painful and so good I want to push back hard against his fingers, but hold myself back, knowing there is no hurry. No penis to be coaxed into erection, no foreplay to be hastily gotten over with, no potential premature ejaculation to be smoothed over and, like so many dreams, deferred.

With his fingers still inside me, he pulls my panties down around my thighs. Hearing the sound of a zipper, I place my palms flat out on the stone windowsill, spread my legs, push up on my toes to raise my ass. His fingers slip from between my legs, but before my feelings of loss turn back into yearning, the fingers are replaced by the fat, hot head of his dick as it slides inch by inch into my wet pussy. Greedily, I push back now to meet my Earl, move my feet to open my legs wider, hungry to take in all of him. It is not until I feel the hairs on his pelvis meet my ass, as he finally thrusts all the way inside, that I relax. I hold him inside me for long moments, clenching the muscles of my pussy to grip his penis until he moans softly. I hold him, motionless, accept the length and breadth of him inside me as he traces the pattern of the earring in my left ear with his tongue. Steadying himself with his left hand along the side of the window, with the right one he cups my breast, strokes the nipple through the fabric of my dress until it is hard and burning. He simultaneously begins to move in and out, his penis pumping slow, then fast, always steady, maintaining his own rhythm even when I push excitedly back against him. Occasionally, in exquisite punishment for my haste, he pulls his penis back so all that remains inside is the head, frozen there for long seconds, then thrusts his length back inside me with gentle force.

Still fucking steadily, his hand moves from my breast to my hot, swollen clit and begins to squeeze it gently, the motion of his hand synchronized with his thrusts. Like a dancer accommodating herself to the moves of a graceful partner, I easily read the signals from his body, move in response to the rhythm he sets. Every now and then I alter the motion or pace of our fucking with a twist or turn of my ass, and can feel the brushfires ignite in my body, baby orgasms all firing up for the final conflagration. We go on, the only sound an occasional gasp or moan, until I feel a sensation as if a rash, oddly pleasurable in its itching, has instantly broken out over my whole body, as a sheen of sweat bathes my stomach and breasts, and my body temperature shoots up. Still on my toes, my legs begin to tremble slightly as the muscles in my pussy contract and ripple violently. "Ready?" he asks, hunching over to kiss my lips, his penis pushing deeper inside.

Startled, I open my eyes, turn my head to see Odell, not Earl, driving his penis into my erupting pussy. Even if I wanted to, it is too late to tell him to stop, as I move into that moment of orgasm beyond speech. I can barely nod yes, I'm ready, as I push back to meet his strokes, close my eyes, and listen to the voices, Earl's in my head and Odell's in my ear, urging me to "Come, baby, come!" I climax leaning into the wind, hoping it will carry my screams away, toward heaven or hell, I don't care which.

11

BY THE TIME ACEY AND ODELL GET BACK FROM CHURCH IT'S AFTER twelve o'clock. I've slept a good three hours, showered, made a fresh pot of chocolate hazelnut coffee, and am up and dressed when I hear two cars pull into the driveway. I'm kinda surprised because I'm not expecting Odell back, but it's cool. I figure the two of them must have hit it off all right, otherwise Acey would have told him politely but firmly to take his tired butt elsewhere. When I open the door they're standing there looking all cool and relaxed, wearing expressions that look like they just put them on before I appeared. I wonder if maybe I've missed something. "Hey. How was church?" I ask.

"I'm saved," Odell jokes.

"I'm healed," Acey adds. She has a small, tight smile on her face, the kind people have when they're trying not to display one of those big, wide, I-just-got-my-shit-off-and-it-was-good grins.

In response, I give her a quick raised-eyebrow, oh-no-girl-you-didn't look. She flashes one of those contented faces folks have after calling a moratorium on cholesterol surveillance and pigging out on baby back ribs at a Fourth of July picnic. Even though I know Acey's a spiritual sister, I suddenly suspect it might not have been the sermon alone that accounts for her unsettled look. I make a mental note to grill her for details later.

If Odell notices any of this fast and furious facial conversation, he doesn't let on, as he's busy looking through the high-tech steel racks that hold my collection of five hundred CDs. Acey plops down on the living room couch like she's totally physically exhausted even though her soul is rested, while I go into the kitchen to fetch mugs of coffee for everyone. Odell puts on Alicia Keyes and the three of us lounge comfortably for a few minutes, nodding our heads along to the music and sipping coffee. The atmosphere is so chill and comfortable, I'm ready to doze off again.

"We need a questionnaire for the men who want to work at the spa," Odell suddenly says, sitting up. "A written application they can fill out."

"I already told you, I envision more of a live audition-type format," I say lazily. Acey throws a pillow at me, says, "The application is our pre-screening. If they pass that, then we'll give them a live audition."

"Somehow, I don't think the application exists for this job," I snicker. Odell's straight up, listening.

"Get a grip, Lydia. We need to write our own application. After all, we're looking for something more than hard penises."

"Really? And what might that something else be? Long tongues?" Odell laughs, but Acey rolls her eyes at me and says, "It's not all about the sex, but about healing, too, making sisters feel beautiful and appreciated. Gimme a pad and let's write it down before we forget." I stumble up, go to the desk against the far wall, and toss Acey a yellow legal pad and my lucky Mont Blanc pen with the dark green ink. "Okay. What's first?"

"Besides the standard name, address, Social Security number, we need to ask questions that'll tell us if the brother understands pleasing women," Odell suggests. I nod.

"Sisters have enough complaints when the sex is free. You know they're not going to stand for any problems if they're laying down their hard-earned cash."

"The question is, besides the physical, what makes sex good?" Odell asks sincerely, only a hint of fishing for compliments in his voice.

"Attitude."

"Experience and stamina."

"A willingness to experiment."

"A sense of humor."

"Tenderness and creativity."

"And no damn hang-ups."

"No rolling over and falling asleep. The man's gotta talk." Acey and me blurt out suggestions while Odell, who's grabbed the pad, starts taking rapid notes.

"He's got to have the balance between being hard and being tender just right—the same way Odell does," Acey blurts, then looks stricken. Too late.

"Say what?"

"The balance between being firm and gentle," Acey murmurs.

"I heard that. But wasn't your point of reference Odell?" I laugh,

point my finger at the two of them, stopping at Acey. "Give it up, sister."
The info, I mean, 'cause now I know she already gave up the other thing.

"Can we talk about this later? Privately?" Acey's voice is pleading.

"This is private. We're all business partners aren't we? If we're going
to start a brothel, we damn sure better be comfortable talking about sex.
So, you did do the wild thing, am I right?" Odell nods shyly, but Acey just
sits there, looking mortified.

"Acey. Come on, relax. It's cool. Odell's a nice guy, a new friend,
and a great lay, but he's not my man. You know I'm not looking for that."
Acey's expression relaxes slightly.

"I just thought, you know, maybe, of course I wasn't thinking about
anything . . . I mean we just met, and he and you . . . but we were up in
the bell tower and I was thinking about Earl, the sermon, and just . . . it
just . . ."

"Happened." Odell says, grinning that easy grin of his.

"What*ever*," I say, and wave my hand in dismissal. "So how was it?"
Acey looks embarrassed. "Acey, you were the one who got all freaked
out when I told you I'd offered Odell a job after last night, remember?
No offense, Odell, but now you can see why, can't you?" Acey nods in
agreement.

"I mean, let's give it up, the brother knows how to please a woman,
am I right?" Now it's Odell's turn to look embarrassed, but Acey can't
keep that big old smile off her face.

"Okay, okay, you're right," she laughs. "It's just really strange sleeping with the same guy as your best friend within twenty-four hours, and
no one being angry or hurt."

"Yeah, it's not the norm—and being honest and upfront about it
sure isn't. But we're best friends, we've been through a ton of shit together, and we always make it through. Let's not start letting a little dick
mess with us now." I notice Odell flinch, so I add, "Little dick is only an
expression, brother. Don't trip."

"You're right," Acey nods. "It's just this is all so different, almost
like we're creating our own little parallel universe, where the old rules
we've been obeying most of our lives don't apply."

"Amen to that. No more possessiveness, jealousy, competition between women over men."

"Still, it feels weird."

"Yep. It is a whole new way of doing things for women, and if we
don't have our shit together, I mean between us, it won't work. Remem-

ber, the point of A Sister's Spa isn't to meet your mate and live happily ever after; it's to have fabulous, uncomplicated sex, then go back to your real life satisfied, happy, and planning your next visit. Like we just did with Odell."

"Hey, wait a minute," Odell interrupts. "You make me sound like some kind of gigolo."

"That's not what I said, Odell. But you know the saying, if the shoe fits . . ."

"Which means what?" Odell bristles.

"Which means there's a long tradition of men working as male escorts or high-end gigolos, catering to the needs of rich, older, mostly white women, so what's the big deal if black women who aren't necessarily wealthy want to get a piece of that action?"

"But that's not *my* action. Or is it?"

"Nope, you're right. We have other plans for you."

"Cool. Because my understanding is that to be an escort or a gigolo, money has to change hands," Odell says. "And in this case, it didn't." Acey nods.

"That's true. Apologies, Odell. But once the spa opens, money will be paid for the services of the gentleman who work there."

"Then what makes A Sister's Spa different than any escort service?" Odell asks, frowning.

"That's a good question," Acey nods. "Because you know the average woman, much less the average black woman, isn't going to call an escort service. And while it's true in some circumstances we may essentially be paying for sex, it's usually more subtle than cash on the barrelhead."

"You're right. A Sister's Spa is more than an escort service, it's a total experience," I say.

"Good line, but what does it mean?" Odell asks.

"I can't speak for Lydia, but to me it means that we create a complete environment in which women can relax, be pampered, and have great sex. The spa will be gorgeously decorated and offer all the amenities sisters need to de-stress and feel special, including great sex. It's not like they'll be sitting in a hotel room waiting for an escort to arrive and run their MasterCard."

"Hey, we've got to accept credit cards," I pipe in.

"Credit's cool, but I understand what Acey's saying, it's how and when it's done," Odell says. "It's hard to create the right ambiance if sisters are peeling off bills, writing checks, or weighing the service rendered with the price charged. The monetary shit needs to be taken care of before they arrive."

"I agree. We should structure the spa like Club Med: once you choose a package, book it, and pay up front, everything's all inclusive. You can check your pocketbook at the door."

"Of course women are going to be hesitant at first, that's natural," Acey adds. "It's up to us to create a welcoming, controlled environment, where discreet, celebratory sex is available 24-7 and there's never a need to feel sleazy, furtive, or like a loser."

"Yep. If we do that, I think women of all ages, sizes, and economic brackets will be happy to plunk down those benjamins to come to a place full of sexy men all ready, willing, and able to give sexual pleasure," I say.

"Now, that brings me to the issue of the men we're gonna hire," Odell says. "It's not just about them being good lovers, they have to be able to perform with any and all kinds of women."

"What do you mean?" Acey asks.

"Just this. Any man can make love to a fine woman, but we're going to have all kinds of women at the spa. Old, young, middle-aged, and probably at least a few who aren't that attractive. We need to find sex workers who can get turned on by all types of women, or else we're back where we started from."

"Which is where?"

"Which is any damn bar in America on a Friday night. Or anyplace else there're more women than men and men hold most of the cards," I say.

"And if that's the scene, we'll be out of business before we really get started. Maybe we should put some questions on the application to help us identify those men who are turned on by a broad spectrum of women."

"Great idea. Then we can push them on it in the interview."

"Just like I was pushing you about how the sex was with Odell a few minutes ago until he gallantly changed the subject," I tease. Acey gives me a frown.

"Excuse me, Miss Sexual Liberation, but I guess I'm not as highly evolved as you are. Could we *please* talk about this some other time?"

"Cool. But I expect the complete play-by-play later. Right now, we need to get back to the questionnaire. Okay, how do we structure the questions to get the most honest answers?"

"How about multiple choice? Give the brothers more than one option. It'll be harder to figure out the right answer that way," Odell suggests.

"We should have some questions where there's more than one right answer, too, designed to find men whose priority is pleasuring women."

"Yeah, and we can plant some wrong answers. Red flags that if any-one checks they go immediately into the circular file," I suggest.

"Maybe a few short essay questions at the end, in case an applicant wants to elaborate," Acey adds.

"Good idea. And the multiple-choice questions will save us time weeding through every single application," Odell says.

Acey turns to him, asks hopefully, "You think we'll get a lot of them?"

"Hell, yeah," Odell says. "Brothers like myself looking for a transi-tion gig, one between the bad one they're in and the great one they're moving toward, not to mention men who are temporarily unemployed. And take it from me, even when they're not working, they're fucking. It's like a brother's dream job, boning women for pay." We all laugh.

"But we don't want A Sister's Spa full of unemployable losers," I say.

Odell bristles. "Damn Lydia, you're kinda hard on the brothers. Just because a man's not working doesn't mean he's unemployable. He just can't find a job. Besides, I'll wager a few men who already have gigs will be eager to work at the spa if it's a vertical move."

"Okay, be cool, point well taken," I say, rolling my eyes.

"Lydia, I'm not trying to get on your case, but I want you to hear me," Odell says gently. "You're talking about starting a business that em-ploys mostly men. I think it's important that you like and respect the men who work for you. It'll make managing them easier, and result in more satisfied customers."

"Good point, Odell." Acey, who knows me well enough to know I'm now probably offended, interjects smoothly before I can go off. "And you're right. Our job is to make sure they deliver satisfaction with a smile to the sisters, and they need to be well treated to do that."

"All right. How about a question on foreplay . . ." Odell suggests. We've all got our thinking caps on and little grins on our faces, when the telephone rings.

"Hello? Oh, hi Mom," I turn to Acey and make an "Arrggh" face. "I'm fine. You? Dinner? I don't think so. I've gotta work today. Actually, I'm in a meeting now." I pause as my mother goes into a monologue about Sunday being a day of rest, not working too hard, and have I spoken to Lorenzo.

"No, I haven't returned his calls . . . . Because I'm really busy and actually have nothing to say to him, Mom." After I say this, I claw the air as if I'm trying to escape from an invisible cage. Acey smiles, while Odell watches impassively.

"No, I don't usually work Sundays, but we just got a big new account. Huh? Well, um, it's a new business, based in Nevada . . . Mom, you're not really interested, are you? You are? Well, it's a, uh . . ." I turn away from the telephone inquisition toward Acey, give her a pleading sister-help-me-out-with-this-one look. Acey gives me a you're-on-your-own-sister shrug, closes her eyes, and ends our silent conversation.

"No, I can't get you comped at the Sands when Nancy Wilson's there. No, mother, it's not gambling . . . Okay, okay. It's a brothel," I blurt out. Enough of the International Mommy Telephone Torture, she's broken me. What does my always unpredictable mother do? She laughs.

"What's so funny? Yeah, I think it's strange men want to pay for sex with all these women out here, too. But to each his own, Ma, I'm just trying to do my job. What? Hold on." I cover the receiver and turn to Acey and Odell, who are both now snickering evilly and patting their feet to the rhythms of Heather Headley singing about understand the nature of a man. "She wants to help me! What should I do?" Acey throws her hands up in the position of surrender. She's known my mother long enough to know that once she fastens on to an idea, she won't let it go. Desperate, I turn to Odell, not that he knows my mother, but he's got one, too. How different can the genre be?

He grins, whispers, "Didn't you say your mom's a librarian? Research. Ask her to research the history and laws about brothels in Nevada. We're gonna need to know that. What she doesn't need to know is you're gonna open one for women."

"Mom. I'm back. Do you really want to help? All right, could you find out the history of brothels? When they started, how they're run, what the laws are, shit like that . . . Sorry, I meant to say information." I pause, listen as my mother switches into research librarian mode, fires off specific questions.

"Just pull whatever you think I can use, and I'll weed through it . . . Mom, gotta go, I've got people here . . . No, not a man, and definitely not Lorenzo. Okay. Thanks. I'll talk to you later." I replace the receiver and fall into a chair, exhausted and shaking my head.

"Not a man?" Odell teases. "What do I have to do to prove myself?"

"Your mom is wild," Acey laughs. "But we're going to need that info, and it'll be less for us to do." She frowns at the pad covered with notes that Odell's tossed back on to her lap.

"Okay," Odell says, sitting up straight. "First things first. After we dispense with the basics, the first question we should ask is about fore-play . . ." I give Acey a smug glance of sexual bonding, hoping to elicit acknowledgment of Odell's proficiency in that area, just gimme some kinda sign, girl. But the sister's already scribbling and doesn't even notice.

(12)

A Sister's Spa Employment Application

Name: _____

Age: _____

Address: _____

Telephone Number: _____

Penis Size When Erect (in inches. Please answer honestly.
All information will be verified manually.): _____

Hand Size (tip of pinkie to tip of thumb outstretched, in inches): _____

Shoe Size: _____

Can you touch your nose with your tongue?: Yes _____ No _____

Are you double- or triple-jointed? If so, what limbs? _____

Total Number of Female Lovers: _____

Total Number of Female Lovers Brought to Orgasm
(no, this is not the same question as above!) _____

Have you prematurely ejaculated since high school? Yes _____ No _____

What is the longest period of time you have continuously penetrated a
woman without ejaculating?
_____ seconds _____ minutes _____ hours _____ days

What's the longest amount of time it's taken you to get from
a woman's lips to her poonani?
_____ seconds _____ minutes _____ hours _____ days

Will you perform oral sex on a woman having her period?
Yes _____ No _____

Will you participate in a menage a trois? Yes _____ No _____

Will you perform anal sex? Yes _____ No _____

MULTIPLE-CHOICE QUESTIONS

(Feel free to check more than one choice. If you would like to elaborate, use a separate sheet of paper. Please be specific if you check "other.")

1. I usually begin sex with:
☐ kissing ☐ a massage ☐ ask for a blow job ☐ other

2. My favorite sexual position is:
☐ on my back ☐ my partner on her back ☐ doggy style
☐ I don't have a favorite position, I enjoy them all

3. To find out a woman's sexual desires, I:
☐ talk to her before sex ☐ talk to her during sex
☐ read her body language ☐ don't care and never have

4. I enjoy having sex to:
☐ jazz ☐ hip-hop ☐ R&B ☐ no music at all
☐ all the above ☐ other

5. I think condoms are:
☐ essential ☐ for other people ☐ okay, but they don't make them big enough for me ☐ I'm not familiar with them

6. I go down on a woman:
☐ some of the time ☐ all of the time ☐ never
☐ don't understand the question ☐ only when she goes down on me

7. When a woman grabs my head during oral sex it means:
☐ she wants me to continue ☐ she wants me to stop
☐ she's trying to guide me to the right spot
☐ could mean any of the above

8. When a woman says "stop" or "I can't take anymore" during oral sex it means:
☐ it doesn't feel good and she wants me to cease and desist ☐ she wants me to put it in ☐ I should lessen the pressure, it's getting good to her ☐ She's reached her maximum orgasm limit ☐ other

9. I go down on a woman because:
☐ I like it ☐ she likes it ☐ because most women's orgasms are clitorally, not vaginally stimulated ☐ because I understand a man's gotta eat that pie ☐ other

10. A woman's breasts are:
☐ places where fat is deposited ☐ an erogenous zone
☐ where babies get milk ☐ things that look nice in a low-cut dress
☐ things I love to suck and fondle

11. When I smell a woman's sex I am:
☐ turned on ☐ turned off ☐ indifferent ☐ inspired

12. I'd describe the way a woman's vagina smells as:
☐ earthy and stimulating ☐ fishy ☐ stank ☐ other

13. When I make love to a woman, my intention is to:
☐ please the woman ☐ please myself ☐ please both of us
☐ other

14. When an older woman approaches me, I:
☐ assume she's asking for directions ☐ am attracted
☐ think about my mother ☐ am turned off

15. When I come before a woman, I:
☐ roll over and go to sleep ☐ maintain my erection
☐ figure there's something wrong with her ☐ fall down on my knees and ask forgiveness ☐ I never come before a woman

16. When a woman talks shit during sex, I:
☐ get aroused ☐ tell her to shut up so I can concentrate
☐ talk shit back to her

17. Have you ever spoken any of the following phrases in bed?
☐ "whose pussy is it?" ☐ "call me daddy" ☐ "tell me it's the best"
☐ the name of any woman other than the one you're with
☐ none of the above

18. When a woman asks me to do something new sexually, I:
☐ immediately say no ☐ immediately say yes
☐ ask her if I do it will she respect me in the morning
☐ ask her where she learned that shit ☐ other

19. If a woman wants to have anal sex, I:
☐ jump for joy ☐ am willing and gentle as long as it's safe sex
☐ repulsed ☐ other

20. I regard a woman's feet as:
☐ something to walk on ☐ a neckbone to be savored and sucked on
☐ a repository for corns, bunions, and calluses ☐ other

21. If a woman brought hand-cuffs, vibrators, physical restraints, or other sex toys to bed, I would:
☐ get up and leave ☐ ask her what she wants me to do with them
☐ tell her this ain't *Roots* and I don't play that shit ☐ other

22. When a woman has a multiple orgasm, I:
☐ pat myself on the back and am happy for her
☐ become extremely jealous ☐ demand she do the same thing for me

23. After sex I like to:
☐ go to sleep ☐ talk ☐ eat ☐ rest up and have sex again

24. If a woman tells me she gets pleasure from satisfying me, I:
☐ roll over on my back and tell her to hit it ☐ convince her that my priority is her sexual pleasure ☐ suggest ways we can mutually satisfy each other ☐ all of the above ☐ other

SHORT-ANSWER SECTION

25. Please list all of the erogenous zones on a woman's body.

_____

_____

_____

26. Do you have any special or unusual sexual talents? Please describe.

_____

_____

_____

27. Describe your most erotic experience with a woman.

_____

_____

_____

28. Tell us your favorite place to have sex and why.

_____

_____

_____

29. Is there anything we haven't asked you that you'd like to tell us about your sexual self?

_____

_____

_____

30. Please give a brief physical description of the last three women you made love to.

_____

_____

_____

31. Please tell us why you want to work at A Sister's Spa, and what unique contribution you feel you would make.

_____

_____

_____

32. Please attach a full-body photograph of yourself in gym wear to the last page of this application. Head shots are not accepted.

⓭

I DON'T FREAK WHEN THREE WEEKS LATER ON THE WAY TO THE BANK
to discuss getting a business loan, the taxi gets a flat tire five blocks from
my destination. Of course this crisis occurs less than a quarter of the way
up one of San Francisco's steepest hills, and I have to hoof it the rest of
the distance in three-inch Bruno Magli heels. Not surprisingly, when I
get to the bank I'm sweating and puffing like I've just run—and lost—the
Kentucky Derby, and have a tear up the back of my stocking.

It doesn't help when Acey, impeccably dressed in a fabulous beige
Armani pants suit, low-cut blouse, and the usual flawless make-up, isn't
even curious as to why I've arrived on foot with a face dripping perspira-
tion, but simply snaps, "Finally. Girl, if you can find a way, you'll be late
for your own funeral." Cool as she looks, I know the sister is stressed
when she doesn't even crack a half-assed smile when I retort, "Hell, if I
can figure out how, I intend to miss it altogether." All she does is say,
"Come on, we don't want to be late," and hurry into the bank.

The Old Western Bank is one of those old-fashioned banks with
marble floors and walls, ceilings two stories high with frescoes painted
around the rim, and pre-automatic weapon wrought iron instead of
Plexiglas in front of the teller's windows. Whatever the temperature is
outside, the air inside Old Western Bank is always chilly, slightly thin,
and smells of money. Being inside feels like it must feel to be inside a
vault: protected, secure, and impregnable. This was where my mother
brought me when I was nine to open my first real savings account, where
I'd taken out my college loans, where Lorenzo and I had come to borrow
money for our first mortgage.

The sharp tap of heels on marble punctuates our progress as we walk
toward the area of the bank where the loan officers are clustered, past
people lined up patiently in front of teller windows, older women bent so
far over the high, marble-topped tables as they squint and fill out deposit
slips, their foreheads almost touch the cool surface. Past three security

guards in navy blue uniforms who lounge casually, not one of them look-ing like he could stop me, much less Queen Latifah and her crew from *Set It Off*. I comfort myself with the thought that even though their guns are holstered and two of them look old enough to be collecting Social Secu-rity, they are secretly alert and ready. Even though Acey's pulling me rap-idly forward, I have time to notice that the younger guard is more than a little attractive. I can't help turning my head to check out his buns as I pass by, and I'm not surprised to find him giving us the same attention. Years of being female and observing men have taught me that it's a rare black man who can let an ass roll by without looking, whatever a woman's age, countenance, or size. Busted, we both laugh and Acey turns too. Scoping out the situation in a moment, she snorts, "Girl, let's go! This is business," slips an arm through mine, and yanks me ahead.

"This is research," I laugh. "I'm checking out the potential pool of employees for the spa. You know some women are turned on by men with guns. And uniforms. We should most definitely have some fine law-enforcement type and one of those young buffed brothers with good teeth, bulging arms, and his name embroidered on his shirt pocket. You know, the ones who come to your house to fix, deliver, or install some-thing and you have to restrain yourself?"

My voice fades away as my mind fills with images of the various brothers I've lusted after in my life and the possibilities for the spa. Hell, why discriminate against white guys? I'd seen more than a few who I wouldn't mind nibbling my nugget. Just as I'm about to go off on an in-teresting internal jag, Acey pulls me back from possibility to the present.

"Maybe we'd better concentrate on getting this money, or there won't be any need for research," Acey says. "But that's not a bad idea, let's talk about it later. The spa will be a full-service establishment. Now, come on."

I can see it clearly. We're not about sex alone, but fantasies realized. We will offer not just the sexually satiating booty call, but a total experi-ence with the man of your dreams, whatever your dreams are. Who hasn't fantasized about sex with a man with a body so sculpted it looks like carv-ing, with a professional athlete who can sail through the air or tackle any-thing? With a brown-skinned man with muscular thighs who takes you back to Africa, with an easy man who plays in bed and makes you laugh and come simultaneously? With all the beautiful black men we pass on the street, see on a movie screen, even the guy with the gorgeous back selling the cologne from the insert stuck in your Macy's bill? I'm so giddy with the notion that I can't help it, I laugh out loud and chortle, "The possibilities are endless!"

Acey grunts. "Listen, don't put the dick before the dough. We're almost there. Remember, as far as the bank's concerned, we want the money to start a spa, plain and simple. Now, stay focused and let's do this."

Just ahead of us is a four-and-a-half-foot-wide mahogany door, in the middle of which a thick brass nameplate announces that behind lies the inner sanctum of Gardiner Roberts III, vice president of Old Western Bank. But of course the gateway to the cash is not unattended. The sentry guarding the portal beyond which Gardiner Roberts waits to loan us money is a woman whose name, according to the tin nameplate on her desk, is LaShaWanda P. Marshall. From her demeanor, she's one of those women who can smell bullshit from twenty yards away. Ms. Marshall looks to be about thirty, although if she told me I was off by a decade either way, I'd believe her. She is brown-skinned, full-bosomed, size sixteen and then some, and flaunts square-tipped, two-inch fingernails painted in an elaborate red, black, and green design. She wears her hair in beaded extensions halfway down her back, what me and Acey refer to as gypsy curtains, after those floor-length strands of beads that guard a fortune-teller's inner sanctum. She's wearing a gray pinstriped business suit that looks like an Emanuel Ungaro (bad, if a little tight) over a silk blouse in a paler shade of gray. I can't decide if her conservative attire clashes with those beaded braids or if they play off each other. Even though I can't see them, I'm willing to bet her shoes are in pristine condition: no run over heels, unsightly scuff marks, or creepy bunion bulges. As with so many big women, her hair and shoes would be together.

Women like LaShaWanda P. Marshall make up an army of sisters in cities across America. You see them every morning before nine on their way to work and every evening on their way home. Usually they wear sneakers and tired, occasionally sour expressions, and why shouldn't they? These are the women who work thankless jobs for lousy pay, who come home to too many children and no man, or a bad man and no children to hug and help take the edge off. They spend their days protecting and lying for their bosses and are never protected themselves. They bust ass for whole lifetimes and still don't ever get ahead. The mistake that those of us with what we consider to be better jobs, or better lives, or better taste often make is thinking that these women are content, without ambition, or not too bright. It is a judgment that can be fatal. The LaShaWandas of the world are seldom stupid or without ambition. They are never ambivalent or wishy-washy. If they are friend, your back is eternally watched. If a LaShaWanda decides you are foe, it is best to give up any designs on who or what is under her control; there is no escaping her wrath. Ever. Better to admit defeat, get smart, and move on to other, hopefully more hospitable pastures. Pray that the Arleathia or JacQuanda or Shaneequa encountered up ahead will be more positively inclined.

But I don't understand that yet, so I stride up to her desk and say, "Mr. Gardiner Roberts, please. Lydia Beaucoup and Acey Allen to see him. Our appointment is for two o'clock." No "How are you," no sister-bonding, no nod to LaShaWanda's humanity, much less her enormous power as gatekeeper and censor. The tone of my voice says I am the important one, so put a move on.

Bad move. LaShaWanda, who's been typing steadily since we came in, doesn't look up, speak, grunt, or acknowledge our presence in any way. The only indication that she heard what was said is that the click-clack of her keyboard slows down, almost imperceptibly, definitely ominously.

I stand before Ms. Marshall's desk, tapping a high-heeled foot, impatient and oblivious to the subtle power dynamics at work here. I'd like to blame it all on having to scramble up that damn hill and the run in my stocking, but that would be a lie. Interpersonal relations aren't my strong suit.

Acey pushes me aside unceremoniously, and before I can put my Magli'd foot in my mouth, she smiles and says, "Good morning, sister. How you doin' today?" all respectful and friendly, yet dropping that G and doing that subtle I'm-a-down-sister bonding voice. Ms. Marshall's chin ascends. Slowly. She looks at Acey with violet contact lens-colored eyes that are sharp as knives. With a desultory glance she looks her up and down, and finally says in a voice that, while not quite icy, is definitely cold, "Not very well," and turns back to her keyboard.

"I know just what you mean," Acey says, talking fast, trying to keep LaShaWanda's fingers from that keyboard, knowing that once she starts typing again we don't stand a chance. "It's hardly afternoon and it's already been a tough day. The masseuse at my spa called in sick at the last minute, although I suspect she's either lazy, hungover, or got lucky last night, and by the time I got the message there was a client waiting. I haven't given a massage in years, never was very good at it, but I put that woman on the table and did my best, but, as the song says, I guess my best wasn't good enough. I kneaded that flesh for forty minutes, and she complained throughout. 'Too hard, too soft, ouch.' Then, to add insult to injury, I broke one of my new nails. You want to talk about bad days?" Acey shakes her head, wiggles her left index finger, the polish chipped and the nail a quarter inch shorter than the others, in front of LaShaWanda's eyes.

LaShaWanda leans slightly forward so she can see, says, "Nice color. Chanel's 'Ribald Red,' isn't it? I had that last week."

"Mm-hm. What I like about it is that this shade goes with every-thing. You know how some of these colors are so strong, you have to match your outfit to them." LaShaWanda laughs, holds both hands in front of her face.

"I know what you mean, that's why I got red, black, and green this time. I figure, fuck it, black liberation colors go with everything." Acey nods in agreement while gently examining LaShaWanda's nail art, makes low cooing noises of approval, the kind patient, sensitive people make when someone shows you her new engagement ring or baby. Damn, Acey's good. I watch the two of them, feeling both embarrassed by the way I'd spoken to the sister and left out.

"You think you all have had a tough day? Check this: my mother called me the other day and disturbed me when I was making love with Denzel!" I feel like I did as a kid when we picked teams in gym, as if I'm jumping up and down with a hand in the air yelling, 'Choose me! Choose me!' only this time the gymnastics are mental.

"Washington?" LaShaWanda condescends to let me onto her radar screen, signaling a tentative forgiveness. Denzel'll do that for you.

"Is there any other?" We share a chuckle. Denzel as object of desire is one thing about which black women have no argument. Acey observes our interaction cautiously. I can almost feel her waiting for me to fuck up, and willing me not to.

"So, is he as fine in person as he is in the movies?" LaShaWanda asks intently.

"Well, the truth is, I don't know what he looks like in person, but in my fantasy he's definitely better looking than in the movies," I say. LaShaWanda looks confused for a moment, the way people do when they're not quite sure if you're joking with them or making a joke at their expense. Then she laughs.

"You had me goin' for a minute there. I was ready to beg you for the brother's number."

"I truly wish I had it. If I did, I'd share it with you," I say. "Times are tough."

"Now that's the truth," LaShaWanda agrees. I can tell by the way she's stopped typing, has both elbows on her desk, and has cocked her head to the side that she's warming to the subject. "I had to leave the man I was dating back East a year ago, and there's nothing happening here."

"That's terrible," Acey says sympathetically. "I know you must miss him." LaShaWanda gives her that wide-eyed incredulous look most often seen in B movies, then does that black woman's neck move, the one that announces, before a word's been spoken, that either the shit's about to hit the fan or profound words are about to be uttered.

"I'll tell you the truth, I don't miss a damn thing about him but the sex," she says flatly. Acey looks a bit startled by her candor, but I guffaw agreeably.

"Well, it couldn't have been my ex Lorenzo, because I don't even miss that about him." We cackle nastily.

"Are you dating someone now?"

LaShaWanda tosses her braids, smiles smugly, smoothes the skirt of her dress over thighs as plump as pillows.

"You know, I may be big, but I've always had a man," she says, just in case we thought otherwise. "My point is, right now I don't have time for one. I just moved out here from back East in October, and this is definitely not my dream job." When she says this she tilts her head backward toward her boss's door, then slowly rotates her head left to right. Her eyes fill with disgust as they rake the perimeter of the bank. If her pupils were a semi-automatic weapon, no one would be left standing. "I gave myself a year to find something better, and the clock is ticking. So a man is rather low on my list of priorities at the moment."

'What'd you do before?" Acey asks. LaShaWanda's eyes sharpen, she looks uncomfortable.

"I was in finance," she responds vaguely.

"Oh, you worked in a bank?" Acey says perkily.

"Not exactly," she says, begins shifting her body toward her computer.

"What would you like to do next?" I interrupt, taking my shot on the rebound. LaShaWanda looks relieved.

"Something with money, but not as a secretary. And I'm sure not interested in being promoted to executive, executive assistant." Her voice is full of pride and contempt. My kinda woman. "Anyway, my year'll be up in the fall, so I gotta find something and make that move." I nod in agreement because I feel her and because the effects of my night with

Odell continue to linger. That's one thing about being old enough to distinguish good sex from bad: you realize the good sex is sort of like a time-release capsule. It keeps on giving, and even though you might want more, you don't need it, you can modulate your dosage. When you're younger you're so happy to get some good loving you convince yourself you're *in* love, can't live without it, and chase the dick like a crack addict after the pipe, or chase the bad sex hoping something happened to the man overnight and the next time it'll be good.

"What about sex?" Acey cuts to the chase.

'What about it?" LaShaWanda looks her dead in the face. "You making me an offer?" She stares at Acey hard, then laughs. "Just kidding. Don't trip." Acey looks relieved. I know her well enough to know she's taken aback by LaShaWanda's words but doesn't want to offend, is trying to figure out a polite, nonhomophobic way to assert her heterosexuality without putting us back on that wrong foot I'd started out with.

"Don't you miss having it?"

"Hell, yeah. You know, I bought one of those vibrators, but it just isn't the same, although I will say it's more efficient than some of these men, a few twirls of that dial and I'm satisfied, at least physically. But there's a big difference between cold rubber and warm meat. Add that to the fact that it's over in two or three minutes and there's nobody's heat except my own, no cuddling, no one to talk to," LaShaWanda sighs wistfully.

"Yeah, I miss those things too. But there're also no sexually transmitted diseases, no one to clean up after, no one to cook home fries for," I interject. She laughs then, because she knows I'm telling the god's truth.

"I guess it's like my grandma used to say, huh? 'Can't live with 'em, can't live without 'em,'" LaShaWanda says, then adds, "Damn, don't you hate it when not only are the old people right, but you find yourself quoting them?"

"Now hold on." I put both palms flat out on her desk and lean so far toward her our faces are almost touching. Out of the corner of my eye I can see the brilliant purple background of her screen saver propelling the message "It's Better To Eat Nothing Than To Eat Shit" in two-inch Day-Glo orange letters. "What if I told you me and my girlfriend have figured out a way to have hassle-free great sex, with live, cuddly, affectionate men?" LaShaWanda looks me dead in the eye. Even through the violet veneer of her contacts, I can tell she thinks I'm crazy, lying, or possibly both. Even so, among sisters hope springs eternal. I'm counting on that to make the spa a success.

"I'd say where, and how do I get there?"

I reach out and cover one of LaShaWanda's hands with mine, squeeze it. I feel like a preacher at a revival meeting, deep into the call and response. It's time for a laying on of hands.

"I will tell you. Seriously, I will. But first, we need to get some money from Gardiner Roberts." Before she can respond, one of the lights on the telephone on her desk starts blinking. She puts up her hand to still my open mouth, picks up the receiver.

"Mr. Roberts's office. May I help you?" she says officiously, listens for a moment, then relaxes her voice and posture. "Hey, Muffin. What's going on? Girl, me too. I know that. So what do you need? I have people here," she glances at us as she speaks, gives that this-will-just-take-a-minute look, speaks into the receiver.

"You're damned straight I'd sell, and fast. Haven't you been follow-ing the tobacco hearings? Looks as if any profits will be going to settle suits against them for the next hundred years. What's hot? Haven't you heard about SecurityConcept? They build personalized steel shelters, supposedly guaranteed to protect you from nuclear war and terrorists. What? Shit no, I don't think they'll work, but so what? The share price is steadily going up and will keep going that way until someone dies in a SecuriCave, and what're the odds of that? And buy Griff-Margetson Pharmaceuticals. I just bought some of that myself, would've bought more if I had your money. The share price is high, but so what? You know it can't go anywhere but up. Yeah, im-po-tence, don't pretend you haven't heard the word, with that old-ass husband you've got." She pauses, studies her nails, frowns. Eavesdropping shamelessly, Acey and I exchange raised eyebrows. "Girl, you know it's flying outta drugstores. Then just sit back and watch it rise," she guffaws at her own joke. Acey and me stand in front of her desk shuffling our feet, glancing around at nothing, and trying to pretend we're not listening, but my ears are so wide open they hurt and I bet Acey's are, too.

"What? Muffin, I am not your personal investment advisor, al-though I should be since I'm smarter than that fool you have on retainer, the one who told you to buy all that airline stock because the interna-tional fear of flying would, I believe 'just blow over' were his exact words." She pauses. "Of course I have your back, girl, it's just that some of us have to work. Call me tonight at home if you want to go over those other stocks. Okay, talk to you at eight, bye." LaShaWanda hangs up. The ex-pression on her face is simultaneously put upon and smug.

"Sorry about that. My girlfriend needed some advice, and you know how these chicks who don't need a job are, call you up any time and think you've got nothing better to do than solve their so-called problems." Acey gives one of those tell-me-more nods, but LaShaWanda ain't going for it.

"Funny name for a sister. Muffin," I roll the name across my tongue, but it doesn't roll well.

"Who you tellin' about funny names?" LaShaWanda asks. "Listen. My father's name was Lawrence, my mama's name was Wanda, and my mother's grandfather was a Native American from the Shahaptian tribe from along the Columbia River in Oregon, so they named me La-Sha-Wanda, can you believe it? Black people and their names! But shit, I've heard much worse. Anyway, Muffin Dixmoor ain't no sister. See, white folks got horrible names, too, they're just shorter and easier to spell and pronounce."

"*The* Muffin Dixmoor, as in the wife of Dick Dixmoor?" Acey chokes the words out. LaShaWanda tosses her head, rolls her Elizabeth Taylor eyes.

"Is there any other?"

"How'd you meet her?"

"We went to prep school together in Connecticut, one of those programs where they take smart kids out of the ghetto and educate them with the elite. At first they only did it with black kids, but you know white folks, can't let us have anything for ourselves—at least nothing that's good—so they started squawking about reverse discrimination and started taking white students, too. Enter Muffin Dixmoor, nee Sullivan."

"And you're still friends?"

"Yeah, we've kept in touch over the years, although we didn't see as much of each other until I moved out here last year after—" She stops herself, an uncertain look on her face. She's barely lost a beat when she concludes, "I decided to move out here," although she's already said that and even Ray Charles could see there's something she doesn't intend to talk about.

"What kind of business you sisters planning to start?" She abruptly changes the subject. I start to open my mouth and tell all, but before I can Acey jumps in, says, "Another spa."

LaShaWanda looks bored. It's clear that the last thing she's interested in doing is jogging, sitting in a dry-ass sauna, or anything else that could cause her to break a sweat. I guess Acey senses her lack of interest, because she adds, "A full-service spa, exclusively for black women." Her eyes brighten, ever so slightly.

"What do you mean by full service?"

And then Acey, who usually takes her time judging character and getting close to people, surprises me. "Men!" she whispers, leans towards LaShaWanda. "Along with massage, sauna, whirlpool, steam, pool, medi-ation, foot reflexology, we're going to offer the services of men. Whatever you want, you'll be able to get it at A Sister's Spa." LaShaWanda guffaws.

"That is, if we can get some financing, with the help of Gardiner Roberts," Acey adds, always Miss Focused.

"Good luck." There's a sneer in LaShaWanda's voice when she says this, and it's clear the mention of his name has snapped her back to an unpleasant reality. "Roberts is so tight, you'd think it was his money, not the bank's. Folks come out of that office cryin' every day." LaShaWanda shakes her head. "It's a goddamn shame."

"Can you give us any tips on how to best handle Mr. Roberts?" The tone of Acey's voice is wheedling. She has on her best begging look, the one that resembles the expression on the face of that last unsold puppy. Slowly, LaShaWanda nods agreeably.

"First off, the man's a total idiot and the only reason he keeps his job is his great-granddaddy founded the bank. He knows next to nothing about money and finance, and why should he, since he lives off a very large inheritance. I think his wife just sends him here so he won't drive her insane around the house. As for strategy, it's very basic: Let him see as much of those titties as possible when you're talking," she suggests, look-ing at Acey. "And you, work them legs, you know, the old cross and un-cross move like Sharon Stone in *Basic Instinct*, although I hope you're wear-ing panties. For my money it's been so long since old Gardiner saw any snatch he might have a heart attack at the slightest glimpse, and I will not be performing CPR. Not today." She sniffs righteously and tosses her head again, her beaded braids clanking together like a plastic waterfall. I laugh, but Acey looks shocked and shaken.

"Now, you're not one of those feminists, are you?" LaShaWanda asks.

"Well . . ." Acey hesitates. Feminism is frequently a bad word among black people, including black women. I can tell Acey's trying to weigh the honest answer against the pragmatic one, but before one of them tips the scales LaShaWanda laughs, waves her hand dismissively.

"Well, I am. But you know these men cannot deal with that. Since Gardiner's got the money—and the power to give it away—relax, sister, and show him some tittie. Like James Brown says, 'A woman got to use what she got to get just what she want.'" Acey, a James Brown fan from way back, laughs too. The tension falls from her face. You can never go wrong when you speak the international language of James Brown.

"Guess I better listen to the Godfather."

"And me." LaShaWanda adds, just to make it clear who's in charge, even if the tension with which our meeting began has dissipated and she is going to let bygones be bygones.

"Rap, Godmother," Acey says.

"I'll tell him you all are here," LaShaWanda says, pressing a button on the telephone on her desk and murmuring into it. "Y'all go on in," she says. "Good luck." We glide past, me smoothing a bubble in my stocking and hoping the run doesn't spread, Acey trying to be subtle as she pulls gently at her breasts, trying to plump them up for maximum cleavage.

"Thanks," I say, smiling, and pledge always to remember to treat the LaShaWanda Marshalls of the world with respect, not just because they're human but, quiet as it's kept, they're the ones who know where all the shit is and keep everything running.

"Don't thank me, you're gonna need it," LaShaWanda says, already turning back to her typing. Then, before either of us can reach for the knob, the door in front of us flies open and a thin voice infused with false ebullience chirps, "Good afternoon! And what can I do for you ladies today?"

14

THE ONLY TIME I'D EVER REALLY DEALT WITH A BANK OFFICER WAS years earlier when I was married and Lorenzo and me applied for a mortgage. Even then all I really did was fill out my portion of the forms and sit there with my legs crossed while the men hammered out the specifics in between singing the praises of Michael Jordan and the Chicago Bulls. What can I say? It was during the playoffs. I signed on the dotted line beneath my hubby's signature, a move I regretted after I kicked Lorenzo's broke and tired behind out and had to assume full responsibility for the monthly payments. Acey, though she owned the spa and ran her own business, hadn't had much more experience than me. She came from old colored money. Her grandmother had been a successful manufacturer of hair products designed to tame black women's unruly hair, and she'd used Earl's life insurance settlement to finance the spa. So we were flying blind when we walked into the office of Gardiner Roberts, but if there is one thing we see immediately, it's that it was going to be a bumpy ride.

Gardiner Roberts is six feet tall and a pale pink color tinged with the faint yellow of incipient jaundice. Even though there isn't much hair left on his head, you can tell by what remains that as a young man he'd had a headful of fine, curly hair. All that is left is a fringe around the sides. His eyes are a watery blue, set deep in his gaunt face. The only thing bright about him are his cheeks, an alarming, robust red, a color that in his case I associate more with the generous consumption of alcohol than healthy living and exercise.

In spite of his lack of physical appeal, or maybe because of it, Gardiner Roberts is impeccably dressed. His gray pinstriped double-breasted Brioni suit is perfectly tailored, the waist pinched in ever so slightly to make the most of his slim form, the French cuffs of his sparkling white Turnbull and Asser shirt exactly turned. His cufflinks of dark jade edged in silver are subtle, precisely chosen to complement his dark green tie, picking up the tiny flecks of silver barely discernable in the rich fabric.

His Ferragamos are dark gray wing tips. They even look soft. Everything he wears screams care, deliberation, and money. If it is true that clothes make the man, Roberts looks the part of a serious banker, someone to be reckoned with. I file LaShaWanda's scathing description of him in the back of my mind as he ushers us to an arrangement of chairs in a corner of his enormous office.

"So. You ladies want to start a business. Is that right?" Roberts says in his chirpy voice once we're seated.

"Yes, sir. A spa for women. We'd like to—" Acey starts to say, leaning over to unzip the black lizard Bottega Veneta briefcase beside her on the floor. Roberts interrupts, waves her aside with an abrupt motion of his hand.

"I'd *like* to be on my boat. Or in Tuscany sipping a glass of wine and nibbling freshly picked olives. Or on the seventh hole with Tiger Woods. I am not. Instead, I am here. With you ladies. Doing business." He pauses, peers at us with his pale eyes. "And my point is . . ." He smiles when he says this, exposing his teeth for the first time. With the exception of the small, yellow, pointed canines on either side of his mouth, all of his teeth are beautifully capped. His eyes move back and forth between us, waiting for a response. I feel as if I've suddenly been beamed from Old Western onto the set of *Jeopardy*, and should be racking my brain for the correct question so I can hit that buzzer. His look of expectation gradually turns to disappointment. I suspect that by the time we get to Final Jeopardy, me and Acey will be in the minus column and out of the running.

"My point is that banking has nothing to do with what you or I would *like* to do. As Calvin Coolidge, perhaps this nation's most under-appreciated chief executive, put it so succinctly, the business of America is business." He pauses, maybe waiting for us to agree, or applaud. I just sit there willing my expression to stay neutral and thinking, this mother-fucker is crazy.

"So let us all agree that we are here to do business, not because we like this or like that. Like and money do not mix," he finishes pompously.

"Okay." Acey drawls out this tiny word, stretches it into many syllables, probably trying to get her language together so that when she finally states our case Roberts won't go off on another tangent. "I'm Acey Allen, this is my partner Lydia Beaucoup. I already own one spa here in the city, and we're looking for funding for another one. In Nevada." Roberts sniffs and the nostrils of his thin nose contract, exposing a web of tiny blue veins.

"Nevada. Disgusting state. Fraught with gamblers, mobsters, and all variety of malcontents. Why there?" Acey reaches into her briefcase, pulls out a sheaf of photocopied pages, all articles written about Nevada: the medical benefits of desert air, the surplus of cheap labor, the low costs of operating a business there, the state's popularity as a destination for conventioneers. She hands a stack to Roberts.

"According to our research, the accessibility, climate, and economy of Nevada make it a prime location for a luxury spa. It is served by all major airlines, with frequent daily flights from most areas of the country. The warm temperatures and dry heat make it an ideal vacation destination year round. And of course, Nevada is one of the most popular destinations for annual conventions. Over the last decade, the state's image has been transformed from simply a place to gamble to a vacation destination for the entire family, with theme parks, day camps, and other kid-friendly activities. One reason we're convinced the spa will be successful is that thus far resort areas have not focused specifically on the needs of women. Women who visit alone, or with their spouses and children, but would like to spend a day of relaxation by themselves." Roberts' expression is simultaneously bored and impatient.

"Possibly. Let us examine your loan package. Do you have a business plan?" Acey hands it to him. He flips through it with raised eyebrows, nods, and looks surprised.

"I suppose you haven't yet completed the bank's application?" he says smugly, but can't hide his disappointment when Acey forks over the completed twelve-page form.

"You'd like to borrow $500,000?" I call tell from his voice that he wants to laugh, but knows better. "What about your spa license? Income projection data, investments? Copies of both your personal and business taxes for the last three years?" He fires these questions at us like bullets, with Acey steadily handing over documents and me sitting there feeling smug. Every time he requests something and she has it, he looks amazed and I want to holler, "Faked you out! Faked you out!" I resist, barely.

Once he's gotten everything he asks for, we sit for long minutes as he goes over the paperwork not once, but twice, searching for problems. Finally he looks up and says, "Everything seems to be in order." But before we can get happy, he adds, "Thus far." He inhales portentously. "Now. There is the matter of collateral. What assets do you ladies have to secure the loan?"

"We both own homes valued at $200,000. In addition, my partner

owns the building where her spa is located, most recently assessed at
$359,000," I say, passing over the appraiser's valuation of the proper-
ties. That I-smell-shit look passes over Roberts's face again. But hey, as
we say in the neighborhood, our shit don't stink, at least not this time. My
boy looks outright displeased.

"Credit reports?" Coolly, Acey passes them to him, a slight smile on
her lips. In our younger days, we'd both signed up for every credit card we
were offered, without a thought to interest rates or paying the bills, focused solely on what we desired. Together, we'd been through our shop-
aholic phase in a big way, buying anything and everything that caught our
fancy, juggling credit cards and paying the monthly minimum to keep
afloat. By the time we were in our late twenties we were both overwhelmed,
so busy juggling bills and trying to keep ahead of impending bankruptcy
that shopping just wasn't fun anymore. One Sunday we'd gone down to
Fisherman's Wharf armed with a blue money-attracting candle from the
botanica, incense, and all our credit cards. We lit the candle and incense,
said a prayer for financial restraint and stability, then cut the credit cards
in half and threw them into the bay, where, in spite of the buoyant properties of plastic, they sunk like the stones they were. We spent the next several years paying off bills and making purchases in cash, then reapplied
for credit cards, confident we controlled them, not the other way around.
I catch Acey's eye and we grin.

"These look to be in order." Roberts sounds truly miffed. "Now to
the subject of cash. On a loan of this magnitude, the bank requires that
you have 20 percent of the loan amount in cash. That's $100,000 on a
loan this size," he adds, as if we can't figure it out ourselves.

"I've brought along a statement from George Washington Carver
Savings and Loan, which reflects my current balance of $56,229.14, and
any other information you might need." Acey passes him a sheet of
paper. Roberts snatches the letter from her hand, takes a quick glance,
and turns to me.

"And you, young lady?"

"My savings account is right here, at Old Western. I currently have a
balance of slightly more than $40,000 in my money market account.
Here's the account number." I smile when I say this, but Roberts doesn't
look pleased. He abruptly turns away and picks up the telephone on the
table beside him.

"Ms. Marshall. Please check the balance in this account," he says,
barking the digits into the receiver. We sit waiting, confident. I'm hum-

ming the words to "We're in the Money" in my head when the phone buzzes. "All right. Read that figure back to me," Roberts says, scribbling numbers on a small pad. "When? Right. Thank you." He replaces the receiver, swings around. For the first time he actually looks pleased. I smile, too. Maybe I've read old Roberts wrong, mistaken his business acumen for ill will. Could it be I have that familiar Negro chip on my shoulder, that I have misinterpreted his fiscal caution and superior financial knowledge for racism, sexism, and condescension?

"Ms., uh, Beaucoup is it? According to our records, your account balance is currently $122.09. Added to Ms. Allen's balance, that gives you ladies a total of $56,351.23 cash. Insufficient funds." There's no mistaking it, the son of a bitch is grinning to beat the band.

"That's impossible!"

"I am sorry, but it's quite possible. Ms. Marshall checked the figures. Twice."

"On no it's not quite fucking possible!" I shriek, flying out of my chair toward him. He looks terrified. "Let me see that!" I reach out to grab the notepad from his fingers and he holds it over his head, moving it back and forth as I try to snatch it. We're playing some high-stakes, adult version of monkey in the middle, him smiling smugly and me screaming "Give it to me, give it to me!"

"Lydia. Sit down," Acey commands, standing between us. "Mr. Roberts, there must be some mistake. The balance was checked last week. At that time it was more than $40,000."

"Well that was then, this is now," Roberts snaps. "According to our records, a withdrawal of $40,000.91 was made March 21. Two days ago. See." He thrusts the pad in front of him, holding it out so Acey can read the figures. She swivels around to face me, the expression in her eyes pleading say it ain't so, tell me you didn't suddenly decide to make a down payment on a Porsche, haven't become a crackhead overnight. I shake my head.

"I sure as hell didn't withdraw any damn money. There must be some mistake."

"Old Western Bank does not make mistakes."

"Then you'd better find my $40,000. And don't forget my ninety-one damn cents."

"If you want to recover your funds, I suggest you contact . . ." Roberts looks down at the paper, "Mr. Lorenzo G. Hicks."

"What? *Lorenzo?* That sniveling, slimy, goddamned, soon-to-be-no-dick son of a bitch!" I scream. "He stole my motherfuckin' money!" Acey's eyes go dead when she hears Lorenzo's name. She knows him well enough to comprehend there's no possibility of keeping hope alive when he's around. All she says is, "Well I'll be damned."

"I take it you are no longer associated with this . . ." he pauses here, searching for the correct word, which makes me think he knows Lorenzo, too. "Person?"

"He's no person!" I snarl. "He's my lying, cheating, lazy, no-count almost ex-husband."

"You left his name on the account?" Acey inquires softly. I moan like an animal caught in one of those traps that eats through your leg when you try to escape.

"I forgot," I sob. "I remembered everything else. The credit cards, the checking account, the car loan, the mortgage. I just forgot one little thing." I collapse into my chair, sobbing. Tears, mascara, and foundation run down my face, drip onto my red Tahari suit.

"Not such a little thing, at that," Roberts peeps.

"Shut the fuck up, asshole," I say. He does. The three of us sit there until my sobs turn into sniffles and the whole front of my suit is soaked.

Finally Acey says, "I guess we might as well go." Roberts pops up like a jack-in-the-box from the chair where he's been sitting impassively, eager to show us the door. Acey puts a hand under my elbow and damn near pulls me out of the chair, touching me in that fragile, careful-or-she-just-might-break way usually reserved for the elderly or insane. The truth is, I feel both homicidal and as if I've aged forty years in one afternoon. She guides me to the door and my head is low, shoulders bent, footsteps shuffling. If I had a cape, I'd look like James Brown in the old days when he'd finish his show singing "Please, Please, Please," and one of the Famous Flames would throw a cape over his shoulders and drag him off stage. But James was on his way to pick up a fat paycheck, and there's no check in my future except checkmate. I exit empty-handed and pissed as hell.

To add insult to injury, old chickenshit, sorry, racist, sexist, classist, and probably homophobic Gardiner Roberts can't leave bad enough alone. He waits until we're halfway out the door to murmur, "As I said, the business of America is business, but not every American is ready to do business," then slams the mahogany door closed behind us before I can turn around and kick his natural-born ass.

IT BECOMES APPARENT OVER THE NEXT FIVE WEEKS THAT OUR EXPE-
rience with Gardiner Roberts is one of those ill winds that blow nobody
any good. We visited every other bank in the city and were turned down
each time, usually because we lacked the requisite cash, but occasionally
for other reasons. One bank told us the health craze was as good as over—
apparently the desire to be in good health is merely a fad—and they
weren't interested. Another bank refused to accept the appraised value of
any of our properties, obliquely suggesting that whatever the assessed
value, since they were in black neighborhoods the amount should be re-
alistically cut in half, the location making the land essentially worthless.
After the third week it got so bad I suggested to Acey we file a broad discrimination suit against the banking industry and use that money to start
A Sister's Spa. Acey wisely pointed out that if and when we won, we'd
likely be too old to start anything.

Embarrassed as I am to admit it, in desperation we finally even went
to some of those outfits whose late-night television ads we'd snickered at
for years. Sure, they were more like drive-by banks than respected financial institutions, and their interest rates were astronomical, but we'd exhausted all other possibilities. Accepting that we were rejects in the straight
world of banking, we approached them believing their spiels that no one
is turned down. Well, we were, and rudely.

Every time we were refused a loan, I got angry and saw it as a challenge and motivation to try harder. Acey took it as some sort of sign from
on high that the idea was morally and financially unsound, and started
equivocating about starting the spa after all. Between being rejected by
every bank in the city and trying to keep our spirits up, I was exhausted
and stressed, but still convinced the spa was gonna happen. The only
good news came from Odell's side of the business: he'd collected sixty-
five completed questionnaires in just a few weeks, more than enough
prospective employees to get started.

So Acey and me are feeling truly down, but not all the way to hopeless, as we wait for Odell to pick us up and take us to Sapphire's, another watering hole for the hipoisie. We'd planned the evening a week earlier when we were still hopeful about getting a bank loan, figuring it was a great place to scope out prospective employees. Even though we had no idea where the money was coming from, I wasn't willing to give up on A Sister's Spa, and convinced Acey it couldn't hurt to have our workers lined up. We both need a break from going to banks at lunchtime, feeling beat-down and depressed for the remainder of the afternoon, then getting together almost every evening to plot strategy. So, we're sitting in Acey's beige-on-beige living room, the only hint of color the African mud cloth pillows trimmed with cowry shells tossed here and there, sipping blush wine and waiting for Odell. We're listening to Dinah Washington on the box, not only because the sister had a gorgeous set of pipes but also because no matter what she's singing, she always sounds powerful. Dinah could take the corniest, saddest, most victimized love song and transform it into a song about women's sexuality, resiliency, and liberation.

"You know, Lorenzo was always strange," Acey says, apropos of nothing and everything. I laugh, not because there's anything funny about that thief, but because I'm thinking about him, too.

"You always said that. Wish I'd listened."

"I could never put my finger on what it was. If he was anything, he was clearly affair, not marriage, material. There was just something about him that seemed wrong."

"Not seemed, is. Too bad I had to marry him to find out he's a lazy, mooching, stealing creep." Acey nods agreeably.

"Yeah, all that and then some. But there's something else strange about him. I just can't grab what it is."

"To hell with him. All I know is I should've taken my grandmother's advice and steered clear of pretty spooks with light eyes. She always swore you can't trust 'em." Acey laughs.

"That's sure right. With Lorenzo, it was almost like he was too fine to be true, and he knew it."

"Wish I had, then I wouldn't have spent ten years married to a salesman who never sold a damn thing, and who I had to fight every morning to get to the mirror, even though there wasn't any hurry because he didn't have a job to go to."

"He did always look good."

"That's an understatement. That man was prettier than a pretty boy."

"Refresh my memory as to why you married him?"

"Shit. I'd been dating him for two years, he kept on begging me to get married, I hadn't figured out he was a loser, I thought I wanted children, he could cook his ass off, and he was neat."

"I hear you, especially about the kids. Whoever thought I'd be over forty, single, with no children? That's one of the reasons I hang in there with Matthew."

"You still want kids?"

"I'm not sure, but I still think about it. But sometimes it's hard to separate what I want from what I've always thought I wanted, or was supposed to want. Know what I mean?"

"Do I ever. When I married Lorenzo, I hadn't thought out anything about life and what I wanted from it—hadn't even asked myself the questions, to be honest."

"Didn't you tell me the sex wasn't all that?"

"There wasn't enough of it, but when it was good, it was very, very good. When Lorenzo was on, he was on. That man truly had no hang-ups, no off-limits erogenous zones. He loved me to be on top, didn't get into that whole silly domination trip, and I figure I sucked his titties as much as he did mine." Acey laughs.

"Lyds, you're wild."

"Hey, I just tell it straight. Remember, I was raised by an agnostic librarian who believes that somewhere there's a book that has the answer to any and every question. Unfortunately, even she hasn't found the volume yet that explains Lorenzo."

"Have you heard from him?"

"I got some weird message last week. He was pretending to cry and mumbling some shit about he was sorry, but I'd eventually understand. I've been trying to track him down, but his phone's turned off, so whatever he stole my money for, it wasn't for paying his bills. The phone company's probably looking for him, too. He hasn't even called my mother, so he must know he's really fucked up this time."

"He'll be back. Men always come back."

"Like a bad penny."

"Why is it always the small change?"

"Yeah, well when he shows it better be with my $40,000."

Acey starts to say something, but the doorbell rings. We grab our bags and go outside to meet Odell.

Sapphire's, with its antique oak bar running along the front window, wainscoting, muted peach décor, and serious food, is an upscale, more affluent, slightly more mature version of the Piranha Bar. If the patrons of the Piranha Bar are the newcomers and wannabes of the financial, music, publishing, and fashion industries, the clientele at Sapphire's are those who have made it. As much as the Piranha loudly announces its patrons' beauty, talent, and ambition, Sapphire's quietly confirms those same qualities. Its owner, Hyacinth Jones, is an ageless sister from Charleston, South Carolina, who first came to San Francisco as part of a gospel caravan when she was seventeen and refused to board the bus back home once the revival was over. She got a job waitressing and spent her weekends dancing at underground, mostly gay clubs. It was at the urging of a few drag queen friends that she entered one of the club's talent contests when she was twenty-four. She won easily, belting out a disco version of "How High the Moon" clad in thigh-high boots and a black lace bodysuit. This led to a thriving career as a vocalist and theatrical fag hag, a persona and career she modeled after those of her three idols, Bette Midler, Donna Summer, and Josephine Baker. By the time she was thirty, she'd toned her act down slightly and moved into the larger, more mainstream venues of hotel dining rooms and rooftop cabarets catering to San Francisco's endless flood of tourists. She was a short, round, deep black woman with thinning, cropped hair plastered to her head and small, pointed, ferret-like teeth. She swathed herself in brilliantly colored, draped clothes made especially for her by a gay designer friend, made up her face perfectly, read everything, knew everyone, and was so striking, charming, and seriously ambitious that she became, if not exactly beautiful, then at least mesmerizing. Hyacinth cultivated friends in high and low places, straddled the line between the risqué and obscene, and was beloved by all. It didn't hurt that Willie Brown, back when he was serving as speaker of the California State Legislature, was an impassioned and vociferous fan, regularly taking visiting dignitaries to hear her sing. By the time Brown was elected mayor, Hyacinth Jones had shed her cat suits for Versace and saved enough money to open her own restaurant and club. She limited herself to the demure activities of hostess-diva with the mostest, singing only on special occasions. She christened her restaurant Sapphire's after both the gemstone and the name of Kingfish's wife on the old *Amos 'n' Andy* show. It was just icing on the cake when Mayor Brown decided San Francisco needed an official chanteuse, and named Hyacinth Jones the Official Throat of San Francisco.

"Hey, girlfriends, how you doing?" Hyacinth squeals when Acey and enter the restaurant. We'd first met while clubbing back in the days of disco fever and she'd become a regular client of Acey's when her spa opened. We'd always been friendly and stayed in touch, and I'd been more than happy to help out when she called me for PR advice just before Sapphire's opened. Beneath the peacock chic, Hy was a down sister and a loyal friend. She'd created a bar restaurant that was not only beautiful, but one where women without men felt welcome, appreciated, and safe. We all hug, kiss air so as not to disturb our make-up, and exchange sincere pleasantries as Odell stands by patiently.

It's Saturday night and Sapphire's is packed. Over the racket of voices, laughter, and the tinkling of ice in glasses, Norah Jones puts her own spin on Hank Williams' "Cold, Cold Heart." I make note of a clump of nice-looking men in suits at the far end of the bar. Women in short dresses and crossed legs perch on stools along its length.

"I see business is good."

"Hey, you know how it is. Folks with some money always looking for a place to spend it and showcase with their own kind." Hy laughs when she says this. Acey arches an eyebrow.

"And what kind is that?"

"I call them OKOP," Hy laughs. "Our kind of people. Other folks who've arrived, or think they have. In the twenty-first century, it's all about class bonding. The women want to meet a fine man with a credit card that won't be rejected and a legitimate, embossed business card—and it better not say 'international business consultant,' that's jive talk for unemployed. The men are looking for an attractive woman with a better than decent job who isn't looking for a man's back to climb on to get them over, although they all favor a freak in bed."

"Who wouldn't?" I ask. Hy and I delicately slap palms. She winks, casts her eyes on Odell.

"Looks like you're set, girl."

"Hyacinth Jones, Odell Overton. Odell, meet Hy." Odell extends his hand, but instead of shaking it, Hyacinth raises it to her lips.

"Enchante, Odell."

"Oh no, it's my pleasure," he says easily. Back to business, Hy drops his hand like a stone, turns to survey her domain.

"Where you all wanna sit, the bar or at a table? You having dinner or what?"

"We may eat later, but right now we need a few stiff drinks. It's been a tough week," Acey says.

"Cool. What about a table by the bar? That way you can drink, observe the action, and if you decide to eat, I'll move you." As she says this she sashays through the crowd, the three of us in tow, greeting patrons and kissing air as she makes her way to a corner table. "This okay?"

"Wonderful," Acey says, sinking into one of the plush upholstered armchairs. "Thanks, girl."

"My pleasure. Catch up with you all later. My public calls." She twirls around on four-inch heels and disappears into the waiting arms of said public.

The three of us envisioned this evening as a joyous collective scouting trip, but that was prior to being turned down by every source we'd approached for a loan. When the waiter comes we order three double Remys, straight up. While we're waiting we dig furiously into the bowl of salted almonds and cashews in front of us, ignoring their fat content. We chomp along silently, lost in our own thoughts, until Odell finally says, "Well. Isn't this supposed to be a working evening? Neither one of you has looked at anything but those nuts since we got here." Acey looks up, shakes her hair. She's been wearing a massive, way below the shoulders, Diana Ross-esque weave for the last week. I catch Odell's eye, start to make a joke about different types of nuts, but I'm not feeling funny and his serious expression makes me think better of it.

"You're right, Odell," Acey concedes, pushing the bowl of nuts away. "It's been a tough week, but as Mrs. Beaucoup always says, they're not obstacles, they're challenges."

"Having $40,000 stolen by your ex-husband is a pretty damn big challenge," I grumble.

"Let's not go there," Acey says, holding up one hand and gazing toward the bar.

I follow her gaze and my lips slowly curl into a grin. "Let's go *there*," I say, jerking my head toward the bar.

The man's back is to us. Both his forearms rest against the brass railing as he leans forward talking to the bartender, one foot crossed behind the other. He's over six feet tall, his hair close shaven and brushed back, razor cut at the neck. From what I can see of his body through his dark suit, he is big, but not fat. My eyes travel down from his head, across his broad shoulders, along his back, and then, bingo! There it is, sitting hard and round, its two globes clearly delineated by the careful drape of his slacks, accentuated by the way he's standing.

The perfect ass.

There are four basic types of asses for men. There's the flat ass, the fat ass, the okay ass, and the perfect ass. A flat ass offers nothing to look at and very little to hold on to. The fat ass offers too much for the eye to behold and rolls like a woman's when a man walks. The okay ass is just that, okay. Neither turn-off nor turn-on, its form is purely utilitarian. Blessedly, the invention of the Stairmaster offers the possibility of butt transformation, and not only for white women. Climb enough steps at a fast enough speed and possibly, just possibly, the okay ass can move up that critical notch. Finally, there is the perfect ass. This ass protrudes subtly, just enough so you can't miss it. When a man with a perfect ass moves, the muscles of his ass never roll or bounce, they ripple. Whether standing or in repose, the cheeks of the perfect ass never collapse lazily against each other, but always remain separate and distinct. The perfect ass offers a woman something gorgeous to look at and firm to hold on to (but not soft enough to sink into). The perfect ass can overcome a bad to middling face and sorely wanting personality. And baby, a perfect ass is hard to find.

"I have died and gone to heaven," I whisper. "Is he alone? Do you think it'd be too bold to send him a drink and invite him over to our table?" Odell's eyes follow ours.

"What's the attraction? You can't even see his face." Odell comments.

"His ass," Acey and I say in unison. While Acey raises two fingers and summons our waiter, I scribble "We'd love to buy you a drink" on a cocktail napkin, thrust it into the waiter's hand, and send him toward the bar. Odell laughs.

"Damn, you two are sure aggressive," he says.

"Why not? This is business."

"Assertive, not aggressive," Acey corrects. "Look, it worked." I lick my lips as I watch the man walk toward us, fresh drink in hand. Okay face, nice smile, no urgent dental work needed.

Odell rises and shakes his hand, offers an empty chair. "Did you ladies send me this drink? Thanks. I'm Kevin Thompson." He bows slightly and nods to me and Acey, folds himself into the chair.

"I'm Lydia, and this is my friend Acey. You already met our friend Odell." I want to make it clear right out front that we're both unattached.

"Nice to meet you all," Kevin says. His voice is low and relaxed. "You come here often?" he asks, then catches himself, laughs. "That sounds like a real come-on line, but I mean it. I just moved out here last month from Chicago, heard this is the happening spot, and decided to check it out."

"What brought you out here?" Acey asks.

"The weather. I got tired of fighting the hawk every winter."

"Welcome to San Francisco. Now you can fight the fog."

"What kind of work do you do?" I ask.

"I'm a painter, but I make my living as a graphic artist. Gotta pay those bills, and I'm not willing to live in a freezing garret for my art," Kevin laughs.

"What kind of painter? Realist, abstracts, what?"

"Abstracts, mostly, but I've done a portrait or two."

"How do you like San Francisco?"

"Beautiful city, nice enough people. A little white, but then Oakland's right across the Bay. The best part is it isn't cold."

"Sure ain't cold like Chicago," Odell says, and we all laugh.

"Where're you working?" asks Acey.

"I'm not," Kevin says. Maybe he sees that oh-no-not-another-unemployed-brother-trying-to-make-it-as-an-artiste look come over my face, because he quickly adds, "I start at Kensington Images International in a few weeks. I took some time off when I moved to settle in and get acclimated." I try to keep an overt expression of relief from my face, but it ain't easy.

"How does your wife like the Bay area?" Am I subtle, or what? Kevin grins.

"No wife, no children, just me. Now, let me buy you a round and you can tell me about yourselves."

Leaning toward him I start to tell Kevin my abbreviated and expurgated life story while Acey angles her chair around for a better view of the crowd, chatting lazily with Odell. The music's switched to Anita Baker, but we can barely hear her, the place is so crowded. Gales of raucous laughter come from one end of the bar, where a group of six or seven attractive men are clustered around something or someone I can't see from this distance. "I'm going to the powder room," I announce to the table. Kevin, gaining points with his impeccable manners, stands as I rise, but Odell and Acey are deep in conversation and oblivious. The truth is I'm less interested in freshening up than I am in seeing what's going on at the end of the bar that has the most attractive men in the place mesmerized. Lord, don't let it be a white woman.

I weave my way through the crowd, steadily scoping, and work my way to the knot of men. By divine intervention, since there are no accidents, the circle parts to let a waitress laden with a heavy tray of drinks through. I catch a momentary glimpse of long, beaded, extensions, a wave of nails painted red, black, and green, and hear a laughing voice say, "Honey, believe me. I am too busy and not interested." Unmistakably LaShaWanda P. Marshall.

Mumbling "Pardon me," I squeeze my way through a three-deep circle of brothers, not rushing and enjoying the feel of their hard bodies against mine as I make my way forward. Finally I'm clear and there's LaShaWanda, perched on a barstool in a hot pink minidress, sipping an over-sized margarita and holding court. When she sees me she extends both arms in dramatic welcome, and as if we're long lost homegirls, says, "Lydia Beaucoup, right? Girrrrllll, how's it going?"

Me, I fall into those big open arms, hug her back, and whisper, "Not great. We didn't get the money." Before she lets me go she hisses, "We'll talk later," adds, "I told you I could pull the men, didn't I?" then pushes me away from her and starts introducing her fine fan club. After a few minutes of chatting, LaShaWanda drains her glass, declines several offers of another one, and announces, "Cute and sweet as you men are, me and my girl need to talk. I want each of you to give me your card—home number on back, please, and if you can't give up the home digits, forget it—and maybe I'll be in touch." She pauses as her disappointed minions obediently place their information in her outstretched palm. "Now, go forth and share your handsome selves with some of these other ladies." She dismisses them with a wave of her hand and a laugh. They straggle forlornly away.

"Damn, you're good." I slide onto the seat beside her. LaShaWanda studies her nails.

"Nothing to it but being friendly. Women come to these places to cruise, then act like they're too good to speak. What's the point of that? If I want to be alone, I keep my ass home with the only two men I know who never give me any shit, Ben and Jerry. What's the point of fronting? You can catch more flies with honey, et cetera, et cetera? Anyway, where's your sidekick?" I gesture toward our table. She casts a quick, appraising eye over Acey, Kevin, and Odell.

"Nice meat. Sorry about Gardiner and the money, but I told you he was useless. And did I mention mean? No luck anywhere else?" Being careful not to rant lest any bile fly out of my mouth, I give her a brief run-down of our financial crisis. She nods sympathetically, says, "All is not lost. The idea's too good to let go."

"That's why we're here trawling. We're hoping the money'll come, although I have no idea from where. You here alone? Why don't you join us?" LaShaWanda looks toward the door, eyes sharp.

"I was supposed to meet my girlfriend, but she's late, as usual." She slides off the stool. "I'll join you for a few, but if the heifer doesn't show up soon, I'm outta here."

As we walk toward the table the door to Sapphire's opens wide, a gust of chilly air sweeps over us, and a voice hollers, "Wanda, my sweet. I have landed. Let the games begin!" and in glides Muffin Sullivan Dixmoor. Although I've never seen her in person, it is all but impossible to live in America and not be familiar with Muffin Dixmoor's face. Her mug graces the *Chronicle*'s social pages just about every Sunday, grinning from the dais as honorary chairperson of some charity or attending the opening of a new exhibit at a museum endowed by her hubby. Barely a week goes by when Muffin isn't featured in a photograph or print coverage of one local crisis or another. In the last month I swear I'd seen her hugging AIDS babies, delivering meals to the housebound elderly, saving beached whales, and tutoring inner city kids. Even though I hate the husband, I've always been curious about the wife.

In her early thirties, Muffin Dixmoor, philanthropist and volunteer, has been profiled in all the local newspapers, some national ones, and twice by *People* magazine; everything about her makes good copy. Tall, with short, naturally blonde hair, and handsome in that aloof, serious way Wasps sometimes have, she wears only couture. She was raised in a trailer park in Connecticut, attended Yale on scholarship, has been married to one of the richest men in America for almost ten years, and is about half his age, twice his height, and way to the left of him politically. The odd thing is that when Muffin and Dick Dixmoor are photographed together, they both always look relaxed and happy. They respond to the questions of skeptics and naysayers with assurances that they are still very much in love, and regularly swear that it is the demands of ruling the Dixmoor empire and Muffin's charitable commitments that keep them apart, rather than choice.

LaShaWanda gestures for Muffin to follow us to the table. "Wanda. I am really sorry. I know you think being late has something to do with being rich, but it doesn't. If you remember from high school, I was late when I didn't have a dime, too. Dick flew into town unexpectedly for an emergency meeting. He's angry as all get out because Griff-Margetson just announced the official release of ViriMax, and beat his own impotence drug to the punch. He insisted I go to the meeting with him, where he proceeded to go ballistic on the pharmaceutical research staff. What a scene! The man screamed, yelled, accused the chemists of industrial espionage, vowed revenge, and cancelled all vacations. We were supposed to have a peaceful dinner before the corporate jet flew him to New York, but he was so pissed he couldn't stop raving to chew or swallow, just kept ranting about getting even. It was the most I could do to get him to have a cup of chamomile tea and an Alka Seltzer and put him on the plane, and I'm still worried about his blood pressure. That's why I'm late. I couldn't just leave him, could I?" She looks wide-eyed at the five of us at the table. Four of us nod sympathetic "no's." LaShaWanda sucks her teeth.

"Girl, please. We're trying to have some fun here. Spare us tales from lifestyles of the rich and fascist, people here have real problems. What're you drinking?" Muffin orders a double Tanqueray martini, extra dry, six olives, takes a healthy gulp, leans back in her chair, and sighs contentedly.

"Did I interrupt the conversation?"

"You're right on time, we were just about to start a new one," LaShaWanda says. "Acey and Lydia are trying to start a business, but can't get the loan."

"What kind of business?" Muffin asks.

"A spa. In Nevada," Acey says.

"I love Vegas," Muffin says, "And after a few days drinking, gambling, and sweating amongst the masses, I can use a massage and a peel. Great idea," she pronounces.

"We know it's a great idea. The trouble is, no one else thinks so," LaShaWanda says.

"And we don't have enough cash to secure the loan," Acey adds.

"Cash? Do they still have cash? I charge everything," Muffin says mischievously. "Hardly ever carry a purse anymore, just this." She digs into the pocket of her slim skirt and fishes out an American Express Ultra Platinum card. LaShaWanda snorts derisively.

"So, why don't you just take a $500,000 cash advance, lend it to my girls, and they can get rolling?" Me, Odell, and Acey look hopeful, but Muffin looks embarrassed, then laughs.

"See the name on this thing, Mrs. Dick Dixmoor? My bills go directly to Dick and he'd be mad as a hornet if I took that much cash. Even rich people have budgets."

LaShaWanda looks disgusted. "Girl, I been telling you for years to build a nest egg. Shit, steal from the grocery money if you have to. Can't you skim anything off your toiletries budget?"

"Wanda, you know Dick owns the World O'Drugs chain. I just call up, order what I need, and they send it over."

"Nice life," I mumble.

"You are truly useless to be so rich," LaShaWanda teases.

"Have you really been to all the banks?" Muffin asks Acey and me thoughtfully.

We nod, glumly.

"What about foundations . . ."

"This is a for-profit venture, not a charity," LaShaWanda snaps. Muffin waves her words away impatiently.

"Wanda, as I recall we *both* graduated with honors," Muffin snaps right back. "I'm thinking maybe there's a way to structure the idea so they can get some not-for-profit money, then pay back the grant and change status once it's up and running . . ."

"Possible, but wouldn't work here. Once you got that 501(c)(3) status, the foundation trustees are all in your business—not to mention Uncle Sam," Wanda says.

"That's too much scrutiny for what we want to do," Acey adds.

"What's the big deal? What's to keep secret about a spa? Planning to heat the whirlpool past the legal limit?" Muffin laughs, signals for another round.

"Odell, would you and Kevin excuse us?" I say.

"Huh?"

"Go to the little boys' room," LaShaWanda orders. "And don't hurry back." They obey. She turns to me. "Tell her."

"Are you sure?" Acey looks uncomfortable.

"I'm sure. It's okay. Tell her."

I lean in toward the center of the table and the others follow suit. We gather into a chic, feminine huddle.

"Look, it's not simply a spa we're opening, that's just one of the services we plan to provide. It's a brothel. For black women. We're selling men." Muffin sits there for long moments staring, her green eyes get bigger and bigger until they look as if they might pop out of their sockets. Finally, she exhales so forcefully I can feel her breath against my face.

"A whore house?"

"Yep, except this time the ho's are men. Don't you love it?" LaShaWanda snickers when she says this, breaking the tension. The four of us ease back in our chairs.

"Is that legal?" Muffin whispers, but before I can answer, a hand clamps onto my shoulder and a deep, familiar, and definitely unwelcome voice booms, "Ho's? Did I hear someone say ho's?" I look up into the smiling, predatory face of journalist for hire and notorious gossipmonger Barbaralee Edison.

Just over five feet tall, with her reddish brown skin, cat-like eyes, and silver hair cut close to her head, Barbaralee Edison is a short woman whose affect makes her seem taller than she is. This is a woman who never walks, but strides, as if confidence is part of her molecular structure. Her makeup is always impeccable, and she's partial to cat suits, many of which she has custom-made in a variety of colors and fabrics. Invariably, they hug her compact, muscular body in all the right places. There's something sleek, coiled, and waiting about her, like she's always poised to pounce.

Barbaralee is the West Coast editor of *Girlfriend!*, a popular weekly tabloid for black women. I met her years ago when she interviewed me for a story she was writing on the advertising industry. Barbaralee won a couple of awards for the story and gave her career a nice boost, but in the process cost at least one source her job when she used her name in the piece after swearing the interview was on background—a pattern that's continued throughout her career. She is smart, talented, funny, and amoral: journalistic ethics, sworn promises, friendship, nothing matters to her in pursuit of the story and greater glory. I try to steer clear of her without offending. This isn't easy, since for some reason she acts as if we're ace boons.

"Barbaralee. How you doing, girl?"

"Lydia Beaucoup, you'd know how I was doing if you returned my calls," she says in admonishment, her grating voice at odds with her smooth exterior. "How *you* doing? That's my question. And what ho's are we talking about?" I look beseechingly at Acey, my eyes telegraphing for help.

"Clothes, we're talking about clothes," Acey says smoothly. "Not ho's." Barbaralee looks disappointed.

"And I thought something hot was going on at this table, fabulous gossip that the readers of *Girlfriend!* need to know. Damn. Clothes, that's a subject for the fashion editor, which I definitely am not, thank goodness." Amen to that. If Barbaralee had her way, every woman in America, regardless of her shape, would have a closet with nothing in it but spandex cat suits and bolero jackets.

"Sorry to disappoint you, Barbaralee," I add. "Want to join us for a drink?"

"And talk about boring clothes? Like hell. I'm here to scare up a hot topic for *Girlfriend!* You know I'm doing a column now, 'Believe It,' news, gossip, information, whatever scandalous shit I can find."

"Sorry, no scandal here, just Donna Karan," Muffin says sweetly. Barbaralee shrugs.

"Yeah, well, ciao then, babies. And Lydia, let's have lunch, I need to pick that little brain of yours for some juicy tidbits. Call me," she throws over her shoulder as she prowls away.

"Yeah, sure," I murmur, exhaling.

"Who the hell was that?" LaShaWanda asks, then shrugs. "Never mind. Do I really care? Back to the business at hand."

"Muffin, you asked about the legality," Acey picks up. "Prostitution for women is legal in certain counties in Nevada, so we plan to put the brothel in one of them. As far as we can tell, it isn't illegal for men to work as prostitutes. It's just never been done before."

"A brothel. Just for black women. Isn't that discrimination?" Muffin asks.

"Oh please," LaShaWanda says. "Not that shit again. No, it's not discrimination. Look at it this way; it's reversed reverse discrimination. Let's call it voluntary segregation." Acey and me exchange a quick approving glance. LaShaWanda is definitely on it.

"All black men?"

"Mostly, but we plan to hire all types; we're equal opportunity employers," Acey responds. "And let me add that we don't have anything against white women, we just know their presence will change the ambiance."

"Fuck with the vibe," I chime in.

"How?" Muffin says this in that hurt, don't-have-a-clue tone of voice that even the liberal white people usually have when the subject is race and the black folks in the conversation aren't humming "We Are The World" or some other sappy integrationist theme.

"Competition. Rape fantasies. The arrogance of inherent white privilege. Put some horny white women in a room with some sex-starved sisters, both of them after some black dick, and it'll never work. Bitches will be too busy fighting to fuck. We won't make a dime."

Muffin looks thoughtful.

"Maybe you have a point. Okay. How many employees do you plan on having?"

"We thought we'd start with about twenty to provide spa and support services and forty sex workers, then hire as necessary. If the spa takes off like we think it will, we could eventually employ a hundred," Acey says.

"A thousand," LaShaWanda laughs.

"If you can pull this off, you're going to be rich," Muffin says.

"They're not gonna be shit if they don't get some money," LaSha-Wanda barks. "Doesn't that rich fascist hubby of yours have a little slush fund he's forgotten all about that you can sneak into?" Muffin laughs.

"Wanda, be real. You know Dick's as tight as that Kevin's ass." She smiles conspiratorially, brushes back a hank of blonde hair that's fallen over one eye. This chick is observant. "Let me think. There must be something . . ."

The four of us fall silent. I don't know what anyone else is doing, but ambivalent agnostic that I am, I've got my fingers crossed and I'm praying to a higher power that this rich white girl I just met will come up with the cash we need to build our Promised Land.

"I've got it! 1-800-HEP-BROS," Muffin suddenly blurts. I feel my blood pressure spike and curse myself for praying to this blonde ninny for salvation. It's LaShaWanda who finally says, "Cut to the chase. How's that gonna help them?" Unruffled, Muffin smirks, takes a long, slow sip of her martini, plays the moment out for all it's worth.

"Dick just announced this new $100 million dollar foundation dedi-cated to getting rid of black superpredators, but he didn't say how, did he? I know most people hate him, but he's really not an evil man, just confused and a bit rigid. He sincerely believes black men are the cause of most of America's problems and wants to do something to help them . . ."

"Like shooting losers wielding Boy Scout knives at the Dairy Queen?" I can't help interrupting. Muffin looks hurt.

"Look, I was repulsed by that, too. But I sincerely believe Dick was frightened. He's almost seventy years old and not used to going anywhere without his bodyguards. But he'll do anything for Little Dickie, not that he's very little anymore, and besides . . ." Her voice fades away.

"Can we get back to the cash?" LaShaWanda's voice cuts through our anger and Muffin's reverie.

"Right. So the foundation's mission is to fund projects that will help get black superpredators off the streets. It doesn't say what kind of projects. Why not a brothel—I mean, spa? You do plan to pay decent salaries, Social Security, and taxes, don't you?" Acey and me nod our heads up and down so fast we look like two bobblehead dolls in the rear window of a car.

"Good. Dick's put together a committee to review projects, but that's just for show, it's really up to him. And me. I'm codirector," she says proudly.

"That's my girl," LaShaWanda says, reaches over and hugs her. "That's the Muffin Sullivan I first met." Muffin beams. "How long does it take before we get the money?"

"If I present the idea to Dick, a week, max," Muffin says confidently.

"Are you serious?" Acey's mouth is so dry she rasps out the words.

"Absolutely."

"Let me get this straight. You're suggesting that we use money from your husband's 1-800-HEP-BROS foundation to finance our brothel?"

"Why not? Money's money, isn't it? And you'd be adhering to the foundation's mission, to get black men off the streets. No one said anything about where they're going." She giggles.

"What do you need from us?" I ask eagerly, before Acey can talk her out of it. "A proposal, loan package, the life of my unborn child, what?"

"Because of the nature of your business, it's probably better not to put anything about the brothel in writing. Just give me a copy of the documents you took to the banks. I'll show them to Dick and fill him in on the more innovative and nontraditional aspects of the business myself. By the way, do you have a name yet?"

"A Sister's Spa," Acey says. Muffin laughs, but before she can say anything, Odell and Kevin reappear. Kevin slides into his seat while Odell stands behind me, gently massaging my shoulders. I lean back into his hands and arch my body like a contented cat as Miles Davis' "So What" wails in the background. If I could, I'd purr.

16

IN THE TWO WEEKS AFTER MUFFIN DIXMOOR AGREED TO GET US THE
money to fund A Sister's Spa, everything accelerated, since we were determined to open in early summer. Odell has been rushing through his
route so he can finish and meet Lydia to review applications. They're trying to cut the number down to only those men who appear worth a personal meeting. Meanwhile, I'm still running my spa and training L.E.,
my assistant, so she can take over when I head to Nevada. Most evenings I
spend on the Internet, looking for a suitable property in Storey County,
just outside Reno, which we've targeted as our optimal location for the
spa. It has to be in a relatively deserted area, have at least thirty bedrooms,
a dozen bathrooms, space we can use as dormitories for the workers, and
an institutional-size kitchen. So far I'm not having much luck.

I haven't been alone with Odell since that afternoon in the bell
tower, thank goodness. I'm not exactly saying that the devil made me do
it, but sleeping with some man I don't know just because he's fine and
sexy, and I'm feeling needy, is Lydia's thing and not mine. I'm not saying
I didn't enjoy the sex when we were doing it, I certainly did. But ever since
I've been feeling confused and guilty, and at the same time alive in ways I
haven't in years, and it's just . . . too much, I guess.

I've seen Matthew several times in the last few weeks, but, as hard as I
try, no sex. If he's not busy with the cases on his schedule, he's obsessively
working on his speech to the National Bar Association in August. I suspect he's thinking of running for office the following year and wants to
make a big impression, but when I ask him he just tells me not to "be premature" and goes back to his legal pad.

I haven't seen Earl in the pantry since that first time, either, although I probably look for him there several times a day. I could really
use him now to help me sort out these jumbled feelings, but maybe he
can't get back from that someplace else.

I've been hunched over my computer screen so long my back and eyes hurt, and the cup of tea on the table next to me is cold. I walk into the kitchen, put on the teapot, sit down at the table and unroll the newspaper I haven't had a chance to look at all day. Terrorism, war, corporate chicanery, unemployment—same story, different day. I flip the paper over and a headline beneath the fold catches my eye:

LOVE GURU'S BEDROOMS ON THE BLOCK
by Jacques Westin

The hundred-acre retreat built by Bhagwan Fhree El-Bootai, the mysterious mystic whose doctrine of free love and sexual experimentation attracted thousands of followers in the early 1990s, will go on the auction block next week.

El-Bootai, who at various times said he was from India, "somewhere in the Southwest," or Providence, Rhode Island, established his ashram in Storey County, outside Reno, in the early 1980s. According to published reports, the property cost in excess of $4 million dollars to build and includes dormitories, numerous private bedrooms with bathrooms, a communal sauna, massage rooms, and outdoor swimming pool. In addition, the property has a waterfall and several small dwellings that were allegedly inhabited by El-Bootai's several wives and numerous children. El-Bootai consistently asserted that he had "spiritual, not sexual relations" with his female followers, and never admitted fathering any children.

Residents of the area, where El-Bootai lived for five years, had mixed feelings about his midnight departure for points unknown four years ago and the subsequent closing of the ashram.

"Good riddance to bad rubbish," said Nell Cousins, who runs a legal brothel several miles up the same road. "I make my living selling what that weirdo coot was giving away. He was bad for business, and I'm glad he's gone."

Dirk Dietrickson, a local handyman who often worked on El-Bootai's property, disagreed. "It's a sad day for free love," said Dietrickson. "I sure do miss those female followers, I'll tell you that."

According to local authorities, Bhagwan Fhree El-Bootai is still wanted for questioning by the Nevada office of the IRS for tax evasion, and anyone who knows his whereabouts should contact local authorities. The property has been for sale for three years, and will be auctioned off a week from today. Proceeds will go toward settling Bootai's tax debt and several paternity suits.

I read the story twice, call my real estate agent, read it to her, and instruct her to get the details, find out who's handling the sale, and make them an offer. The facility sounds perfect, and I can't help but giggle at the symmetry of A Sister's Spa taking over where Bhagwan Fhree El-Bootai left off.

I start to call Lydia, then decide to wait until the agent's called me back and, hopefully, I can give her the good news. I flip on the small television on the kitchen counter and sit down at the table, trying to resist drumming my nails impatiently and chipping my nail polish. My eyes scan back and forth over Jacques Westin's story, and I can't stop grinning.

I flip the dial to BET hoping for some news, but there's nothing on but music videos. I start to click onward, but then Snoop's "The Dogfather" comes on and I stay put, enjoying the music and ignoring the relentless images of black women's disembodied asses, thighs, breasts, and hips humping to the beat. I'm casually scanning the newspaper and waiting for the phone to ring when I'm startled by a knock, look up to see Lydia peering through the glass pane of the kitchen door. I motion her in.

"Hey, what's up, girl," Lydia says. "Thought I'd drop by on my way home." I turn to grab the remote and turn the TV off, and my eye catches the image on the television. Gone is Snoop Doggy Dog, replaced by the Right Reverend T. Terry Tiger.

"Isn't that your favorite minister?" I ask, staring at a screen full of black men wearing everything from dark suits to full African drag, a few with clerical collars. They're lined up four rows deep in solemn formation. If they weren't all way past puberty, they could be the Boys Choir of Harlem waiting for a signal from the choirmaster. I hit the volume button. Lydia looks up.

"Yeah, there's the rhyming preacher, T. Terry Tiger. And Reverend Cliff Bear and that guy from the United Federation of Promojites. Damn near every black preacher or leader's up there except your man Rutledge. At least he has more sense than to align himself with this tired group." I peer at the television more closely. The camera pans rapidly across the faces of those assembled. The ministers are gathered for what looks to be a press conference, probably about "the black problem," since they're all wearing grim expressions. "Isn't that a coffin behind them?" I ask, leaning in toward the screen and pointing my finger. Lydia moves closer.

"Damned if it ain't. What's that about? Don't tell me that after *Survivor*, *The Real World*, and the rest of that so-called reality shit, we're now going to be tortured by televised funerals? They call this civilization?"

"Let's hear what he's saying," I say, waving a hand to shush Lydia's mouth and turning the sound up. T. Terry Tiger steps to the microphone.

"Thank you all for coming. We are gathered here today because there has been a death in the family. Some of you might ask, who died? Right now some of you are probably shaking your heads and reaching for that remote, telling yourselves, no one in my family died, I haven't heard about any death, whatever this is has nothing to do with me. Turn the dial! Bring on MTV, ESPN, The Playboy Channel!" T. Terry pauses here. "Well, do not touch that dial! Put that remote control down! Because I am here to tell you that whatever you've heard, this funeral involves you. And yes, you are correct. We are not burying Aunt Florence or Uncle Mike. No, it's not Mama or Daddy who's gone to meet their maker. No. Today we are burying a member of all of our families who died alone, forgotten, neglected and disrespected. We gather together today to bury morality, who died while we were so busy pursuing life's earthly and carnal pleasures that we didn't even notice. God rest his soul and God help his people.

"Without morality, we are a people adrift, in crisis. Lost. In despair. Wandering in the wilderness. Enslaved by our carnal desires and those who feed them. Yet most of us don't even realize this. We think that we are free because we have seven hundred channels on our television, because we fornicate without marriage, because we create children without taking responsibility. That the absence of the old family values of commitment, hard work, and fidelity liberate us. That as long as each of us can 'do our own thing,' we're free. But life absent a moral compass is not freedom, but a subtle and debilitating form of slavery. So we are here on this sad, sad day to mourn the death of morality." T. Terry turns, gestures toward the gleaming casket behind him. "Let us pray," he says, closing his eyes and dropping his head.

"But wait!" he roars, head snapping up. "Morality has died, but just like Jesus raised up Lazarus, moral men can raise morality up! Morality can be resurrected! Unlike the resurrection of Lazarus by the son of God, no one of us can resurrect morality alone. The body blows of immorality that led to its demise were too many. The flesh has putrefied for far too long. The people have willfully ignored morality's cries for recognition, sustenance, and human embrace, and the substance of morality has almost disappeared." As he says this, a tear runs down his brown face.

"He's good," I whisper.

"He's insane," Lydia grumbles. I quiet her with a wave of my hand. "Hear me now, hear me," T. Terry continues. "I said, 'almost.' Morality is almost dead, but not quite." He cocks his head toward the gleaming coffin behind him. "If we listen closely we can faintly, faintly, ever so faintly, hear a heartbeat. Why? Because morality does not want to die! Morality knows that if it dies we as a people will fall further into the fiery hell of immorality. Morality lies in that coffin struggling to live so that we may live too, crying not just for release, but our loving embrace! Silence!" He roars, whirling and walking away from the podium. He stalks the six feet between himself and the casket, reaches out with both hands and flings open the lid. All that can be seen is the pale pink satin that lines the top of the coffin. Apparently morality's shrunk so small that not even its nose peeps above the rim. T. Terry stares down.

"Breathe, morality, breathe!" he yells. "Rise up, renew yourself, and help my people return to their former glory. Help my people to recognize the error of their wicked, wicked ways. Hear my call!" Spellbound, both Lydia and I jump when the telephone rings. Eyes riveted to the television, I reach behind me and grab it without turning, mutter "Hello?"

"Is this spook crazy?" LaShaWanda's voice asks.

"Like a fox. Call you back," I say, hanging up the receiver.

On the tube, T. Terry walks away from the casket looking both profoundly exhausted and deeply hopeful. "My people, morality is alive but not risen. Unlike Lazarus, he has been in the crypt for far longer than three days and his resurrection will be neither quick nor easy. Bringing morality back to life will require the energy and commitment of many. It will require that we examine and re-examine our lives with a revived moral compass. That we confront sin not only in ourselves but in those around us. That we have the moral courage, yes, I said moral courage, to say no to hedonism, sin, and rampant sexuality wherever we find it. In short, it will require sacrifice! This will not be easy, but it is up to those of us who mourn the near-death of morality, and want it to live again, to breathe new life into it. Join me. Join me and save the life not only of morality, but of yourselves and of our race. The Baptist Brotherhood and Boulé, in coalition with numerous other organizations dedicated to the upliftment of the race, invites each of you to join the Crusade to Resurrect Morality. But as I have said, such a great crusade demands not only great moral fortitude, but financial sacrifice. Sin doesn't come cheap, nor does morality. Righteousness has its price. We must set a river of righteousness to flowing. We must save ourselves through sacrifice. I ask you to dig into your pockets and pocketbooks, now, to support this Crusade to Resurrect Morality. Your fives, tens, and twenties can help banish amorality and breathe new life into morality. Help recreate a world where men are men, women are women, and the blessed family reigns supreme. There is an address flashing on your screen where you can send contributions and find out what you can do to make this twenty-first century crusade a success. Do not hesitate. Amen. And let us pray."

T. Terry steps away from the podium and bows his head. The heads of the assembled men, like dominos, fall with his. Members of the fourth estate, irreverent to the solemn moment, begin shouting questions. Is it my imagination, or do I hear Jacques Westin's deep voice among them? T. Terry, seemingly deep in prayer, ignores them.

"Crusade to Resurrect Morality? Is he kidding?" I say.

"Unfortunately, probably not, but he should be. Hasn't he had a mistress for years? You know he doesn't have morality or black folks interests at heart. Strange. What do you think T. Terry's agenda is?"

"Scam is more like it. Forget morality, he's trying to revive that tired career of his. You know he's been overshadowed by the ministers who take an active role in the community, try to solve some of black folks' problems, like Rutledge, instead of haranguing them once a week and asking for money. He just wants to be back on top of the Negro Leaders heap," Lydia says, sucking her teeth.

"I guess," I say, flicking off the television. "But this doesn't look good for A Sister's Spa. All we need is a pack of desperate ministers after us . . ."

"Be cool, Ace. They don't know about us, and remember, we're gonna keep the spa's specialized services on the DL—especially now that we know T. Terry has a crusade going."

"Yeah, well we'd better. The church is about the most powerful institution black people have, and if T. Terry manages to get folks riled up about immorality and then finds out about the spa, we're doomed," I say.

"Hey, I'm not planning to take out an ad in *Girlfriend!*" Lydia grins. "Although I'm sure its readers could appreciate our services. Anyway, let's not stress because of a press conference, that might be all there is to this bullshit. Any luck with finding a place?"

I nod, toss Jacques Westin's article across the table to her. Lydia flips me a copy of the report on brothels in Nevada that her mother wrote, neatly bound in clear plastic folders, indexed, and footnoted.

I pick up the report, begin to read. As aggravating as Mrs. Beaucoup can be when it comes to some of her opinions, her skills as a research librarian are superlative. Lydia gave her a Toshiba laptop for her birthday two years ago, and she's been an Internet junkie ever since. She'll log on and cruise the net for hours. She devours information and lives by one of her favorite credos: you can never know too much and you never know what you'll need to know.

She's written her report in her unique narrative style, which includes lots of personal asides, tangents, and explanatory addenda. I pour two tall glasses of San Pellegrino with lime, curl up in my chair, and read as follows.

A SHORT HISTORY OF BROTHELS IN NEVADA
By Mavis Ransom Beaucoup, MLS

How It All Began:

According to a number of sources, several brothels operated illegally in rural Nevada into the 1950s, one run by a former GI named Joe Conforte, the other by a madame named Sally Burgess. Perhaps because great minds think alike, they eventually got married and started the Triangle Ranch on the border of Washoe, Storey, and Lyon counties. Even though prostitution was illegal, business was booming. There was barely a blip in profits when Conforte went to prison in 1960 for tax evasion and trying to frame a district attorney. In 1967, Joe and Sally took over the Mustang Ranch. Sadly, in 1967 a judge ordered both brothels closed, and told Joe to pay Storey County $1,000 a month for the cost of patrols to make sure the brothels didn't reopen. Undaunted, Joe kept his business running, continuing to pay $1,000 a month to the county for three years.

Legalization:

Finally, in 1970, no doubt seeking to avoid giving up that steady revenue, the county commissioners legalized prostitution. Ironically, the brothel-licensing ordinance took effect on Christmas Day. In order to keep brothels off the Las Vegas strip—after all, gambling causes enough trouble, doesn't it?—brothels were banned in counties with more than 200,000 residents in 1971. The implicit message was that other counties could make up their own minds. At the present time, prostitution is illegal in the following Nevada counties: Las Vegas, Reno, Carson City, and Lake Tahoe. (Put another way, prostitution is legal in more counties than not!)

Fascinating Tidbit No. 1:

Mustang Ranch went into bankruptcy in 1982 due largely to tax arrears, a situation that appears to be more a result of greed and bad bookkeeping then lack of interest in sex for hire. In 1990, the IRS seized the ranch for $13 million in back taxes. Initially, the federal government intended to own and operate the brothel, but then Arsenio Hall got wind of it and called President Bush the First a pimp on his late night talk show. Not surprisingly, the government decided not to become whoremongers. (Although to my mind they're already warmongers, and incompetent, so why split hairs? Also, am I the only one who suspects this, not low ratings, was the real reason that nice Arsenio Hall's talk show was canceled?!)

Opposition:

Although youthful or simply ignorant politicians regularly try to make the evils of prostitution into a campaign issue, the truth is that revenues to the state from the more than 30 legal brothels are substantial. Then there's the fact that, win or lose, gamblers—and, let's be honest, most men—want easily accessible women who they control and who are paid to do their bidding.

Brothel Format:

Most brothels have a large common room where a client selects an available woman. Negotiations for sexual acts do not commence until you have chosen a woman and are in her room. Some brothels actually offer printed menus, and men can just point to what they want, although prices are negotiable. Once the sex act—or acts—is agreed upon, but prior to any activity, payment is made. Brothels accept Visa, MasterCard, American Express, Discover, and, of course, cash. (Good thing, too! Can you imagine the hell there'd be to pay when the wife finds a charge for sex beneath those from Home Depot?) After she checks your credit card and you sign the slip, the sex worker—prostitute seems so cold, and these are hard-working women trying to make a living—washes the man's penis and her vagina, and the sex act commences. Condoms are mandated by law in the State of Nevada.

Prices:

It should be noted that prices usually begin at $100 and can go anyplace from there, depending on what the client wants and for how long. Obviously, group sex is more expensive. Typically, sex workers receive half of the amount paid. The rest goes to the brothel's owners.

Fascinating Tidbit No. 2:

Some brothels allow clients to take the sex workers off the premises, although this costs much more and is up to the woman's discretion. One married CEO of a Fortune 500 company regularly hires a sex worker to spend the four days of his annual convention with him in his Vegas hotel, though for obvious reasons she's not allowed to leave the room. This service costs thousands of dollars.

Fascinating Tidbit No. 3:

You must be eighteen years or older to patronize or work in a Nevada brothel.

Fascinating Tidbit No. 4:

While women are welcome to purchase the services of female sex workers at most brothels, there are no brothels in Nevada where women can purchase sex from men.

Fascinating Tidbit No. 5:

Sex workers receive thorough medical exams on a weekly basis.

In My Opinion:

Basically, prostitution is piecework, with the sex workers as exploited laborers. Often, their contracts require that they work three to five weeks on with one week off. (A grueling schedule for any type of work, but can you imagine? Those poor girls must be sore as hell!) Even when off duty, their movements are often severely proscribed by their employers, who do not want them seen by or fraternizing with prospective clientele. What hypocrisy! Even though prostitution's legal and lucrative, the bad girls have to stay out of sight! Men! It would serve them right if some smart woman started a luxurious, worker- and patron-friendly brothel for women in Nevada, where not only the patrons, but the workers, are respected, welcome, and treated in a style commensurate with their difficult and important labor.

Love,
Mom

ACEY FLIPS THE FINAL PAGE OVER, STANDS UP, AND STRETCHES. "Wow, your mother's something else. And thorough! Don't you love her "in my opinion" section, where she practically advocates brothels for women? Maybe we should take her in as a partner. She's wild."

"It's funny, too, because I haven't told her about the plan."

"Are you going to?"

"Sure." My mother can be a pain with her adages, opinions, and ability to talk without breathing, but on the flip side she's a problem-solving type, and a great researcher. Skills I'm sure we'll need again, soon. "Hey, did I tell you she won the Senior Most Proficient on the Internet award from her community center?"

Acey laughs. "You know, that's an age group we haven't even seriously considered as patrons, seniors, but we should. Is your mom still dating that guy down the street, what's his name?"

"Mr. Blanchard. And yeah, as far as I know they're still an item, if my mother hasn't killed him."

"Nice way to go, huh?"

They say your ears must be burning, and you're going to live a long time, when people are talking about you and you appear. If that's the case, my mother's going to live forever, because right then the telephone rings.

"Hello?"

"Hi, honey, did you get the report? I slipped it in the mail slot on my way to the supermarket and wanted to make sure you found it, what do you think? Fascinating subject isn't it? I learned a tremendous amount. Anyway, I hope it helped."

"Hi, Mom. Yes, I got the report, it was great. Me and Acey just read it and were talking about you," I respond.

"Only nice things being said, I hope. Give her my love."

"Absolutely. Listen, Mom, we're working on a project and thought you might be interested in doing some more research for us."

"I thought this brothel stuff was something for your job at the agency?"

"Actually, it isn't. Remember what you wrote in your last paragraph, the one called 'In my opinion?' "

"Of course I remember," my mother snaps. "I may be old, but I am not senile." Like all elderly people, she is incredibly sensitive to any suggestion, real or imagined, that the deterioration of her body has any correlation to her mental acumen.

"Sorry, didn't mean it that way," I apologize hastily. "Anyway, we're planning to do exactly as you suggested and open a brothel for women in Nevada."

"We who?" my mother asks when she finally stops laughing.

"Me and Acey."

"Alice Clothilda Allen, baby girl of the dear departed Reverend Esmont Allen, ace boon coon of Reverend T. Terry Tiger, self-appointed leader of the Negro people and guardian of our morality? That Acey Allen? I know her daddy must be spinning in his grave at the thought of any daughter of his having sex out of wedlock, much less selling it," my mother pronounces, laughing heartily.

Though Acey and I have been best friends since we met, the same can't be said for our parents. Acey's mother was a small, silent woman who always deferred to her husband and never voiced an opinion of her own unless it agreed with his. She died a horribly painful death from pancreatic cancer five years ago. Reverend Allen was a squat, short-armed man who strutted like a peacock, had a judgment about everything, and dominated conversation by raising his voice decibel by decibel until he drowned out the competition. That's the way he raised Acey, according to his own strict beliefs and with no interest in what she or anyone else had to say. He had a biblical justification for every one of his rules and regulations: no parties, no loud music, no sex, even no soft drinks, with or without caffeine. He died the year after his wife, and along with grief, Acey's still struggling to reconcile her mother's timid silence and her father's booming judgments with the life she wants to lead.

"Yes, it's Acey, and no one knows about this, so please, don't you say a word."

"Me? Who's still alive to tell?" my mother says. "You know, there

are many ways to love the Lord. People have forgotten that Mary Magdalene was a prostitute at one time herself."

"I don't know what people have forgotten, mother. Just make sure
you don't breathe a word about this to anyone, including your boyfriend."

"No one will find out from me," she says huffily.

"Okay. Could we talk about the brothel? What do you think?"

"I said what I thought in the report," she says impatiently, "Although the way I expressed myself may have been tongue in cheek, I was
serious. Even the most incompetently or meanly run brothels are lucrative. Besides which, why should men have all the fun? Not only do women
want and need sex, but the truth is we're able to have it longer than most
men, you should hear the women at the senior center talk. So yes, I think
it's a great idea as long as it's done right, with respect, safely, and in an attractive setting. It's a chance to show these men that women do it better."
She winds down, exhales. "What can I do to help?"

"Could you find out how we apply for a brothel license, get a hold of
the applications from Nevada, and help us get that aspect rolling? We
want to be open by summer, and that's just a few months from now. And
Mom, please keep this under your hat." Before she can respond, I hear
the beep on the line signaling another call coming in. Before I can ask
her to hold on a minute, she says, "What brothel?" and disconnects. I
depress the button on the phone, switch over.

"Hello?"

"Lydia, it's Odell. What's happening?" Odell's easy voice asks. "Any
word from Muffin?"

"Not yet, but I got her all the information she asked for, so I'm
thinking positive. What's going on with you?"

"It's all good. I went to the game last night with a bunch of guys I
play basketball with on the weekend, mentioned our business, and think
I've got a few more great prospects."

"Really?" I squeal. "It's raining men!"

Odell laughs. "I gave out about fourteen applications, and as soon as
I get them back and we look them over, we can set up personal interviews."

"Yum. No one thought you were crazy?"

"More like kidding. But when I broke it down, a lot of the fellas were
interested. Like I told you, having sex and getting paid for it is a winning
proposition."

"Great. Acey thinks she's found the perfect place outside Reno, and if it works out we're gonna have to shift into high gear to open in July. If we get the money from Muffin, that is."

"Good. Oh yeah, I went by the Piranha after the game and mentioned it to my man Tom L. Remember him?" An image of bedroom eyes and a great physique flash onto my mental screen. How could I forget?

"Yep."

"He's interested, said he knew some other men he'd talk to."

"Fantastic. Now all we need is the check."

"All right. Let me know if I can do anything." I hang up and fill Acey in on Odell's progress. She smiles.

"Now if Muffin just comes up with the cash, we're in business," I say.

"So we're really gonna do this?"

"We have to do it. Look at the response we're getting to just the idea. Even my mother thinks it'll fly."

"Yeah, but . . ."

"But what?" I'm praying my girl isn't about to bail now that we're so close.

"But Matthew."

My ears perk up and alarms start going off.

"What about him?"

Acey twitches uncomfortably in her seat.

"I've been thinking about what we were talking about the other day, you know, the fact that I'm in a relationship with Matthew and about to open a brothel at the same time. I'm lying to him and I just don't know if I can do it."

"You're not lying to him, you're just not telling him the whole story."

Acey gives me a stern look, rolls her eyes.

"Please. That junior high school rationale will not work. Maybe I should tell him . . ."

"Tell him? Are you kidding? Mr. Straight Arrow will never go for it. He won't even understand the point of the spa, since according to you the sex, what little there is of it, stinks, but he thinks it's okay."

Acey just shakes her head.

"I feel like maybe there's hope for Matthew. Maybe I need to focus, be more committed, and that means be honest. Maybe I shouldn't be putting all this energy into A Sister's Spa, but should rededicate myself to the relationship . . ."

"Maybe there is and maybe you should. But what does that have to do with our business? Why can't women's business life and personal life be separate, the way men's are? If you're not going to screw the men who work at the brothel, what's the problem?"

"I hear you, but . . ."

"But what? You want to pull out of a business that not only will make you rich and, if you'd let it, ensure your sexual satisfaction but, think of it this way, will also be a public service for sisters, because *maybe* Matthew's going to snap out of his sexual lethargy and get a new lease on sexual life? Acey, that's crazy. You're just creating problems for yourself."

"Exactly how is wanting to be in a relationship making problems for myself?" Acey asks, frowning. "You may have become the queen of not getting involved since you and Lorenzo split up, but as I recall you were Miss Committed while you two were together."

"That's true. I spent so much time hoping Lorenzo'd maybe this and maybe that and trying to be supportive, I didn't have time to think about my needs and my dreams. Those went on the back burner. I never want another relationship like that, where I'm doing most of the work, investing most of the energy, and trying to convince myself that's okay. And as your best friend, I'm going to say something if I see you heading down that road to nowhere."

"What's the alternative?"

"Hey, I haven't got it all figured out, but I do know that the only thing I've got to have every morning is a job, not a man. I want to wake up excited about the work I do, not dreading it. I've only got a little more paid leave and then I have to decide whether to go back to Believe The Hype. We're both risking a lot with A Sister's Spa. But that's what life's about, taking risks, no?"

Acey looks both hopeful and dismayed. "Maybe you're right."

"No maybe about it. Let's do it, and if your relationship with Matthew works out, that'll be wonderful. And extra."

"I guess. But still . . ."

"Listen, let's agree that we'll go for it, but if you have reservations at any time, we'll sit down and seriously talk. Okay?" Actually, I'd rather run over and slap some sense into her, but I'm making an effort to be both sensitive and a pacifist. "Until then, maybe you need to summon Earl back to the pantry. Besides," I add coyly, "there's no way I can screen all the applicants by myself. I know it's a sacrifice, but I need your help."

Acey holds up her hands in surrender, laughs. "Okay, okay, you've made your point. I'm in. For now." Right on time, my cell phone rings.

"Hello? Hello?" I pause, hear breathing on the other end. "I'm going to say hello one more time, then I'm going to hang up, press star-69, call the police, and tell them you're harassing me. Hello?" I hear sniffling in the background.

"Lydia, don't hang up. It's me. Lorenzo."

"Hang up? You motherfucking son of a bitch, I'd like to hang you! I want my money! I want the fucking money you stole from me!" I shriek.

"I didn't really steal your money, it was in our joint account."

"Lorenzo, the only joint you're gonna get near is the one they'll put you in when I find your ass and have you arrested. Joint account? You never put a goddamned dime into that account. What makes you think you have the right to *one cent* of my hard-earned money? What? Tell me, what?" I'm screaming and clutching the phone so tightly my hand is sweating. Acey impassively hands me my glass of Pellegrino.

"I should have known you wouldn't understand." Lorenzo has the nerve to sound huffy. "You never did. But you will. After I'm gone."

"Gone? Where the hell are you going? The only place you can go for me is to hell, but just in case you're planning to take the final leap, let me know where I can pick up my $40,000."

"You know I don't believe in suicide," Lorenzo says self-righteously. "I'm leaving San Francisco, though. You won't see me for a while, maybe ever, but if we do meet again, you'll understand. There'll be no need for me to explain."

"Lorenzo, what are you on? Because you sound crazy as hell, Negro. And let me make myself perfectly clear: If I have to stalk your tired ass for the rest of my days, you will not only explain your stealing self, but give me my money back! You always were full of shit."

"Lydia, I am not the same man I was. Everything has changed. I've got to follow my new path. That's why I took the money," Lorenzo says.

"Path? Don't tell me about your New Age path paved with my gold, you creep. There's nothing you can say or do that'll ever make what you did all right. Remember this, Lorenzo: life is a long hard road that doesn't bend." I'm yelling so hard the mouthpiece is flecked with spittle. Just then a recorded voice says, "Please deposit five cents for the next minute or your call will be disconnected."

"Well, I'd better go," Lorenzo says.

"Stole my money and don't even have a nickel for the phone, you cheap bastard. What the hell did you call for?"

"To say goodbye. And tell you I dropped the alimony suit. Guess I better be going, anyway."

"Where are you? Don't hang up!" I yell.

"Goodbye, Lydia. I want you to know I always loved you, in my own way," Lorenzo whispers. "Forgive me."

"I'll forgive you when motherfucking hell freezes over!" I shout, but the only thing on the other end of the line is a dial tone. I throw myself down on the couch and sob tears of rage. Acey rubs my back with circular, soothing motions as I spew invective and epithets aimed at Lorenzo. After a while I'm all cried out. If it weren't for the money, I wouldn't be crying, and both the money and Lorenzo are gone. Concerning the latter, good riddance to bad rubbish. I go into the bathroom to put tea bags on my eyes and pull myself together just as the doorbell rings. When I come back into the living room there's LaShaWanda. She gives my ravaged face more than a quick glance, but is thoughtful enough not to say anything but hello.

"I was telling Acey I was in the neighborhood and thought I'd drop by, see if Muffin delivered."

"Not yet, but we're hopeful," Acey says.

"And waiting," I add.

LaShaWanda flips a hand in dismissal. "Rich folks. What I love about them is they have no idea how important money is to other people 'cause they've got so much of it. Muffin's probably somewhere getting her hair trimmed or serving meals to the homeless and simply forgot to call and tell y'all the deal is done."

"Let us pray."

"It'll happen," Wanda says confidently. "Anyway, I was thinking you all need to set up a money market account when you get the cash. That way you can earn the best interest rates and still write checks. If start-up expenses aren't too much, I advise you to invest $100,000 in some fast-growth stock, maybe Griff-Margetson, so you're spending your capital on one end and replenishing it on another. I also checked into mortgage rates, and now's the time to buy. If you can put twenty-five percent of the purchase price down in cash, I think I can swing a three percent interest rate on a fifteen-year mortgage."

"Slow down and let me get some paper."

"Wanda, how do you know so much about money?" Acey asks intently. LaShaWanda gets the same look on her face she had when we first asked what she did before she came to San Francisco, but this time she shrugs it off.

"Just picked the shit up here and there."

"LaShaWanda, come work with us at A Sister's Spa," Acey blurts out. "We need someone who knows business, money, and men, and that job description has your name written all over it. You've been fantastic helping us get the spa together, why not hang in and enjoy the success?" I nod my agreement.

"You all serious?"

"Hell, yeah. Plus, if you work with us, you'll beat your self-imposed deadline for finding a new job by five months."

"You know you're asking me to be your chief financial officer?"

Acey nods. "Yes, we do."

LaShaWanda looks thoughtful. Me and Acey hold our breath and pray, something, oddly enough, both of us seem to be doing a lot of lately.

"All right, but we need to talk about salary, benefits, and a percentage. You know I don't come cheap," LaShaWanda smirks.

"All that can be worked out," Acey assures her. Before I can chime in my assent, the telephone rings.

"Hello?"

"Lydia. How are you doing? It's Muffin Dixmoor."

Even though I'm holding my breath and have every limb on my body crossed superstitiously, I manage to choke out, "Hey, Muffin. How are you doing? What's up?"

Muffin sighs lazily. "Not much. I just called to tell you I transferred $500,000 from the 1-800-HEP-BROS Foundation into your account ten minutes ago. You're in business."

I'm so happy I'm damn near slobbering as I say "Thank you, thank you" about two dozen times.

Muffin laughs. "Don't thank me, thank Dick. He's intrigued by the idea, thinks it might work. He's just read some study on sexual activity and promiscuity among black men and its effect on birth rates, and thinks paying men to have intercourse without any resultant pregnancies might truly make a dent. He also has a theory about violence being the result of repressed sexual tension, so he thinks fucking in a controlled environment might decrease the crime rate, too. He was really excited by your project. It's the first thing that's taken his mind off Griff-Margetson for weeks. He wants to see the operation and stay involved once you're up and running. So do I."

"Great. We'll keep you posted, Muffin. And thank you." I hang up, ready to tell Acey and LaShaWanda the good news, but it's obvious from the hugging and squealing going on in the middle of the room that they've figured it out from overhearing my end of the conversation. I head for the kitchen, grabbing three bowls from the china cabinet as I pass by. There are moments where the only way to respond is with an enormous bowl of Cherry Garcia ice cream, and this time, we're not even depressed.

19

JUST AS THEY DO AT LOCAL 802, THE MUSICIANS UNION, WHEN THEY
need instrumentalists, or at Radio City Music Hall when they want more
long-legged women to be Rockettes, we finally hold our auditions for
men to work at A Sister's Spa. It seems only practical, since after culling
the applications there are still over seventy-five men who seem to be serious candidates.

Odell's network of friends and acquaintances has yielded a wealth
of applicants. LaShaWanda and I even went through our address books;
we identified the men who were, as Wanda put it, "strictly affair material," good for a booty call at two in the morning, and contacted them
about A Sister's Spa. After much teasing from Acey and Odell, I had to
put greed and temptation aside and admit it was both impractical and—
probably—physically impossible for me to hold one-on-one sessions
with each of them.

Odell suggested we meet in his loft along the waterfront, since it
was centrally located and spacious. It was perfect, because if there were
any irate rejected applicants, they wouldn't know where me, Acey, or
LaShaWanda lived.

LaShaWanda had become an essential part of A Sister's Spa. Not
only had she brought Muffin Dixmoor into the picture, but she'd also
made herself indispensable in countless other ways. She volunteered to
negotiate the purchase of the property outside Reno and managed to get
the IRS to knock the asking price down to a figure that was within our
budget. She also hooked us up with that fifteen-year mortgage at three
percent interest through some banker, she vaguely explained, who "owed
her from when I worked in New York." She was all-around great when it
came to money, numbers, and organization. She'd revised our business
plan, helped us decide on appropriate fees for the various packages and
services, and determined basic salary and benefits structures. She even
created scales for bonuses, and savings and pension plans. And of course

she negotiated a tough (but worthwhile) deal with Acey and me to become our official chief financial officer.

Neither of us could figure out exactly why someone who was clearly as smart and well-educated as LaShaWanda had been working as secretary to a vice-president of Old Western Bank, but it was useless to ask her direct questions. Wanda, as we'd come to call her, was savvy, helpful, and funny, and she kept information about her past very close to the vest. Every now and then she'd let something slip, but if I asked her about it, she'd clam up. Like one time she picked up a copy of *Business Week* from the coffee table in my living room, glanced at the cover photograph of a bunch of white guys in suits under the headline, "The Smartest Businessmen in America?" and tossed the magazine down in disgust, muttering, "Those assholes. It's no wonder the economy's in trouble if they're the smartest men in America." But when I asked her where she knew them from, she she didn't want to talk about it and then asked me if I'd seen some segment of Oprah.

Curious as I am, I'm too busy to spend much timing trying to figure out who Wanda really is. That's her business, and the important thing is that she's a godsend for our business. She's also the perfect bridge between my usually unbridled and sometimes irrational enthusiasm about the brothel and Acey's recurring flashes of guilt motivated by memories of Earl, loyalty to Matthew, and old-fashioned Christian morality. Odell's a doll and tries to mediate sometimes, but sweet as he is, he just can't fathom the dynamics of a thirty-year friendship between two women. We'll get into discussions where I'm advocating A Sister's Spa as a revolutionary concept that's as important to the lives of black women as the overthrow of Batista was to Cuba, and Acey'll be philosophizing about if it's possible and permissible for a good Christian woman to be into uncommitted sex, and Odell, well, he'll just try to bring us both back down to earth so that we can deal with whatever decision we need to make. LaShaWanda will usually just sit and watch us, smoking a Newport and sipping from a glass of wine, until the argument starts to double back and loop over itself to where she either realizes it's going nowhere, gets sick of listening to us, or both. "Okay, enough," she'll suddenly say, crushing out her cigarette. "Neither one of you's gonna win this argument, but we need to move on and resolve the issues at hand." Then she'll remind us what the issues are, more often than not something mundane—like what the A Sister's Spa logo should be (we eventually decide on a drawing of a black woman, eyes closed, looking blissful) or whether the male staff should wear short shorts or spandex unitards (we agree on both, and then some)—we'd somehow managed to spin off of into something profound.

Since she was the mistress of cutting to the chase, we asked Wanda to come to Odell's and help us choose the forty initial employees of A Sister's Spa, which is why we're all sitting in Odell's loft, legal pads and photocopied applications on our laps, about to invite the first hunk in. I'm so excited my legs are shaking like they do after I have an orgasm.

"Everybody ready?" Odell asks. "I'm gonna call out a number, he'll come in, and we'll have five minutes for the interview." Acey and LaShaWanda nod, but me, I can't resist yelling, "Let's get it on!"

"Number one!" Odell calls. The door opens and in walks DMX. Well, not actually DMX, but I swear this brother could have been his twin. Chocolate brown, six-pack abs, small waist, shaved head. As required he's wearing shorts, and it's obvious that above his muscular calves and thighs he's got a dick that demands respect. "Hello," he says, smiling and strutting over to stand on the taped X on the floor in front of us. "I'm King. Thank you for having me." I can't keep the grin off my face, but I do manage to refrain from screaming, "And I'm your queen, and I want you to have me, too!"

"So, why do you want to work at A Sister's Spa?" Odell asks.

"Hey, I love women," he laughs.

"What is it about women you love?" says LaShaWanda.

"Everything."

"Could you be more specific?"

"Yeah, sure, no problem. The way they look, smell, taste, feel. That little sound they sometimes make in their throat just as I make them come, when they're beyond words. The way they like to throw their leg over mine and talk afterwards—"

"Wait. You like to talk after sex?" Acey asks incredulously.

"Yeah, that's when women are most open."

"Sign him up," Acey whispers to me.

"Amen," I whisper back at her.

"What part of sex don't you like?" Wanda asks.

"Oral sex."

"Well, that ain't gonna work, honey. Since all women love oral sex."

"I mean, I don't like getting blow jobs," King says.

"You don't want a blow job, but you like to give head?"

"That's about it. I hope that doesn't disqualify me," King says anxiously.

"Are you kidding? I have died and gone to heaven," I squeal as me, Wanda, and Acey look at King reverently. Flipping through his application, Odell brings us back to earth.

"It says here you're willing to move to Nevada. Great. Do you have any problem using ViriMax in order to be able to service multiple women?" King grins, stretches.

"No, although that's probably not necessary. I'm twenty-six and don't have any problems in that area. But if I need help to do the job, I'm happy to have it."

"You work out, King?"

"Yeah, five days a week."

"What do you bench-press?"

"350, on a good day 400."

"Good. Because A Sister's Spa welcomes women of all sizes and you may be required to do some lifting," Odell says. King nods.

"That's fine. I'm into taking women higher, any way I can."

"Okay. Thanks for coming in," Odell says, rising to shake King's hand. "We'll get back to you," he adds as King walks toward the door. When the door closes Odell turns to the three of us. "What do you think?"

"Get back to him? I'm ready to hire him on the spot," I say.

"He's a yes, definitely," Wanda adds and Acey nods. So does Odell.

"Okay. Number two!" Odell calls.

Number two, whose name is Alton, is a dark-skinned brother, on the short side and kinda beefy, with legs and arms like tree trunks. He must pump serious iron; he may be big, but there doesn't seem to be an ounce of fat on him. He walks to the X, grins, and I swear, his teeth are so big, white, and pretty it's as if a lamp's been turned on in the room.

"How y'all doin'?" he says in a voice so thick with the South I can almost smell the magnolia blossoms. LaShaWanda sits bolt upright.

"Fine. You?"

"Wonderful, ma'm. I am really excited about this opportunity," he says shyly. Looking at the thickening in the crotch of the shorts spread tight over his pelvis, I almost say, "You telling me?"

"Why is that?" Acey asks.

"Well, I'm from Currituck County, North Carolina. I came out here two years ago 'cause I didn't want to work my uncle's hog farm. Thought I'd make my fortune, find myself, or both, but so far, no luck. I been unpacking stock at Home Depot for two years, and don't want to keep doing that. When I ran into Odell at the court and he told me about your spa, I figured, why not? Sounds exciting."

"What excites you about it?" Wanda asks.

"Just about everything. I'm a stock guy at Home Depot, remember?" Alton chuckles. "Seriously. I like women, I love sex, and have never gotten any complaints in that department, not to be immodest. I've got no real ties to the area, and wouldn't mind seeing more of the country. Besides, I promised my family if I didn't find my passion in three years I'd come home and learn hog farming. I surely don't want to do that, so it's time for me to try something new."

"Now, on your application you said you can touch your nose with your tongue. Would you show us?" Acey says. Alton's fat pink tongue darts out of his mouth, the tip of it touching down not on the tip of his nose, but on the bridge. Beside me, Acey lets out a faint gasp.

"You checked the first three boxes on question three, the one asking how you find out a woman's sexual desires. Can you explain?" Odell asks, passing Alton a copy of his application to refresh his memory. He scans it quickly.

"I try to do them all—talk to her before we start making love, watch how she reacts while we're making love, and ask her what she likes while we're going at it. That's why I checked all three. Was there only one answer?" he asks nervously. The four of us shake our heads simultaneously.

"You also checked "No music at all," when asked what type of music you like to fuck to. What's up? You anti-music?" LaShaWanda asks.

"Naw, music's cool with me if the woman wants it, I can work with that. Myself, I prefer the music of bodies making contact and our voices, but if the lady wants to hear music, that's okay with me."

"You said you'd be willing to participate in a ménage a trois. So, you'd feel comfortable with another man and a woman?"

"As long as he ain't gay and that's what the woman wants, I'm cool," Alton says. "I've been in scenes with two women, so I can see why a woman would want to be with two men, as long as it's about pleasuring her and not each other."

"No doubt," I respond.

"Could you turn around?" That's Acey, always into the buns. Alton swivels and shows us a big, tight ass. Acey grins.

"Thanks. We'll be in touch," Odell escorts him to the door.

"I like him. He's sweet," Wanda says.

"And sincere," adds Acey.

"And willing to experiment," I add. "Two down and seventy-three to go."

I'm in fantasyland, enjoying myself and thinking it's all going to be smooth sailing until, that is, number eighteen.

Raymond Buckman is about five-ten, a rhiney brother with freckles and an air of confidence that's appealing until he starts talking and you realize it's bordering on arrogance. He's thirty-five and has a nice body, but it's ten pounds from being overripe and squishy, and it doesn't look like he's doing any exercise at all to keep gravity at bay. When Odell calls his number he saunters in with a slight smirk on his face, as if he's doing us a favor, not asking us to do him one. "I'm Raymond, but my friends call me Buck," he announces, standing spread-legged on the X and licking his lips suggestively. Even though his words and stance make for a rather crude come-on, he exudes a sexuality that's unmistakable.

"Okay, Buck," Wanda says in a tone of voice like an arched eyebrow and meets his challenge. "What is it that's special that you can bring to the spa?"

"You name it, I've got it. Just tell me what you're looking for," Buck smirks. LaShaWanda rolls her eyes, impatiently flips through the application on her lap.

"It's like that, huh?" Wanda snaps. "Okay. On question five about condoms, you answered that condoms are 'For other people.' What's that about?"

"It's about the feeling, mama. It just doesn't feel right. Besides, I'm clean. I get my joint checked once a month, and I don't fuck no stank ho's."

"Whatever," Wanda erases him with her hand.

"Employees of A Sister's Spa are required to use condoms. Is that going to be a problem?" Acey asks.

"Not if you can find some big enough for Mr. Mighty Meat."

"Mr. Mighty Meat?" Acey echoes.

Buck doesn't say a word, just grabs his crotch, pulling the silk of his shorts against a not insubstantial wad, and gyrates his hips. Oh, he means that Mr. Mighty Meat.

"All right, for question twelve, you checked three answers. You said a woman's vagina smells "earthy and stimulating," "fishy," and "stank." Could you elaborate?" I ask.

"Sure. It depends which bitch I'm fucking and for how long. She can start out earthy, but by the time I finish with her she's fishy, stank, too, and either passed out or hollering for more. That's why they call me The Terminator."

I can't help it, I start to laugh. Buck grabs his penis again, and it's not my imagination, it's getting hard.

"You laugh now," he says, "But you won't be laughing once you ride this shit. I guarantee it. Giddy-up."

"Giddy-up? Did you say giddy-up, motherfucker?" Wanda growls. Buck grins as his penis swells inside his purple silk shorts.

"Oh but I did, baby. Big-ass bitch like you could ride my shit like a bronco, now couldn't you?" His penis is fully erect now, the outline pressed against the thin fabric. And his shit is fat, too. But who'd want to fuck an asshole like him, even with outstanding equipment?

"Who you calling a big-ass bitch?" LaShaWanda yells, pushing herself up from the couch. Odell puts his hands up for silence.

"Er, Buck. Did you read the application? We're opening a spa where the most important thing is giving women pleasure. It doesn't sound as if that's the right job for you," he says diplomatically. Buck laughs.

"Listen, I wrote the book on pleasuring bitches. You got to ride 'em like dogs, fuck 'em 'til it hurts, and spank their ass if they complain. Fuck all that tender loving care shit, I know bitches, and what a bitch wants is to be dominated. They're all searching for their lost daddies anyway. What a black woman wants is dick and discipline, in that order, and I got the equipment to give it to them."

"You're crazy!" Wanda yells. "Get the fuck out." Buck dismisses her with a movement of his head.

"Cool, you one of those fat repressed bitches, stay that way. What do you foxes have to say?" he says, and turns toward me and Acey. By now his dick's so hard I'm looking for it to burst from his pants like a heat-seeking missile. I just hope I'm out of target range. This brother's getting turned on by his own bullshit. I glance over at Acey and she looks stricken dumb, as if she can't figure out what to do with her mouth except leave it to hang open. So I step to the plate.

"Buck. It is Buck, isn't it?" I say sweetly. "This fox wouldn't let a jerk like you anywhere near the hen house, much less A Sister's Spa. You're gross, crude, arrogant, and frankly, I'd rather fuck a sex-starved orangutan than you, and the sex would probably be gentler. Ya got to go." But does Buck put his tail between his legs and leave? No way. He turns expectantly toward Acey who manages to squeeze out "I agree," before she's struck dumb again.

"Well, thank you for coming in," Odell says, rising and motioning toward the door. Now it's Buck who's paralyzed, as if he can't believe we're not interested in his sadistic brand of pleasuring women. He stands there frozen, his penis still squirming against his shorts for release. Odell finally has to grab his elbow and almost drag him to the door.

Luckily, Buck is the only applicant we reject because he both hates women and is insane—which, come to think of it, is probably the same thing. The other men who don't make the cut fail for more benign reasons, paramount among them bad teeth and bad attitudes. By the time we get out of the twenties, we can pretty well tell before a man reaches the X, with a quick look at his eyes, mouth, and crotch, if he's even worth interviewing. But at Odell's urging we give every man his five minutes of fame. "Y'all don't need to be so cold," Odell admonishes after Louis, number fifty-three, slinks out of the loft after Wanda looks at his package, shakes her head, and tells him straight-up, "I am not impressed," as Acey and I dissolve into giggles.

"You need to give each applicant the benefit of the doubt. You never know who might rise to the occasion," Odell says, reminding us that it is a job interview and some of the men are nervous.

We spend the most time with number thirty-one, a brother named Robert who is the deep copper color of a well-used penny, with a powerful, lithe body and high, chiseled cheekbones. He's at ease with his body, well endowed, eager to get the job, and doesn't seem conflicted about the prospect of being a sex worker.

"I can't put my finger on it, but there's something not quite right with him," Wanda says when he leaves the room.

"Are you saying you're not impressed?" I tease.

"Oh, I'm impressed, all right. He's got everything we're looking for. Still . . ."

"Still what, Wanda?" Odell asks impatiently. "We need to make a decision, we've still got forty-four men to interview."

"Anyone seen *American Gigolo*?"

"With Richard Gere? Hell, yeah. Now he is a fine white man."

"True that, but remember how in the end, when times get tough, he goes back to finding male customers?"

Acey perks up. "We all saw the movie. What's your point, Wanda?"

"I've got no evidence, and this would never be admissible in court, but Robert strikes me as a switch-hitter," Wanda says. "Don't ask me why."

"You think he's into women *and* men?" Odell asks incredulously. "I didn't get that vibe from him at all."

"That's my point, Odell. That shit's hard to know for sure."

"Haven't you read any of E. Lynn Harris's books? I mean Basil's always poking a woman, that doesn't mean he isn't sleeping with a man, too," Acey says.

"Or doesn't want to," I add. Odell looks confused.

"You lost me. Who's Basil?"

"A character in E. Lynn Harris's books," Wanda says.

"Let me get this straight, for want of a better phrase," Odell says incredulously. "Even though he has all the necessary characteristics, you want to reject Robert because he reminds you of a character in someone's novel?"

"Not just a character, Odell, a bisexual character. And E. Lynn's sold about a trillion books, so it's not just someone's novel," Wanda says. "Look, I know you men are all intrigued by the lesbian thing, love nothing more than seeing two women going at it, but you'd have a hard time finding a woman who's down with her man getting his dick sucked by another man, much less getting fucked in the butt by one."

"I'm with you, Wanda. Something about him reminds me of a guy I dated briefly years ago. He gave the best head in the world but infuriated me out of bed. The affair ended soon after I discovered that his dresser drawers were so neatly organized he'd shame Martha Stewart. Once I saw that, something clicked in my mind, connecting to other miscellaneous impressions I'd formed since we'd hooked up, and it began to occur to me that possibly he was gay. There was a quality of something missing there, or that didn't quite add up right, and the obsessive arrangement of those drawers wasn't a good sign. I'm not a homophobe, but I don't want to be with a man who doesn't have a solid fix on his own sexuality. Usually women who fall for sexually confused men end up suffering."

"Yep. A woman's got to go with her gut when her gay-dar starts beeping," Wanda says.

"My friend Jeffery swears he's not gay because he's never taken it in the ass. 'I serve, I'm not served,' is how he puts it. Whatever works for him, but serve or served, sisters ain't into it," I say.

"If there's any question, it's a no. Robert's out," Acey says firmly. Wanda and I nod our agreement as Odell raise his hand in a gesture of surrender.

Even though Odell lost that round, having him with us keeps us from going to that cold zone where we forget these guys are human, see them as nothing more than meat, and treat them the same way women are too often treated by men. Without Odell here to slow us down from snap, superficial judgments, we would have passed over a few men who we ended up hiring, including Christian, a kinda short, balding brother with the most seductive French accent. Originally from the island of Guadeloupe, he'd gotten as close to a perfect score on our questionnaire as anyone and during the interview described making love to a woman's feet in such detail that my toes cracked involuntarily. *"Now* I'm impressed," is how Wanda succinctly put it.

But mostly, I think we're all impressed. Even though I'm not about to do a mea culpa right then and there, what Odell said about the way sisters mistakenly stereotype men as being interested only in the booty was true. The men we wanted to hire had more going for them than being attractive and sexual. They were also different combinations of smart, funny, adventurous, artistic, intellectual, creative, musical, and gentle. And they all actually seem to like women when they're not fucking them, too.

I never thought I'd tire of looking at attractive, scantily clad men, but by the time we see David, aka number seventy-five, a painter with salt-and-pepper hair and beard, full wet lips, and a sultry voice that could make a less tired woman cream just listening to it, I'm exhausted. The good news is we've found the forty men we need to open and a handful more we could hire immediately if our supply isn't adequate to the demand. The men range in age from twenty-one to fifty, although most are under thirty-five. Twenty-five are black, ten Latino, and five white. We've got a Latino guy with burnished bronze skin and fabulous cheekbones; a beefy brother from St. Lucia with dark black skin, massive shoulders, and a smoldering gaze, and a slim, intense white guy with that sexy working-class vibe. And of course we hired Tom L. Livingswell, from the Piranha Bar. A lot of them are easy to agree on, since we all like them fairly tall, able to speak English, and with a sense of humor. But it's LaShaWanda who fights for Wes, a short, plump hairdresser of twenty-seven who Acey and I aren't feeling at all until Wanda tells him to give us a scalp massage and he rubs my head so intensely I can feel it between my legs. When I ask Wanda how she knew, she just murmurs something about "the look of his hands," and moves on.

And it's Acey who insists on a thirtyish brother named Spider, a light-skinned guy with a barrel chest, pretty legs, and a great laugh, but not right off my type. Something makes Acey ask him if he knows any songs by Luther Vandross, and he bursts into a gorgeous baritone rendition of "A House is Not a Home." Honey, I'm ready to open my triple-locked front door when that song ends, and he's hired.

Me, I press for Ahmad, a deep brown twenty-two-year-old with dreads and dreams of being either the next Master P or an astronomer. He has the body of life, beautifully muscled and toned. On his left bicep is a tattoo of a gorgeous night sky streaked with light with an ornate "A," I guess for Ahmad, in the center. He's exuberant, full of himself, and vibrates with energy. Hey, I'd fuck him, and I know some of our clients will be turned on by his dreads and his head.

We started at eleven that morning and it's eight that night when Odell puts an Angelique Kidjo CD on and finally says, "So that's it. I'll call the chosen forty tomorrow morning and arrange for them to be at the spa for training next week." He bends down and rips the taped X from his living room floor.

"You still think we can open by July 4?" Acey asks. The four of us are languidly collecting applications and notepads, throwing scraps of paper into a garbage bag, straightening up after a hard day's work.

"Yep. It's not going to be easy, but I think we can finish pulling everything together by then, give or take a day," Odell nods.

"Odell, it's got to be July 4, we can't give or take a day," I say.

"Tell me again why it has to be the Fourth of July?" Wanda asks.

"Come on, think about the resonance. The fourth's a national holiday, Independence Day. What better day to open A Sister's Spa, a place that will offer sister's a level of independence and sexual liberation we've never experienced. Ya gotta love it."

Wanda laughs. "Cool, though I don't know how happy the Founding Fathers would be with our equating their triumph over colonialism with opening a brothel. But to hell with them, they didn't liberate our ancestors, did they? Is that it?" she asks, holding the open trash bag in both hands and glancing around the room. "I'm beat. I need to go home and take a long bath." Odell glances around the loft. It's as pristine as it was when we arrived that morning.

"Looks good," he says, taking the bag from LaShaWanda and tying the ends together. "I'll walk you all to your cars. Since no one's interested in dinner, I'm gonna head down to the Piranha Bar and have a few drinks."

We walk slowly down the two flights to the street, Odell bringing up the rear. On the sidewalk, Odell hollers, "Wait a minute," runs into the alley alongside the house to throw the bag into the garbage can there. Me, Acey, and Wanda silently wait for him in the dusky evening. The water-front is alive with people on their way to dinner or to hear some music, or simply enjoy a stroll on a beautiful spring evening. Throwing my head back and turning my neck to try to work some of the tension out, I catch a glimpse of a silver-haired woman in a cat suit turning the corner a half-block away.

"Hey, isn't that Barbaralee Edison?" I ask Acey, but by the time she turns around to look, the woman's disappeared around the corner. I shrug. "Probably not. Just another sister in a cat suit," I say as Odell emerges from the alley and somehow manages to wrap his big arms around the three of us. "A good day's work, ladies, a good day's work," he says as he gathers us into a group hug. "We've come a long way, babies," he adds, and our soft laughter floats away into the warm twilight.

20

THREE WEEKS LATER I'M SITTING AT MY KITCHEN TABLE, LAPTOP open, sending the last few e-mails to a select group of sisters inviting them to spend a complimentary day and night at the grand opening of A Sister's Spa. Lydia had come up with the idea of inviting forty carefully chosen women to our inaugural weekend, and along with Wanda we'd culled the list from our various address books, inviting women who were discreet, sexual, and plugged into a network of women they'd be sure to pass the word on to if they enjoyed their time at A Sister's Spa. Of course our carefully worded invitation never mentioned sex. We emphasized black women's need for relaxation and stress relief, and promised that A Sister's Spa could help via a regimen of facials, shiatsu, foot reflexology, various spa services, and what we discreetly called "total stress relief through intense deep tissue massage."

We were gambling that once women arrived, unpacked, and met our scantily clad, totally solicitous, and willing-to-do-anything-to-make-sure-their-stay-was-a-pleasurable-one employees, they'd be stripped down and enjoying themselves—on the massage table, in the sauna, sunning on the deck, splashing in the pool, or in their bedroom—in no time. Lydia and I were home taking care of the California end of things, while Wanda and Odell had been at the spa training the workers, not least in how to let our clients know, wordlessly, that sex was most definitely an option. Cold drinks should be served with a brief brush against breast, arm, or hip. Workers were to enter the sauna periodically and gently wipe the sweat from clients with a cool towel. Massage was to include the breasts and inner thighs, and water aerobic instructors were to initiate water sports that maximized the gentle colliding of wet, slippery bodies. All contact with clients, from taking a food order to changing linen, from the moment sister girl checked in until she turned out of our long drive-way, was to be ended with the words, "Please don't hesitate to let me know if I can do anything to make your stay totally pleasurable."

We'd covered the walls in nubby raw silk in mild shades of orange, red, and gold, and made sure that the lighting was soft and flattering, placing small lamps with beaded shades around the rooms. Each was equipped with a king-sized bed, plush chair and ottoman, dresser, CD player, and private bathroom, but no television. After a brief discussion, we'd all agreed that television was depressing and stress-producing, and its presence would serve only to negate the positive attitude we were trying to promote among the women at the spa. As Wanda so aptly put it in that blunt way of hers, "Any sister who spends time here watching TV doesn't get it, is just taking up space, and needs to take her ass home." We'd framed bright illustrations from the *Kama Sutra* and hung several of them in strategic places in each room. All of the rooms had mirrors opposite the bed and a few had them on the ceiling. Just in case some women were too dense to get it or couldn't believe it when they did, the shelf on the bedside table in each room held copies of books of black erotica and nude photographs. In the drawer of each night table, instead of a Gideon Bible, was a new, complimentary vibrator in a discreet leather case. We'd tried to do everything first class and, I think, succeeded, although I hadn't been out there yet, just had several virtual tours thanks to Odell's digital camera.

I type in the last e-mail address and lean back in my chair, knitting my fingers together above my head and arching backwards to get the kinks out of my shoulders and scan the words on the screen. Sudden as that, the light in the pantry flicks on and Earl's voice says, "Hey, baby darlin'. I see you took my advice."

Startled, my fingers hit the keys as I stand up, walk into the pantry, and there he is, handsome as ever. "Hey, yourself. I've been looking for you every day. And yes, I guess I did take your advice. A Sister's Spa's going to open in a few weeks, Lord willing."

Earl grins.

"Yeah, I think she's willing. But I wasn't talking about the spa. I meant you and what's his name, Odell, in the bell tower." I feel the hot flush of a blush begin around my hairline.

"Earl, I'm sorry, you see, I had my eyes closed, for a while there I swear I thought it was you, or maybe just wished it were you, I don't know. But until Odell said something . . . it was *you*, and by then it was too late—" Earl waves a finger in a line across my lips and even though he doesn't actually touch me, I feel its coolness.

"Hush, baby. It's fine. I told you before that just because I'm not there to give you pleasure doesn't mean you shouldn't have any. I wish I were Odell, or any man able to make love to you, to touch, stroke, and lick you, to make you happy. Maybe, in a way, I am, since we are all part of the same divine force, both the living and those of us in this some-place else."

"Oh Earl, I miss you."

"I know, baby, but you shouldn't. When our bodies die our energy lives on. It just disperses into more pieces than we have names for. You and me, we're blessed to be able to be together in this way, most people never get back into one piece after they pass." He smiles at me tenderly. "But I came to tell you some things, and don't know how long I'll be able to stay, so I need you to listen."

"What, honey? What's wrong?"

"I'm not sure, I'm not God," Earl laughs softly. "But I can sense things. Most of what I see is good, but there's something bad up ahead."

"What? Tell me what it is," I moan.

"I'm not sure, but you need to watch out for it and be prepared for a struggle."

"With who? What?"

"I don't know, baby darlin'. What I do know is that it's coming, and you, Acey, Odell, and LaShaWanda have to prepare yourselves for it." The way he says this makes chills run down the back of my neck.

"Earl, I'm scared," I moan.

"Don't be, just be prepared," he says, his voice fading.

"Earl!" I yell, as if I can summon him back with the volume of my voice.

"Watch your back, baby. You can do it." His voice is now a faint whisper. "And don't forget to enjoy yourself. I'm always with you," he says. His body ripples and he's gone, and I'm staring into an empty pantry with my mouth open and the phone ringing.

"Hello?" I say tentatively.

"Girl, I can't wait for you and Lydia to get your asses out here and see what me and Odell have done. This place is really coming together."

"LaShaWanda?"

"Who else? Acey, you are not going to believe the wonders we have wrought. The decoration is looking fabulous, the brothers look even bet-ter, and we're just about ready for business. You gotten any RSVPs for the opening?"

I wrench myself from the pantry, push Earl's warning to the back of my mind, focus on what Wanda's saying.

"Slowly, but it's all good. I'm getting one no for every five yeses, so that's going great. I just sent out the last batch of invites, so I'm confident we'll be full opening night."

"All right. Listen. Odell hired two brothers who just missed the cut on the first round. It occurred to him that we needed some back up, in case someone gets sick or collapses from exhaustion. Cool?"

"Sure. And smart."

"So when are you two coming out here for the test run?"

"Test run? It sounds as if you and Odell have it together."

"We do, but we need you and Lydia to get your asses out here early and sample the wares. You know, pretend you're spa guests and make sure the pool, sauna, food, and men are top notch. A dry run, for want of a better term," Wanda adds, cackling. "We don't want any glitches on opening night or when the paying customers arrive."

"I hadn't thought of that, but I guess you're right," I say absentmindedly, opening my datebook. "I'll check with Lydia. She's got to meet with Jason Hype, her soon-to-be-former boss, next week, but we should be able to wrap things up here by the third week in June and get out there. That'd give us two weeks before the grand opening on July 4."

"Cool," Wanda says. "By the way, Muffin and Dick showed up this morning. He had a meeting in Reno and Muffin was cutting the ribbon at a playground for disabled children nearby, and they decided to drop in for a quick tour. Me and Odell walked them around the place and there's no doubt they were impressed, although Dick, I have to admit, has always made my skin crawl, whether Muffin loves him or not. Even when he's being nice, which he was, he's got 'bad vibe' coming out of his pores. They loved the place. You know who he hit it off with? Chef Marvini. While me and Muffin were giggling about the bedroom's décor, he stayed in the kitchen talking nutrition," Wanda chuckles. "Muffin says he's gotten deep into a healthy diet as he's grown older. They were here a few hours, then left, and all's well."

"Good. His foundation did supply the money, so if he wants to see what we're doing, I guess that's okay. Anyway, Wanda, we'll be there as soon as we can wrap stuff up here."

"You're gonna love it. Listen, Odell has to drive down there every now and then to take care of a few things on the home front. If you guys can get it together, he can pick you up and drive you back out on one of his trips. Just call him on his cell. Gotta go. The seamstress is coming to alter some of the brothers' uniforms and I need to be there to make sure they're showing just enough of what we're selling without being gauche."

"Thanks, Wanda. Couldn't have done it without you."

"You telling me?" Wanda says as she hangs up the phone.

21

AS ODELL STEERS US OUT OF THE BAY AREA AND TOWARD THE ALMOST completed spa, he and Acey converse up in the front seat while I relax and zone out in the back. I've never liked long car trips, but things have been so frantic I'm happy for the opportunity to chill for a few hours and reflect on everything that's been happening. The past several weeks have been a blur, but the one event that stood out in the whirlwind of spa-dedicated activity was my final resignation from my job.

I had been more than a little nervous on my way to meet with Jason and let him know that after my leave, I wouldn't be returning to Believe The Hype. Even if you're bored and quitting to do something exciting, leaving a high-paying job after fifteen years is a gigantic change, even more so if you're leaving to start an untried, some would say scandalous, business and every cent and all your energy's tied up in it's success.

Truth is, I'd had a great run at BTH. Jason hired me months after he'd started his business. He always respected me and my ideas, paid me well, and did his best to create a laid-back, no-bullshit working environment. Fifteen years ago, I'd been out of college a few years and was doing freelance advertising—when I could find work, which wasn't as often as I liked or needed. Jason saw some of the stuff I'd done that helped make Sapphire's one of the hottest clubs in town, tracked me down, and offered me a job.

What kept me at BTH was that for the first ten years I was able to grow there. I wasn't relegated to the Negro products, but handled all sorts of accounts, ending up the executive on most of the biggest ones, including Ricky Craig. That I'd gotten restless during my last five years had nothing to do with Jason and lots to do with being tired of selling crap and working for someone other than myself. I wanted to be more excited and fulfilled by my work. The demise of my marriage to Lorenzo sort of freed me to reimagine myself, I realized now, not just as someone who was no longer a wife or partner, but also in terms of my work. The idea for A Sister's Spa came right on time.

When I enter his office, Jason gives me a big smile and warm hug, then steps back and stares at me. "Lydia. Great to see you. You look fantastic. It's obvious you used the time off to your benefit."

"I did. And it's really good to see you, too, Jason. How's Believe the Hype survived in my absence?"

"We're doing well," he says motioning me to sit down. "But we'll do better when you're back again."

I look away. "So what happened with Ricky Craig and his Cellulite Compactor?" I ask, because I'm both curious and stalling for time. Jason shrugs.

"He left, in spite of Randolph prostrating himself to keep him here. But we picked up Griff-Margetson. They're unbelievably hot since they came out with ViriMax, so everything more than evened out," he shrugs, then smiles. "Plus, it's wonderful not to have to deal with a racist jerk like Ricky."

"So . . ."

"So . . . you're not coming back. Right?"

I take a deep breath. Of course, he figured it out. After fifteen years, Jason knows how to read me. "Right. It's been great being here. But I'm going to start my own business, with Acey." He smiles, his face a combination of warmth and dismay. I can see he's sorry to lose me, and I feel a pang. For a second.

"Lydia, that's great. How is Acey?" Jason knows Acey well, and never minded when I'd help her out with little promotional projects for her spa back in its early days. "What does this mean for her spa? What're you going to do?"

"Basically, we're going to open another one together, a bigger place with a broader range of services."

"Wonderful. That should do well. But are you sure you don't want to work here part-time during the start-up? You could make your own schedule."

"Jason, that's really wonderful of you, but no. I've got to put all my energy into making this work. I'm doing exactly what I want to do."

"Well, I understand," Jason laughs. "I certainly know how gratifying it can be to go out on your own and work for yourself. I'm happy for you. By the time you went on leave, it was hard for me to ignore that you weren't really enjoying it here anymore. Now you look terrific, so much more relaxed. Obviously, it must be agreeing with you. So let me take you to a long, luxurious, drunken lunch, and we'll work out the details." We spend the rest of the afternoon at Sapphire's, where I manage between toasts to suggest that Mi Lan, my former assistant, would make a great replacement. She's smart, hungry, young, and why not do the sister a solid?

I'm so busy pondering my meeting with Jason and the end of all my years at BTH that I don't realize we're almost at the spa until Odell turns the car into the long driveway. As we near the house, forty men clad in shorts, unitards, and biker shorts in various shades of the signature orange of A Sister's Spa, our blissful-sister insignia embroidered on their hips, line either side of the approach to the main building, legs splayed, hands behind their backs, and big-ass welcoming grins on each and every face.

It's like a scene out of *Gone With the Wind* or some other revisionist slavery fantasy, the one when the darkies are told to stop their back-breaking unpaid labor for a few minutes in order to line up out front, grin, and pretend they're delighted about Massa's return to the plantation. But except for the visual reminder, it's not really like that at all. These forty men are well housed, fed, and clothed, and their labor is far from grueling. Me and Acey aren't Massa or Miss Ann, but two sisters trying to deliver a service, and have some fun and get ahead at the same time. There's no need for chains, slave catchers, or nigger-hunting dogs here; Odell's got a fat file full of men who want to work at A Sister's Spa.

We pull up to the front door and there's LaShaWanda, her smile so big her cheeks almost cover her eyes. "Welcome to A Sister's Spa," she says, skipping down the steps and wrapping me and Acey in a bear hug. "Wait'll you see what we've done," she says, grabbing our hands and pulling us into the quiet, cool interior.

Even though I'm dog tired, Wanda's excitement is contagious. The transformation of the ashram is truly amazing. The enormous main salon, where the workers will hang out waiting to be selected, has pool and ping-pong tables and pinball machines against the wall, a dozen slot machines, and lots of plush orange ultra-suede couches and chairs piled with beaded and embroidered silk pillows. Chaise lounges are scattered poolside, there's a floating bar staffed by two men in the skimpiest of Speedo trunks, and six orange canvas cabanas furnished with massage tables and waterbeds are placed a discreet distance away.

Each bathroom is equipped with a tub, shower, bidet, a fat package of complimentary toiletries from Carol's Daughter, and enough towels for the Grambling football team. I could stay right in there for the weekend and be, if not perfectly satisfied, part of the way there.

"So, what'd you think?" Wanda asks, hands on her hips. Odell stands beside her, beaming proudly.

"Everything's gorgeous," Acey says. I nod.

"Absolutely perfect."

"Not quite," Odell says, "but it will be in a few weeks."

"And you haven't seen the employee dorms, kitchen, laundry facility. Acey, I even had them put in a little pantry in case you-know-who wants to visit you," Wanda blabbers, but I interrupt.

"Later, girl. I need to chill. I'm whipped. I'm gonna go lie down. Where're my bags and where's my room?"

Wanda presses a button in the wall behind her and seconds later a vaguely familiar man appears with my bags. "Trevor will show you to your room and get you settled," Wanda says with a wink. I turn and follow him down the hall.

When we get to my room I throw myself face down on the bed. Trevor moves quietly around, lighting scented candles and adjusting the air conditioning. "Would you like some music?" he asks softly, and when I nod he puts on a John Coltrane and Johnny Hartman CD. Perfect.

"May I help you get out of those clothes?" Trevor purrs as he slips the Jimmy Choos from my aching feet. I groan with relief. He gently unbuttons my skirt, lifts my hips, and slides it over and off. Warm fingers turn me over as he unbuttons my blouse, lifts my arms out, eases it off my shoulders and away with only the slightest of disruptions.

"Would you like me to finish undressing you?" he asks when I lie there in my bra and panties. I nod sleepily. He reaches down, unsnaps the clasp between my breasts, and the cups of my bra fall away. Trevor gently takes my breasts in his hands and blows warm breath across the nipples, which instantly harden. A thumb runs softly over a nipple as he lifts my back with his other hand and eases my bra off. Now he rubs both of my nipples, still blowing softly. I moan, and he leans over and traces the areola of one breast and then the other with his warm, wet tongue as his hands coax my panties down over my hips and legs, stopping to massage my calves. My breasts swell and it is as if I can feel the gently licking motion of his mouth, first on one breast and then the other, between my legs. I push my chest upward and he takes my nipple in his mouth and begins sucking. "Harder," I whisper and he responds immediately. I turn my chest slightly and he knows exactly what I want, takes the other nipple in his mouth, alternately sucks one, then the other, his teeth just begin-ning to lightly nibble at my breast. I lie there in a state of exquisite arousal as his hands caress my hips, stomach, sides, slide down my legs and up the inside of my thighs, kneading firmly. My hips rise up to meet his fingers, my poonani already wet. He slips the tips of two fingers just inside me and begins to probe gently, his mouth still working my breast. I spread my legs and raise my hips and gasp as his long fingers slide fully inside. His mouth sucks my breasts harder as I thrust myself onto his fingers as they move in and out, varying the rhythm, reaching to touch that spot deep inside me that screams for the release of orgasm, then darting away.

Then my breasts are suddenly cool and I feel his tongue lick smoothly around my clit. Now, I raise my hips to both his fingers and mouth. His lips wrap around my button and he pushes the skin back with his tongue, takes the firm bud of flesh in his mouth, and begins to suck gently. Inside me, the fingers of one hand play counterpoint to the rhythm of his mouth as the other reaches up to squeeze and caress my hard nipples.

I lie there, hands listless above my head as Trevor works my body, bringing me to the brink of orgasm and, just before that moment, pulling gently back with a change of rhythm, skillfully resisting my efforts to climax.

Full, hot lips touch mine and begin to kiss softly. A tongue begins to trace the outline of my lips, its tip darting into my mouth and away. It forces my lips open and slips inside, tracing my teeth in a motion that both tickles and arouses, as the intensity of the sucking on my clit intensi-fies. My eyes open to behold Trevor sucking the hot spot between my legs and another brother whose name I can't remember kissing my lips.

His lips still on mine, the man pulls my arms forward until I am first sitting, then, as Trevor's mouth slips from my pussy, on all fours. His lips leave mine and he slips between my open arms, squeezes my breasts to-gether, and begins sucking the nipples. I hear Trevor behind me, feel the head of his hot dick slide along the crack of my ass and rest against my sopping pussy. He spanks me lightly and I moan. The other man—Alton? Spider? Christian?—moves his lips from my tits and thrusts his tongue inside my mouth as his arm stretches back to tease my swollen clit.

Trevor gently slaps the cheek of my ass. The other man increases the pressure of his lips on mine and squeezes my bursting clit between his fingers as Trevor pushes deep into my cunt from behind, not hesitating this time, driving his dick up inside as the other man's lips smother mine and his tongue fills my mouth. I spread my legs wider, push back to meet

Trevor's thrust, hungrily kiss the other man and crush my pussy into his fingers, every inch of me alive and coming oh so slowly again and again and again. "Where one relaxes on the axis of the wheel of life, to get the feel of life, from jazz and cocktails," Johnny Hartman sings the words to Billy Strayhorn's "Lush Life" from far, far away.

JACQUES WESTIN SITS AT THE TINY LINOLEUM TABLE AT SYLVIA'S SOUL
Food Restaurant on 126th Street and Lenox Avenue, and tries not to gape
as he watches T. Terry Tiger demolish a breakfast of fried chicken, eggs
sunny side up, grits, and biscuits. The reverend eats passionately and me-
thodically, tearing a piece of chicken from the bone, dragging it through
the runny yellow egg yoke until it is coated, swishing it in grits divided by
small rivers of butter, then stuffing the whole mess into his mouth, followed by a quarter of a biscuit.

Across from Westin, his Palm Pilot with expandable keyboard is set up
on the table, wedged between a vase of plastic flowers and bottles of
ketchup, hot sauce, and greasy salt and pepper shakers. As Tiger's open
mouth grinds food between his teeth, crumbs flying, Jacques Westin discreetly covers the keyboard with a napkin and takes a bite of a single piece of
cornbread as he waits for Tiger to finish eating and begin their interview.

As always, the small restaurant is packed, the din from many voices
drowning out the jukebox, which plays futilely in the background. Sylvia's
is the eating spot of choice for local residents, office workers, Harlem's
elected officials and clergy, real estate developers from downtown, and
busloads of European and Japanese tourists in search of an authentic soul
food meal after enjoying a morning of gospel music or an evening of jazz.

Sylvia's is not the place to go when discretion or secrecy are needed,
since it is impossible to set foot on the block, much less walk through the
door, without running into someone you know. Instead, Sylvia's is the
place to announce one's importance and acknowledge allegiances, to
publicly declare war or wave the white flag. It is the place where the movers
and shakers of Harlem eat when times are good and there is a message they
want put out on the drum of observation and gossip that pulses through
the black community. Eat at Sylvia's and inside of an hour everyone who is
anyone in a ten-block radius will know not only who you ate with and what
you had, but also will be speculating on what was discussed.

194

T. Terry Tiger pushes his plate away, pulls the napkin from where it's been tucked into his collar, looks over at Westin, and belches contentedly. "Now, you sure you don't want more than that measly piece of cornbread?"

"No, sir. Just that interview," Westin says. Tiger sighs, looks around the room, waves and smiles at a table of clergy huddled in a booth against the wall. Spying a waitress hurrying by, a pot of coffee in hand, he motions toward his cup. After she fills it he extracts four packets of Sweet and Low from the dispenser in front of him, tears them all open at once, dumps them into his coffee, takes a gulp, and looks at his watch.

"Okay. What do you want to talk about?"

"The Crusade to Resurrect Morality," Westin says, adjusting his keyboard. "You announced it last month. What's the response been?"

"Overwhelming, absolutely overwhelming. We have touched something in the people, and they are responding."

"In what way?"

"Calling, writing, asking how they can help, what they need to do to become foot soldiers in this new crusade."

"What do you tell them?"

"I tell them to set their own house in order, pray to the Lord Jesus, and be ready to march when the bugle call for moral righteousness sounds. I tell them that it is not enough to pray, but they must also pay. That just as sin don't come cheap, they must open their pocketbooks for righteousness and dig deep. I tell them they don't have to be sinners, they can join the crusade and be winners. That's what I tell them."

"You mentioned the bugle call for righteousness . . . ?"

"You heard me right, Jacques. And when the bugle sounds, you will hear that, too. Loud and clear. After that the only sound to be heard will be the pounding footsteps of the army of the righteous. "

"When and where will that be?"

"Soon, soon. As we speak my staff is reviewing reports from all over the nation of sinful activity sent to us by the little man and woman, average people tired of their communities harboring sexual profligates and perversion, of unwed mothers and deadbeat fathers. Old people sick of going to the pharmacy to pick up their heart pills and having to fight past thugs and overflowing condom racks. These are our eyes and ears on sin, and it is from them, along with the divine guidance of the Lord, that we will find our direction."

"How much money has the crusade raised so far, and how is it being used?"

"Ah, now you ask the real question your white masters sent you up here for, 'What's the black man doing with the money?' White folks can't stand the thought of a black man with a few nickels to rub together, can they? And a righteous black man with an army and a few dollars . . ." Tiger hesitates, looks dramatically behind him. "I might just get assassinated, ain't that right?"

Westin glances at the people around them, intent on their chicken and waffles and oblivious to T. Terry.

"Are you saying you've received death threats?"

"No, I am not saying I have received death threats!" Tiger snaps. "But I am confident I will. Do you think that the Crusade to Resurrect Morality will proceed unopposed, that the immoral will simply fall away in the face of our righteous example and demands? Do you?"

Westin nods. "Probably not. Now, about the money you've raised."

"Those funds are being used for research and development of the crusade and to cover day-to-day expenses. A man's got to live, doesn't he? People have to be paid, do they not? Jesus worked as a carpenter, did he not? Just as man does not live by bread alone, a man needs bread to buy bread. We are also building a war chest in anticipation of the battles ahead."

Mentally, Jacques Westin sighs. It isn't the first time he's interviewed Tiger and probably won't be the last, and it's always a combination of innuendo, pulling teeth, and personal attack trying to get specifics before T. Terry's willing to give them, and that's usually at a press conference. Even so, he's got to hand it to Falwell, Jackson, Robertson, Tiger, and the rest of the Christian leaders, and give up a grudging respect for their ability to sway people with their rhetoric. But they still need to account for the money.

"The battles ahead?"

"You heard me right, son, the battles ahead."

"Would you be more specific about what those battles might be?"

"So that mine enemy should have warning that we approach the gates? No, I will not be more specific, other than to say, sinners, set your house in order or beware! We will come for you when you least expect it, as you writhe and hump in flagrant fornication, as you make babies you do not want and cannot care for, as you seize cheap sexual gratification with the passion with which you should embrace the Lord, we will be there, and we will bury you under a mountain of morality upon which we shall build a temple of righteousness!" Tiger falls back again his narrow chair, hyperventilating after his impromptu sermon.

"Sin? Did I hear someone say sin? Is that the king of sin, T. Terry Tiger?" a voice asks, loud enough to be heard above the din and Tiger's panting. "Jacques, how are you?" Barbaralee Edison, in a pinstriped cat suit, says, pulling out an empty chair and plopping down at the table.

"Hey, Barbaralee, long time," Westin says, unplugging his keyboard. Between Terry's rant and Barbaralee's arrival, it's clear the interview is over.

"Too long," Barbaralee says, patting his cheek with one hand. "You too, Reverend Tiger. It's been a long time." Recovered, T. Terry smiles, places both hands over hers.

"Barbaralee, looking gorgeous as always. Have you had breakfast?" She laughs.

"Now Reverend, you know the only thing I like to eat this early in the morning is a handsome man or some equally juicy information. What've you got for me?"

"Me? Nothing but the word of the good Lord," Tiger says piously.

"Didn't I hear someone talking about sin?"

"I'm interviewing the Reverend about the Crusade to Resurrect Morality for a piece for the paper, that's probably what you overheard," Westin says, but the fact that she interrupted the interview either falls on deaf ears or Barbaralee chooses to ignore him.

"Yes, I heard about your crusade. As a matter of fact I mentioned it in my last *Girlfriend!* column. Got an update for me?"

"Not at the moment, but you'll be one of the first calls I make, you can believe that," Tiger says.

"I hope I'll be the second," Westin says, folding up his keyboard and Palm, dropping it in his briefcase, and standing. "Well Reverend, thanks for your time." T. Terry manages to tear his eyes from Barbaralee's cleavage long enough to look up.

"Any time, Jacques, any time. And mark my words, you'll be hearing from the crusade shortly. The armies are amassing as they prepare to strike!" he calls to Westin's retreating back, then turns to Barbaralee.

"And what brings you East to my town?"

"The National Association of Black Journalists is holding its convention, so I'm here for the rest of the week before heading back to San Francisco. I figured while I'm here I might as well try and shake loose some stories, and Sylvia's is a mandatory stop for that," Barbaralee says, hunching toward him and scanning his handsome face with sharp eyes. "I know you didn't tell Westin anything to take back to his masters at the *National Chronicle*, but you've got something for *Girlfriend!*, haven't you?"

"You've received the press release and daily e-mail updates, haven't you? As I told Jacques, we are still in the process of collecting information and formulating an effective strategy for our assault on immorality." Hearing this, Barbaralee smiles, revealing sharp, pointed incisors.

"Not to offend, Reverend, but cut the crap. It's me, Barbaralee Edison, the same Barbaralee who didn't publish the story a few years ago when you had my cousin the choir girl sucking your Johnson underneath your desk—who, by the way, called me last week and told me your check is late. Just a reminder. You owe me, so give up the goods." Anger, embarrassment, and defiance pass over T. Terry's face, and he sighs.

"Truly there are no goods to give up. The campaign is foundering. Apparently no one cares about immorality, however egregious, blatant, and thriving, with the exception of a few old codgers who are broke, couldn't attend a protest rally to save their lives, and probably only care what other people are doing because they can no longer get it up."

"You're kidding."

"I wish I was, Barbaralee. We've been holding focus groups for a month and nothing. Talk to black folks about Bill Clinton's philandering in the White House and they damn near break into applause and proudly claim him as America's first black president. Jesse Jackson's love child? No one gave a damn about that either except a few of those black feminists, who don't count, and even they put the blame on that woman who had his baby, not him. We've tried 'em all. Apparently when it comes to the black man, morality is passé."

"What about the black woman?' Barbaralee asks softly.

"She's the victim in the story, so ain't nothing there, either. Shit, don't tell Jeanette I said this, her head'd swell up bigger than it already is, but if it weren't for black women, the black man would be lost, quiet as it's kept. Raise our children, work like dogs, fuck us when we ain't got no job and ain't looking for one, defend us even when we're loud and wrong. Black women. Nobody cares about the black man's sins, and black women don't have any. Often misguided, but always willing to sacrifice themselves for the brothers. Saints, that's black women. I don't know where we would be without them," T. Terry finishes, raising his hands in a gesture of both emptiness and supplication.

"So, what are you going to do?"

T. Terry shakes his head.

"Pray for guidance. And if worse comes to worst, sell the air rights above the church to some developers from downtown who've been after it for years. Wanna build luxury lofts or some such, say Harlem is the last frontier. Take that money and go back down home to Itta Bena, start that autobiography I've been promising to write, maybe get a little church there . . ."

"Let's not be hasty," Barbaralee cuts him off. "Or melodramatic. I may have something for you." T. Terry pulls himself back from the rural church he's building in his imagination, looks at her intently. She smiles.

"Maybe we can make a deal. If the crusade takes off, I get exclusive rights to all one-on-one interviews. When it comes to Jacques Westin, Ted Koppel, CNN, BET, the networks, Terry, give them those simple rhymes you're so good at. But if you ain't rhyming, the only one you're talking to is Barbaralee."

T. Terry draws back.

"That's asking a lot. Your information would have to be sweet indeed for me to agree to that."

"Oh, it's sweet all right, and just what you're looking for. Raw, vivid sin about to break out in a big way." T. Terry licks his lips in anticipation as if she's describing a sumptuous meal.

"Deal."

She laughs softly. "Not yet. I also need you to put me on retainer as, say, a public relations consultant at, let me see, five hundred bucks a week."

"That's steep. And what am I paying for?"

"Immediate, exclusive access to *Girlfriend!*'s million black women subscribers. I'll feature the crusade and you in my weekly column, "Believe It!," the second thing our readers look at, after their horoscopes. The good news is you don't have to worry which side I'm on, like you do with some principled Negro like Jacques Westin who actually believes in truth, justice, and trying to be objective, not to mention the white folks who like nothing better than to bring a black preacher down. For $500 a week, I'm yours. That's cheap."

Terry stares at her, mutters to himself, "I suppose some of the contributions to the crusade could be diverted from direct action and used for publicity purposes . . ."

"So, we have a deal?" Barbaralee interrupts, extending her hand across the table.

T. Terry reaches over and shakes. "This better be good."

Barbaralee grins, reaches into her briefcase, and pulls out a wad of wrinkled pages, some the long yellow pages of a legal pad, others neatly typed. Spreading them out on the small table, she pushes the condiments aside. "Okay, check this. A couple of Sunday's ago I was down by the San Francisco waterfront hunting for some scandal for my column and noticed dozens of black men going into the same building. Of course that piqued my interest, so I found a bench, sat down, and watched. Nothing but men going into that building, one after the other after the other, mostly black. So I'm thinking, maybe it's a new hot club or some shit. Just as I start to walk over and check the buzzer, out comes Acey Allen and Lydia Beaucoup, two sisters I know from around. One runs a spa, the other's in advertising, although I'm checking a rumor that she had a niggerbitchfit in a client meeting and got fired. They were followed by a brother and a fat chick I've seen them with at Sapphire's. They're laughing and looking happy and he's got a big-ass garbage bag over his shoulder. Of course I want to know what the hell's going on, but they're not going to tell me, we don't have it like that, so I don't let them see me. After they leave I take my ass into the alley, rescue that trash bag, grab a fisherman's platter to go, drive home, empty that bag on the dining room table, and start going through it.

"Never did eat that fisherman's platter, much as I love shrimp and scallops, too busy piecing together scraps of paper, tedious work, but doable, which is why I invested in a shredder years ago. Check this, Rev," Barbaralee says, sliding a stack of reconstructed pages toward him that have been criss-crossed with scotch tape.

T. Terry reads aloud, "20. If a woman brought handcuffs, vibrators, physical restraints, or other sex toys to bed, I would, a) get up and leave b) ask her what she wants me to do with them c) tell her this ain't *Roots* and I don't play that shit, d . . . Where's d?"

"Who the hell cares where d is? Look at the next page," Barbaralee commands.

"'Packages: The In and Out, The Slow Ja . . .'" T. Terry looks up. "What the hell am I reading?"

"Read on," Barbaralee smirks, passing him another page.

"18. If a woman wants to have anal sex I, a) jump for joy b) am willing and gentle as long as it's safe sex c) repulsed d) other," Terry shakes his head, turns to the next page.

"Please tell us why you want to work at A Sis—" he reads. "They're all torn. What's this about?"

"Doesn't matter. Look at the next one."

The legal sheet in his hand is covered with elaborate geometric doodles and scribbled notes in purple ink. He squints to read the writing.

"Nice buns!"

"Great smile, bod, but too laid back."

"Definite hire."

"NO! NO! NO!"

"Love the dreads."

"Very sexy white boy."

He leafs through the rest of the papers, lips moving as he reads softly to himself, finally looks up. "Barbaralee, what's this all about?" Barbaralee laughs triumphantly.

"Wait. Read this." She slides a printout of an e-mail toward him. "An acquaintance who works as the vice president of an insurance company forwarded this to me."

T. Terry looks down and reads.

Dear Sister:

You have been carefully selected and are cordially invited to join an exclusive group of like-minded black women and spend a complimentary day and night at the Grand Opening of A Sister's Spa.

A Sister's Spa represents a new concept in luxury especially designed to respond to the unique personal needs of the black woman. The spa, nestled on 20 acres of land in beautiful Storey County, Nevada, just minutes from the Reno Airport, offers luxurious suites with the finest of accommodations, healthy gourmet meals, and numerous spa services in an atmosphere in which the pleasure and relaxation of our guests is our highest priority.

A Sister's Spa offers all of the traditional spa services, including massage, meditation, sauna, facials, seaweed wraps, manicures, pedicures, and foot reflexology. But what makes A Sister's Spa truly unique is that we also offer a special set of services designed to meet the most intimate needs of black women. For those who are interested, we offer a series of packages carefully designed to gently and lovingly work out the tension and stress that comes from our often high-powered and always demanding lives. We have structured these packages at varying price ranges to make them accessible to sisters of most tastes and income brackets. We are so confident of our offerings that we feel we can say with certainty that your first visit to A Sister's Spa will not be your last.

Please join us on Friday, July 4, for the opening of A Sister's Spa, the first facility of its kind exclusively designed for and dedicated to the pleasure of black women. We guarantee that a good time will be had by all and look forward to seeing you. Please RSVP to this e-mail address, and please do not forward this invitation as accommodations are limited and it is your unique company that we desire.

Acey Allen and Lydia Beaucoup
A Sister's Spa

"What the hell," T. Terry sputters, looking up. "What is the meaning of this?"

"I don't know, but here's what I think: I think they're opening a sex club with male ho's. A brothel. Why else go to Nevada? The exploitation of the black man once again, this time by those long suffering paragons of virtue, black women. Perfect for your crusade," Barbaralee smiles. "And my career."

A smile creeps into T. Terry's eyes, spreads slowly until it covers his whole face.

"If you're right, this is gold, absolute gold," he whispers, leaning toward her and catching another glance of her cleavage. "Help me, Jesus."

"He already has," Barbaralee smirks. "Your prayers are answered."

Across the street, Jacques Westin is still trying to hail a cab, not easy in the morning rush hour. Waiting for the light, he glances across the street at Sylvia's, and through the glass front sees T. Terry and Barbaralee still at the table, heads close together, two pairs of lips moving rapidly, looking conspiratorial. As the light changes and cars speed toward him, he raises his arm for a taxi to take him downtown to his paper's New York office, at the same time pulling a reporter's notebook from his pocket. He flips it open and makes a note to read Barbaralee's recent columns and try to figure out her connection to T. Terry, and to call some ministers and activists and suss out what they know about the reverend's crusade. As a cab screeches to a stop in front of him, he scribbles a final note to himself regarding another story he's been working on: he needs to check in with Dick Dixmoor's office to see if an interview has been set up yet for a follow-up story on the Dairy Queen shooting months earlier.

23

JULY 4 BREAKS HOT AND DRY UNDER A CLOUDLESS AZURE SKY. UN-
able to sleep between worry, anticipation, and excitement, I get up before
dawn, make coffee, and sit by the pool to watch the sun rise. I have that
weird fluttering and tightening feeling in my stomach that comes when
you're simultaneously excited about something and dreading it at the
same time. I envy Lydia, Wanda, Odell, our sex workers, and the twenty
other people—masseurs, reflexologists, manicure-pedicure specialists,
chambermaids, et cetera—who make up the support staff their ability to
sleep soundly even on this most important of days, although the truth is
we're ready, and the hard work won't start until the guests begin arriving
this afternoon. As the sun rises I sit on the still-cool tiles around the pool
in the lotus position, meditating, and say a little prayer asking that all go
well. I also throw in a request for a visit from Earl, but when I go inside
and check the pantry, there is nothing there but flour, canned food, and
several cases of condoms and ViriMax.

Even though it seemed that I was rattling around by myself forever,
by eight o'clock A Sister's Spa has come alive with last-minute prepara-
tions, and the air crackles with excited energy. Me and Lydia make sure
that the orange fanny packs the sex workers are required to wear are properly stocked with an assortment of condoms, massage oil, and lubricating
gel, while LaShaWanda walks through each bedroom, checking that the
candles are fresh, towels soft, beds smooth, and that each has an assortment of CDs from Monk to Miles, Al Green to Luther, Usher to Eve, as
well as a list of the thousands of CDs in the library that can be delivered
with the touch of a button.

Odell takes the men into the lounge for a last run through and pep
talk. They line up before him at attention. Fiddling nervously with an already beautifully arranged bouquet in the entrance hall, I can hear his
deep voice through the thick oak double doors.

"Brothers, today is the day we have all been preparing for, the day the mandate of A Sister's Spa is put to the test. At noon the first of forty women will begin arriving from cities all over this nation. Hard-working, tired, stressed-out women we have lured here with the promise of relaxation and pleasure. If they receive it, they will not only return themselves but, and this is key, tell their friends what a wonderful place A Sister's Spa is. And that is crucial, since we are a business that relies on word of mouth.

"Myself, Lydia, Acey, LaShaWanda and the rest of the staff have done all that we can to make their experience a pleasurable one. The accommodations are top notch, the setting is beautiful, the food is sumptuous. But the most important element in making each and every woman's stay fabulous is each and every one of you. You who have been carefully chosen because we know you have it in you to give pleasure that takes women beyond the ordinary to extraordinary." I swear, he sounds like a general preaching to his troops before battle. I'm so inspired I'd enlist myself if I could.

"On the outside each of you in different ways represents an exemplary specimen of manhood. Yet you are here at A Sister's Spa not simply because of what is on the outside, but for what you are capable of, what is inside, too. Every one of you was hired not only because you have the necessary physical attributes and external equipment, but because you like and love women as well. Because you are committed first to her pleasure, not your own.

"We ask that you focus all of your prodigious skills on being thoughtful, tender, and intuitive. To giving pleasure to the women you will soon meet. That you dedicate yourselves to helping our guests reach heights they have seldom visited or only imagined. That you subvert your own needs and ego to those of the sisters who will soon arrive at our doors tired, stressed, and horny.

"We've all worked for weeks toward this moment. I know you can do it. Now, go relax for a few minutes. Check that your skin is oiled, teeth sparkling, stomach full. Most of all, that your attitude is focused on giving women pleasure however, whatever, wherever, and whenever the women want it. The moment is almost upon us. I know you will acquit yourselves like the superior men you are!" Odell finishes, and damned if those forty fine sex machines don't spontaneously start shouting, "Beep-beep, ahh, beep-beep!" Go figure. I guess they're as delirious with anticipation as we are.

By noon Lydia and I are behind the deep orange granite reception desk in the foyer, fiddling with the list of confirmed guests, most of whom we know, and speculating about their sexual proclivities while we wait for the first of the fleet of limousines Wanda insisted we hire to deliver our first clients from the airport. Wanda herself, our official greeter, is outside on the air-conditioned front porch, watching the driveway and tugging nervously at her hair. Most of the sex workers are lolling around in the lounge, shooting pool, or huddled around the PlayStations. Ahmad, the young blood with the dreads, sits cross-legged in the middle of the room, eyes closed, chanting as if preparing himself for a transcendent experience, and maybe he is.

The only one who isn't chilling or trying to is Odell. He hurries from room to room, a headset in one ear, barking orders to the kitchen and maintenance staff and anyone else he can get a hold of. We'd decided that he should always wear tailored slacks and a muted orange polo shirt so as not to be mistaken by a client for an employee, who always wear shorts and are encouraged, weather permitting, to go topless.

"Here comes a limo!" Wanda shouts. "No, two limos, three, hell, the party's started!" she hollers. I can see the cars kicking up dust as they cruise up the driveway.

"I guess we're really doing this, huh Lyds?" I say tentatively. Lydia laughs, reaches over, and gives me a quick hug.

"Hell, yeah. It's too late to change our minds now," she says, just as a car door slams and LaShaWanda's voice says, "Hello, ladies, and welcome to A Sister's Spa. Where your pleasure is our only concern."

Even though either me, Lydia, or both of us know just about every sister who'd been invited, once they start rolling in they don't stop, and it's hard to get out more than a quick, "How are you?" or "So glad you could come," check them into a room, and summon the man we've assigned them to take their bags before the next batch of sisters arrive. And come they do. Watching them arrive reminds me of standing with my mother, brothers, and father at the door to Daddy's church every Sunday morning when I was growing up, "welcoming the faithful," as Daddy called it. Tired, overworked, dressed in their finest, and full of expectation, the sisters flood into A Sister's Spa as they did for Sunday sermon. Underneath their laughter, chattering, and lovely clothes the effects of hard work, accomplishment, and still unachieved expectations are clearly visible in the frown lines between their foreheads, the tension visible in their backs, even beneath the surface of the perfectly applied make-up that creates their faces to meet the world. Yet unlike church, these women are coming to A Sister's Spa not as supplicants to a shrine, but as pilgrims in search of one. The weight of their expectations and need can be heard in the tenor of their voices and their laughter as they enter, wondering if this was a place where they can finally, in the words of the old Negro spiritual, lay their burdens down.

We'd tried to assign each woman an escort based on what we knew about her and the type of men we'd either seen her with or thought she'd like. Lizzie Stone, a labor organizer from Chicago, who'd been married and divorced three times and tended to both scare men and take them too seriously, got Ahmad because he was young, fun, and impossible to take seriously. We assigned Trevor to Marsha Adams, a plump, brown-skinned sister from South Carolina who was a VP for the Girl Scouts and as far as I know hadn't had sex since her heart was broken in college twenty years earlier. We figured even if Trevor couldn't cajole her out of her drawers, they'd have a good time talking about down home.

We gave David, the slightly dreamy painter, to DeeDee Bolly, a thirty-year-old actuary who works for Equitable Life Insurance, because she throws pottery on the side and loves museums and salt and pepper hair. We sent our Eminem wannabee off with Elise Houghton, a mother of four who's been married for twenty-five years, and who scouts new artists for Arista Records. To Amore Holder, an entertainment lawyer with a successful doctor husband recovering from prostate cancer and two gorgeous sons, we gave Jackson, who's triple-jointed and indefatigable, according to Lydia, and who'd told us he wanted to work a few years at the spa to earn enough money to finish med school.

Betty, the hottest woman singer in hip-hop, arrives dripping with too much Versace and diamonds, two members of her female posse in tow. Lydia vaguely knows her because she was the star of an advertising campaign for a brand of forty-ounce beers represented by BTH. She has a great set of pipes and her music is always funky, though the lyrics of her last CD had gone from celebrating life to bemoaning the superficiality of superstardom, not to mention the difficulty of getting laid without being pimped when you are rich and famous. We sent her off with Tom L. Livingswell. He was smooth, confident, fine and we'd prepped him on the importance of making sure Betty has a fabulous time. If she does, we're sure she'll spread the word to the women in the music industry who, like her, are looking for some great, discreet sex that doesn't come attached to a man with his hand out, or with a demo tape in his pocket.

Nervous as I am, it's great watching those sisters walk through the door, full of tension, and seeing them immediately begin to relax as they are first warmly greeted and offered a cold drink, and then get an eyeful of all those gorgeous, barely clad men at their beck and call. Even I can't help thinking that Lydia is right: this is a sure thing. Then the door opens and in sweeps a tall, thin, elegant woman with short, silver hair brushed straight back, a long, patrician nose, enormous sparkling brown eyes, and skin the color of cappuccino, and I know we have arrived.

At eighty-two, Evangeline Worthington is a legend, and deservedly so, a sister who's been the first at damn near everything for sixty years and still is. First woman to interview Martin Luther King, Jr. after racists bombed his house in Birmingham back when she worked for the influential but now defunct newspaper, *The Negro Day*. First black woman hired as a reporter at the *National Chronicle* in the early 1960s. First to work for the mayor and then governor of New York, then the president of the United States, for all of whom she became an indispensable confidant. First to join the modern-day Republican Party, first woman elected to Congress from Harlem, first to wear white after Labor Day and make it chic, first to make baseball caps acceptable at formal events. Most recently she'd opened a chain of cyber cafés in urban communities across the country, a venture that many had viewed skeptically, arguing that black people were so far from the information superhighway there was no way for them to get on. Of course they were immediately successful, making her what Mrs. Beaucoup would call money's mammy, most of which she pumped back into the project.

Evangeline is on the boards of a half-dozen Fortune 500 companies, lives in a fabulous brownstone in Harlem, and is known for giving parties to which people struggle frantically to be invited. No one is more charming, smart, or superbly connected. She can make or break everyone from community activists to political candidates without losing her ever-present smile, breaking a sweat, or putting a wrinkle in the impeccably tailored black Armani pants suits she always wears. Rumor is she has dozens of them in her closet, all gifts from her personal pal Giorgio.

Even though she insists it's not that she thinks much of holy matrimony but simply doesn't know how to say no to a proposal, Evangeline has been married four times. Among her husbands have been a pro basketball player, a banker, a civil servant, and her current spouse, a concert pianist who earns his living as a watchmaker. Men are among the many subjects Evangeline Worthington knows a great deal about.

As if it would be impossible not to notice Evangeline in Grand

Central Station at rush hour, Lydia elbows me in the ribs, whispers, "Evangeline Worthington! We're over like fat rats. What'd I tell you?"

"Who's her escort?" I'm so nervous watching her walk toward the counter my mind's gone blank.

"King, the one who doesn't like blow jobs, and Frank, the political science professor on sabbatical trying to finish his book, remember?"

Right. We weren't sure what Evangeline's tastes were, so we've assigned her both a burning young stud and an intellectual, smoldering older lover, trying to cover all bases. We know that if she enjoys herself, we'll be plugged into a national network of discreet sisters of all ages and classes, who'll come because Evangeline had. Once they check out the spa, we're confident we can keep them coming back. Anyway, we've planned a cocktail sip later that evening, so the guests can mix and mingle and we can get a bead on any problems and make the necessary adjustments.

"It's raining men, hallelujah!" one woman sings as she stands in the lobby waiting for me to check her in, and three well-oiled men in the hottest of shorts descend upon her, murmuring words of welcome. One whisks her suitcase from her hands, another hands her a frosty pina colada, while the third, after asking permission, of course, guides her to a chair and massages her shoulders with firm hands. "I must have died and gone to heaven," she sighes when we've checked her in and assigned her an escort. "And if I'm asleep, please don't wake me!"

"Welcome. And enjoy," I call to her retreating back. "Hope to see you at the cocktail reception at five!"

"Acey, thank you, thank you, thank you! This place is gorgeous. And now I know where all the fine black men are, besides prison," a voice laughs.

"Amen," several voices chime in.

"Yep. And here you can look *and* touch," someone adds.

"It'd be impossible not to."

"Lord, take a look at that one in the corner," a voice whispers.

"Shit. Kunta Kinte, here I come," someone giggles.

"He can massage me any day."

"And anywhere," someone else adds, to raucous laughter.

"Have you checked out the list of services? This place has everything."

"I'm going to have it all, too. Massage, foot reflexology, seaweed wrap, facial, even if I have to stay up all night," a voice chuckles.

"Not me. I've been pulling all-nighters for the last month trying to close a big deal. All I want to do is sleep, eat, and not have to lift a finger for twenty-four hours. That'd be heaven," a weary voice sighs.

"I'm going to go lie by that pretty pool and get some of those fine-looking motherfuckers over there to massage my ass for hours. Did you see how on the brochure it says, 'All the employees of A Sister's Spa are trained in the fine art of deep tissue massage, and it is their pleasure to relax you.' Come on with it, brothers!" another laughs.

We're checking in the last of the guests when the door opens and a woman I've never seen before strides in. She looks almost a foot taller than I am, which would make her at least six-two or so, definitely WNBA material. Her hair's reddish-brown and beautifully cut tight to her scalp, framing a large, impeccably made-up face and eyes covered by gigantic sunglasses. She wears a beige linen sheath that falls from her broad shoulders to subtly outline her small waist and slim hips, and has a matching sweater tied casually around her shoulders. Her clunky necklace of gold nuggets and matching earrings are definitely the real thing, and on her feet are the fabulous pair of Manolo Blahnik sling-backs I'd denied myself a few weeks earlier because they were so outrageously expensive when I saw them at Neiman Marcus.

"Welcome to A Sister's Spa," I say, picking up the guest list. "May I have your name?" I ask, even though I know every name's checked off and accounted for.

The woman smiles. "Lorene Cunningham, but I'm not on the guest list," she says, in a voice like the throaty purr of a snoring cat. "I heard about this place and it just sounded so fabulous, I had to come! I'm here to beg you to take me in, to make room for one more."

"Heard about it how?" Lydia, standing next to me, asks suspiciously.

She waves a hand dismissively. "On the Internet, where else? Someone forwarded me the invitation and I said, how wonderful, how fabulous, how brilliant, I have to be there. So here I am."

"Acey, didn't you block forwarding when you sent out those e-mails?" Lydia hisses. Oops, I may have forgotten to on that last batch, what with Earl popping up in the pantry.

"Ms. Cunningham, I'm sorry, but we're just about full to capacity—" Lydia begins to say, but Cunningham cuts her off.

"Just about full means there's probably room for one more. It's just little old me. I hardly have any luggage, and believe me, I have come a long, long way to get here. Won't you sisters welcome a weary traveler?"

I turn to Lydia, a question in my eyes, and she whispers, "Hey, you know you've got the slammin' party when the high-class crashers arrive," gives me an it's-up-to-you shrug, and resumes putting the finishing touches on the arrangements for the cocktail sip. I turn to Cunningham and smile.

"Sure, I guess we could fit you in. But please understand that after today we require advance reservations and won't be able to accommodate you otherwise," I say, sliding our brief check-in form and a pen across the counter. As she begins writing I notice several sizable and nicely cut stones on her large fingers, one of them apparently a wedding ring. I have a flash of yearning for the dead Earl, or at least a healed Matthew and something like a happily ever after, but I squash it. Lorene Cunningham's just one of the many married women currently under our roof, so obviously matrimony sometimes leaves something—although it's not clear exactly what yet, in her case—to be desired.

I ring a silent buzzer and in moments the last two available employees of A Sister's Spa appear; I send a telepathic thank you to Odell for anticipating the need for a few extras. I give them a quick once-over, but it's a no-brainer to select a brother we call Sequoia, because he's six-eight and built as solidly as one of those huge ancient redwoods. "Sequoia, would you escort Ms. Cunningham to Room 18, please? And see that she has whatever she needs and desires to make her stay at A Sister's Spa the ultimate experience in pleasure."

"Oh, I am so glad I came. And thank you for accommodating me. I can see I'm going to have a glorious time," Lorene Cunningham calls over her shoulder as she follows Sequoia down the hall, tottering gently on her four-inch heels.

"Who's the giant bitch with all the gold?" LaShaWanda asks as she walks into the foyer. Lydia and I shrug.

"Said she got a forwarded invitation on the Internet, but she's not on the list," Lydia says.

"Heifer told me she knew both of y'all, that's the only reason I let her in," Wanda explains, balancing on one foot and rubbing the toes of the other with her hand.

"Yeah, just like I told the goons at the stage door I was Prince's long-lost cousin last time he played San Francisco," Lydia says, laughing. "Hey, my hat's off to the sister, at least it worked for her."

"You know, she did look kind of familiar," I say. "But I can't place her."

Wanda laughs. "Then you probably don't know her. Big woman like that'd be hard to forget. But whatever," Wanda says, shaking her braids dismissively. "We've got more important shit to think about. The cocktail party's in two hours and the caterer and DJ haven't shown up yet."

The caterer soon appears with a sumptuous assortment of finger foods, something for carnivores, herbivores, and dieters, too. The bar is well stocked with champagne, freshly squeezed juices, and San Pellegrino water. The DJ rolls in and starts spinning mellow music that runs the gamut from Ella Fitzgerald, Red Garland, and Dinah Washington to Mary J. Blige, Norah Jones, and Aaliyah. I decide to call Matthew, still busy working on his speech to the National Bar Association. I haven't yet told him about the more specialized nature of the services the spa is providing; as far as he knows we're simply opening a second spa somewhere outside Reno.

"So, how did it go today, honey?"

"Really great. Everyone we invited came, and then some. Even Evangeline Worthington's here," I say excitedly.

"Evangeline Worthington? She came all the way from New York for a massage?" Matthew asks incredulously. "Women."

I can feel myself begin to get defensive, but before I can go there, Matthew says, "What else is happening? Any problems?"

"Can you believe it, none. Oh, the caterer was a few minutes late and the DJ thought we were having an oldies but goodies party, but that was easy to straighten out. I'm about to take a nap before the reception and was thinking about our—"

Matthew interrupts.

"Great, great. Acey, how does this sound? 'In this rapidly changing judicial landscape, the role of the African American attorney is more important than ever. A decade of right-of-center Supreme Court rulings have served to at best undermine and at worst decimate the hard-won civil rights legislation that has characterized the mandate of black attorneys since the 1920s.' What do you think?"

"Sounds wonderful, baby. Listen, I'm about to take a nap and was just wishing you were lying here beside me so I could—"

"Do you think 'right of center' is too forceful?"

"No. If anything, it's too mild a description of Thomas and Scalia. So, I'm lying here in my lacy bra and panties, all alone. Now, if you were here we could—"

"Are you suggesting my wording is too mild?"

"No, it's fine, Matthew, just fine. But what isn't fine is that I'm missing you, thinking about feeling you kissing me, inside me—"

"Maybe 'the Court's new conservatism' is a better way to put it, not 'right-of-center.' More diplomatic. What do you think?"

"I think either one is fine, sweetie. Mostly, I think about you easing slowly inside me as I lick your—"

"Acey, stop!"

"Why? If we can't be together, we can at least talk about sex."

"No, we can't. I've got to finish this speech."

"It's not even three o'clock, and the NBA meeting isn't for almost a month, correct?"

"Be that as it may, I do not care to have phone sex."

"Hey, it's better than no sex."

"Acey, we are both too old for that sort of mess."

"Speak for yourself," I say, irritably snapping the waist of my panties against my stomach. "I thought it might be fun, especially since we haven't had real sex for months."

"Acey, I am recovering from triple-bypass surgery, on multiple medications, and under a doctor's care."

"Matthew, your doctor said he didn't care if we fucked," I say sharply but under my breath. "In fact, he said he thought fucking was actually a good idea."

"I am sure that he did not say anything about 'fucking.' You may not agree, but as an attorney I understand the need for precision in language," Matthew says pompously.

"Okay! Enough! I don't care if he said having intercourse, making love, or doing the nasty. He meant fucking, something we no longer do."

"Another exaggeration, Acey. As I recall we made love several weeks ago."

"Not unless several now means fourteen. It's been over three months, Matthew. And as I remember you barely got hard, rushed through it, and then went to sleep."

"I work long hours and at the end of the day I am exhausted. Surely you can understand that," Matthew says defensively.

"I work hard and I'm beat at the end of the day, too, but I'd still like to make love to and with my man, even if it is over the telephone. Is that asking too much? Is it?" I don't realize I'm screaming until the intercom beside the bed pings softly and a man's voice purrs, "I thought I heard you calling. Is there anything you need, Ms. Allen?" I want to howl, "SEX!"

but instead simply mutter "No, thanks," and ram my finger on the off button.

"You are too excitable," Matthew says, his voice growing even more pedantic, a sure sign he's upset with me. "Could we please talk about this at a later date? I am committed to completing a first draft of this speech by next week, and time is passing. In addition to which, after this contre-temps I think I should go and check my heart rate and blood pressure."

I ignore his bid for sympathy and his effort to put me on a guilt trip. "Okay, I'll call you in a few days," I say tersely. "Bye." I hang up and stare at the ceiling, fuming and resisting the urge to call Matthew back and curse him out, and wishing Earl would appear so I could feel his loving warmth, be in the presence of a man who, even though he couldn't have me, at least still wanted me. I'm simultaneously angry, lonely, and sexually frus-trated on what should be one of the happiest days of my life.

Even though we have wisely sound-proofed each room, lying here I swear I can hear the sound of hot, sweaty skin colliding, smell the musky, salty odor of orgasms in the air, feel the electricity of passion crackling along my skin, as all around me our guests have exuberant, ecstatic sex. It crosses my mind to buzz Odell and ask him to send in that last brother to relieve my tension, but I don't. I'm lonely, but I'm not ready for casual sex. Besides, I remind myself, between Lydia and me one of us has to ab-stain and stay focused this weekend, and, maybe unfortunately, I'm the most likely candidate. As I did when I was a child and needed to comfort myself, I put one hand underneath my cheek on the pillow, the other be-tween my thighs. My fingers caress the outer skin of my hot spot sooth-ingly as I drift off to sleep, angry and confused.

24

"I GOT ONE. WHAT'S BLACK, WET, AND DOESN'T NEED FOOD, DRINK, or sleep?" LaShaWanda drawls, letting the issue of *Girlfriend!* she's been idly flipping through fall into her lap. The four of us are sprawled on chaises around the pool. Stacks of completed exit questionnaires litter the tiles around us. "A woman at A Sister's Spa!" she crows, breaking into laughter at her own joke. It's Sunday in the late afternoon, and the last guest at our opening weekend has just stumbled into her limousine to the airport.

I'd laugh along with her, but who's got the energy? It's enough for me to lift my champagne glass and take a sip, and I've yet to muster the strength it'll take to reach the plate of fresh mango, papaya, and watermelon on the table in front of me. Leave it to Odell to summon the requisite vigor.

"Ladies, a toast," he says, sitting up and lifting his glass. "To a wonderful beginning. And to our continued success." The three of us listlessly raise our glasses, too tired to make the stretch needed to actually touch them. Acey tries, falls back laughing, and says, "The clink is implied." We all nod in lazy agreement, thinking about the past twenty-four hours.

"I was really worried for a long moment when only ten sisters showed up at the welcoming cocktail sip," Acey finally says.

"Yeah, and all they did was gulp some bubbly, load up their plates, and go back to their rooms," Wanda says.

"I know, you kept telling the DJ to play something different, like the music was the problem," I giggle, teasing Acey.

"As I recall, you were the one compulsively rearranging the hors d'oeuvres," Acey retorts. "When I saw you building a pyramid of grilled shrimp and a geometrical arrangement of the caviar blinis, I was sure you had finally lost your mind."

"I almost did. I was trying to distract myself from thinking the worst. Had the sisters passed out from exhaustion and not even sampled the pleasures of A Sister's Spa? Had we managed to hire four dozen psycho women haters who were torturing our guests while I obsessed about the miniature seafood quiches? Or, worst of all, were our sex workers futilely trying to bring sisters to orgasm? Yeah, I was worried."

"Weren't we all," Wanda laughs. "I don't know if my pressure can take this shit full time."

"I wasn't concerned," Odell says coolly.

"Oh, no? And why was that?" I ask.

"Hey, I've been working with these men for weeks and I knew their shit was tight. I also know women. Wanda was joking, but it's true: When you don't get out of bed to eat, drink, or network, you're either sick, dead, or there's something going on in the boudoir you don't want to miss."

"Yeah, hindsight's always twenty-twenty. But I recall more than a few drops of sweat on your brow, Mr. Cool," I tease.

"That was because of logistical issues, trying to meet the needs of my staff so they could fulfill the desires of our guests. We thought we'd anticipated everything, but who really knows what a woman wants until she tells you? More condoms, fresh batteries, chocolate whipped cream, crushed ice, a James Brown CD with both 'Lickin' Stick' and 'Sex Machine' on it, more massage oil, red grapes, a banana, jasmine rose incense. Shit, I knew from the requests rolling in that a good time was being had by most." Odell grabs a pad from beside him. "That reminds me, I need to order more whipping cream and an assortment of incense," he murmurs, scribbling.

Acey laughs. "I know it sounds silly, but I was worried about all that food going to waste."

"Shit, I was worried about all our hard work and money going down the drain."

"We're cool on both counts. Once it became clear the sister's were getting their cocktails in bed, I had most of the food moved to the workers' dining room. They devoured it whenever they could slip out for a few minutes. I think it's safe to say A Sister's Spa is a success," Odell grins. "Listen to this," he says, picking up a stack of papers and flipping through them. "For the most part, we're rated 'excellent' in every category: ambiance, décor, and, most important and thanks to me and my guys, 'staff services.' 'Would you return to A Sister's Spa?'" he reads from a questionnaire. "'Would I? Hell, yes. In fact, here's my American Express number. Book me for the weekend of August 14.'" Odell grabs another paper. "Now dig this: 'Do you have any complaints about your stay?' 'TOO SHORT!!!!!,' and that's in capital letters, followed by many exclamation points." Listen to this, 'Do you book private parties? If so, can I specify which men I'd like to party with my group? Let me know, my twenty-fifth birthday is in two months. P.S.: Thanks for a marvelous time!'" Odell grins. "It just doesn't get better than that."

"You said 'for the most part,' Odell. What were the complaints?" Leave it to Acey to zoom in on what's wrong. Odell looks down, shuffling pages.

"Nothing major, Acey, all things we can fix. Someone complains that they're weren't enough condoms in her bedside table, but I personally made sure there were six in each room for overnight guests, so whoever she was with, he's a candidate for the employee of the month award. I've instructed the staff to put ten rubbers in each room from now on," Odell says, taking a sip of champagne.

"That was probably the gate-crashing Amazon. When she stumbled out of here her eyes were rolled up in the back of her head and her legs were so bowed you coulda driven a Hummer through them, and she's already booked for next week," Wanda cracks.

"What else?" Acey asks, alert and taking notes.

"'Oral sex was good, but could have been better,'" Odell reads.

"Does she say who she was with?"

"Will. I'll talk to him."

"A cutie," Wanda nods. "Isn't he the one who described himself as the Mack Daddy of head at the interview? I guess that was all in *his* head."

"It'll be a sacrifice, but let me know if you need me to give him a refresher course," I volunteer.

"Okay, and?" Acey asks. The four of us begin skimming through questionnaires.

"Someone wants a larger selection of CDs in the room."

"'More candles.'"

"Here's a good suggestion, 'A small refrigerator beside the bed would preclude having to leave the room for food or drink.' Damn. These chicks are serious."

"'My escort talked too much intellectual shit. He shoulda talked dirty or not at all.'"

"A-fucking-Men."

"'Soft leather straps.' How about that? Tie me up, tie me down, huh? Whatever gets you off, my sistah."

" 'More mirrors!' "

"Dig this one: 'My escort seemed highly reticent about allowing me to suck his cock.' Now, ain't that a blip?" Wanda asks. "A Sister's Spa is all about women being pleasured, and here's some chick begging to lick the lollipop."

"Some women actually enjoy that particular activity, Wanda," I say.

"Hey, it takes all kinds," she shrugs. "And she's paying for it. Like they say, have him your way."

"If that's what turns her on," I say. Odell nods.

"I told the men never to ask for head, and to accept it only if the client insists. Maybe I wasn't clear what 'insists' means. I'll go over that with them. No problem."

"Now this could be a problem," Wanda says, sitting up, a sheet of paper in her hand. " 'Fabulous sex, but too much time between erections.' Odell, aren't all the workers aware that we've got a few cases of ViriMax available and they should take it if they feel the need?"

Odell nods. "Supposed to be, but I'll go over it with them again. A few insisted they didn't need it, that it messed with their chi or something."

"What's their chi? New Age-speak for male ego?" Wanda asks.

"Whatever it is, it isn't doing the job. If it's all right with you three, I'm going to start dispensing a ViriMax along with vitamins twice a day." The three of us nod agreeably.

"Anything else? Because so far we're doing great, a few wrinkles but overall a great success," I say. "And if there's nothing more, perhaps I'll go and retrain that inept Will in the fine art of, as my mother would put it, gobbling the goop."

"Wait, listen to this," Acey says. " 'My escort got carried away when I was sucking him off, pushed my head down, and wouldn't let go until he'd shoved his thing against the back of my throat and come in my mouth.' "

"Yuck. No sister is gonna' pay for that type of sex when she can get it at home for free. That is a problem," I say.

"True that," Wanda agrees. "Does she say who she was with?"

"Yeah, Mbenge, whose slave name is probably Jerome, LaMar, or some silliness. Remember him, the kinda cultural nationalist brother with the slight attitude, but fine and with a real big penis?" Acey says.

"Oh, yeah, him. I was not impressed. Something about him rubbed me the wrong way," Wanda chips in.

"Yeah, until he gave you a lap dance," I retort. Wanda giggles.

"Hey, we all make mistakes."

"He's got to go. Today," Acey says.

"Fire him? After the brother's moved out here and gone through training? We've invested more than a little time and money. Maybe I can talk to him," Odell suggests.

"The only thing you need to say to him, Odell, is adios."

"I'm with Acey," I chime in. Odell looks hopefully at Wanda.

"Sorry, O, but I gotta vote with the sisters. Last thing we need is for word to get out that a man at A Sister's Spa does that goddamned let-me-palm-your-head-like-a-basketball-and-come-in-your-mouth-while-simultaneously-choking-you-with-my-dick move. Sorry, we can't take the risk. He's bad for business. He's out," Wanda says, case closed.

"Damn, y'all are cold," Odell says, shaking his head.

"This is business, Odell," Acey says. "It's not about being cold. A Sister's Spa exists to provide women pleasure as defined by women, plain and simple. If an employee demonstrates he's not with the program, and on opening weekend I might add, he's gone. Nothing personal."

"Right on!" Wanda laughs.

"Preach, teach, and amen, too, Sister Acey," I add.

Odell throws his hands up in a gesture of supplication.

"Okay, okay, but that leaves us a man short. And judging from the overwhelmingly positive responses, I'd say we need to hire three or four new workers immediately."

"Already?" Acey asks. "Where are we going to find four workers by tomorrow when the first paying customers arrive? We don't know any men in Nevada." The four of us sit there staring out into the desert as if we could conjure up a few men if we try hard enough.

"I know where we can find three," Odell finally says, hesitantly. "My brothers, DeJuan, DeQuan, and DeMon."

"The basketball hunks? I thought they were in school."

"They were, but as of Friday they're on three weeks' athletic and academic suspension, and the last thing they need is to spend that time loose in Las Vegas with nothing to do."

"Suspended for what?" Odell closes his eyes and shakes his head in embarrassment. "For what, Odell?" Wanda demands. Odell exhales mightily.

"According to the officials at UNLV, they stole the keys to the gym in order to give some ladies a tour and were found in there at three A.M. in, well, let's say, compromising positions."

"What the hell kind of 'compromising positions'?"

"Having sex three-wide doggy-style on the foul line," Odell murmurs.

"Say what?" Wanda shrieks, laughing so hard the beads on her braids clank together, tinkling musically. "That sure must have been a sight to see. Didn't you say your brothers are six-six or some shit?"

"Six-nine."

"How'd they get busted?" I ask, giggling.

"Fools turned on the overhead lights, damn near lit up the whole campus, and security came running. Apparently the campus cops rushed in, guns drawn, and were greeted by the sight of DeJuan, DeQuan, and DeMon's big asses pumping into three coeds on all fours. They're lucky they didn't get shot."

"Damn. Can we go to the videotape?" I say.

"Fortunately, there isn't one," Odell says. "They're lucky they weren't kicked out for good, but this is their last chance. I was going to drive to Vegas later this afternoon, try and talk some sense into those knuckleheads and figure out what to do with them for three weeks. I don't want my parents to know about their latest fiasco, so they sure can't go back to Oakland. Given that we need some temporary workers until we can move a few of the brothers we interviewed up from San Francisco, I was thinking . . ."

"That your loser brothers would be suitable employees for A Sister's Spa? Sounds like they'd be nothing but triple trouble," Wanda snarls.

"They're not losers, they're knuckleheads," Odell says.

"Pray tell what the difference is?" Acey asks.

"A loser is hopeless, a brother who will not or cannot get it together," Odell explains. "Now, a knucklehead is a brother who has some, but not most, of the characteristics of a loser, but underneath is okay and has the capacity to become something better. A knucklehead doesn't have enough sense, but has a chance of getting more, under the right circumstances and tutelage. Like most knuckleheads, DeJuan, DeQuan, and DeMon aren't really thugs, they're wannabes. Young, arrogant, and hard-headed, but not hopeless. Still capable of redemption, if you will," he adds, turning toward Acey and tossing in a little religious terminology in a transparent bid for her support.

"Besides the fact that they're your baby brothers and they need help—and those are serious considerations—what do they have to offer the spa?"

"They're young, good looking, and they don't seem to get any complaints from the ladies," Odell says. "And we need more sex workers, now."

"Yesterday would have been even better," Wanda says, pulling a sheaf of reservation slips from her pocket. "Shit, I don't know when the bitches had time to do it between the sucking, fucking, and coming, but they must have been working those cell phones, because the reservations started rolling in Saturday night and haven't stopped since. Hell, my phone's probably ringing now, we just can't hear it because I turned it off. And did I mention that a third of the sisters who just left have already rebooked? We're full for the next two weeks and I haven't been able to return half the calls yet."

"How'd they find out about A Sister's Spa? We haven't even advertised," Acey asks.

"Word of mouth, Acey. You know black women talk, and when we have some good sex to talk about, especially if we're not married to it, ain't no stopping us. Anyway, we need help, so if it's all right with you folks I'm gonna ask Muffin if she can come up for a few days. She's smart, organized, discreet, and doesn't have any use for a paycheck. Besides, she's curious about what we've done with hubby's investment."

"Cool," I say. Acey and Odell nod their agreement.

"That'd work for me, since I'd like to sneak home for a few days and see Matthew. He's really nervous about his speech to the National Bar Association."

"Isn't that, like, a month away?" I ask sarcastically.

"Yeah, but he's already working on it, and I want to be there to help him."

"To applaud and carry his nitroglycerin, no doubt," I mutter.

Acey turns toward me, eyes narrowed, but before she can respond, Wanda says, "Matthew. How's he doing, anyway?"

"Physically, great, according to his surgeon, but he's still sort of reticent . . ."

"No sex, huh?"

Why is it that Wanda can say whatever she wants and get away with it? Now, if I'd said that shit, my best friend would have killed me with a look.

"Not much, but we're working on it."

"Which translates, the Ace is trying to get some and Matthew's withholding," I interject.

"Whatever works for them. Matthew seems nice enough, he's got a good job, and if the sex once was good, it can be again. Brotherman just needs some TLC," Wanda says diplomatically.

"What about sistergirl's need for some TLC, not to mention a few orgasms?" I ask. Wanda spreads her arms wide to encompass all that surrounds her. "It's here if she wants it, that's what A Sister's Spa's about." I snort.

"Acey's too uptight for that."

"Ladies, about DeJuan, DeQuan, and DeMon?" Odell pulls us back from the brink of an argument toward the business at hand. "We need sex workers, they're available, and I'd feel more comfortable if they were where I could see them."

"You sure they can do the job?"

Odell smiles. "Oh, I'm sure. And I'll run them through the standard training. So, can we try it?"

"Shit, yeah. Six-nine triplets? Yet another unique service we can offer," Wanda says.

"It's fine with me, Odell," Acey agrees. "Just make sure they put their knucklehead impulses on hold while they're working."

"And don't start no shit," Wanda yawns, picking up the copy of *Girlfriend!* from her lap.

"Is that all for now?" I say, standing up and stretching. "Duty calls. I need to give Will that tutorial and, after him, take a long nap."

"And I'd love to take a swim," Acey says, standing up and pulling her beach cover-up over her head to reveal a matching bathing suit.

"That's all I had on my list," Odell says, rising. "If we're done here, I'm going to drive into Vegas and pick up the triplets."

Wanda closes her eyes, lowers her chair back, and falls back onto it as Odell and I lazily gather up our papers and other paraphernalia. We may all be tired, but we're also happy and mellow. And if our grand opening is any indication, we're also on our way to being very successful.

25

"SO WHAT DO YOU THINK?" BARBARALEE EDISON ASKS. T. TERRY Tiger sits across from her in the deserted and dimly lit offices of the Baptist Brotherhood and Boulé, his eyes scanning a tear sheet from the next issue of *Girlfriend!*.

"Let me finish reading," he growls, waving her back with his free hand and suppressing the smirk that wants to spread over his face with every word he reads of Barbaralee's next column. Finally he looks up, a slight smile on his lips.

"It's good."

"Good? It's brilliant," Barbaralee preens. "And it's exactly what you need to breathe spiritual and financial life into the Crusade to Resurrect Morality."

"When will this issue be on the newsstand?"

"To our million subscribers in four days, on every corner newsstand in seven."

"Now, you're sure this isn't libelous?"

"Shit, yeah. I've been sued for libel more than a few times, but that's just the fate of any serious journalist. This is so hot I had the lawyers go over it twice, just to be certain. Anyway, if that's all, I'd like my check," Barbaralee adds. "Oh, and my niece asked me to thank you, too. She got her money a few days ago."

"All right, all right. Let me read through this one last time," T. Terry says, picking up the sheet of paper.

A HO' BY ANOTHER NAME WILL RUB YOUR FEET

Rumor has it that customers can get more than a facial, a foot massage, and good vibes at a retreat for black women recently opened outside Reno, Nevada. Reliable sources tell Believe It! that the all-male staff of this so-called spa offers sisters personal services with a rock hard P, if you get my drift. Am I the only one who finds it troubling and ironic that just as the foremost Leader of the Negro People begins a Crusade to Resurrect Morality, black women have literally laid down their sword and shield, and embraced the ranks of the hedonistic masses? Am I the only one who awaits the roaring response of the Reverend Tiger?

The grin he's been suppressing spreads over his handsome face. "Brilliant, no?" Barbaralee asks. Terry nods.

"It's good, but its rather vague, don't you think?" Barbaralee rolls her eyes.

"That's the point. Just give them a little taste in each week's column, let the curiosity and outrage build, then spell it all out over the next four or five issues. After that, the ball's in your court."

Before he can respond, the door of his office flies open so hard that it slams against the wall and Jeanette, eyes throwing sparks and hands gesticulating, barges into the room.

"Terry, are you having a meeting or not?" she demands, walking to the middle of the room, hands on her hips. "I've been trying to keep these men entertained, but you're running more than two hours late and I've done all that I can. They've sucked every chicken bone dry, drunk the pot liquor from the collards, and the banana pudding pan's so clean you wouldn't believe a Nilla Wafer had been anywhere near it. On top of that, the scotch is at the halfway mark. You'd better call this meeting to order, because you know as well as I do that when the booze is gone, half the men of the Baptist Brotherhood and Boulé will be gone, too. Those that're left will be too stoned to be of any use."

T. Terry looks startled.

"Ah, Jeanette. The time got away from us. Has everyone arrived?" he asks.

"Everyone but the cat, and I'm waiting for someone to drag him in," she snaps. "You got those tired old fogeys from the central committee of the Baptist Brotherhood and Boulé, scarfing down food as if they're at the goddamn last supper and looking down their noses at the cultural nationalists from the United Federation of Promojites, who are wearing so much fake kente cloth and cheap musk oil my eyes hurt. There're a dozen of those insane Chocolate Canaanites, you know, the ones who stand on 125th Street and verbally abuse every black woman who walks by? Well, they're down there in full drag: badly wrapped turbans, MC Hammer pants, black leather wrist cuffs with silver spikes; don't let me forget their hostile looks. They're on one side of the room glaring at the other, where you've got the suited, booted, and bow-tied representatives from that unrecognized Islamic splinter group, looking stern, righteous, and like they're gonna dart across the room and try to sell me a pamphlet. Add on to that an assortment of men whose affiliation isn't clear but whose vibe is unsavory, and you got the picture. I've been trying to be polite and keep that motley crew from each other's throats. It's your party, Terry, you come deal with it."

"I shall, I shall, momentarily," the Reverend intones. "But first Jeanette, baby, come over here and let Daddy show you what Barbaralee has brought us," T. Terry says in his most soothing voice.

"Don't baby me, Terry," she says, one leg thrust slightly forward and a foot tapping angrily against the parquet floor. "I'm tired and I just want to go home and take a hot bath. We haven't had a day of rest or been near Itta Bena because of this crusade. Instead I'm stuck here taking care of a room full of jackasses, and that is not in my job description. I'm your executive assistant, Terry, not your mammy on call."

"Jeanette, darling, there is no man on earth who could appreciate your work more than I do, your versatility in coping with a plethora of situations, not the least of which is keeping the tribes downstairs from each others' throats," Terry purrs. "You are not simply an executive assistant par excellence and the sunshine of my life, you are, truth be told, my secret weapon, my very own Agent Double-O Soul of the new millennium." Jeanette snorts.

"Cut the crap, Terry. You're using me to baby sit a room full of angry wannabe powerbrokers while you and Barbaralee sit up here in peace and quiet and conspire. Well, I ain't no wet nurse. The bottom line is I'm going home in five minutes."

"Jeanette, Jeanette, hear me. This evening is but a passing moment in the scheme of my plans to resurrect morality and revitalize the coffers of the Baptist Brotherhood and Boulé. Moments before you so abruptly interrupted us, Barbaralee and I were discussing a very delicate mission in service of this crusade that only you can accomplish. Isn't that right, Barbaralee?" Still sitting in the chair behind Jeanette, Barbaralee looks puzzled, opens her mouth to say something, but before she can T. Terry flashes her a look that is simultaneously imploring and demanding. She says nothing, but simply nods in agreement.

"What mission?"

"In the next few weeks I shall need you to go on a very delicate re-
connaissance mission, one which only someone with your intelligence,
feminine wiles, and gender can successfully execute. I will give you the details later, Jeanette. Now is not the time. Suffice it to say that there are big
things afoot in the land, and you are an essential element in them. Read
this," he says, rising and approaching her, his hand extending Barbaralee's column.

Jeanette's eyes rapidly scan the page as she slaps away the arm that has
snaked around her waist. As she reads, the muscles of her face, squinched
up into a frown, begin to relax. By the time she's finished reading, she's
laughing.

"What in God's name is so funny?" T. Terry demands.

"Say what? A whorehouse for sisters? That's just plain old brilliant," Jeanette says between chuckles. "Lord knows we deserve some
TLC. You'd better get yourself downstairs, call this meeting to order,
and make your move to squash this fast. Next thing you know these
women will be selling shares on the New York Stock Exchange and you
won't have a chance in hell. Oh, and I'm your woman if you need someone to do some undercover work," she giggles.

"Are you suggesting that the moral fortitude of the black woman is
not the underpinning that keeps the black man from descending totally
into the abyss of immorality? That black women are not the ones who
struggle each day to keep our families, our communities, our very selves
intact, such as they are?"

"It's Friday, Terry. Save the sermon for Sunday," Jeanette snaps.
"And no, I'm not suggesting anything. I'm saying that sisters need some
good, *reliable* dick"—T. Terry winces inwardly when he hears the slight
stress she places on "reliable"—"and selling it isn't a bad idea at all."

"I beg to differ," Barbaralee interjects.

"You can beg to do whatever you want, and I'm sure it won't be the
first time," Jeanette says. "But if you're too proud to beg, this spa's the
place for you," she adds, laughing heartily.

Raking her fingers through her silver hair, sucking her teeth, and
stifling the urge to fly across the room and beat the shit out of the meddling Jeanette, Barbaralee turns to T. Terry.

"Listen. I've been writing for *Girlfriend!* for almost twenty years, and
one thing I know is that sisters are more into the black man than they are
into themselves. You know what issues are always our biggest sellers? The
ones with men on the cover. It doesn't matter if he's a misogynist rapper,

a convicted batterer, or only dates white women, the issue always sells through the roof, as long as the brother on the cover isn't pug ugly. You know what sells least? The money issue, closely followed by any cover that includes the words 'feminism' or 'empowerment.' Sisters are not interested in that shit. They want a good job, nice hair, and a husband, and they are willing to rehabilitate a brother if they have to. That's what black women want."

T. Terry looks relieved, but Jeanette looks at Barbaralee and rolls her eyes.

"Has it been so long that you've forgotten about sex, orgasm, the desire for the dick, dear?" she purrs.

"No. Sure black women want sex, but not without love and commitment. I have a direct line to a million women, and that doesn't even include the pass-along readers. I know what black women want. Believe it. Between T. Terry's network and my column, we cannot fail to build a movement that will not only resurrect morality, thereby increasing the number of marriageable brothers, but also will fill the dwindling coffers of the Baptist Brotherhood and enhance all our economic portfolios, rest assured," she says, reaching out to pat his forearm reassuringly. Like a child, T. Terry gives Jeanette one of those I-told-you-so smirks. She shrugs.

"Hey, I'm not the enemy, remember? I'm just saying you'd better get on it fast. And get downstairs to the conference room and start the meeting before those bums start drinking the vermouth."

"Amen, amen," T. Terry intones, rising from his desk and collecting his papers, paramount among them the copy of Barbaralee's new column. "You are both right. I accept my mandate to expose this spa as the decadent, hedonistic, immoral, exploitative venture that it is. A place that instead of lifting up the black man, pulls him further into the morass of corruption, and encourages the black woman to jump in after him. That undermines black women's historic and contemporary legacy of self-sacrifice in the name of the betterment of The Race—"

"Don't you mean The Black Man?" Jeanette interrupts irritably. "Let's call a spade a spade."

"Calling a spade a spade is not a part of the pedagogy of the Baptist seminary. Or any seminary for that matter," T. Terry says smoothly, turning off lamps as he moves about the room, all the while herding the two women toward the door.

26

A FEW WEEKS LATER, JEANETTE IS LYING ON HER STOMACH, FACE TO one side, staring at the ornate "A" in the midst of a color-streaked night sky tattooed on the arm of the man beside her. She can feel the warm air from his nostrils against her face when he exhales. His eyes are closed and his smooth, almost hairless chest moves steadily up and down with each breath.

Jeanette points her toes downward and again clasps the wooden lattice of the headboard, stretching her petite body. Several hours of lovemaking have left her with the contradictory sensation of being both loose and slightly stiff. She supposes this is because of the variety of ways they'd made love; it had been a while since her legs had been over a man's shoulders, rather than being locked into the familiar and sometimes boring missionary position T. Terry had grown fond of in the last few years.

Jeanette's mission is accomplished. She's infiltrated A Sister's Spa and can now confirm what T. Terry already suspects, that the specialized service offered at this exclusive spa is sex. Everything's gone perfectly, she's been treated royally, and it really is a fabulous place. Too bad Terry's got it in for these sisters, but there's nothing she can do about that. Terry was hell bent on finding, or if need be, creating an issue that would bring him more prominence and fatten the coffers of the Brotherhood, although there was no need for either. If she had her druthers, he'd step down from leadership of both the Brotherhood and the church in New York, and they'd pack up and go back to Itta Bena. Terry could finally write that book he'd been promising a publisher for years and preach only when the spirit sincerely moved him. She could relax, help him as needed, and make every effort to resurrect the introspective man and creative lover he'd once been.

But she knows Terry is waiting for her return and her report, already planning to organize a march and rally to the spa once she confirms his suspicions. It really burns her up that once it was clear that no one was about to get riled up about the moral fiber of black men, he turned his gaze on black women. But when she tried to talk to him about what he was doing, he wouldn't listen or respond, just told her, "It goes without saying that you and the multitude of other righteous black sister are exempted," as if that made his plans to judge and publicly attack A Sister's Spa, and any other black women whose conduct he didn't agree with, okay. She shrugs mentally and flips over on the bed. Since Terry refuses to go anywhere with her and relax, she'd agreed to visit the spa and let him know what was going on when she got home. At least she'd spent a few days getting some peace, quiet, and great sex before all hell breaks loose.

"You okay?" Ahmad, eyes now open, asks.

"Never been better, sweetie," Jeanette purrs. He grins.

"Look, I'm really sorry about that last condom breaking. I would have stopped, but you said—" Jeanette puts a hand over his lips.

"Not a problem. I read in the brochure that the staff get medical check-ups every week, and since I've never gotten pregnant in all these years, even when I was trying, I think we're cool." She reaches over and traces the tattoo on his bicep, with its creamy streaks and arcs of green, red, and purple against a night sky.

"What's this supposed to be?"

Ahmad sits up, shakes his shoulder length locks, twists his arm to the side, and glances down.

"That's the aurora borealis, the northern lights. It's a natural light show in the sky caused by electrically charged particles from the sun trapped in the earth's atmosphere," Ahmad says, his voice excited and face animated. "When they hit all the atoms and molecules that hang around the North and South Poles, shazam!, the aurora borealis. Mostly they occur in the far North or South, but sometimes they spread across thousands of miles, and you can see them other places, too. Alaska's supposed to be the best place to see them, and I'm thinking maybe when I get tired of working here I'll go up there and check it out."

"I've heard of it," Jeanette says, "But never seen it. There's so much ambient light in New York, it never even really gets dark. What made you decide to have that tattooed on your arm? Why not 'thug life,' your girlfriend's name, or a picture of Tupac?"

Ahmad laughs.

"I'm not a thug, and girlfriends come and go, and I figured if I was going to let someone stick needles with dye into my arm, I wanted something unique."

"Okay, but why'd you choose this?"

"In memory of my mom, she's the one who told me all that shit about the northern lights. Did you want to do something else before check-out time? We've still got about an hour," Ahmad asks, rubbing his strong hands from her shoulders down to the small of her back, gently kneading the cheeks of her ass. Jeanette flips over, smiles up at him.

"Nope. I'm going to take a long bath before I go. But I've had a wonderful time. Thank you," she says, rising from the bed and going into the bathroom to turn on the tub. Ahmad stands, stretches, begins pulling on his clothes.

"My pleasure. Maybe I'll get to serve you again," he says.

"You never know," Jeanette calls to his departing back, even though she's certain that if T. Terry has his way, A Sister's Spa will be nothing but a memory in a few weeks.

Steam rising, she slips into a tub scented with mango and full of bubbles, the latest issue of *Girlfriend!* in her hand. She flips the pages, idly looking at the photographs and thinking of Ahmad's lips, hands, and cock. Not for the first time in the last five years she wonders if her time with T. Terry is drawing to a close, if it's time for her to move on. But she has no idea where to go, she's been with Terry so long. She's passed up marriage, children, and a career to be with him while his wife was alive, and look where she was: forty-five, single, childless, and still a secret. Except now she wasn't only Terry's secret lover and partner, she'd become his spy, Agent Double-O Soul, her mission to infiltrate A Sister's Spa and bring the intelligence back to a sixty-seven-year-old man afraid of his own mortality and about to wage a campaign against a couple of harmless black women trying to start a business. A nontraditional business, for sure, but a legal one, and judging from everything she'd experienced in two days, a pretty hip place for a tired sister to chill out.

Jeanette slides down into the tub, the water covering her breasts and licking at the back of her hair. She isn't tired of Terry, just the life they lead—too much scheming, too many assholes and predators around them, most recently Barbaralee Edison. Why was it, she wonders, that men so often see age as an adversary to fight, not a companion to welcome? For more than forty years Terry had done his best, and what he thought was right, and even if it turned out not to be, he couldn't change the past. She could see them back in Itta Bena now, T. Terry on the porch with a glass of lemonade scribbling on a legal pad while she tended tomato, okra, and collard plants in the garden, and the sun went down in the Mississippi Delta . . .

Then the words "Believe It!" in inch-high purple letters jumped out from the pages of *Girlfriend!* and dragged her back to the business at hand.

R-E-S-P-E-C-T OR S-E-X?

Wasn't it Negro icon and Supreme Court Justice Thurgood Marshall who said a black snake will bite you the same as a white one? Well, ditto that for a black woman. As if we don't have enough to overcome being insulted and abused by the white man, white women, and those we call our brothers— what's next, small children and dogs?—now we've got pseudo-sisters offering us meaningless sex. For a price.

You may not have heard of A Sister's Spa, the first resort exclusively for black women in America. They've tried to keep it on the DL, but I'm not down, and it is low. What makes this spa so exclusive? Would you like sex with your sauna and steam? That's right, ladies, it's a whorehouse, except here the pimps call themselves sisters. For a price, sisters can go and get their brains balled out by the brother—or, depending on your tastes, white man—of their choice.

Don't get me wrong, girlfriends, I'm not against sex, but what happened to commitment, love, the rejuvenation and upliftment of the precious black family? Who'll hoist the banner for black love and sacrifice if sisters become the sexual predators too many of our brothers already are? And don't get me started on the white man factor: Sally Hemings must be twirling in her grave. Have we returned to the plantation or is this just genocide by any other name? Whatever, it stinks.

Luckily, there's one man poised to take affirmative action against this latest defilement of black women. For more information, check out his web page: *www.tigeroars.com*.

Jeanette reads the column several times, then steps out of the tub, wrapping a towel around her body and shaking her head. She starts to dry herself, then picks up *Girlfriend!* and rips out the page with Barbaralee's column. Cursing softly, she tears the paper into small pieces and drops them into the toilet, watching the brightly colored pieces swirling and dancing in the bowl before the water sucks them down and they disappear.

"I'M SORRY, BUT THOSE ARE THE RULES. THE TOTAL HEALING DELUXE is the only extended package we offer. No exceptions. Your car is waiting to take you to the airport. You can re-book for next weekend if there's space available, but you cannot stay here any longer." Even though I'm in the office working the reservation lines, I can tell by the sound of Wanda's voice floating in from the foyer that she's on the edge of going off.

"Noooooo!" a deep voice wails in reply.

"Ms. Cunningham. Get a hold of yourself. Unclasp your hands, relax your arms, and remove them from around Sequoia's waist," Wanda instructs firmly. "He has been working with you for three nights and he needs a rest. It's time for you to go."

"I can't. I need it," the voice of Lorene Cunningham manages to squeeze out between sobs. "I'll pay, whatever you want, I just can't leave."

"Money is not the issue. And you must leave. Please don't make me call the triplets to carry you to your car. That would be embarrassing, wouldn't it, and we don't want anyone to get hurt, do we?" There's more than the hint of a threat in Wanda's voice, and apparently Cunningham hears it, too.

"Can I make a reservation for next week now, before I leave?" she sobs.

"Certainly. We can set that up while I walk you to your car," Wanda says smoothly, her voice fading as she moves away. The faint chime of the front door being opened sounds.

"Lydia, there's some woman from Delta on the line. Wants to know if she can book a block of rooms for the weekend of August 12," Muffin whispers to me. Dick is in Vegas for a meeting, so the copter'd dropped her at the spa for the afternoon. She thought she'd have a massage and a swim and relax for the day, but we're so busy Wanda had pressed her into service helping us with reservations.

"What Delta, Muff? The Mississippi Delta, Delta Airlines? Find that out and then ask her how many sisters and for how long?" Muffin nods, speaks into the receiver, listens, then presses the hold button.

"Twelve women from ages twenty-five to eighty, for one night, so that's the Wrap and Roll, right? And do we offer a group rate? She's from something called Delta Sigma Theta. I don't know what that is, do you?"

"Delta Sigma Theta? The sorority? Thank you, Jesus," I crow. "It's nothing but one of the largest sororities for black women in the country. I'll take that call," I say, snatching the receiver from her hand. "Cover the other lines, would you?" I add, looking down at the console of ten lights that almost never stop blinking as women call to book reservations.

A Sister's Spa has been open a month and business is booming. The women who attended the grand opening have generated more clients simply by word of mouth than we could have gotten from a full-page advertisement in the *National Chronicle* or *Girlfriend!*. Every time a satisfied customer falls into her limo on the way home, we're confident that not only will she be back, but she'll tell all her girlfriends about the experience and they'll come running.

We've got bookings for six months ahead, not only individuals but organizations, too. The National Organization of 400 Black Women; One Hundred Hip-Hop Hoochies; the Right On! Sister Book Club; the Caucus of Sister Social Workers; the United Caucus of Women Against Workfare—they've all made reservations to visit the spa in the next few months. We've even been contacted by something called Sisters in the Choir, a national organization of women who sing in their local church choirs, who asked for an "educational tour" of the facility. We figured we'd let a fully clothed and charming Odell show them the more public areas of the place, and if they wanted to go more in depth, so to speak, that was up to them.

According to LaShaWanda, if business keeps up like this we'll be in the black in twelve months, sooner if we take her advice and add another twenty rooms. Even though Muffin insists that the money from her husband is a grant from the 1-800-HEP-BROS Foundation, the four of us agree we want to pay him back, and as soon as possible. There's something more than a little unsavory about having taken money from a paragon of racist, right-wing virtue. Even if his wife is cool.

This is Muffin's third visit to the spa, the first time without Dick. We never know when to expect them. The first time, a helicopter landed on the far end of the property and out the two of them jumped. Dick seemed fascinated by A Sister's Spa and insisted on touring every aspect of the place, from the guest rooms to the men's dormitory to the main lounge. He even wanted to see the gardening shed and laundry room, and was fascinated by the kitchen. He spent hours sitting on a stool next to Acey's pantry, talking to Brother Marvini, our resident chef, about what meals were popular with both the guests and the sex workers. He was a health-food enthusiast, which surprised me; I know it's a stereotype, but I would have thought a cutthroat capitalist running dog like Dick Dixmoor would eat his meat bloody and his vegetables soft. When I thought about it, though, I could see the logic: He wanted to live as long as possible to keep making money and get his revenge on the makers of ViriMax for beating him to the punch. He sang the praises of McGinley's Oatmeal so strongly, praising it as the ideal food because it gave you strength, sustenance, and kept you regular, that Marvini put it on the morning menu, throwing in some raisins or blueberries and doing a crème brulee sugar crust to make it more appealing. The men ate it up, too.

Health food or not, Dick gave me the creeps, and I didn't trust him or like having him around, in spite of Muffin's protestations that "Dick's just an old softie once you get to know him."

"Tell that to the brother he killed at that Dairy Queen," LaSha-Wanda told her more than once.

"Not to mention all the people addicted to one or another of the drugs manufactured by Dixmoor International," I'd add.

"Or killed by guns or bombs he makes," Odell would say, and Muffin would shake her head, murmur, "You all don't understand him," and shut up.

Anyway, even though never would have suited me just fine, he really wasn't there much, and when he was he spent most of his time with Marvini, watching him cook, talking about food, and not interfering with our business. Marvini was a poker-faced brother who was always slightly spaced from two decades of smoking herb. He was funny as hell, and he would cut the throat of anyone who messed with me or Acey in less than a heartbeat. When we were in college, he was the resident pot dealer and a baker of superlative hash brownies, which is how I'd met him, and even though I rarely got stoned anymore, we remained friends and became part of his small but loyal following when he started cooking at restaurants around San Francisco. He was an adult, single, trustworthy, and a tremendous cook, and he'd said yes without hesitation when we'd offered him a job at the spa.

"Can you believe that Cunningham woman? That sister has lost her mind," Wanda announces, walking into the back office where Muffin and I are working the phones.

"You handled her well, though, Wanda," Muffin says.

"Girl, I was at my wit's end," Wanda says, plopping into a chair and taking a sip from a can of Diet Pepsi. "If she hadn't left when she did, I was gonna go off and get street. Tell her, 'Bitch, let go of my employee before I slap you upside your fucking head,'" Wanda cackles.

"Glad it didn't come to that."

"Me, too," Wanda agrees. "I really cannot let that broad work my nerves, but damn. She's been here every week since we opened and still doesn't want to leave when she's supposed to. I have the utmost respect for Sequoia, but I swear I'm afraid she's going to wear him out."

"Not to worry," I say, laughing. Wanda turns to me.

"You know something I don't?" she asks, grinning. "Give it up."

"You didn't check him out, did you?" Muffin says, eyes wide.

I shrug. "Hell, yeah. I couldn't resist and didn't try to."

"And?"

"And, at least in his case, it's true what they say about the size of a man's hands and feet directly corresponding to the size of his penis. That Johnson is all redwood."

"You didn't," Muffin whispers. "He's enormous."

"Oh but I did, carefully. I told him to lie on his back so I could control the action. There was no way I was going to let him get on top of me. One slip up and he could have punctured my uterus," I say. Wanda snickers.

"I squatted on top of him and fucked him for as long as I could. He didn't shudder, buck, or otherwise respond, just lay there and let me work him. That night I was after a purely dick thing. I came three times, and the only reason I rolled off him was my arms were exhausted and I was afraid they'd give out and I'd slip and impale myself.

"Anyway, I'm ready to go to sleep and the next thing I know Sequoia's mouth is between my legs and he's nibbling my sweet spot expertly, and I'm about ready to come for the fourth time. Which I do."

"What happened next?" Muffin asks breathlessly.

"I passed out, so I couldn't tell you. But an hour later when I woke up he was lying there with the same hard-on, ready for more. I had to send the brother back to the dorm so we could both get some sleep. All that's to say that I'm sure he can handle anyone, including Lorene Cunningham."

"You are one greedy sister," Wanda chuckles.

"It's market research. Just checking out the merchandise."

"You're pulling my leg. You didn't, really," Muffin says, shaking her head.

"Hell yeah, we did. If you don't believe me, check him out for yourself, Muff."

"I couldn't," she demurs.

"Why not? Dick's not here, is he?"

"No, but I just can't. I promised him I wouldn't."

"Go 'head, girl. We're not gonna tell," Wanda says.

"Oh, I know that, but Dick and I have a thing about trust. Before we got married we agreed that we'd always tell each other the truth, a vow he reminded me of when I was begging him to give you the money for A Sister's Spa. It'd feel wrong, lying to him now."

"You don't have to lie, just do it and keep your mouth shut," Wanda suggests.

"And what am I going to say when Dick comes back and asks me if I've been a good little girl?"

"A good little girl?" I can't keep the scorn out of my voice. "You've got to be kidding."

"Every couple has their little rituals and secret language, Lydia—something you've probably forgotten since you haven't been in a real relationship in years," Muffin bristles. "A promise is a promise. I'm gonna keep mine as long as I can or until Dick breaks his, as hard as that may be."

"Okay, cool," I say, backing off. "But what do you do for sex? I mean, Dick's pushing seventy, isn't he?"

"Yeah. He'd be mad as hell if he knew, but when I want to make love and he's not up to it, I slip some ViriMax into his dinner. He doesn't have a clue, thinks he's just a virile older man. He drags me off to bed and we're both happy."

Wanda laughs. "Girl, and here you are going on about trust. Still, it's slick, but dangerous. He'll kill you if he finds out he's indirectly helping make Griff-Margetson rich. Not to mention the ego puncture learning that he's not the aging but virile love stud he thinks he is."

"But he'll never know, will he. Wanda? Lydia?"

"Our lips are sealed," Wanda laughs. "Now, I'd better get back on those phones."

"Thanks," I say, standing up and stretching. "I'm going to sit out on the porch and go through that stack of newspapers I haven't had time to read in the past month. Call me if you need me."

Tall, brown, and fine, Odell's brothers turned out to be great for business. At twenty-one, they are like enormous children: overwhelmingly sweet, sometimes naughty, and responsive to discipline, which Odell didn't hesitate to give them. We put them in shorts, oiled them up, and stuck them outside the front door wielding enormous bamboo fans and welcoming smiles, the first men sisters see as they roll up to the spa. I give them a wave on my way to the porch, fall into a chair, and pick up the day's newspapers. I page rapidly through the newsprint, confident as I read that the world hasn't gotten any better or worse while I was too busy to worry about it. I'm halfway through when I get to the *National Chronicle*, page seven, and read the latest from Jacques Westin.

PROMISCUOUS BLACK WOMEN ENDANGER SPECIES, TIGER ROARS: NEVADA TO BE FOCUS OF MORALITY CRUSADE

by Jacques Westin

The Reverend T. Terry Tiger, the veteran civil rights activist whose Crusade to Resurrect Morality appeared to be stillborn since it was announced, held a press conference yesterday. Tiger announced that the Crusade would kick off August 14 with a mass demonstration at an as yet undisclosed location "somewhere in Nevada," adding that the focus of the first phrase of the Crusade would be on black women's immorality.

"Who do we think of when we hear the word immorality? We think of black men, in all their totality. Yet black women too are corrupted by sin, and without our pure sisters, the race cannot win," Tiger said in his press statement, all of which was delivered in his trademark rhyming style.

He asked that all "soldiers in the army of morality" be in Reno by August 13 for the rally.

Tiger's forty-year career as a civil rights leader has been a checkered one. He was expelled from Dr. Martin Luther King Jr.'s Southern Christian Leadership Conference in the 1960s. Tiger subsequently moved to New York City, where he founded the Baptist Brotherhood and Boulé, a quasi-religious organization which serves primarily as a clearing house for donations from corporations and developers that are either in trouble with a black community or interested in access to a black market. In addition, the Brotherhood and Boulé holds several annual fundraising social events, most notably the Brotherhood Awards. Past recipients include Ward Connerly, Condoleezza Rice, and Justice Clarence Thomas.

With Tiger at the press conference were representatives of the governing bodies of the United Federation of Promojites, Christians Against Moral Turpitude (CAMT), and several dozen other small but vocal black organizations.

The only woman in attendance was Edna Mantz Thompson, president of Righteous Ebony Women After Respect and Power (REWARP), who was more forthcoming. "My organization was formed to fight against the image of the black woman as the oversexed, voracious temptress of plantation fantasies. We're here to say that yes, black women were raped on the plantation, and no, black women didn't ask for it. We're here to let America know that contrary to popular belief, real black women don't ask for, want, or even like sex. It is something we submit to for purposes of procreation only. To give birth to princes who we will raise as kings to liberate our people. A black woman having sexual relations for fun sets the race back two hundred years."

Tiger declined to answer questions, but promised that, "The Crusade will commence in just a few weeks," adding, " If you believe as we do, but cannot join our ranks, send us contributions from your credit cards or banks."

"Shit," I mutter to myself, and begin digging in my bag for my cell phone. Acey's in San Francisco for Matthew's speech, and I want to warn her about Westin's article.

"Lydia, do you have a moment?" I'm so frantically trying to find my phone I didn't even hear Odell come up behind me.

"O, this isn't a good time. Can it wait?"

"Well, we've got a little problem, and I want to take care of it right here, before it becomes a big one," Odell insists. I toss the *National Chronicle* toward him.

"Check this shit out. We've already got a big problem. T. Terry's apparently pulled together every organization he can find that's out of touch, reactionary, hungry, hates women, or in a few cases all of the above, for his insane crusade, and guess who he's coming after? I'm sure you'll agree that whatever you've got on your mind can wait." Odell reads the article, the slight frown on his face deepening.

"Damn. That's some convoluted logic. You think Tiger'll actually get anyone to go along with this?"

"Look at the organizations who were at the press conference, Odell. He's already got people behind him, and not all crazy losers like those jerks from the United Federation of Promojites. I mean, most of the churches in the Baptist Brotherhood and Boulé were there, and not only the old-time jackleg preachers. I gotta get in touch with Acey before she sees the article, panics, decides this T. Terry bullshit is God's will or something, and throws herself on the mercy of the church. So whatever problem you've got, Odell, it's small potatoes compared to this shit, am I right?"

"Lydia. Listen. It's this: A few of the workers aren't able to achieve erection as frequently as necessary."

"How many is a few?" I ask as my stomach clenches.

"Six."

I stop. "Damn. Are they taking their ViriMax?"

Odell nods. "I dispense it myself and watch them swallow it, but it doesn't seem to be working."

"Maybe they're just exhausted. I know I am, and I haven't been making love five or six times a day. Come to think of it, I've been too busy to have sex for days. Are they eating properly? Can you give them a few days off and let them just sleep?"

"That'd be hard right through here. We're almost full now, and don't forget we've got that Black Skiers group coming tomorrow. Not to mention the return of Lorene Cunningham, who's booked the Total Healing Deluxe, which means she'll need at least two men at her disposal."

"Can't we use the triplets?"

"I'm not sure they're ready."

"I think you're being a bit over-protective, big brother. They flunked calculus, not fornication, am I right? They sure as hell look ready to me," I say, glancing toward the front door where the triplets stand at attention, muscled bodies gleaming in the sun. "Besides, what choice do we have?"

Odell nods slowly. "Okay, we'll give them a try."

"Listen, since you're nervous I'll ask LaShaWanda to run them through their paces before tomorrow. If that's it, I need to go on line and see if Westin's story has been picked up by other news outlets, and then I have to track Acey down."

Odell looks down at his clipboard.

"The rest of this stuff can wait, then. I'm going to go talk to the boys, go over the training with them one last time, then let Wanda do a test run. When you reach Acey, beep me and I can conference in. We need to figure out how to deal with the Crusade to Resurrect Morality. Maybe there's a way this crap can work for us," Odell says thoughtfully.

"I'm with you. You know what they say, the only bad press is no press."

Just as I open my phone and am about to hit Acey's number, it rings. I'm certain it's Acey, either just checking in or because she's seen Westin's story, so I say, "You're gonna live a long time, girlfriend," and a voice—not Acey's—that sounds vaguely familiar says, "I'm not sure if that's a curse or a blessing. Is this Lydia Beaucoup?"

"Yes," I say, trying to recover gracefully. "And you are?"

"Exultia Wallace, founder and president of Feminists United," the girlish, high-pitched voice replies in a tone that makes it clear she's not used to being asked to identify herself. And the truth is, if I wasn't so pre-occupied, I definitely would have caught her voice, since I've been hearing it for most of my life. At seventy, Exultia Wallace is the grand dame of white feminists. Since the summer forty years ago when she disrupted the Miss America Pageant by streaking across the stage in Atlantic City nude except for a billboard declaring, "This Contest Degrades Women," Exultia Wallace has been a leader in the feminist movement. And though there were some women who condemned her naked jaunt as merely a "publicity stunt," which it was, or dismissed her popularity with the media as a result of the fact that she was physically attractive, which she also is, it ensured that anything Exultia Wallace did was news. And everything she did was in service of the fight for the political, economic, and social equality of women. After five decades of activism she is still going strong: writing books, organizing actions, speaking at rallies, traveling around the world to advocate for women's rights. The last I'd read, she was the only white woman included in a delegation of women going to Nigeria to protest a young woman's death by stoning for the crime of adultery and having a child out of wedlock. So what was she doing calling me?

"Exultia Wallace from F.U? I'm honored," I stammer.

"The pleasure is mine. I've heard exciting things about what you're doing out there for black women."

"What we're doing?"

"Providing women with necessary services in a discreet environment," she says.

"Oh, that. We're just running a spa for sisters, that's all."

"According to my sources, that is not exactly all."

"Your sources?"

"I am closely allied with several women who have spent time at A Sister's Spa, so there's really no need to be coy. We are all sisters under Her eyes, are we not?"

"Exactly who is Her?"

"The fecund and fertile female deity from whom all life springs. The eternal She who Western society has draped in a false cloth of maleness in order to justify the oppression of women. But I digress," she interrupts herself. "I shall overnight you a copy of my book, *God is a She*, in which I explain all this. For now, back to the business at hand . . ."

"Exactly what is the business at hand?"

"My sources tell me that your facility is exactly what women want, that you provide essential sexual services in a clean, beautiful, healthy, and welcoming environment."

"We try," I say tersely, trying to figure out where she's going with this.

"Such an egalitarian and liberating idea, to provide women with erotic pleasure on women's terms. Commendable indeed, in so many ways. And yet there is one major flaw . . ." she says portentously.

"Yes, what would that be?"

"The exclusion of your white sisters."

I can't help it, but I start to laugh.

"Ms. Wallace, I'm black, and unless you've been secretly bleaching your skin for seventy years and suddenly run out of Nadinola, you're not. Why is it that the only time I have any white sisters is when I have something you all want?"

"I beg your pardon?" It's the first time I've ever heard Wallace sound taken aback.

"No need, and pardon me if that sounded rude, it wasn't meant to be. I'm just saying that with all the shit black women have to handle, this is the first I've ever heard from you or F.U. And are you calling to offer assistance? Hell no. You're calling to tell me what I'm doing wrong, according to your superior judgment. A wrong that, by the way, only the presence of my white sisters can make right."

Wallace laughs, an uncomfortable high-pitched sound.

"There's no need to be defensive. Feminists United simply wants to be included."

"Yeah, but there're reasons why you're excluded—it's not as if we simply forgot you. And while I really don't have the energy or time to go into them with you chapter and verse, suffice it to say that your calling up out of the blue to tell me what A Sister's Spa's 'flaw' is just about sums them up. But you white women never seem to get it."

"Get what?"

"That just because we've all got pussies doesn't mean we're all alike. That a lot of sisters are oppressed not only by men of all colors, but by white women, too, and that we want a place that's just for us, where even if there are men around, sisters—black sisters—call the shots. Now do you get it?"

"I'm not sure if I totally get it, but I do hear you. But please, hear me out, if you will. The executive committee of F.U. would like to be supportive of A Sister's Spa. We have discussed what you are doing and think it's radical, courageous, and necessary. We also think your spa is a place our 200,000 dues-paying members would happily patronize, if there were a way to make that possible. We are also aware that the ever-odious T. Terry Tiger, aided by that anti-feminist tabloid that calls itself a newspaper, *Girlfriend!*, seeks to lead the reactionary forces of so-called 'Christian Morality' against you. We have battled those forces of evil before, and could perhaps be helpful. The annual convention of Feminists United is next week in Reno. I'd like to arrange for myself and some of our local chapter chairs to visit the spa, take a tour, and meet with you and your staff to further discuss matters."

"What's that you said about *Girlfriend!*?" I ask. Wallace chuckles.

"You have been busy, haven't you? For the past month Barbaralee Edison's column has been dropping hints about your spa and pumping up Reverend Tiger. They are obviously in cahoots against your endeavor." I just sit there holding the phone, my brain a jumble of panicked thoughts.

"Hello? Are you still there? Can Feminists United visit next week?"

"Next weekend's pretty busy . . ."

"What about Sunday morning, say eight A.M.? We could be gone in a couple of hours, before," she pauses and chuckles, "most of your clientele are even awake, given the strenuous activities I'm told go on there."

Damn, this chick is persuasive, and pushy. If I weren't so stressed about this other shit, I'd admire her chutzpah.

"That sounds okay. But just to look around and talk, right? No contact with the workers. You're cool with that?"

"Yes, I'm cool with that, my sister. For now. I'll see you then." The last thing I hear before the line goes dead is her squeaky voice declaring, "Sisterhood is powerful!" before she hangs up.

28

"I'M GOING TO BE LATE!" I GRUMBLE TO MYSELF AS, CLAD IN BRA AND panties, I hop on one foot around the kitchen of my house in Oakland, trying to maneuver my left leg into a pair of super-sheer panty hose and keep the right leg from dragging along the floor and either snagging or tripping me, while I simultaneously listen to the messages on my answering machine and hobble toward the stove so I can turn off the screeching tea kettle.

Even though I'm usually able to pull off similar contortions numerous times a day (just part of a woman's ability to multitask), today I'm overwhelmed and already running late to meet Matthew at the National Bar Association dinner. I end up sticking a finger through my stocking, tripping over the loose leg, and falling flat on the kitchen floor, back against the stove. At least I can reach backward, turn off the burner, and silence that shrieking teapot.

I'd like to indulge in a session of stress-induced, self-pitying sobs, but I've already spent a half-hour meticulously applying my make-up and can't afford to wash it all away. I settle for carefully resting my forehead against one hand and feeling sorry for myself without tears. Then I do an exercise Lydia got from her therapist and try to go back through my day and figure out what's making me feel so overwhelmed.

In the twenty-four hours since I got in from Nevada I've: cleaned my house, berated the lawn guy for not taking care of business, gone through a four-inch stack of mail, paid the bills, gone to the bank, gone by my original spa to check on how things are running, had a meeting with my manager L.E. to troubleshoot problems, interviewed a masseuse to replace one who's AWOL, gone by Lydia's apartment to pick up her mail, been assaulted by the horrid stench therein, cleaned her refrigerator from which the odor emanated, aired the place out, gone to her bank to make deposits, gotten my nails done, spent too much time at Dekar's Natural Wonder Salon getting my current curly bob touched up, gone to

Nordstrom to pick up 150 more pairs of 100 percent cotton orange shorts in assorted sizes and fifty new fanny packs, dropped them all by the woman who embroiders the A Sister's Spa logo for us and begged and bribed her to get the work done in a day and a half, picked up the messages both from my service and Lydia's answering machine, returned twenty important calls, and, now, damn near broken my tailbone trying to have a cup of soothing chamomile tea before I have to rush to the Ritz-Carlton to meet Matthew.

I rub my forehead, because the truth is, that's not an atypical day in my life. It doesn't usually result in this level of stress, not to mention the headache I can feel rousing itself for a serious attack. I can hear my imaginary shrink gently asking, "What do you think is the underlying issue that's so upsetting?" If she were here, I'd simply say, "men!" In this case, Matthew, the elusive Earl, and the sex workers employed at A Sister's Spa.

Maybe it's a case of be careful what you wish for, because I've gotten it, and I haven't even had time to enjoy it. I feel overwhelmed and confused, not to mention so tightly wound sexually that I could probably turn myself on by sliding against the cool tile floor. Okay, so I'd been praying for Earl to come back to me ever since he transcended, and I was certainly glad to see him when he first appeared in the pantry, but this version of Earl is something the real Earl never was—unreliable and untouchable. He doesn't come when called, but only appears at random, and apparently he doesn't like Nevada, since he's yet to materialize in the pantry at A Sister's Spa. When he does arrive, we can't touch, which, although I'm happy to see him, leaves a *lot* to be desired.

Meanwhile, of course, A Sister's Spa depends on scantily clad, accommodating, and highly sexy men to make it work. And it gets better all the time. Right before I left to come home, Odell introduced me to two new employees. One is a twentysomething light brown brother with a wild Afro, leather pants, and come-hither eyes, and the other has a body like Ali's back in the day. It took my last vestiges of restraint not to attack both of them, and I probably would have if my limo to the airport hadn't arrived.

For almost two months I've spent all day, every day in an atmosphere of sexual experimentation, abandon, and satisfaction, but do not partake of these pleasures myself. Lydia says I'm an idiot not to satisfy myself with one of the workers if Matthew isn't doing the job, especially since he'll never be any the wiser, but the thing is, *I'll* know. With the exception of that hazy afternoon in the bell tower, as long as I'm trying to get it together with Matthew I've vowed not to mess around with other men, even if, as Lydia tries to rationalize for me, it's the cost of doing business. I'm trying to hang in there and build a relationship, but in addition to his fear of post-bypass sex, Matthew's more interested lately in making a big splash with his speech at the NBA convention, as opposed to showering me with love and affection.

Then there's the Reverend T. Terry Tiger hurricane gathering strength in the East and heading West. Lydia says I'm a victim of too many years of mean-spirited Christian propaganda, but I can't get the image out of my mind that it's just a matter of time until Tiger appears, dressed as Moses, casting lightning bolts of divine retribution down on the spa as naked women and men flee in terror, not to mention various states of coitus interruptus.

Given all the confusion in my life, if I had a shrink she'd probably be at a loss to come up with a probing query.

"Damn it, Earl! Where are you when I need you?" I yell out loud.

"Right here, in the pantry, baby darlin'.'"

I yank off the ruined stockings, push myself up from the floor, limp toward the pantry, and there he is.

"Earl, honey, I am so glad to see you. I've been at the spa for weeks, we put in a pantry there and I look for you, but you never come. There's so much going on and I need help. Where do I start?"

"You don't have to. I know. Don't ask me how, but I do. We can talk about the problems, but first, congratulations are in order."

"Congratulations for what?"

"For turning a wild idea into a successful business. For providing a service to black women. For still having those gorgeous legs after all these years. Maybe even for resisting temptation and trying to make a go of it with Matthew."

"You still think my legs are great, even with all this cellulite?"

"Can't see a dimple," Earl grins. "You are still the sexiest woman I know." He makes a motion in the air as if stroking the side of my face and pinpricks of desire ripple from my hair line to my chin.

"You said 'maybe' it's a good thing to hang in with Matthew, Earl?"

"Baby, you know how you are. Sometimes you hang on to one place because you're not sure exactly where to go next. There's no way you can be certain about anything except you've got to close one door for another one to open."

"You mean close the door on Matthew?"

"No, not necessarily. I mean decide what you're going to do, how long you're going to do it, and move forward. Don't let the fear of making a decision lock you in. The only one locked anywhere is me, in this pantry, and that's because I'm dead."

"Don't say 'dead'!"

"What should I say?"

"Passed, transcended, gone to meet your maker, I don't care. Just something . . . softer."

"Death is soft. You'll see. But okay. How about 'no longer there'?"

"Better."

"Now what's going on with you and Maybe Matthew?"

"I've decided to have a long talk with him after the banquet tonight. I'm going to tell him I love him, want to be with him, and suggest we go to a therapist and try to work on his fear of sex."

Earl arches his eyebrows skeptically.

"I mean, Matthew's not you, but who is? Maybe I can't ever have a relationship like I had with you, but what's my alternative? I don't want to grow old alone and sexless, or be like Lydia, having recreational sex with no strings attached."

Earl busts out laughing.

"Why not? Lydia seems pretty happy to me."

"I guess she is. But remember, my father was a minister, my parents were happily married for fifty years, and they raised five children."

"Happily? Acey, it's me, Earl. Isn't that revisionist history?"

"All right, so maybe my father was a bit bossy and a chauvinist, but what do you expect? He was a black preacher, he had a whole congregation depending on him, for God's sake."

"Baby darlin', being a preacher doesn't excuse his refusal to see your mother's passion and talent for photography as more than a hobby, his forbidding her to take photographs of anything other than church functions or to exhibit professionally, and his throwing away all her negatives after her death. Baby, your father was way beyond being a bit of a bossy chauvinist," Earl chides.

"So, what's your point?"

"My point is don't be your mother. Be what she was afraid to dream she could become, or dreamed of being but was too frightened to go for. Figure out what your passion is and follow it, regardless of what Tiger, Matthew, Lydia, or anyone else says. Life's too short not to, believe me." As he finishes speaking, the antique clock in the living room chimes five.

"Shit. I'm already late to meet Matthew," I say, standing up, torn between the flesh and blood man waiting for me and the ephemeral one in the pantry. "Earl. Can you wait for me? I'll be back around midnight."

Earl laughs.

"Isn't this the night you planned to listen raptly to Matthew's speech, seduce him, and afterward have a deep discussion about your future?" he asks in a teasing voice. "Are you sure you won't leave me standing?" Is it my imagination, or is his voice growing faint?

"I don't know. But wait for me, or come to Reno. There's a pantry for you there," I cry.

"I'll try. But as T. Terry might say, you don't really need me, you just think you do, the important thing is to thine own self be true," Earl rhymes, laughing softly. Then he's gone with a ripple, and I'm standing by the pantry door in a bra and panties, a torn pair of stockings in my hand, and running late.

Less than forty-five minutes later I'm in the lobby of the Ritz-Carlton on Nob Hill, scanning the cocktail hour crowd for Matthew. The lobby's packed with black folks, all headed like pilgrims in the direction of the enormous bar set up outside the grand ballroom. Most of them, men and women, wear dark, lawyerly looking suits and expressions that are simultaneously stressed out, hopeful, and determined.

Like most black professional conventioneers, they're here to make contacts and spend a few days collectively releasing a year's worth of the tension inherent in having high-powered, demanding jobs in primarily white work environments. You can almost smell the anxiety in the stale hotel air of a year's worth of frustration from repressed feelings and the constant demand on black people for diplomacy in all their dealings with whites. By the last day of the conference, this pressure will have largely dissipated as a result of strategic lectures and intense conversations, not to mention many, many drinks, secret trysts, and several late-night dances.

Occasionally someone walks by sporting a flash of color or a hint of some more individualized identity. There's a man with a fabulously striped shirt, another in a kente cloth tie, one wearing a kufi on his head. And I see a woman with beautifully groomed locks, some clunky, in-your-face jewelry, and a sharp purple suit.

Me, I'm wearing the black dress I found at Loehmann's, accessorized with a Coreen Simpson necklace and matching earrings made of some pale green, opalescent stones, and, of course, high heels. I haven't seen Matthew in person in six weeks, and I'm relieved to find that absence has made my heart at least grow fonder. Those weird pantry visits from Earl probably have something to do with it too, since he's a reminder that sometimes, just sometimes, it's possible to have it all: good life, good man, good sex.

Wandering around looking for Matthew in the crowd, I hear his booming laugh and his voice saying, "My man! My main man," before I see him standing in a circle of laughing lawyers, one of whom is grinning up at him adoringly as her hand rests cozily on his forearm. As I walk toward him I recognize the woman as the infamous Debi Mountain, a Yale law grad and Harvard M.B.A., a successful criminal defense attorney whose specialty is representing those who are rich, famous, and, to my mind, indefensible. Her current star client is a well-known singer she's defending against charges of statutory rape on the grounds that his four-teen-year-old victims took advantage of a man's "natural desires" and se-duced him against his will. There's nothing special about her one way or the other until she smiles. Her teeth are sparkling white, and when she smiles her whole face, and the room, lights up.

I ease up beside Matthew, slip a hand as far around his waist as I can get, whisper, "Hi, honey," as I stand on my toes and give him a kiss. Out of the corner of my eye I see the woman's hand slide from his sleeve.

"You're late," Matthew mutters. No "Hey, baby," or "You look great," not even a chummy, "Long time no see." "I was about to go into dinner without you," he adds, almost taunting.

"Sorry, traffic was horrendous," I say apologetically.

"Shall we go in to dinner?" Matthew says as much to the crowd around us as to me. "Everyone got their ticket?" Debi Mountain fumbles in her purse for a few moments, then looks up, confused.

"I swore I put my ticket in my bag, but I must have forgotten it in my hotel. I'm only a few blocks away, so I suppose I can dash back and get it," she says, her voice rising at the end of her sentence as if she's asking a question. The people around her laugh, and one, a familiar face from Sunday news shows, teases, "Damn, Debi, for someone who never misses a trick in court, that's pretty sloppy planning."

Debi Mountain grins. "Now Fred, get off my case. Court is a matter of life and death, the NBA dinner isn't, although I was looking forward to hearing your remarks . . . and Matthew's," she adds, looking up at him.

"Don't you go anywhere," Matthew says gallantly. "We'll just squeeze you in at my table. That way you won't miss a thing. Shall we?" he says, offering a grateful Debi his left arm. Me, I have to grab his right elbow so as not to be left behind.

"I'm sorry I'm late. I tried to get here early enough to run through your speech with you, but Dekar was so crowded today, I'm lucky I got my hair done at all. Are you ready to give your speech, honey?" I ask Matthew once we're seated at our table

"Acey, as I have said more than once, sorry does not help. I suppose I am as ready as I can be. I ran into Debi at the bar earlier, and she was kind enough to tolerate a preview of my brief remarks."

"Tolerate? Oh, Matthew, don't be modest, it was an honor to hear such an insightful, witty, well-documented critique of the current state of the black bar."

"And you remain convinced that I am not overstepping when I characterize Justice Thomas as 'a right-wing ideologue bar none'?"

Debi whinnies appreciatively, her teeth glistening. "Absolutely, absolutely. Clarence will probably be flattered when he hears that description, which I will make sure he does."

"Ah, so the two of you are friendly?" Matthew says admiringly.

"Of course. Clarence sits on the U.S. Supreme Court and where is Anita Hill teaching now, does any one know?" We're surrounded by a group of grinning sycophants hanging on Debi Mountain's every word, so I don't even bother to say Brandeis University.

"Debi, I hope I'm not being too forward," Matthew says, leaning toward her as I stab lettuce leaves with my fork, "But did you feel any conflict defending Thomas when in fact it was a black woman, one of your sisters, who he was alleged to have harassed and abused?"

"Alleged? Oh Matthew, I have no doubt Clarence did everything Anita said he did, and probably some she didn't even mention. But was that really a reason to deny him a seat on the Court?"

"I'd certainly say it was," I growl through gritted teeth.

"But you would be in the minority, and you would lose. You did lose," Debi says dismissively. "You're not a lawyer are you?"

"No. I own two spas for black women."

"Spas? How interesting. I've never been to one, although I read somewhere there's a new one that, allegedly, provides some very intimate services. Can't remember where it is, but that might be amusing. The truth is, I really have no time, even for that. I relieve my tension and stay in shape working out on a treadmill in my bedroom while I read legal documents or watch Court TV. Are you a spa man, Matthew? You certainly are in good shape," she asks, smiling and undressing him with her big brown eyes. I join her in looking at Matthew expectantly, as if the revelation of his exercise habits is breaking news that will impact the world order. Anything to move the conversation away from spas and whorehouses.

"NordicTrack," says Matthew. "I read while I work out too, and leave the peel-me-a-grape spa stuff to Acey."

Debi nods her head vigorously, coos, "Yet another thing we have in common, how marvelous. Work is my master, and your mistress, too." Is that the sound of Duke Ellington shifting in his grave?

"Debi, tell me this: What is Clarence Thomas really like?"

"Charming, absolutely charming, not the big black bugaboo these feminists and lefties would have you think. And so sentimental, why last year on my birthday he . . ." And she's off on some long-ass story. Without even listening I know the punch line is what a fabulous, reconstituted New Negro Clarence is, and the worst part is that Mathew, my man, is sitting there looking absolutely fascinated by Debi Mountain's goings on. Just when I'm about to open my usually demure mouth and ask her what self-hating, deeply in denial tribe she comes from, I am, for the first time in my life, saved by my cell phone. I excuse myself to punch the answer button.

"Hello?" I yell, one finger pressed against an ear to drown out the rumble of voices.

"Ace. It's me. Where are you?" Lydia's voice asks.

"At the NBA dinner at the Ritz, slowly being driven mad by Debi Mountain rhapsodizing about Clarence Thomas and, even worse, Matthew lapping it up. Everything all right there?"

"Have you seen the *National Chronicle* today?"

"What?"

"The *National Chronicle*."

"I haven't had time to read the paper in weeks. Why?"

"Jacques Westin has a—"

"Funny you should mention him. He just walked by, I should catch up with him and say hello. I guess he's covering tonight's speeches for the paper. Matthew'll be pleased."

"Jacques Westin has an article—"

"Lydia, you're breaking up," I say into the phone.

"We're in trouble! Read today's *National Chronicle*."

"What? What'd you say about the *National Chronicle*?"

"I can't hear you. Can you hear me? Hello, hello?" Lydia yells, but she's fading.

"Read what?"

"Westin. Westin. I think the shit's about to hit the fan!"

"What shit? What fan?" I yell into the mouthpiece, but Lydia's gone, there's only dead air, and suddenly Matthew's looming over me, shaking my shoulder and hissing angrily, "Would you lower your voice? Put that phone away and get a hold of yourself. Johnnie Cochran is about to introduce me!" When we sit back down at the table, Debi Mountain gives me a bitchy smile, delicately claps her hands, and whispers, "Give 'em hell, Matt."

Moments later Cochran summons Matthew to the podium. I sit there for a few moments with the cell phone in hand, thinking about smashing it into the side of Debi Mountain's head, but it's really Matthew I want to go off on, and he's standing up on the stage next to Johnnie, listening to himself being introduced and trying not to look smug. I stand up, murmur more excuses, and head out of the ballroom in search of a bathroom, a copy of the *National Chronicle*, and better cell phone reception, in that order. And of course, what do I almost collide with at the ladies room door but a yellow spandex cat suit containing the not insubstantial body of Barbaralee Edison.

"Acey, are you alone? Where's your shadow, Lydia? Did you girls get my messages? I left several. We've got to talk."

"Barbaralee, sorry. Just got into town and I've been running all day. Can I call you tomorrow?" I don't add that right now I need to take a pee and a Valium, simultaneously if possible.

"Tomorrow may be too late. That's when the new issue of *Girlfriend!* hits the newsstand. Did you read my last column?"

I shake my head no.

"Well, you should have. You might have recognized someone and someplace in there."

"I don't know what you're getting at. And I've got to go, if you know what I mean," I say, backing toward the door.

"Cut the crap," Barbaralee hisses, reaching over my shoulder and yanking the door closed.

"Pardon me?"

"I said cut the crap, Little Miss Goodie Two Shoes. I know you and Lydia's so-called spa is nothing but a whorehouse for women, and after tomorrow, so will all of *Girlfriend!*'s readers."

"I don't know what you're talking about."

"Do you mean to tell me you really haven't been reading my columns?" she says incredulously.

"Barbaralee, I've been working so hard the last few months I haven't had time to read anything. I have no idea what you're talking about."

"Too late to plead ignorance, girlfriend. Me, or my spies, are everywhere, including A Sister's Spa. I know all about the Total Healing Deluxe; I know what 'deep tissue massage' really means. And by tomorrow afternoon, so will my million readers—sisters searching for relationships, not sexploitation. The tide is rising," she intones threateningly.

"What tide is that?" I ask, because if I don't say something I'm going to burst into tears and wet my pants.

"The tidal wave of the righteous indignation of Christian women everywhere, of self-respecting black women across this nation, the waters of Reverend Tiger's Crusade to Resurrect Morality that will sweep away you, Lydia, and those studs at A Sister's Spa."

I'm speechless, searching for a snappy response, but all I can do is stare at Barbaralee delivering her own version of the sermon on the mount.

"Unless . . ."

"Unless what?"

"Unless you, me, and Lydia can work out a little deal, let's say, in which case I can hunt up a bigger scandal for next week's issue, maybe even print a little retraction, too. You know, my readers have short memories."

"A deal? What sort of deal?"

"The financial sort, is there any other kind?" Barbaralee barks. "You can comp me at to the spa for a few days, and, when I'm not having deep tissue massage," she says, grinning lasciviously, "we can play 'can you top T. Terry Tiger.' If you can, that's the last critical mention of A Sister's Spa in *Girlfriend!* I guarantee. So, have we got a date?"

"You want money? What about the Crusade to Resurrect Morality?" I stammer. Barbaralee leans toward me and laughs so hard drops of spittle hit my face like mist on a windshield.

"Morality, schmorality. Do I care? And neither does T. Terry. Come to think of it, if there's one thing we can agree on, it's that it's all about the benjamins, and I'm going with the highest bidder. Now what about that meeting?"

"Okay. When do you want to come?"

"Next weekend would work for me. You?"

"I guess that's fine," I shrug.

"Girl, don't look so traumatized. This could be the start of some-thing big," she thrusts a few photocopied pages into my hand. "Here, read my columns and you'll see there's nowhere T. Terry Tiger—or you, if we can strike a bargain—can't go with Barbaralee Edison and *Girlfriend!* on your side."

All I can muster is, "Right now, I'm going to the bathroom," as I stagger through the door and toward an empty stall. Not only have we been busted, we're now being extorted, and I've got to get back to the spa as fast as possible to talk to Lydia, Wanda, and Odell about this turn of events. In addition to peeing, I add take two Valiums, throw up, and commit hara-kiri to the list of what I need to do before I catch the last flight to Reno.

29

"FUCK ME!" I INSTRUCT NO ONE IN PARTICULAR AS ME, THE TRIP-
lets, and LaShaWanda contort into and around each other on my king-
size bed. I lie halfway on my side, propping myself up with one elbow and
a knee in the air as one of the boys eases his penis in and out of my sopping pussy from behind, hitting the perfect angle. Another one kneels at
the side of the bed, exploring my mouth with his hot tongue, while
Wanda crouches underneath him on all fours, sucking his dick as triplet
number three slides into her pussy.

I reach down and rub Wanda's head. She looks up at me with a
mouth full of dick, and flashes a lopsided grin. When she does, the
penis falls out of her mouth, dangling above her. She licks the head in
slow circles like it's a Popsicle on a hot day, running her tongue lightly
along the ridges and flicking it over the hole at the end. As she does so,
the triplet's tongue in my own mouth becomes harder and more insistent, and his hands reach over and begin playing with my nipples. I
thrust my ass back to meet and envelop the penis moving steadily in and
out, and in response that triplet pushes deeper inside me, coaxing my
coochica to open more to accommodate him. Wanda swallows the head
of the penis and I can see the motion of her sucking, feel it as the man's
hands leave my breasts and slide down to fondle my swollen love plug. I
push my ass back faster and harder and so does Wanda, and the triplets
match our pace. Then we are coming, the five of us, in a tangle of orifices, members, sweat, and P funk. It's just luck that we don't tear the
roof off the sucker, and thank goodness the rooms are soundproof.

Wanda climbs onto the bed and lies down, her naked body a lush
landscape of hills and valleys, the bushy hair between her legs a forest. I
reach over and stroke it, feeling her hard clit underneath my fingers.
Wanda moans and shifts her body slightly to meet my touch. My index
finger strokes her clit in circles and I feel it respond. Two of the triplets

take her nipples into their mouths as I slip two fingers easily into Wanda's wet pussy and feel her thrust down to meet them.

One of the boys lying next to Wanda gently rolls her into her side, spooning her soft, ripe body with his hard one. Our hands collide as he touches her pussy, rolling his fingers gently in the wetness. His hand retreats and I feel Wanda stiffen as he eases the tip of a finger into her ass, then removes it to coat it with lubricating gel. My fingers still in her pussy, I shift my body around, flick her clit with my tongue, feel her shudder. Beneath me I can see a long, slick finger pressing deeper into Wanda's ass as she groans with pleasure and my mouth and teeth gently encircle her engorged love spot. The four of us make love to Wanda slowly, and that is the way she comes, too, slow and flowing, with a smile on her face, the contractions of her pussy pushing my fingers away.

The triplet behind her shifts his body again so that his sheathed penis rests against Wanda's impressive behind. He coats her orifice with more gel and slowly slips the head into her ass. Wanda gasps, relaxes, pushes slightly back against him, her mouth open as his cock slips further inside. I crawl onto my knees, lean over and give her a kiss. Our tongues play tag. Behind me, one of the triplets spreads the cheeks of my own ass and slowly slides his dick into my cunt. I can feel his hip bones against my behind as he begins to pump away. I groan, then push back against him as someone's mouth sucks my nipples and unknown hands playfully spank the cheeks of first my ass, then Wanda's. And that is how we come again and again and again until I pass out.

And I would have been happy to stay that way, perhaps rousing occasionally for another visit to the sexathon, but instead there's a pounding on the door that sounds like a battering ram wielded by members of the LAPD, and Odell's voice yelling, "Lydia! LaShaWanda! Are you in there?"

I grab a UNLV T-shirt from beside the bed, slip it over my naked body, and climb over eight legs, eight arms, and four prostrate bodies to open the door.

"Odell, what's up?" I say, rubbing sleep from my eyes and yawning. "What time is it, anyway?"

"Almost six in the morning," Odell says, glancing at his watch. "Acey just got back from San Francisco. She's in the kitchen with Marvini making breakfast and coffee. Get Wanda up, get dressed, and meet us down there ASAP."

"What's Acey doing back? I thought she wasn't supposed to be coming home until Saturday night."

"Supposed is the operative word. Acey ran into Barbaralee Edison, some deep shit went down, and she's back to fill us in. Also, Exultia Wallace left a message confirming a meeting with us and a delegation from F.U. on August 14, but we can't figure out who made that arrangement," Odell looks at me quizzically.

"Oh yeah, that. I meant to tell you about that, but me and Wanda got caught up."

Odell looks over my shoulder at the tangled bodies on the bed and whistles softly.

"I can see that. How'd they do?"

"Words cannot express," I say, stretching. "Suffice it to say they're ready, willing, and extremely able."

"Good. We're almost full, and there're a couple of last minute bookings, one Slow Jam and an In and Out. I've now got ten members of my staff with erection issues, so we desperately need the boys. Get it together and come downstairs. We've got a lot of shit to talk about. Apparently Barbaralee is in on T. Terry's plans to descend on Reno, and I think that means us, next week."

"All right, all right. I'll get Wanda and we'll be down in a few minutes."

An hour later the four of us are sitting around the big butcher block table in the kitchen, the *National Chronicle* article and copies of Barbaralee's columns spread out on the table, cradling second or third cups of coffee and looking grim. Plates stacked with Marvini's blueberry waffles, home-made turkey sausages, home-fried potatoes, and salmon eggs benedict sit in front of us, along with a big pot of Dick Dixmoor's favorite oatmeal, untouched and rapidly congealing. I'm usually starved after a night of boning, but this morning's conversation is enough to make me lose my appetite.

"Let me get this shit straight," Wanda finally says. "T. Terry's summoned his army of anti-sex reactionaries to Reno for a rally, and we suspect he plans to make A Sister's Spa the focus of his new crusade. Barbaralee plans to bust us out big time in her next column, although she's willing to make it all go away if the price is right. Exultia Wallace and her band of merry white feminists feel excluded by their 'black sisters' and arrive for a tour and what unfortunately promises to be a 'sisterhood is powerful' tete a tete next week. Have I forgotten anything?"

"I've now got ten workers whose hard-ons are unreliable and, according to a few exit questionnaires, unimpressive," Odell says. "That's about twenty-five percent of the staff, and we're almost booked solid. We can probably manage with a little juggling, but if any more workers go down, it'll start hurting business."

Acey shakes her currently curly head and rubs her forehead.

"Is *that* it?" She glares at each of us, as if daring someone to add to the bad news.

"Now, don't blame the messenger," Wanda says. "But when I cleared the machine of overnight bookings, there was also a message from Jacques Westin, the *National Chronicle* reporter. He says he was at the NBA dinner, spoke to Barbaralee Edison, and wants Acey or Lydia to call him back ASAP."

"I'm gonna kill that fucking bitch," I yell.

"Be sure to use a silver stake and carry a cross," Wanda mutters.

"We were doing so well. I can't believe everything's falling apart," Acey wails. "What are we going to do?"

"After I drive the stake through Barbaralee's heaving chest, I'm going to talk to Jacques Westin," I say.

"Talk to him? For what?" Acey asks.

"Look Ace, what choice do we have?" I say. "Westin's smart, tenacious, and if he's calling us he already knows something, and we need to find out what it is. If we don't call him back we'll look as if we have something to hide. If we do, at least we can get our side of the story out." Acey nods thoughtfully, staring into the pantry.

"Remind me what our side of the story is, besides providing much great sex and getting paid in the process," Wanda says.

Before I can open my mouth, Acey says, "We're black women who had a dream and made it a reality. Sister entrepreneurs building a successful business serving the needs of black women in an entirely legal business. The nature of the service we provide really shouldn't be a part of the equation."

"Yeah, and I shouldn't eat this waffle, but I'm going to," Wanda says, spearing one from the plate in front of her. "What about the moral issue, as it were?"

"What moral issue? The only reason there is one is because T. Terry says what we're doing is immoral, an analysis none of us, or the hundreds of women we've serviced in the past month, agrees with," I say.

"I hear you, but we've got to spell that out, elaborate on what our position is," Odell says.

"Women wanna get fucked, men wanna fuck 'em, and we use condoms," Wanda says, chuckling through a mouthful of waffle.

"That's about it, Wanda, although we've got to put it in language that's suitable for publication," Acey says. I can see something in my old boon Ace toughening up by the moment. I don't know what went down with her and Matthew when she was back home, but something seems to have changed—for the better, as far as I can tell.

"The truth is that we're black women, we love black women, and we want to enable sisters to have their sexual needs met in a clean, safe, loving environment for a fair price. Our men are required to wear condoms, have weekly medical check-ups, and are carefully chosen and trained to provide pleasure without pain. What's the problem with that?" Acey says, her brown eyes flashing.

"Nothing. As far as I'm concerned, that sounds like an award citation from the local Chamber of Commerce," Odell says, adding, "Maybe you should say something about the employment opportunities for black men."

"That's a good point. We should big up the service-to-the-black-man aspect since it's there, but also because you know these men—and more than a few demoralized, misguided women—go ballistic when black women do anything that in the end ain't about uplifting the brothers," I agree.

"True. Let's emphasize that A Sister's Spa now provides gainful employment to, including the support staff, more than sixty black men, at least some of whom might otherwise be a burden on society," Odell says. "Don't forget to let him know we pay unemployment and disability benefits, taxes, and even offer a pension plan after three years of service."

"That's all well and good. But the bottom line is, we're still running a whorehouse for women, aren't we? How do we get around that?" Wanda drawls.

"Compare and contrast," Acey says. "Talk about what it's like out there picking up random sex. The increase of STDs and AIDS in the black community, unwanted pregnancies, a woman getting beaten up just trying to get a piece—"

"Not to mention all the plain old bad sex floating around out there," I say.

"That too," Acey agrees. "We're providing sex in a safe, satisfaction-guaranteed environment. Jobs. A contribution to the economy. If

T. Terry had any sense, he'd back off and give us one of those Brother-hood Awards."

"He can keep his jiveass award as long as he backs off," I say. "Wanda, can you follow up with Jacques? Odell, can you talk to the afflicted men again and see if you can find something they have in common that might explain their impotence? That way me and Acey can try to figure out how to deal with the Reverend Tiger and Barbaralee. And Wanda, do you think you can persuade Muffin to come up for a few days and organize the meeting with F.U. next week? Okay?" Everyone nods but Odell.

"Listen, I need help: I've increased the workers' vitamins and their dose of ViriMax, made three meals a day and an hour in the gym manda-tory, shortened the work load, and they're still petering out. I'm stuck," Odell says, frowning and shaking his head. "I've done everything except crawl into bed with them and do observational research."

"Well, I guess that's next," Wanda says.

Odell bristles.

"Listen, we agreed when I took the job I wouldn't be a sex worker, but part of management. If that's going to change, I'm out of here."

"Be cool, Odell. Nobody wants your ass in bed with the clients, just your eyes in the bedroom," Wanda says.

"And that means what?"

"We've got to catch them in the act, like people do those psycho nannies who beat up children. It means we need to put one of those itty-bitty surveillance cameras in a few of the rooms and tape what goes down behind closed doors. Maybe that way we can figure out what's turning the workers off."

"Spy on the clients?" Acey asks skeptically. "I'm sure that's uncon-stitutional."

"Only if they find out, which they won't," Wanda says.

"It's still not right, Wanda. It makes me feel like a combination of Larry Flynt and Richard Nixon."

"We're not paranoid, obsessed megalomaniacs, nor are we pornog-raphers, Acey. We're just trying to figure out why some of the workers are having penis problems," I interject.

"Who's going to monitor them?"

"The four of us can take turns. If there's nothing on them, into the incinerator they go. How's that? If nothing turns up in a couple of weeks, we take the cameras down and move on to plan B." Acey nods slowly.

"What is plan B?"

"Damned if I know, but hopefully we'll come up with something," Wanda says.

"That sounds fair."

I grin at Wanda. "Great idea, girl."

"Yeah, wish I'd thought of it when I was on Wall Street," she mutters.

"Wall Street? What?"

"Forget it," Wanda says. "Listen, we can buy the cameras at the Radio Shack in town, but we need someone we can trust to install them."

"The boys can do it," Odell offers. "When they were in high school they earned money by secretly taping themselves having sex and then charging their friends to watch the videos in the garage."

"Damn! Those triplets just have a plethora of skills," I laugh, glancing at the clock over the stove. "All right, it's almost seven o'clock; we need to get to work, since the paying customers will start waking up and arriving soon. Odell, can you take the twins, get the cameras, and start putting them into the rooms?"

"Sure. We'll do the bedrooms during the changeover and the lounge, kitchen, pool area, and other public rooms in between."

The four of us stand up and put our coffee cups in the sink, getting ready for a long week. The good news is that the mood of unavoidable impending doom of a few hours ago has been replaced by, if not exactly determination and defiance, then at least a plan. On our way out, I stop Acey.

"Ace, I almost forgot. How was Matthew's big speech?"

She closes her eyes with a wince, then exhales. "Matthew's speech. I totally forgot." She starts to massage both temples, as if trying to prevent a headache from emerging. "After that encounter with Barbaralee, all I could think about was getting back here as soon as possible."

"I'm sure he'll understand."

"If he even noticed I was gone," Acey says bitterly. "Between nerves and being sucked up to by Debi Mountain, he hardly seemed to notice I was there. Don't assume he realized I left."

"Guess there was no chance to have a meaningful conversation," I say, putting oral quotation marks around the last two words.

"Lydia, back off," Acey snaps. "I've got enough shit to deal with today without getting more of it from my best friend."

Before I can respond, the back door opens and Chef Marvini steps inside, his arms full of fresh basil from his kitchen garden. "You kids didn't eat anything," he says, admonishing us with his index finger. "What's the matter, forgot to put your teeth in? You could have at least gummed some oatmeal," he adds, gesturing toward the untouched pot on the table.

30

LIFE DOESN'T STOP WHEN THERE'S A CRISIS. INSTEAD IT EITHER accelerates or goes into slow motion, and what Lydia calls "the every day shit of life" keeps coming, even when life, death, or the potential demise of A Sister's Spa demands all of our attention and energy.

It's been almost a week since we read Jacques Westin's article and Barbaralee's columns, and since I left the NBA dinner without a word. I've been calling Matthew every day, but haven't been able to reach him, which in itself is strange, since he has a secretary, a cell phone, and a beeper and is one of those people who definitely never likes to be out of touch. I'd left three sets of messages, but the truth is I was kind of relieved. I was looking forward to talking to him and dreading it at the same time. I figured he'd be furious, of course, that I'd left the NBA convention without a word and missed his speech. I'd lost the neutral ground I'd been on the night of the dinner by leaving abruptly. That action had put me far in the wrong and given Matthew license, which I'm sure he'd take advantage of, to be angry with me. I also know from almost two years with him that talking about his feelings, and our future together—which was the first thing on my agenda—wasn't something he'd feel comfortable with.

As we have been since opening weekend, the spa is incredibly busy, which I guess is good since it tires me out and there's too much that has to be done to worry about the storm of the righteous that's brewing. Meanwhile, everything at the spa is going well. Several clients had asked for a more romantic way of easing into the spa experience, and Odell had come up with the concept of The Chance Encounter. Women were told to go to the baggage claim area once they landed and someone would come and meet them. We'd let them wait fifteen minutes and then send in a sex worker in a suit or golf clothes to present himself as a safe, legitimate type who had a car waiting and just happened to be going their way.

I was skeptical when Odell first came up with the idea, and argued that women wouldn't get into an unknown man's car in a strange city, but

Odell assured me that he'd met many women that way and that it all depended on a brother being smooth, well-dressed, and having a chauffeur. Even though we all know that criminals and perverts don't look a certain way, and don't all drive rusted Chevy trucks, at the same time we think we can judge who's safe by the way they look. Odell was right, because The Chance Encounter worked every time.

Once one of our guys got the sister in the back seat of the car, his job was to chat, relax, and seduce. By the time they got to A Sister's Spa, the women were usually so eager to get to the bedroom we had to speed up our already express check-in, and it wasn't until later that they realized all of this was a carefully contrived set-up, part of our full service. We'd then rush the sex worker who'd been driving back into his shorts so we could assign him to the next arriving guest.

In some ways A Sister's Spa is becoming like the national headquarters of a vast, vibrant sorority, with members of all types dropping in unexpectedly twenty-four hours a day, seven days a week. A sister I knew from high school arrived with a contingent from Black Women United, a community-based group that reclaimed and rehabbed abandoned housing. A woman I went to college with brought her daughter and six bridesmaids for an overnight visit in lieu of a wedding shower. My assistant, L.E., busy running the San Francisco spa, sent a group of customers for an overnight visit, along with the message that business was booming and she regretted that she couldn't find the time to come along. A contingent of women between ages sixty-five and eighty, members of the Black Grey Panthers, came for a two-night stay. Afterward, the workers joked that they had to work hard to keep up with those ten elderly women; their libidos might have been old, but they were mighty powerful.

And then there is the now-ubiquitous Lorene Cunningham. She comes as often as allowed, once a week. She always asks for Sequoia and we try to give him to her, since a few of the other workers had complained of soreness in their dicks after servicing her. Apparently her sexual tastes focus on giving blow jobs and occasionally having anal sex. Sequoia is reliable, steady, and completely unfazed by Lorene, who plainly adores him.

"That bitch is over the top. I mean truly dick-whipped. We need to ban her from the premises," Wanda suggested. But Wanda was given to overstatement and, besides, we could count on her for a steady $1,000 a week.

Two more men are now having penile dysfunction issues, which means that twelve workers are sporadically out of commission. We have all of our customers covered with no complaints, but just barely, thanks in no small part to the triplets, each of whom is doing a yeoman's job. Like their big brother, they love sex. The other good news is that unlike him, they have no problem being perceived purely as studs. To compensate for the men who couldn't be relied on to get it up, we have the triplets doing secret double duty: when one woman goes to swim, eat, or have a massage, we send her triplet off to service a new client, then back again before the first woman even knows he'd been gone. Overgrown kids, they seem to love being able to satisfy the sexual needs of multiple women at a time, and we promised them big bonuses once staffing was back to normal.

Besides doing what they were paid for, the triplets had finished installing video cameras in a third of the bedrooms and the common areas, the better to see what was affecting the lagging workers. They hooked it up so that me, Lydia, LaShaWanda, and Odell could monitor the rooms from our private bedroom televisions, and even stuck an extra monitor in the back of the kitchen pantry for convenience.

I must admit that even though the idea of secretly taping our workers and clients made me squeamish, once DeQuan explained to me how it worked, I was fascinated. With the click of a special remote I could move from room to room, or I could split the screen into as many as eight windows and watch what was happening in that many locations simultaneously. At first I was mesmerized by multiple images of twats, dicks, mouths, and fingers in every imaginable combination (and some I personally never would have thought of), but after a few days the novelty pretty much wore off. I guess repetition desensitized all of us toward the erotic aspect of what was actually occurring. We scanned for odd behaviors, kept a sharp eye out for limp penises, and moved on.

More fascinating than the fucking was watching Odell finesse information from the twelve affected brothers during a meeting in the lounge. They'd all gotten a clean bill of health from the doctor on staff; there was no physiological reason why their erections were sometimes less than erect. Odell was hoping something would come to light during a casual conversation with the men, so that he could get them back to functioning at the high level we required and preclude anyone else from coming down with a similar malady.

"Listen brothers, I know what you're going through is not easy. But I thought if we all talked maybe we could come up with a solution to your mutual problem," Odell says. Twelve gorgeous men sit or sprawl in chairs, all in various stages of orange and undress. Black, Latino, white, from twenty-one to forty-five, to a man they look as if they'd rather be anyplace else but in that room.

"Everyone's eating a healthy breakfast, lunch, and dinner and working out, right?" The men nod. "Getting enough sleep?" The men in the room burst into laughter.

"Odell, we're sex workers, we never get enough sleep," King drawls. "Anyway, that never had this effect on us before we started working here."

"Why don't each of you tell me, briefly, what problems you've been experiencing," Odell says. The room is silent, the faces of the men blank. Odell clears his throat. "Look brothers, I know talking about this isn't easy. I'm not trying to get in your shit; I just want to find the problem so we can figure out how to correct it. No biggie."

Phil, a young white worker, guffaws morosely. "That's the problem right there, bro. It sure ain't no biggie."

"It's so small I don't even recognize my shit," Alton says. A couple of the men around him twitch uncomfortably.

"Okay, that's a start. Can someone tell me when this first happened?" All eyes in the room are cast down or stare out the window. No one says anything.

"Then I'll read from the forms the doctor filled out after your visits," Odell suggests, leafing through the stack of papers on his clipboard. "Now, it says here that one of you told the doctor you knew something was wrong when you woke up without a hard-on."

"For fifteen years my dick's been hard when I wake up and suddenly, nothing," says King, the first man we hired. "I'd been in a marathon ménage with two freaks from that sorority the night before, so I'm thinking, okay, maybe I'm just tired. I shower, work out, eat me a three-course breakfast, go back to my room to check my man out before my next client arrives."

"And?"

"And nothing, Odell. Zip. I haven't seen Peter looking so small since we were little boys." Around him, a few of the men nod knowingly.

"Did you take any actions to address the situation?"

"Shit yeah, a nap. I thought I was just tired," Alton says.

"I spanked the monkey, but the monkey did not respond," says Phil.

"I spent an hour looking through my favorite issue of *Big Butt Broads* and couldn't even get a rise from those sweet big asses. That's when I knew something was seriously wrong," Will adds.

"Look, I went to work, figuring that being with a lovely lady would do the trick," Oscar sighs. "Well, she didn't. I had to eat that pussy until she fell asleep so she wouldn't see how limp my shit was."

Odell nods. "Other than that, you feel okay?"

Trevor lets out a loud snort.

"Other than that, Odell? Shit man, I know you're management and not a sex worker, but you're a man. Get real. There is no other than that. If my dick don't work, all the rest of my shit is messed up."

"My bad," Odell says. "Let me put it this way: Anyone have any other signs of illness?" Around the room, heads shake no.

"Hey, I'm probably in the best shape I've ever been. Living out here in this clean desert air, eating three healthy squares courtesy of Chef Marvini, with a gym right on the premises? And getting paid for boning appreciative women? Shit, I'm living such a righteous life, I woulda thought my dick'd experience a growth spurt," says Wesley as the men around him laugh.

"If my dick would just get his shit together, life would be perfect," someone says as others nod their agreement.

"What you gonna do, Odell? You think it's some sort of flu or what?" Alton asks.

"I'm not sure. That's why the doc took more blood from each of you, and he's gonna run another set of tests, for anemia, mono, shit like that. We'll figure out what's happening and fix it. Now we need to decide what to do until then. We're packed this weekend and need all hands on deck."

"Should we bring our limp dicks, too?" King asks angrily. "What good's that going to do our clients?"

"Maybe you could see this not as an obstacle, but an opportunity," Odell begins.

"An opportunity to be humiliated? I'll pass," someone grumbles.

"No, an opportunity to see for yourselves once and for all that women's orgasms are clitoral, not vaginal. I mean, most women might like penetration, but science says most of them don't need it to get off."

"What are you saying, man?" Trevor asks.

"Until we solve this problem, why not take the dick out of it, that's what I'm saying. What would you all think about being part of a new package called, let's say, Serious Eating. Bringing women to multiple orgasms using only mouths, fingers, and toys, dicks off limits?"

Will laughs. "Yo, that could work. Truth is, most of these women seem as interested in my rocking their little man in a boat as they are in any other shit anyway." Around him other workers nod.

"Cool. I'm getting tired of bed rest, man," says Paul, a honey-colored former fireman who retired on disability at thirty-one after a fall from a ladder. "I look at bed as a place to work, not chill," he adds, chuckling.

"Everybody down with that idea?" Odell asks. The twelve men around him nod.

"Okay, let me go talk to the bosses and I'll get back to you ASAP," Odell says, standing up.

"Listen man. This arrangement's cool as a temporary thing. But I know I speak for all of us when I say we want our dicks back the way they used to be," says King. "Hey. I love eating pussy, but you need a dick to rock a woman like her back ain't got no bone."

Later that evening I run into Odell in the hallway on my way to the kitchen to meet Lydia and grab a quick supper, but when he sees my raised eyebrows and questioning look, he shakes his head in frustration.

"Nothing. I've talked to each of them, and I still haven't a clue what's turning these brothers off. Neither do they. They don't feel bad, they're healthy, they enjoy the work, and they all say getting hard hasn't been a problem before now."

"All men always say that. Did you push?"

"As hard as I could," Odell laughs. "A couple were willing to admit to having experienced PJ issues—"

"PJ issues?"

"Pre-jac, premature ejaculation," Odell explains. "But they all insisted they'd never been incapable of getting hard. As a man, I can tell you this shit is strange."

"It is that," I agree. "What's the prognosis?"

"The doctor's got no clue. Phil, Trevor, and Wesley are all vegetarians, and they've been on a juice fast for two days and swear Jimmie's on the rise. Hopefully they can get back to work tomorrow. As for the other nine, there's no improvement."

"Suggest that they drink lots of liquids, stick to veggies and grains, and cut out the dairy and flesh. That might help," I suggest.

"Cool," Odell says, making a note on the pad he always carries. "We've got a full house starting tomorrow, and I'm thinking that since none of them feel bad—and, as you and Lydia never tire of pointing out, most women's orgasms are clitoral, not vaginal—we tailor a package around everything but the need for a hard dick and put them back to work if they're willing."

"That'll work temporarily. But Odell, women like to see a hard penis, even if they're not going to do anything with it," I say.

"I know. And we're working on that. Now, I gotta see if my condom delivery came in," he calls over his shoulder as he hurries away.

Lydia loves to call me a pessimist and say I told you so. Maybe she's right, but with the exception of the erection issue, I can't get over being amazed at how smoothly life is going inside the spa. Sure we're busy, but that is a good thing. For the most part our staff is reliable and easy to work with, and our customers are deeply and profoundly satisfied. It's the world outside our property that creates trouble. Even with the phones ringing, sisters constantly checking in and out, and making sure things run as smoothly as possible inside the spa, it's impossible to forget the trouble gathering just over the horizon.

"So, any thoughts on what to do about T. Terry and Barbaralee?" I ask. We're sitting in the kitchen eating salads during a brief break for dinner. Behind us, Chef Marvini cleans shrimp for that night's special, Creole Gumbo.

Lydia can't resist saying through a mouthful of mesclun and goat cheese, "Well, Barbaralee's easy. She'll turn on her own mother if the price is right. All we have to do to get her to retract that column and leave us alone is pay her off. T. Terry's a harder nut to crack."

"Tell me about it. It's hard to hold someone accountable if he believes he's been chosen by the Lord."

"Amen, and pass the apple juice," Lydia chuckles.

"My father had at least two distinct faces. One for the congregation: the patient, thoughtful, gentle man of the cloth. And another for his family: the drill sergeant who tolerated no flaws and ran our house like it was one of those boot camps for bad children."

"Your poor mom. I could never figure how she stood it."

"I think she really did love him. Why else would she have tolerated him for fifty years? I guess she saw something in him we couldn't," I say, shaking my head.

"Did you ever ask her?"

"All the time. Every time Daddy refused to let me do something for no reason—and as you know, Lyds, that was frequently—I'd ask her why she'd married such a mean man. I kept asking too, after I was grown and out of the house."

"And?"

"And she never would give me an answer, would always say, 'Your father means well.' Then when she was sick, a few days before she died, I was at the house helping her take a bath, and the front door slammed. She asked me to go see who it was, and it was Daddy, coming back from the church. When I went back into the bathroom she was lying down in the tub, almost submerged. I told her it was just Daddy coming back in. I was angry with him for slamming the door; he knew Mommy was dying. Maybe she heard the anger in my voice, cause she just shook her head from side to side, I remember the motion made little waves in the water. Then she said, 'Your poor father. He always wanted to be someone else, when who he was was more than enough.'" Even though it's been almost five years, I can feel my eyes fill with tears.

"Damn. Now that is deep. I miss her, too," Lydia says, rubbing my shoulders with the flat of her hand. "What made you tell me that now? You think that's true of T. Terry, too?"

"That he's after us because he feels inadequate about something that has nothing to do with us? Maybe. Why?"

"If we could figure out what's really motivating him, we could use it to beat him down."

"He's been around so long it could be anything," I say. "Daddy was an officer of the Baptist Brotherhood and Boulé for years. I can remember him coming home from meetings and talking to my mother about how desperately T. Terry wanted to be rich, to be more famous than Dr. King, to be the leader of the Negro people and leave a legacy. 'He doesn't understand that the road to redemption is paved with good works, not photo ops or gold,' Daddy used to say. 'He seems to believe that if he's on television enough, that'll make him the leader. Brother Tiger doesn't want to do the difficult work. And tell me why in the Lord's name does he speaks in rhymes?' Then he'd just put his forehead in his hands."

"So you think T. Terry thinks he can make the big time attacking us?" Lydia asks.

"I've heard for years that he's had a steady girlfriend, not to mention more than a few passing fancies. Don't forget, as a preacher he has his pick of church sisters willing to confuse their minister with their man. I mean, he's in his sixties now and still looks great. I seriously doubt if he's truly concerned about morality or immorality, ours or anyone else's. I think he's just looking for a gimmick."

"And unfortunately, we're it."

"It's a shame. We're just trying to do our thing, run our little business that doesn't hurt anyone."

"Don't sound so down, we're not beat yet. Come on, Ace, you're the logical one. There's got to be something we can do," Lydia says plaintively, sounding just like she did when we were teenagers and her mother busted us climbing back into the house through her bedroom window at one in the morning after sneaking downtown to watch the hippies and acid freaks outside a concert at the Fillmore. That time I started babbling about the constellations, the wonders of astronomy, and convinced Mrs. Beaucoup we'd simply been in the park across the street, lying on the grass and looking at the stars.

"Yes, there's something we can do. Pray, and have faith that God's on our side, not T. Terry's," I say, standing up and putting my plate in the sink. "Great salad, Marvini, thanks. And Lydia, I'm serious, a little prayer might help, and it sure can't hurt." I start to ask her to throw in some words for the conversation I'm about to have with Matthew, but don't. Truth is, in that respect I'm not exactly sure what I want her to pray for.

When I finally reach Matthew it's almost midnight and I have to shout into the phone in order to be heard over the bass rumble of his motorized treadmill and the squawk of argument blaring from Court TV.

"Matthew?"

"Yes."

"Matthew, can you hear me? It's Acey."

"I know who this is."

"What's happening, baby? How are you?"

"Perhaps I should ask you that. I take it you are in hospital or making funeral arrangements for a beloved relative. What other reason could you have for your abrupt departure from the NBA dinner, an affair that had been on our schedule for months?"

"In hospital?" And why does he pronounce "schedule" as if he's Queen Elizabeth's nephew? Matthew's never even been to England. Still, I'm the guilty party here, so I say, "Honey, one of the reasons I'm calling is to say I'm sorry. Something urgent came up at the spa and I had to catch the last plane out. I am really, really sorry, baby. How'd your speech go?"

"Sorry does not help. It is, in fact, a useless word," Matthew says huffily, not bothering to ask me what happened at the spa that caused me to run out of the Ritz in terror. But at the moment that's a good thing. I cannot imagine convincing him I'm sorry, discussing our relationship, and telling him what A Sister's Spa is really about all in one conversation. The truth is, I'm not convinced I'll be able to accomplish any one of the above the way this conversation's starting.

"Well then, how about, I sincerely apologize for missing your speech? Hello? Matthew, are you there?"

"Yes."

"Did you hear what I said?"

"Yes. I heard you."

"How'd the speech go?"

"Obviously, you were not interested enough to stay and hear it. Nor, apparently, have you read the paper recently. Otherwise, you would know how it went," Matthew speaks so softly I have to push the receiver into my flesh and hold my breathe to hear him.

"Fabulous, I knew you'd kick ass," I say cheerfully. "And I've been trying to call you for days. Did you get my messages?"

"Yes."

"Well, were you going to call me back, sweetie?"

"I do not think so."

What is it with this man? Does he think not using contractions makes him sound more intelligent? It just makes him seem like an up-tight jerk. But he's my uptight jerk, so I say, "What?"

"I said I did not intend to return your calls."

"Why?"

"Pardon me?"

"You heard me, Matthew. I asked why you didn't intend to return my calls."

"And I could ask you why you left the ballroom so precipitously."

"I told you, there was a crisis at the spa and I had to get back."

"Well, that is the rub, is it not?"

"What does that mean?"

"It means that perhaps we have different goals and are at cross pur-poses. One of the biggest evenings of my life, and you were not by my side. That would seem to me to be clear indication that you are not seri-ously concerned with my life."

"That's not true. I called didn't I, which is more than I can say for you. And you haven't even asked me what was so urgent at the spa."

Matthew gives one of those contrived, condescending chuckles.

"Ah, you are right. What was the problem? A broken treadmill, a whirlpool that would not whirl, an overheated sauna?"

"Excuse me?"

"My point is that whatever crisis you and your little spa encountered pales in comparison to the myriad crises facing African-American attorneys that I addressed in my critically acclaimed speech last Saturday."

"So now the truth comes out," I hiss. I can't believe he's giving me this kind of shit, and something snaps in me.

"What truth is that?"

"That you have contempt for what I do, that it's not important. That my 'little spa' can't hold a candle to your 'big career.' Am I right?"

"As the old saying goes, if the shoe fits . . ."

I'd called Matthew to talk about what we need to do to make our relationship work. Even though I knew I'd have to eat crow for missing his speech, I'd thought once that was done we could move on to the discussion of us. Instead I'm being soundly dissed. I'm speechless. Until that is, I hear a female voice call out in the background, "Mattie! *The Johnnie Cochran Show*'s about to come on."

"'Mattie?' Matthew, who's there with you?"

"A friend and colleague."

"At one in the morning? Who is it, that right-wing opportunist Debi Mountain? I should have known from the way she was acting at the dinner that she was into more than your legal prowess!"

"Perhaps," Matthew says, and I swear he has the nerve to sound smug.

"Well, hand me the phone and let me give sistergirl a heads up not to throw out her vibrator, because she *will* be disappointed. You may be a brilliant legal mind, but when it comes to the bedroom, ain't nothing going on but the rent."

"Acey, there is no need for anger. Relationships end. As the song goes, 'I did my best, but I guess my best was not good enough.'"

"It wasn't, it wasn't good enough, 'Mattie,' and that's an understatement," I yell. "The truth is you never did your best, you barely even tried. And it's not just the sex, although that's definitely a problem. It's your refusal to talk about what you're feeling, to extend yourself the slightest bit, to see what I do as important, to think about anyone but yourself. Top that mountain of crap off with the fact that even before the bypass, sex with you was mediocre, and that now it's nonexistent, and that's serious trouble."

"Are you through?"

"Almost. You always looked down your nose at Lydia, and I want you to know I know why. You're jealous. You know how I know this? Because even though she's my best friend in the world, I'm jealous of her, too. Because she's not afraid of anything, and I know that what you are, and what I really am, is scared. Afraid to admit passions and go after them, afraid to take risks, always playing the safe side, which is why I've spent almost two years trying to make it work with you. Well, it's all over, you lousy Casanova!"

Matthew sighs.

"What venom. Perhaps professional help might—"

I cut him off. "The only help I need is to get laid by a man who likes women and knows how to make them happy. And I've got that right here at my very own little spa, as you call it. Think about me getting my brains balled out by a fine, slim twenty-six-year-old while you and Debi haul your fat asses on that stupid treadmill's road to nowhere!" I yell.

Then I slam down the phone and burst into tears.

31

"HE CUPS MY HEELS IN THE PALMS OF HIS HANDS AND CARESSES THE bones of my ankle with his fingers, then begins slowly moving up my legs, kneading the flesh of my calves. Past my knees he slides his hands inside my thighs so that the tips of his fingers curve under my legs. As his fingers move closer to my vagina, little silvery wings of anticipation flutter through me as I lay face down on the bed.

"His tongue licks and kisses the back of first one knee, then the other as his fingers now gently pull and tease my pubic hair. The muscles in my pussy open as his fingers lightly trace a circle around my opening. I push back slightly and the tips of his fingers slip inside me. He holds them there as I twist my torso around to face him, arch up to kiss his thick dark lips as his hands play just inside me.

"From my mouth his lips drift down to take a hard nipple between his teeth. He nips the end softly but insistently, and I press toward him, wanting to bury myself in his mouth. I shift my body up, then down, enveloping his finger. His mouth rises, his teeth bite that spot on my neck between my chin and shoulder blade, and I moan. He turns me over on my back and kisses me gently, over and over and over. I can feel the ridges on his hard penis swinging against my thighs as he hovers above me.

"Carefully, he places a leg on either of his shoulders, angling my hips upward, then sets the head of his cock against my wet pussy and thrusts forward. His penis enters me and I exhale slowly as my muscles wrap themselves around it. 'Breathe,' he whispers, and only then do I realize I have been holding my breath, as if trying to freeze this moment. I inhale and he slips further inside until his pelvic bone touches mine. His hips do not move back and forth but in slow, lazy circles, until there is no part of my welcoming pussy that remains untouched by his hard, probing penis.

"I reach up, put my hands on his shoulders, and massage the back of his neck. He grunts softly, increases the rhythm of his thrusting. My fingers wander up to caress his neck, cheeks, lips, which open to envelope and suck insistently on my fingers. He stops a moment, then says, 'I want to see you touch yourself.' I place my wet fingers on my clit and rub hard. He increases the motion of his hips and as he circles inside me and they push my fingers harder against my hot spot, dragging my fingers against it and forcing me to increase the pressure. The air flutters with more of those silvery things.

"He leans down, covers my lips with his, and slips his tongue inside my mouth deeper, deeper as his dick follows suit. I lift my neck to meet his mouth, my hips to meet his hot penis, and my poonani opens wider and wider to take in all of him. Over his shoulders, my legs are stiff, toes curled. A thin sheen of sweat covers both our bodies. The motion of his hips slows and he grinds his hips against mine, his dick embedded deep inside me, pushing forward. I gasp as my muscles grasp him and then I come, my whole body contracting and releasing, mouth open and moaning, those little silver, fluttering things raining down around us in a sexual meteor shower."

"Sexual meteor shower?" I say. "I like that, and I know what you mean by those silvery things. All right, so what happened next?"

Acey's head jerks as if she's startled, and her eyes come back into focus. We're sitting in the kitchen having breakfast. Even though we're supposed to be scanning tapes on the pantry monitor, I'm more interested in getting the details of her interlude with Ahmad out of her, but she keeps drifting off into reverie.

"What didn't?" Acey laughs, knitting her fingers over her head and stretching backward. "I feel as if all the kinks are definitely ironed out," she grins.

"Damn straight. There's something to be said for great sex that doesn't have any other meaning than great sex. Oh, and I.T.Y.S." Acey laughs.

"Okay, okay, I know you told me so. But I had to work through my feelings about Matthew. Or what I thought were my feelings. I'm beginning to think I was holding on to Matthew not because I cared for him as much as because I was afraid to let go," she says sadly.

"Hey girl, don't sweat it. We've all been there, done that. Sometimes the shit we know seems safer than the shit we don't."

"You too?"

"Yeah, I've felt that way. Remember, I was married to Lorenzo for ten years. I've got a pretty advanced bullshit detector by now. You were married to a truly good man, Earl, so you're not as sensitized to the bullshit as I am, which isn't necessarily a bad thing. You just can't assume anything."

"Right. Like Mrs. Moore taught us in fourth grade; 'Don't assume, because it'll make an ass out of U and ME.' How did I forget that?"

"Good morning. What's funny?" Muffin says, startling us as she walks into the kitchen. With everything that's brewing, Wanda'd asked Muffin to spend the weekend at the spa and help keep things going if the shit gets crazy. She pours herself a cup of coffee and sips it, leaning against the counter.

"Long story," I shrug. "What's going on with Feminists United?"

"The meeting's set for tomorrow morning at eight. Exultia's bringing the head of each of their regions with her, that's twenty women. I made it clear the meeting has to end promptly at ten. And we've agreed on an agenda."

"Which is?"

"Forging an alliance between black womanists and white feminists, according to Exultia."

"What the hell is a womanist?"

"I think it's a black feminist who doesn't want to be called such because of the historic racism and exclusion of women of color in the traditional feminist movement," Muffin says, chuckling. "I've been doing some research."

"Muff, what kind of alliance with us does Exultia want?" Acey asks.

"I'm not real clear, but I think she wants three things. To bring more black women into F.U.; to gain access for white women to A Sister's Spa; and last, but not least, to kick T. Terry's ass once and for all."

"What's her beef with him?"

"Well, you know T. Terry's always been opposed to women's rights, black women's in particular. Exultia blames him for using the feminist movement as his personal whipping girl, and that's a quote, and undermining opportunities to build a multiracial women's coalition for the last forty years."

"She's right about that. Remember when he organized those prayer vigils outside O.J.'s trial? I almost went ballistic every time I saw those simple-minded sisters marching around with placards saying 'Free Our Brother," and 'O.J. Come Home.' O.J. ain't no brother of mine, and if he tried to come home, I'd have the locks changed."

"How about that national tour of the black community he tried to pull off a few years ago to celebrate Mike Tyson's release from prison? 'Homecoming for Brother Mike,'" Acey says.

"I distinctly recall that the first time I heard Anita Hill accused of being an erotomaniac, it was from T. Terry's lips."

"As your mom would say, Lyds, 'He's a bad cat.'"

"Exultia Wallace certainly thinks so," Muffin agrees. "F.U. keeps tabs on him, along with his pals Jerry Falwell, Pat Robertson, and a bunch of other chauvinist, right-wing so-called Christians; that's a quote, too. That's how she knew he was going to come after the spa almost before we did. It's funny, because she's agnostic, but when she talks about T. Terry, it's in almost biblical terms, as if it's a war between good and evil."

"What's her position about white women coming to the spa?"

"That white women are as much in need of the services we provide as women of color. That operating a racially segregated business is illegal. And that to welcome all women to A Sister's Spa would be a radical step in tearing down the barriers that have existed between black and white women for centuries." Muffin pauses. "Actually, I think she has a point."

"Intellectually, maybe. But I can't see how integrating the spa would work. How you gonna have Miss Ann in the room with Mammy and pretend the cotton field's suddenly level, that hundreds of years of history have just been wiped off the slate? Having vaginas does not true sisterhood make," I snap.

Muffin holds up the palms of her hands.

"Okay, okay. Don't blame the messenger, Lydia, I'm just trying to give you a heads up. I've got to go clear the answering machine. See you all later," she says, picking up her coffee cup. I pull at the earring dangling from my ear.

"This is going to be a hard couple of days." Acey says.

"Let's hope so, especially when it comes to our sex workers with their malfunctioning penises. Heaven help us."

"Will I do?" a man's voice says. I turn and look around the kitchen for Odell, Marvini, or one of the sex workers, and there's Earl, standing just inside the pantry, looking as fine as he did when I last saw him.

"Earl! You're in Nevada," Acey says, standing up. Earl smiles that familiar, lazy, sexy-as-hell smile.

"I told you I'd try and get here, baby darlin'."

"Damn. Damn. Damn! Earl! It's really you, huh? I thought Acey had finally lost her mind when she first told me you were living in her pantry, but I guess I was wrong."

Earl laughs.

"Well, I don't exactly live in the pantry. I visit when I can."

"Whatever. It's really you, right?"

"As much as it possibly can be, yes. Don't forget, I'm dead. Now, allow me to congratulate you on a successful business."

"Successful? Earl, you've been away too long," Acey says. "Since the last time you were here T. Terry Tiger's been organizing a morality crusade against us, the white feminists are demanding access in exchange for their support, a column in *Girlfriend!* has been attacking us for the past month, and—"

"Twelve of our workers' dicks won't get hard," I add.

Earl laughs. "On the positive side, the place is packed, you're making money hand over fist, the triplets have risen to the occasion in more ways than the obvious, and everything you need to defeat your enemies is right in front of you."

"Do they make you talk cryptically once you're dead?" I ask.

"Not exactly, but the way you look at life definitely changes. You suddenly see how much power individuals have, and you realize the challenge isn't to overcome powerlessness, it's to accept how powerful you already are."

"Earl. We need help, not Iyanla Vanzantisms," Acey says impatiently.

"It didn't seem as if you needed my help the other night with Matthew. Or Ahmad." Acey blushes.

"Well. You told me to trust my instincts and go for the pleasure, and that's what I did. Now I need some help from you, baby."

"No you don't, Ace. You all have it covered, believe me. That makes me know I can go and you'll be okay."

"Go where, back to Oakland?"

"No, baby darlin', go on to the next level. It's not natural for me to keep hanging around here. You need to go on with your life and I need to go on with my death."

"Go on with your death?"

"Death's just another kind of beginning. Eventually you'll understand what I mean. I loved you madly, Ace. But it's time for both of us to move on."

Earl's form begins to ripple slightly.

"Earl, wait!" Acey cries, moving toward the pantry.

"Yes, baby darlin'?"

"I . . . I . . . do you know how much I loved you, how happy you made me, how much I've missed you?" Acey says as tears roll down her cheeks. Earl smiles, gestures with his hands across her cheeks, and the tears disappear.

"I know. Me too, sweetie. We got so much more in life and in death than most people ever do. Now smile," he purrs. "Let me remember that gorgeous smile," and Acey grins.

"Beautiful," he says, his voice fading and body rippling. "A picture is worth a thousand words." Then he's gone, and the two of us sit in silence.

"Damn! I feel like I'm Whoopi Goldberg in *Ghost*," I finally say, getting up and walking into the pantry. Acey sits at the table, an odd happy-sad smile on her face, watching me as I scour the pantry.

"He was here, but now he's gone," she says simply. "I wonder what he meant by a picture being worth a thousand words?"

My eyes drift over to the monitor. Images from the hidden cameras in the room shuffle past: A voluptuous sister leans on a dresser as a man rides her from behind; two women and a man create a moving sculpture of arms, legs, and orifices; a man and a women engage in 69, faces buried in each other's genitals; a woman squats above a man's hard penis, gently lowering herself onto its head and then withdrawing; another sister's wide mouth envelopes a man's penis. Then we see an image of Lorene Cunningham, planted firmly on her enormous hands and knees, red silk dress pulled up over her rump. Behind her Sequoia eases his penis in and out of her ass.

"Darn, there is something so familiar about that woman," Acey says, frowning thoughtfully. She turns up the sound. We hear Lorene yelping, "All right, Daddy, all right! Take Mama to the bank! Take Mama to the bank!" I move up until my face is inches from the television. Then there's a flash in my mind like when a lightbulb burns out.

"Damn straight there's something familiar about her! I'd know that tired come line anywhere. That bitch ain't no woman, it's that god-damned bastard ex-husband of mine! Lorene is Lorenzo!"

32

"THAT'S WHAT I SAID. FOUR PLATTERS OF CHICKEN WINGS, A COUPLE dozen shrimp cocktails, and some kind of bread. What's that? No, I would not like a tray of crudités. Black folks don't want any damned miniature raw vegetables. That's correct, you heard me right. And send me a couple bottles each of scotch, bourbon, gin, and vodka, lots of ice, and some mixers. That's all coming to Reverend Tiger in the Presidential suite. And don't take all day." T. Terry slams down the phone on the bedside table and looks around the suite.

"Jeanette! What the hell are you doing in there? These folks are going to be banging on our door any minute, and I still need you to touch up some of these gray hairs. You know what I always say: A smattering of silver is distinguished, but a flood just means you're old!" T. Terry guffaws at his own joke and lies back on the pile of pillows on the king-size bed.

Kneeling on the cold, pink tile of the bathroom floor, her head hanging over the toilet bowl and both hands clutching its sides, Jeanette manages to squeeze out, "Coming, baby," before another mouthful of bile cascades from her lips into the toilet. She leans over the bowl and opens her mouth wide. She spits and, holding onto the edge of the sink, pulls herself up, turns on the cold water, and drops a washcloth underneath the faucet. When it is soaked she carefully wrings the water out, folds it neatly lengthwise, and presses it against her forehead. "I hate Nevada," she mutters to the wan, blotchy skinned woman with the disheveled hair in the mirror.

They'd been together in Reno for four days, preparing for the rally to kickstart the Crusade to Resurrect Morality. Tomorrow, Sunday, they march to A Sister's Spa. It seems to Jeanette that two-thirds of T. Terry's troops consist largely of old, angry, marginalized losers: tired ministers in shiny suits and pinkie rings who drive Cadillacs and think they're the Mack, and disgruntled cultural nationalists who still hadn't grasped that the 1970s were long gone and it was way past time for them to take a bath, comb their hair, and get a job.

Last, and worst of all to Jeanette's mind, were the women who came to follow these men, foremost among them Edna Mantz Thompson of Righteous Ebony Women After Respect and Power (REWARP). It was as if the sisters she led, even the ones born twenty years later, were stuck in the 1950s. As the world had changed and opportunities opened to them, they refused to move forward. They still hard-pressed their hair with hot combs and thought being a school teacher was the pinnacle of professional success. True, they kept black churches all around the country functioning, yet they demanded no voice or power in church affairs, and instead advocated that a black woman could have no greater role than supporting a black man and having his babies.

They clothed themselves in righteous superiority and passed judgment on women who were not like them. This one's too fast, too loud, too confident, too aggressive. This one's a whore, a slut, a temptress. If it was possible, Jeanette thought, their venom towards A Sister's Spa was greater than that of the men. The men, T. Terry first among them, at least attacked the spa for cynical, opportunistic reasons; the women's anger was nothing but curdled envy.

Looking at her face in the mirror, Jeanette wonders how different she really is, once you get past the bad hair and lame clothes, from women like Edna Thompson, wonders how she got to this place with T. Terry.

"'Nette! They'll be here in a few minutes. Are you coming out?" Terry yells as Jeanette finishes applying lip liner.

"Okay, baby, okay. You don't have to yell. My stomach already hurts, I don't need a headache on top of that," she says as she walks into the bedroom.

"Again? You've been sick since we got here," he says accusingly.

"I told you I don't like Nevada. Too dry. I also told you I don't like this whole crusade against A Sister's Spa. I think it's wrong."

"Whoring is right? Casual sex without marriage is right? Making money off lonely, needy, gullible sisters is right?"

"Come off it, Terry. No lectures, please," Jeanette scoffs. "And as for what's right or wrong, talk about the pot calling the kettle black."

"Exactly what's that supposed to mean?"

"You've been a married preacher for forty years and fucking me for twenty-five. I'd say that about covers whoring, adultery, and, Reverend

Tiger, taking advantage of those lonely, gullible sisters you profess to be concerned about."

" 'Nette, what's gotten into you? Has your, ah, little friend come to visit?"

"What little friend?"

"You know, baby, your monthly."

"No. Are you suggesting that I'm out of control with PMS or some shit?"

"Jeanette, I was simply trying to be sensitive to what's going on with you. Let's face it, you haven't been yourself lately, but I could be wrong. Perhaps we are approaching that time in a woman's life when her child-bearing years end, a time that I know is not easy . . ."

Jeanette slips her breasts into a lacy bra, almost wincing when the fabric touches her nipples. She walks toward the closet and yanks an emerald green silk dress from a hanger and steps into it so as not to muss her face by pulling it over her head.

"Enough, Terry. Enough. While we're on the subject, have you heard of male menopause? That's when aging guys lose their goddamned sense and act like idiots. Abandon their families, start sniffing cocaine, or initiate absurd crusades in an attempt to resurrect waning careers. Sound like anyone you know?" She spits this out, yanking the stockings over her hips with such angry force that her fingers go right through them, leaving enormous holes that instantly turn into runs on either side.

"Dammit!" She stomps to the dresser for another pair, but of course there are none. "Terry, I need you to go down to the gift shop and get me some nylons," she says, just as someone knocks on the door.

"Who is it?" Terry calls.

"Room service."

Terry turns to Jeanette, but before he can open his mouth she says, "Forget it, Terry, I'll go myself. I could use some air before all those ass-holes get here, anyway." She quickly wiggles out of the dress and into a pair of capris, a T-shirt, and her flip-flops, nearly colliding with a cart laden with shrimp cocktails. At the elevator she bangs the button angrily, as if doing so will speed its arrival or make the voice in her head still argu-ing with Terry go away.

Not surprisingly, the only pantyhose the gift shop sells are thick, grayish brown, and look like something her grandmother might have worn rolled just below the knee to hide varicose veins. No way she'd wear those. Jeanette threads her way through the lobby crowded with gamblers and men who'd come to visit the whorehouses scattered outside the city. There is something simultaneously furtive and exhibitionist about them, as if they are little boys defiantly doing something naughty. Their laughter is too loud, their clothing too casual, their grins more like leers. It is as if here, in this place where prostitution is legal, the line between women going about their business and women whose business is sex had been erased, and they are all fair game. Jeanette can feel eyes raking her clothes from her body as she weaves through the crowd toward the door.

The drugstore is one of those massive, fluorescent chain stores that are everywhere across America, and everywhere the same, selling everything from Pepperidge Farm cookies to olives to condoms. Jeanette finds the pantyhose aisle, selects what she wants, and wanders lazily toward the check-out counter, stopping to look at make-up, hair accessories, toy displays, whatever catches her eye as she delays returning to the hotel.

In aisle four she stops to stare at a rack of early pregnancy tests. She marvels at all the different brands, wondering if there is any difference between them and impressed that it's now so easy for women to find out if the egg has been fertilized. A group of teenagers surprise her as they swarm into the aisle, laughing and shouting. She grabs a test off the rack and hurries to the cashier, suddenly reminded of the need to get back to the hotel.

She knows the moment she exits the elevator that the party has begun. She can hear raucous laughter, smell a sickening blend of cigarette smoke and musk oil, and hear the muffled rattle of ice in plastic cups. She steels herself for one last night of being T. Terry's hostess to a suite full of drunks, simpletons, and drunk simpletons. When she pushes open the door, a wall of sound envelops her.

"Hey, pretty lady. I was just asking what happened to you," yells Reverend Cliff Bear, head of the southern region of the Baptist Brotherhood and Boulé. He weaves toward her, arms outstretched, his dark drink sloshing onto the carpet as he advances. Recently released from prison after serving a five-year sentence for theft of church funds and spousal abuse, Bear had returned to his large Florida church, which had paid his salary, kept his pulpit open, and acted as if he'd had just gone away for a quart of milk, not five years in a minimum-security state penitentiary.

Jeanette extends the palm of her hand, stopping him before he can collide with her chest and wrap her in yet another sweaty, grinding, dry hump of a hug.

"Evening, Reverend. I had to run out to the store. Now, I'm going to run and change and I'll be right back."

"You be sure to come right back. I want to talk to you about how old T. Terry's held onto a fine little chocolate drop like you all these years." He reaches for Jeanette's ass as she snakes past him, a familiar move she skillfully avoids.

"The only way for the black woman to regain our ancient African status as queens is to conduct ourselves in a queenly manner that is be-yond reproach, beyond reproach, and by that I mean no sexual contact outside marriage," Edna Mantz Thompson declares, standing in the middle of the room and wearing a dark blue sequin and chiffon cocktail dress, circa 1958.

"My sister, that is why the United Federation of Promojites encour-ages marriage at age sixteen, to protect the virtue of our young sisters by legally enfolding them in the protective arms of black kings," a tall brother with salt and pepper hair and a full beard intones.

"My brother, that's absurd. A sixteen-year-old girl should be in school or in church when she is not in her father's house. She is certainly too young to have a husband and children of her own."

"So God has made a mistake?" asks a man with long dreads from RAH, the Rastafarian Association of Harlem.

"Our Lord doesn't make mistakes," Thompson glares. 'What's your point?"

"Why would the Lord give the woman the ras clot if he wasn't ready to give her the children?"

"Ras clot?" Thompson says.

"The menses, mama. That's Jamaican for the menses," the Rasta-farian explains.

"Menstruation is a biological function," Thompson says in her best lecturing-to-the-lumpen voice. "It does not mean that girls are educa-tionally, emotionally, or morally ready to have children. It simply means they can."

"It means that they should," declares a short, slight man from the Chocolate Canaanites, almost overpowered by his turban, leather pants and jacket, and spiked wrist bracelets. "You see them every day in our communities, tight pants up their ass, titties all exposed, faces painted like it's Halloween. They are the whores of Babylon in training. But they are all yearning, whether they know it or not, for the discipline of hus-band, children, family."

"Right on."

"Teach. Preach."

"Tell it, brother."

"Surely you are not suggesting that the solution to the problems of these misguided girls is to have babies?" Thompson asks. "We have enough unwanted children of childish mothers as it is. No, celibacy and education is the answer."

"The juices are flowing, the juices are flowing, the dam that will still them can be found in the arms of a strong man," the Rasta says, his words slightly slurred by the presence of a chicken bone in the side of his mouth.

"Amen," says the Chocolate Canaanite. "If those women over at that spa had a true black man, you think they'd be over there now, fucking, sucking, and licking? It's past time for the black man to reassert his paternalistic rights in our communities. Just like whitey does in his."

"Now, I can't argue with that," Thompson says. "The black man's historic role is to be the father and guide the black woman. But I must insist that marriage at sixteen is out of the question."

"It's those damn feminists. Stirring up already troubled waters, trying to convince our women that the black man is the oppressor, when we are the oppressed. Black women always had it easier than the black man, ever since slavery. It is the black man who is the true victim, first, last, and always."

"Uh-huh."

"True that."

"Break it down, my brother."

"See, this shit is really about divide and conquer, foment some in-group hostility shit so we be so busy fighting each other we won't notice that slavery's back until it's too late," a skinny young brother says through a mouth full of shrimp.

"Slavery?" Thompson asks skeptically.

"Slavery. You seen the growth of the prison-industrial complex. Over two million Americans incarcerated and providing slave labor to corporate America. Who will produce the next generation's warriors if black women can get fucked with no commitment or consequences as long as they have condoms?"

Thompson nods slowly.

"I hear what you're saying, and Lord knows I support you brothers. But I'm sure you'll agree black men need to change their behavior, too.

Grown men must stop preying on young girls, brothers must take responsibility for the children they father, for the spread of disease . . ."

"How we gonna do that when we're victims? Victims! Assaulted by
the state and now our women, too. We an endangered species, you dig?"
the skinny brother sputters. The men who are gathered in a circle around
them nod their agreement. Thompson starts to open her mouth to respond, then shuts it, excuses herself, and heads toward the bar.

Looking around the room, Jeanette feels her stomach turn. She
slips inside the bedroom and then into the bathroom, locking the door
behind her. She unwraps the test, reads the directions, sits down on the
toilet, and sends a feeble stream of her urine over the stick. She feels her
stomach rising again and rapidly wipes herself, flushes, sinks down to her
knees once more, head hanging over the toilet, tasting the sour bile as it
rises in her throat. Just before she opens her mouth to retch she glances
at the wand in her hand: two dark stripes. Positive.

"I'm pregnant with T. Terry's heir," she thinks to herself. "His living legacy! Maybe now he'll settle down and we can get out of this racket."
And then she remembers that evening at the spa with gentle Ahmad and
his northern lights tattoo, and the broken condom, and the bile fills her
mouth and overcomes her.

33

"YOU SILLY, SORRY, THIEVING, LYING DRAG-QUEEN SONOFA *BITCH* !"
I scream. "I am going to kill you so slowly you'll be begging me to take you
out of your misery."

Acey and I stand in the pantry looking down at Lorene-Lorenzo.
His hands and feet are tightly bound to the back and legs of a folding
chair. He's still wearing the red dress, but his make-up's smeared from
sex and crying and the wig's gone, revealing hair that's not quite shoulder
length. I guess he's growing it out.

"You fucking pervert creep. How could you? Not only do you steal
my hard-earned money but you got the gall to use it for a motherfuckin'
sex-change operation? And then you bring your ass to my spa to get your
sick-ass groove on? Now I understand why you weren't interested in Miss
Kitty—you wanted to be the pussy yourself, you sick fuck!" I cuff him a
back-hand lick against his temple.

Acey grabs my hand. "Lyds, I know you're angry, but violence isn't
going to make you feel better."

I make a fist, rap the middle of his forehead with my knuckles, and
smile as he flinches.

"Don't be so sure. I'm feeling better already. This larcenous drag
queen deserves to get the shit kicked out of him for all of my years of married misery and then some."

"Transsexual," Lorene-Lorenzo whimpers defiantly. "I'm not a drag
queen. I am a transsexual."

"Transsexual, transvestite, who cares? What you are is seriously
fucked up," I yell. "How could you do this shit to me? How could you? I
don't give a damn if you want to change your own sorry life, you need to.
But you stole my cash to do it, you creepy fuck." I raise my hand to hit him
again and Marvini, sitting behind me smoking a spliff, catches it mid-air.

"Take it easy, boss, take it easy. Don't go breaking your hand on the
poor brother's thick head," Marvini says. "Anyway, I just read an article

287

on transsexuals in *Harper's*. Fascinating stuff. People who are born with the genitalia of a man or woman but the spirit of the opposite. That's some deep shit, there, if the brother ain't bullshitting."

"Has there ever been a time when you weren't bullshitting, Lorenzo? If this is it, speak now, because I'd just as soon kill your ass right here and leave you somewhere out in the desert for the coyotes."

Lorenzo, his face covered with tears, snot, and rivulets of foundation, sniffles.

"May I have some water? And could someone wipe my face? Then I can try to explain."

Acey runs a tissue along his face and Marvini holds a cup of water to his lips. Lorenzo, or whatever his name is, clears his throat.

"Well, as you know, Lydia, toward the end there we weren't doing much in the bedroom department, which was fine with me, but as I recall a sore point with you."

"Damn straight it was a sore point. Ya didn't work a job, didn't do shit around the house besides cook, and you didn't want to fuck."

Lorenzo shrugs dismissively, as if that's all behind him.

"There were more than a few times I started to tell you how I was feeling, how I'd been struggling with this interior conflict for years, but as you've just made obvious, you wouldn't have been receptive. With you, it's always been 'my way or the highway,' so frankly, I took the highway."

"With *my* cash, Lorenzo."

He flinches. "Lorene. It's Lorene. I'm a woman now."

"Stop me before I kill again," I mutter. Acey puts a comforting hand on my arm, then asks, "How were you feeling, Lorenzo?"

"For a long time, just . . . confused. You know, I tried to be a man, be macho all those years, one of the guys, but inside I knew I was pretending. Finally, I realized that my thing was being a woman trapped in a man's body. I thought like a woman, felt like a woman, in fact I was a woman in my soul. I just had a penis. An accident of birth and chromosomes."

"It would have been nice if you'd let me know about that accident before we got married."

"I wish I'd known myself. I didn't. Back in college I thought I might be gay, but I wasn't attracted to men as a man. I didn't know what I was. I thought I just needed to meet the right woman, settle down, and all these conflicted feelings I had would work themselves out. I didn't intend to hurt you, Lydia, I loved you. Believe it or not, I still do, just in a different way."

"That's an understatement."

"Maybe not. Love changes, and as much as most people don't want to face it, sometimes so does our sexuality."

"What do you mean?" Acey asks.

Lorenzo sniffles, and his voice starts to take on a different tone as he goes on. "Think about it for a minute. In a world where nothing's static, why do we believe our sexuality is? I think it's because we're conditioned that all people are either straight or gay, male or female, and there's an impregnable wall between the two. But maybe that's not so."

Even through my anger, I'm intrigued. He might have been lazy, a liar, and a lousy husband and stingy lover, but one of things I've always liked about Lorenzo is his willingness to think outside the box.

"Go on."

"You both know. This spa's proof of that. You've created a private place where women can come to enjoy and explore their sexuality, without restraints or judgment. That's what makes this place so unique. At least while they're here, women's sexuality is open, liberated, and fluid. That's got to change some of the people some of the time, even after they leave here. When I called you last, I was at the airport, on my way to Bangkok for the surgery. I wanted to tell you then, but you went off. Around the middle of June someone e-mailed me a note about A Sister's Spa. I was finishing up recovery from the surgery. I knew I had to get here."

"The surgery?"

"Sex reassignment surgery," Lorene-Lorenzo nods.

"You had your dick removed?"

"Yes I did. And my balls. I also had penile skin inversion vaginoplasty, that's when they create a vagina, and some cosmetic work done, but I'm not finished yet, just broke."

"A black man volunteering for castration? You must really want to be a woman," I say.

"That's my point. I don't want to be a woman, I *am* a woman, just one given the wrong genitals."

"Damn. He sounds exactly like the cats in that article," Marvini murmurs.

"Are you saying you have a fully functioning vagina? Come on."

"Not fully functioning yet. That's one reason why Sequoia and I always have anal sex. I need another surgery before I'm truly fully operational."

"Unbelievable," I mumble.

Lorenzo-Lorene ignores me.

"Anyway. A Sister's Spa seemed the perfect place to come to explore my new, female sexuality, and believe me, I was totally shocked when I walked through that door opening day and saw you and Acey behind the check-in counter."

"Not as shocked as we were when we saw you on the videotape," Acey giggles. Lorenzo laughs.

"No doubt. Lydia, I know this is asking a lot, but maybe one day you can forgive me."

"Forgive you? As soon as you give me my $40,000 back, all's forgiven, Lorenzo, how about that?"

"Lydia, I spent most of the money to pay for my transportation, the operation, and three weeks in a hotel recuperating. Most of what I had left I've spent here, and I'm still not working yet. Trying to figure out what Miss Lorene wants to do with her new life."

"What've you got left?"

"About $2,000."

"I'll take it. That leaves a balance of $38,000. Are you planning to pay me back, or are you expecting me to write it off under 'expenses for Lorenzo's sex change' on my tax return?"

"I don't think the IRS allows sex reassignment as a deduction, though some advocacy groups are working on it. I'll give you the $2,000. Maybe I could work some of the rest off here until I get a job?"

"How would you do that Lorenzo, uh, Lorene? We employ men who like to fuck women, not the other way around. If you're interested in that, I suggest you take your ass right down the road to Mustang or Chicken Ranch and get a job there."

"I certainly was not suggesting I work as a prostitute," Lorene says coldly.

"What were you thinking about?" Acey asks.

"I'd really be interested in hearing that, too, since I never saw you do a lick of work while we were married."

"I hadn't really figured out the specifics," Lorene says. "I could answer phones, help out cleaning up, or—"

"I could use some help in the kitchen," Marvini says softly. "We're getting busy enough that I could use a sous chef."

"Lyds, you know Lorenzo—sorry, Lorene—is a wiz in the kitchen. And maybe he could help monitor the videotapes, deal with the phones, take some of the weight off us," Acey adds. "We'll pay his salary directly to you until he pays his debt down or finds something else."

"Yeah, well that all sounds open-minded in a 'we are the world' kind of way, but is this someone we can trust?"

"Sure," Marvini says softly through a cloud of marijuana smoke.

"And that's because?"

"Cause maybe now that he's a she, he's changed. Anyway, we've got him by the balls, er, breasts. If he screws up, we can always go to the video-tape."

I look from Marvini to Acey to my former husband, now a woman and tied to a chair in the pantry of A Sister's Spa. Part of me wants to cuff him some more around the head. But what's funny is another part of me wants to burst out laughing, this shit is simultaneously so bizarre and yet so appropriate. I guess the truth is I haven't loved Lorenzo like a woman loves a man in years. Even though I'm angry as hell he stole my money, his story strikes a note that touches me; it adds up with, even explains, a lot of what happened between us, so I know it's probably all true. I figure any-one who goes to all that trouble to become a black woman, the mule of the world as Zora Neale Hurston called us, must have no other choice.

"Lyds. What do you say?"

"Okay, I'm willing to give it a try. But he's—excuse me, she's—got to stay away from the sex workers. No money, no sex, okay?"

"But Sequoia and I—"

"Lorene, don't go there. Sequoia and you have nothing but a busi-ness arrangement, period. Get over it. Now that you're a woman, let me give you a heads up: Just because the sex is good doesn't mean it's a rela-tionship. Keep that as your mantra and you'll do all right. Maybe."

"Would you untie me now?"

"Sure. Then get yourself a cup of coffee, make yourself some break-fast, and start watching those videotapes. We need to find out why these dicks are going limp."

"And we need to find Wanda and Odell and get ready for the meet-ing with the delegation from Feminists United tomorrow morning. Come on," Acey says, grabbing my arm. We turn to leave.

"Lydia," Lorene says.

"Yeah?"

"Thanks. I didn't think you'd be so understanding. It means a lot to me."

"That's cool," I say. "Welcome to the sisterhood," I say, giving Acey a wink that only she can see.

34

"I HOPE IT'S ALL RIGHT, BUT I TOOK THE LIBERTY OF INVITING A close friend and sister in the struggle to this meeting. I'd like to introduce you to the Reverend Irene Morris," Exultia Wallace says, as if an introduction were necessary.

Her trademark cowgirl hat sits high on her head, underneath which are flowing gray locks. She's almost six feet tall, the color of dark honey, with a big gap between her two front teeth, and arms laden with perhaps a hundred gold and silver bangles that make music—sometimes soothing, sometimes discordant, depending on her mood—when she moves. As always, she's got an unlit cheroot stuck in the side of her bright red lip-sticked mouth.

At eighty-four, the Reverend Irene Morris is a legend in her own time. A graduate of Yale Law School, the New York Chiropractic College, and the recipient of a divinity degree from Atlanta Theological Seminary, this sister is bad. Her parents were born in Georgia in 1865, the year slavery ended, and spent their lives as sharecroppers on the plantation where they'd been enslaved. They vowed never to bring children into a lousy world that had visited slavery, poverty, Reconstruction, poverty, the Ku Klux Klan, poverty, and World War I upon them, and were as surprised as anyone when Irene's mother Florence, long since past the change, got pregnant at age 53. Being deeply religious folks, they took the pregnancy as a sign and eagerly awaited the birth of their daughter. She came on December 29, 1918, with a veil over her face and not a peep from her lips, even after the midwife spanked her repeatedly. In later years they joked that was the first and last time Irene was spanked, couldn't see perfectly straight, and didn't have something to say.

Florence and Willard Morris lived into their eighties, long enough to see Irene graduate from law school and chiropractic college and announce she would continue on to divinity school. One of Irene's few regrets was that they hadn't lived to hear her preach.

When she wasn't furthering her own education, Irene moved from city to city, teaching, preaching, adjusting aching bones, and speaking the gospel of women's revolution. In circumstances where most women, black and white, were beaten and frightened away, when the dust cleared Morris would still be standing, chewing that little cigar and speaking truth to power. During a sixty-year teaching career she divided her time between the Ivy League and historically black colleges, never accepting an appointment for longer than three years, and always turning down tenure as "high-siddity slavery."

"My father was a sharecropper, tied to the land by blood, false debt, and violence. He tilled the earth, sowed the crop, picked it, and then started all over again. Myself, I only sow, and my crop isn't cotton, it's young minds. What they do with the knowledge I give them once they're grown is their business," is how she explained her restless spirit.

She'd never married or had children, and rumors of her sexual liaisons were many. According to the tales told, Morris had intimate relationships with every important radical political figure of her time, and neither age nor gender nor color gave her pause. "I make love to minds. The body, while pleasurable, is merely incidental, although some of those incidents were rapturous," she responded with a laugh and wink when asked by Ed Bradley on 60 Minutes if it was true she'd had affairs with Fidel Castro, Shirley Chisholm, Emma Goldman, Kwame Nkrumah, Dinah Washington, Paul Robeson, Miles Davis, Evangeline Worthington, and Tupac Shakur.

I love her because she's brilliant, political, outspoken, uncompromising, and a gadfly, something black women seldom have an opportunity to be. She goes where she wants, works where she wants, says whatever she wants, and leads a fabulous, important life. She lives in Cambridge, Massachusetts, where she pastors a women's church with 5,000 members: black, white, Asian, Latino, lesbian, bisexual, undecided, straight, Christians, Muslims, Buddhists, Jews—all women committed to radical change were welcome. The men who accidentally stumbled up the steps or came to have their feminist credentials anointed were politely but firmly turned away at the door.

"Good morning, my sisters," Morris says, looking first at me, Acey, and LaShaWanda, who we had to drag to the meeting and who's already in her "fuck this bullshit" pose, elbow on the table, forehead in her hand, her extensions almost covering her face. Morris nods to the twenty white women from Feminists United sitting around the table, most of them wearing jeans with T-shirts, although as always Exultia Wallace is chic in a tailored suit. "And thank you for your early morning hospitality. Although it would have been nice if you'd summoned cooler weather. It's hotter than Georgia out here."

"Irene, would you like to say a prayer before we begin? It is Sunday."

Irene waves her hands in a gesture of dismissal.

"Thanks, Exultia, but I'll be preaching at the convention's gospel brunch in a few hours. Let me rest my voice and listen for a change."

Exultia turns to me and Acey. "Again, let me say how much I appreciate this meeting. Would you like to begin, or shall I?"

"Well, since you asked for the meeting, why don't you?" I say.

"Yes. As I'm sure I indicated on the phone, Feminists United is committed to bridging the traditional divisions between white women and women of color. We believe those divisions are false barriers created by our mutual male oppressors to keep us divided. We understand that our black sisters were treated as beasts of burden on the plantation, because we too were chattel, forced by men to submit to an oppressive system—"

"Cut. Wait a goddamn minute. If you came over this morning to give us the Miss-Ann-was-as-oppressed-as-Mammy version of history, we might as well end the meeting right here," I say, rising from my seat.

"I was simply trying to lay down a historical context for the under-recognized commonality between black and white women."

"Maybe you'd better move on past the plantation. Because that really isn't going to wash here," Acey says.

"A frequently heard analysis, but one that the work of feminist historians steadily debunks. Have you read Carla Gottlieb's latest book on white women in the plantation South, *My Name is Mammy, Too*?

"They already stole Elvis, the blues, and half our men. Now they want Mammy, too? Ain't white folks a bitch?" Wanda mutters under her breath.

Me, Acey, and Irene Morris snicker.

"Did I miss something?" Exultia asks perkily. Wanda's head sinks further into her hand.

"No. Go on," Acey says.

"Perhaps we can be criticized for a lack of courage in expressing our support for our colored sisters, but are we not all victims of our times?"

"Yeah, I always wondered what got into Elizabeth Cady Stanton when she sold us out on the vote," I interject.

Acey glances delicately at her watch, says "Could we move on to the purpose of this meeting?" Exultia takes a deep breath.

"Exultia, you really should get to the point here," Irene Morris says quietly, the tone of her voice more a command than a suggestion.

"Yes. I apologize. As you may know I was trained as a historian and even though I never taught, I do have a tendency to fall into teaching mode. One wants to share what one knows." Wanda's head snaps up, she tosses her braids out of her face, and for a moment I actually feel sorry for Exultia Wallace.

"Well, Big Missy, we's sure happy y'all came down from the big house dis Sunday mornin' to preach to the darkies, but we gots a ho' house to run so if you could cut to the motherfuckin' chase, we'd be mighty grateful," Wanda drawls.

Irene Morris meets Wanda's eyes, nods imperceptibly, and says, "Exultia. I really think you should. You do not have the home court advantage here," she says softly. Exultia blushes.

"Yes. Cut to the chase, was it? We have an opportunity to change the course of the troubled history between white and black women. We want to do whatever we can to prove our sisterhood."

"Which is exactly what?" Acey asks.

"We would like to be welcomed here as patrons of A Sister's Spa. We are not asking for any special treatment, discounts, or concessions—"

"I hope not," Wanda interrupts. "That would be affirmative action. Or is that reverse discrimination?"

"As an aside, let me say I support the former and deny the validity of the latter," Exultia says. "So, we would like to know that we will be welcomed to partake of all the wonderful services your spa has to offer."

"Our primary service is sex with black men," I say.

"We are more than aware of what your primary service is, although I understand you have white men employed here, too."

"A few. Listen, to each her own, that's our motto. We provide whatever a sister needs to get her freak on, as long as it doesn't involve pain."

"Not that we make any judgment about the S&M people. We just don't sell that here," Acey adds.

Irene Morris clears her throat. "May I ask the reasons behind the exclusion of white women?"

"Reverend Morris, you're a sister, you know the deal," Acey says, turning toward her. "We aim to provide a space where sisters feel safe, sexy, and sensational just as we are. With our big asses, breasts, and lips.

With our weaves, extensions, dreads, or naturals, even if we're bald-headed. In all our many colors and shapes, whatever our age or nine-to-five. A Sister's Spa is a place where black women are the norm. We don't have televisions in the guest rooms because our clients come here to escape the tyranny of the stick-thin, blond-haired white women who define beauty in America." Morris nods thoughtfully.

"Yes. But we are not part of that tyranny," Exultia squeaks. "Look at me, look at my regional officers. Are we pretty? Are we thin? Are we attractively dressed? Our hair, if it is long, is gray. How are we the enemy?"

"Exultia, no one said you were the enemy. But you're also not the *subject* here. It's not about excluding you. It's about embracing us," Acey says.

"Yes, but surely we can work something out. We lose so many good feminist soldiers to the carnal imperatives a sexist and homophobic society conditions women to believe they need a man to satisfy—"

"I go all ways," Irene says with a laugh, "But truly, Exultia, there are some needs that only a man *can* satisfy."

Exultia laughs. "Irene, that's an argument we've been having for years and will likely never resolve. Yes. So, to my mind it would be therapeutic for my members to visit a place like this where unbridled sexual desire is encouraged and satisfaction is efficiently delivered. No drinking, dating, bar hopping, and rejection, no ties that bind when the call goes out that women are on the move. No possibility of pregnancy to delude our sisters into believing that the mammaries are the message. A weekend here would free feminists to eschew men for weeks, maybe months, and allow them to focus on the women's revolution that must come!"

"Amen," says Irene Morris.

"Ya really think so?" LaShaWanda raises her head and looks intensely at Irene.

"That the women's revolution must come? Absolutely. That white women must come here? Possibly. That said, I understand the pitfalls of pretending we're all one big happy womanist family. History has shown us otherwise."

"Yes. But might this not be a chance to change history?" Exultia says, "We are, after all, sisters under the skin."

Irene glances at Wanda, who's glowering behind her braids, and quickly says, "Let's meditate on a solution."

I do what I always do at prayer time: pretend to shut my eyes and peer out from beneath the lids at the people around me. Irene Morris' breaths are so deep a hum like a cello emanates from her body. Exultia's breath whistles from her nose like a high-strung racehorse's, while Acey's is delicate and even. There's something soothing about sitting in a roomful of women, just breathing.

"Go down, Moses, way down in Egypt Land. Tell old pharaoh, to let my people go." I even seem to be hearing the words of the old spiritual in my head.

"I said, uh, go down, Moses, way down in Egypt Land, Tell old pharaoh, to let my brothers go." The music's getting louder, accompanied by clapping and soulful humming.

"Is church one of the many services you provide?" Irene Morris asks with an arched brow.

"No. We do have a bus to take clients to eleven o'clock services, but it's not even nine."

"Perhaps some of your employees feel inspired to sing a few spirituals after a hard night's work, not unlike our ancestors in the cotton fields?"

"I doubt it," Wanda scoffs. "That song's about slaves escaping, and these brothers aren't going anywhere. Shit, they got the perfect gig. If they were singing, it'd more likely be 'Let's Get It On.'"

"Go down, Moses, way down in Reno Land, tell those whoremongers, to let my brothers go."

"What the fuck?" Wanda says, getting up from the table.

"It's T. Terry," Acey whispers, her face stricken.

"That devil. Let him come so that I may smite him," Irene declares, standing and pulling herself to her full height. She may be eighty-four, but she looks as if she could righteously kick some ass.

We hurry to the windows on the west side of the building, the direction from which the singing comes. What looks like a dust tornado created by the march of hundreds of feet moves slowly up the driveway toward the main house.

"It's on," Wanda says. "If you can't get along, let's get it on." Suddenly, one of the women from F.U., a petite brunette with an intense gaze, sits bolt upright and says, "LaShaWanda Marshall! It is you!"

"Do I know you?" Wanda asks, raising her voice to be heard above the singing.

"I'd never forget that phrase, or the woman I heard using it. Don't you remember me? I used to be Claudia Powell. You worked with my husband at McGruder Forbes."

"*Julius* Powell? He's your husband?" Acey and I shoot each other a confused look, then turn toward Wanda.

"Not anymore, I divorced the bastard last year."

"Did he send you to the poor house, too?"

"He tried. But I'd been photocopying his business papers for years and once I showed him what I had, he settled nicely."

"Well, that's bully for you, but I've always suspected he's the thieving bastard who set me up, and had McGruder Forbes seize $2 million in my hard-earned commissions."

"I know. Some of the papers I have detail how Julius manipulated the partners at McGruder Forbes and the Securities and Exchange Commission to cover his own ass. By the time I discovered them, you'd left New York long before, with no forwarding address."

"Yeah, sometimes it be's that way when you're trying to avoid being indicted."

"Wanda," I interrupt, "what the hell is going on?"

"It's a long-ass story, but for now let me give you the short version. I didn't just work in a bank back East. I was an investment banker. After I graduated from Yale I went to work at McGruder Forbes in New York. I started out as a trainee, but I hustled my ass off and made associate after a year. Those white male MBAs from Wharton, Harvard, and Columbia didn't know what to make of my black female ass, but I knew what I was there to make: money. I worked on a team that structured a billion dollars' worth of deals, and made sure I got credit for my participation. I'd been there six years and was on my way to becoming the first black female partner when all hell broke loose."

LaShaWanda pauses. Her eyes have that faraway look that lets you know she's reliving every moment.

"We were about to close the biggest single deal yet when all operations were abruptly suspended by McGruder Forbes's CEO. Apparently someone had suggested there was unusual activity in one of the banker's accounts, so the company started an investigation. I knew I'd done nothing unscrupulous, and when my employers asked to review my personal account, I said sure. I'd made some money over the years, but not enough to raise any eyebrows. I was building a nest egg and hadn't even checked the account for months, the money was just sitting there. Or so I thought . . . Let me have a glass of that designer water, will you?" I pour her a glass and nod for her to continue.

"Did I ever think wrong. They found $20 million dollars in my account, in addition to the $2 million I'd earned in commissions. I don't know where the shit that money came from, but I sure didn't put it there. I was as surprised as they were. The balances of all the other associates on my team were what they should be, which de facto made me the guilty party. I tried to tell them I didn't know how the money got into my account or where it came from, but no one believed me. They contended that the only place that much money could have come from was profits from insider trading, and threatened to go to the Securities Exchange Commission unless I gave the money back. I told them I'd be happy to give the money back, but to whom? My bosses didn't think that was funny. Then came the ultimatum: transfer the $20 million into McGruder Forbes' general fund, pack up my desk, sign an affidavit waiving any claim to my commissions, and agree never to work in investment banking again, and they wouldn't have me arrested. Not much of a choice, was it? I left, they closed the investigation, and three months later I moved out here," LaShaWanda concludes.

"That's a terrible story," Acey says sympathetically. "Did they ever find out who took the money and put it in your account?"

Wanda shakes those braids. "Never even tried, as far as I know. Once I was gone, the matter was settled, and McGruder Forbes was $22 million dollars richer, including my commissions. By magic."

"Damn."

"Who do you think did it? Did you have enemies?"

LaShaWanda rolls her eyes. "Is a pig's pussy pork? Of course I had enemies, plenty of them. You think it's easy for those Wall Street boys to tolerate a sister proud of the street kicking their Harvard Business School behinds? As for who set me up, it could have been any of my so-called colleagues."

"You must be angry as hell." I say.

Wanda shrugs. "Nothing I can do about it now, and like my granny says, what goes around comes around. Whoever did it will get theirs. I'm focused on getting mine." She turns back to Claudia Powell.

"Now about those papers of your former husband's?"

"LaShaWanda, I'm glad see you again. I think it's terrible what they did to you. And I'd be honored to share Julius' confidential documents with you."

Suddenly there's a fierce pounding at the door.

"Lydia! Lydia, let me in! It's Dick Dixmoor!" a voice shrieks. Before I have time to wonder when he got back, not to mention what the hell he wants, someone bursts through the door—but it's Lorene-Lorenzo, not Dixmoor, still in that red dress and fully made-up, but now accessorized with a stocking cap and giant-sized beaded flip-flops.

"Well my goodness," Irene Morris says. "Who do we have here?"

"My soon to be ex-husband, Lorenzo, who stole my money and is now a woman named Lorene who works here in something like indentured servitude. Long, twisted story." I turn to Lorenzo. "What do you want? And whatever it is, can't it wait?"

"It's Dixmoor! On the tapes! Meddling with some shit in the pantry," he pants.

"It's true, Lorene showed me," calls Muffin, running in breathlessly on Lorenzo-Lorene's heels, a horrified expression on her face. "I don't know what it is, but Dick sure looks like he's up to something on those tapes."

"Those tapes?" Wanda asks pointedly.

"More than a few. You know how when he visits he always spent time with Marvini? Well, he also spent time in the pantry, alone."

"I should have know he wasn't hanging out in the kitchen just to talk to Marvini about a healthy diet. I wonder what he's up to," I say.

"I don't know what the hell he's up to, but when he gets here this afternoon to pick me up, I'm going to find out what he's doing on those tapes," Muffin says miserably.

"I'm going to call Odell and ask him to watch the videos," Acey says, flipping open her cell phone. "Lorenzo, I mean Lorene, go back up to the kitchen and help Marvini start breakfast, and . . ."

Her words are suddenly drowned out by a pounding on the door followed by the booming voice of T. Terry Tiger. "Sinners, come out and answer for yourselves!"

"If you can't get along, let's get it on!" Wanda and Claudia Powell say in unison, turning toward the doorway.

"See! See!" Exultia Wallace gestures toward LaShaWanda and Claudia, "Sisterhood is powerful."

"I certainly hope so," I say, looking out the window. "Because the crusaders are at the gate."

35

"OKAY, ITS HIGH NOON, TIME FOR THE SHOWDOWN. YOU TWO ready?" Lydia says.

LaShaWanda nods enthusiastically, her braids clanking. Now there's a sister who never shies away from a confrontation. I smooth my hair with one hand, my shorts with the other, and wish I had on a conservative, Sunday-go-to-meeting-type outfit.

"What's the plan?" I have to yell to be heard above the umpteenth version of "Go Down, Moses."

"To tell that saggy-assed reverend to leave us the hell alone," Wanda says.

"He thinks we're the ones going to hell."

"Yeah, well, you got any ideas?" Lydia says impatiently. "You're the one whose father was a minister."

"Yeah, and I seldom won an argument with him," I say grimly.

"The key is not to argue. Simply go outside, let him rant and bluster, and as he begins to wind down, figure out what our next step should be," the Reverend Irene Morris suggests. "I would be happy to accompany you if you think I might be of some service."

"That would be wonderful, Reverend Morris," I say, taking her arm, more because I need her support than the other way around.

"Your father was a minister? Perhaps I knew him."

"Esmont Allen. He was pastor of First Shall Be Last Baptist in Oakland before Herman Rutledge took over."

"Of course. Handsome man, very distinguished. Bright, too, but quite the chauvinist. I knew your mother, also. What a talented photographer. In fact, I have one of her photographs in my living room."

"Really? I'd love to see it. My father burned my mother's work right after she died, so there're only a few things left."

"I'd be honored if you came to visit me in Cambridge. We can arrange all that later. Right now, Reverend T. Terry awaits us," Morris says, pushing me toward the door.

"You're leaving us behind? Isn't there anything you'd like us to do?" Exultia squeaks. "This may be the moment to begin to change history, Irene."

"Exultia, at the moment we can handle this. For now, just watch our backs."

I open the door and the four of us step out into blinding yellow-white sunlight, holding hands. The sun is against our backs. Reverend T. Terry Tiger stands before us, resplendent in a purple robe with a kente cloth collar and a matching kufi style hat. His left arm is linked through that of Edna Mantz Thompson, who glares at us menacingly, her cantaloupe-sized breasts heaving either with righteous indignation or incipient heat stroke. On his right is a petite brunette who looks vaguely familiar, decidedly uncomfortable, and slightly sick. Flanking them on either side are four men. I recognize Reverend Cliff Bear from the Baptist Brotherhood and Boulé; Shazam Hakim Shazim of the United Federation of Promojites; Yusef Ben-Israel of the Chocolate Canaanites; and Minister Mal Muhammad Perez, a religious omnisexual who's burnt bridges with the Baptists, the Methodists, and the Buddhists, and is currently affiliated with an unrecognized offshoot of the Nation of Islam. Behind them are probably ten rows of zealots, about 120 people in all. The four of us are definitely outnumbered.

"Reverend Irene Morris. I certainly wasn't expecting to see you here," T. Terry intones.

"After all these years, Terry, you should have learned that you never know where you might find me," Irene says imperiously. "Unfortunately, ever since you screwed up with SCLC and Martin kicked you out, you can too often be found on the wrong side of the issue."

Terry looks as if he wants to respond, then catches himself.

"Are these the harlots who established this outpost of Babylon in the desert?" T. Terry extends his arm and points slowly to me, Lydia, and LaShaWanda. Irene nudges me gently with her elbow.

"We are the proprietors of A Sister's Spa," I say quietly.

T. Terry whirls around to face his followers.

"These are the sinners who seek to bury morality underneath a mountain of sexuality and carnal knowledge! These are the sick, misguided black women who do not seek to uplift our fallen brothers but to lure them deeper into the mire of earthly desires and degradation! Yes, it is these three nondescript women who move within our communities as wraiths, haints, spooks, whispering the false gospel of sexual gratification by any means necessary. Of sexual liberation." He pauses, drawing in a deep breath. "Of the clitoral orgasm!" The words swoosh from his mouth like a gust of wind. Apparently, this last is the final straw. His followers grow restive, begin to mutter, stomp feet, clap hands. T. Terry whirls around, his robes billowing.

"Look at them!" he roars. "Memorize their faces. Know that these are the faces of those who have passively allowed the destruction of our men and now seek to profit from the defilement of our women. Do you see them? Do you see them!"

"Yes, Lord, I see them."

"Amen, amen."

"Right on, brother."

"Break it down."

"Now forget their faces! Erase them from your mind! Why? Because the devil is a shape-shifter. Can take on any form he wants. Can make himself look just like you or me. It is not the face of the devil by which we recognize him. Or her. It is his evil deeds!"

"All right, all right."

"Let's tear this place down."

"What should we do with these women, Rev?"

"Did I hear someone ask what we should do with these sinners? Let me first tell you what we will not do. We will not burn them at the stake, as Joan of Arc and the witches of Salem were burned. We will not turn them into a pillar of salt for their disobedience, like Lot's wife. We will not ex-communicate them. No. Jesus forgives. He even forgave Mary Magdalene for her whoring. We shall do what all good Christians do. We shall pray for their salvation."

I stand in the sandy dirt, Lydia holding one of my hands and Irene Morris the other, surprised that I am not terrified. I'm apprehensive, not knowing where this whole mess is going, and I'm a bit frightened looking out at a small sea of angry men and women, but I'm not terrified. Even though I know that what's happening is serious, there's a new place inside me where I'm able to situate myself and watch the spectacle.

I glance at Lydia. A slight grin plays at the corner of her mouth. Beside her, Wanda's expression is bored, disgusted, and pissed in turns. Reverend Morris looks regal and impervious.

"But before we pray, I have just a few more things to say," T. Terry continues, his voice dropped almost to a whisper. "I want to tell these sisters that God loves them. That he wants to welcome them back into his loving arms. Yes, they are whoremongers, but he can forgive them. Yes, they revel in hedonism and sexual experimentation, but he will wipe their sins away. Yes, they are confused, they want to be "liberated" like their "sisters," those angry, ungrateful white feminists, but he understands they are possessed by the devil. He wants them to come home where he can wash their sins away! Oh, happy day!"

T. Terry breaks into the words of "Oh, Happy Day," and as if on cue his dusty congregation joins him.

Even though the song is part of T. Terry's bizarre exorcism of immorality and resurrection of morality, it's been one of my favorite spirituals since I was a little girl. The voices of a hundred black folks singing in the emptiness of a Nevada morning rise and swoop in the air, floating on beautiful harmonies. For a moment I close my eyes as I used to in my father's church, let myself sink into the music.

"Is there a problem here, gentlemen?" a smooth, familiar voice demands. I open my eyes to see Odell, Muffin, Ahmad, Sequoia, DeJuan, DeQuan, DeMon, Chef Marvini, and the other fabulous men who work at A Sister's Spa strutting down the path toward us. Irene Morris claps her hand delightedly, her bracelets jangling.

Odell positions himself between me and Lydia. Behind us are the men from the spa, suddenly joined by Exultia Wallace and the troops from F.U., who burst out of the house as soon as they saw Odell and the men appear.

"Reverend Tiger. May I help you?" The tone of Odell's voice is both studiously polite and coolly threatening.

"Here are our poor, misguided immoral brothers now!" T. Terry yells. "Let us pray for them, for these poor sisters, for the resurrection of morality," he says, falling to his knees in the dust. Like dominos, his minions follow him, all except the petite brunette, who remains standing.

"Acey, Lydia, Wanda, 's up? Who's this guy?" Ahmad asks, gesturing toward a prostrate T. Terry as he pushes his way forward, rubbing sleep from his eyes. I can't help notice how cute he is in a skimpy pair of orange shorts, his muscled chest, arms, and shoulders gleaming. He looks at the woman standing next to T. Terry and squints.

"Jeanette, right? What're you doing back here?"

"Ahmad. I . . . I . . . I . . . The truth is, I don't know what I'm doing here, but I'm leaving," she says, stepping away from T. Terry. The poor woman looks queasier than ever.

"Jeanette? You know this person?" T. Terry raises his head and looks Ahmad over. "Look at him, standing nearly naked and shameless, his body despoiled by a devil's tattoo."

"Listen, man, I don't know or really care who you are, but don't say shit about my tattoo. You may be old enough to be my grandfather, but I will kick your ass, a'ight?"

"Behold the brand of Satan on his arm! Pray for this poor young brother's salvation!" Terry cries.

"You supposed to be so smart, right? Don't even know this ain't no brand of Satan, it's the aurora borealis," Ahmad says.

"The aurora borealis?"

"For my Moms, may she rest in peace."

"Your mother got you that tattoo?"

"No, I got it in memory of my mother. Aurora Bonaventure, from Itta Bena, Mississippi."

"Aurora Bonaventure was your mother?" T. Terry rasps, struggling to rise from the dirt. "Sweet Jesus. I never knew she married." He looks like he's seen a ghost.

"She didn't. But that's okay, she raised me right. Told me I was her love child every day until she died."

"And your father?" Terry whispers.

Ahmad shrugs.

"Some cat she grew up with who thought Moms wasn't bourgie enough to marry, but sexed her when he was home for a funeral."

Terry steps forward, falters.

"Sweet Jesus," he murmurs, staring at Ahmad. "My son?"

"What the fuck?" Ahmad says, moving away from Terry's outstretched arms.

"Terry, I've had it," Jeanette bursts out, before a startled and confused Ahmad can say anything else. "I want no more part of this jiveass Crusade to Resurrect Morality. I have had enough. I'm forty-five years old, and I've been going along with this crap of yours for too damn long. I'm too old for this shit, I'm sick and tired. And now I've got more to think about than just myself. I'm pregnant. I'm going back to the hotel, taking a long bath, and catching the first thing smoking to Mississippi."

"Pregnant? Pregnant! Thank you, Jesus. What wonders to achieve," Terry yells, grabbing Jeanette and hugging her. "A boy, do you think it's a boy? It must be. Two sons in one day. Hallelujah!" he says, reaching again for a confused-looking Ahmad, who's backed so far away he's leaning against Wanda's ample breasts. "I'm your daddy, boy, your daddy! Let us rejoice!"

By now Terry's followers have stopped singing. Still on their knees, they're watching what's going on up front, although most can't hear what's being said.

"What's going on up there?" a voice calls from the back of the crowd.

"I thought we was praying."

"Who's your daddy?"

"Are we gonna save these sinners or not?" someone whines.

T. Terry releases the mother of his unborn child, stops clawing the air between him and his newly discovered son, turns toward his followers and lifts his arms. Behind him, Ahmad and Jeanette have a complex and delicate conversation with their eyes, full of questions, answers, and an eventual agreement. Even though it's T. Terry who opens his mouth, it's Jeanette who hisses, "Terry, cut the shit and send these people home. Leave these women alone to run their business and live their lives. For once just stop. Let's go home to Mississippi with your son and ours."

"But Jeanette, these people depend upon me to lead them out of the wilderness," T. Terry murmurs.

Jeanette sucks her teeth.

"Terry, look at these people. Look at them! We're talking a hundred folks who are misguided misfits, addle-brained, sexually repressed, or, worst case, all of the above. The *best* thing you could do for them is let them alone to make their own way. They don't need you, they're using you."

"But, Jeanette—"

"I think she has a point, Reverend," Odell says softly. "If you're worried about your safety, myself and the workers would be happy to escort you to your car."

"But Jeanette . . ."

"But Jeanette nothing," she snaps. "Stay here, Terry, and I guarantee you'll never see me again. Or your son. Ever. Isn't losing one child for more than twenty years enough?"

"She's right, you should go on and let them alone. This is a cool place, these sisters been really good to me. You should let them alone," Ahmad chimes in. T. Terry looks around in confusion.

"For once, Terry, be in the right place at the right time, with this good woman and your family," Irene Morris whispers.

Edna Mantz Thompson's eyes glitter greedily. "Go ahead, Reverend," she urges. "I can finish the sermon here."

"Will you come with me, son?" Terry turns to Ahmad, his eyes imploring. "We have lost too much time already."

"Hey, this is all kinda deep, ya know," Ahmad says. "I mean, I don't even know you, and besides, I got a job here. I need to think about all this shit, then we can talk. A'ight?" T. Terry looks devastated until Ahmad adds, "Pops." Then nods slowly.

"I guess I am tired. It has been a long struggle, one that, without heirs, I could not leave. But now that I have found Ahmad and have another son on the way . . ."

Jeanette slips an arm around his waist. "Let's go home baby. Time for me to plant that garden and for you to get to know your sons and start writing that autobiography."

"I'll walk y'all to the car," Ahmad offers.

Slowly, T. Terry, Ahmad, and Jeanette head toward the parking lot in front of the spa's main building.

If the creep hadn't just tried to destroy us, I might shed a tear.

"Where's T. Terry going?"

"Is the Rev all right?"

"What we gonna do about these sinners?"

"Does this mean it's over? Is morality dead?"

"Reverend Tiger has been called away on urgent business, but he has asked me to continue in his name," Edna Mantz Thompson says. "Let us pray."

"No thanks. I'm not even a Christian, I'm Yoruba. I just came out here to do T. Terry a solid. I'm gonna go check out the casino," Shazam Shazim of the United Federation of Promojites says, turning to trudge up the hill with his followers.

"Hell no, it's against my religion for women to lead the prayer. Shit, it's against my religion for men and women to pray together. Come to think of it, women anywhere but barefoot and pregnant are against my religion. I'm outta here," Ben Israel from the Chocolate Canaanites says, stalking away with his followers.

Thompson turns to Minister Mal Muhammad Perez, a beseeching expression on her face.

"Sorry, Sister, but I can't stay either. There's a hip-hop conference in Vegas, and if I leave now I might be able to do some networking with Russell Simmons," he says, scurrying toward the parking area. With him go the last of the men and women present, trotting so as not to miss their rides.

Edna Mantz Thompson stands in the dusty yard exhausted, disheveled, alone, and breathing hard. I exhale.

"Edna. I have warned you for years about throwing your lot in with these egomaniacal, opportunistic men," I hear Irene Morris say as she steps toward a desolate-looking Thompson and gently takes her arm. "What will you do now?"

"I guess that's it," Lydia laughs. "Kinda anticlimactic."

"I would hope that's it, and that's more than enough."

"So what's the deal? Ahmad is T. Terry's son by some woman named Aurora and Jeanette's pregnant with his baby? Shit, that old codger needs to come and work here," Wanda laughs.

"I think he's got his work cut out for him," I say, "Jeanette, too. But she handled him."

Lydia reaches over and grabs my arm, and suddenly me, Lyds, and Wanda are hugging and screaming. Then Muffin, Odell, and Irene join us, followed by Sequoia, the triplets, and the rest of our employees, even Exultia and the F.U. posse. Everyone's telling their version of what just happened all at once and laughing.

The sound of applause rolls down the hill toward us, and when I look up the windows of the main house are wide open and filled with a rainbow of black women's cheering faces framed by hair still unruly from a night of passion.

"The revolution has begun!" Exultia declares, pumping her fist in the air.

"I don't think I'd go that far," Irene says, "But sisterhood is powerful."

"Sisterhood is powerful! Sisterhood is powerful! Sisterhood is powerful!" The women from F.U. begin chanting, dancing in circles around us with such enthusiasm that we're even moved to exchange a few high fives. And you know, maybe it is.

When we quiet down we hear the roar of helicopter blades. Above us, Dick Dixmoor's private copter floats down toward the landing path.

"What'd I tell you? A woman's work is never done. Now we gotta deal with this snake," says Wanda.

"Wanda, I can deal with Dick by myself," Muffin says, glowering.

"No, sister. We've got your back," I say. Lydia nods.

"Can we be of further assistance?" Irene asks.

"Thanks, but we've got this one covered," I say.

Irene Morris, Exultia Wallace, and the F.U. troops begin heading toward their vehicles as we all call out congratulations, thanks, and promises to be in touch soon to see what we can do about arranging for our white sisters to enjoy A Sister's Spa.

"Men, let's get back to work!" Odell calls, shooing the workers back to the house. "You've each got a woman to satisfy, am I right? Do you all need me for anything here? If not, I'm going to finish looking at those tapes," he says, moving off toward the house when we tell him we think we can handle old Dick.

Then it's just the four of us, me, Lydia, LaShaWanda, and Muffin. Everyone's gone—except, that is, Edna Mantz Thompson. She's still standing there looking forlorn until suddenly she wails, "What will I do now?"

And what do you know if it ain't old hard-rock LaShaWanda P. Marshall who slips an arm around Edna's waist, turns her toward the house, and starts her up the path. "Here's what we're gonna do. First we're going to have a cup of coffee and get Marvini to fix us one of his big-ass breakfasts. Then you're going to take a long, hot bubble bath, and after that, I'm going to get you just what you need. Some sexual healing."

36

"DICK DIXMOOR, YOU OWE ME AN EXPLANATION! WHAT HAVE YOU been up to in the pantry?" Muffin shouts to be heard above the roar of the helicopter as Dick alights. Behind him, Barbaralee Edison jumps to the ground, a small tape recorder in hand and her silver hair and matching cat suit glittering in the sun.

"So this is A Sister's Spa," she says, looking around. "Where's T. Terry? I figured we can all sit down civilly and decide which one of you can afford my services."

"What the hell's she doing with Dixmoor?" I whisper to Lydia.

"I don't know, but I'm sure they're both up to no good."

"Muffin, dearest, what is the matter?" Dick says in his squeaky voice, arms outstretched. Muffin swats him away.

"Don't 'Muffin dearest' me, Dick. We have you on tape messing around with the supplies in the pantry. I want an explanation." Dick looks momentarily uncomfortable.

"Muffin, dearest. You know how I feel about healthy foods. I was just checking the food stuffs to make sure the workers were receiving the finest nutrients possible."

"Funny, I've never seen you in the kitchen in any of our houses; you give instructions and leave the rest to the cooks. Now you're suddenly hands on? Something stinks, Dick." An affronted, victimized expression appears on his face.

"I cannot believe you're saying this, Muffin, you who always told me to be less aloof, *more* hands on . . ."

"It's the oatmeal, he's putting something in the oatmeal!" A voice calls, and we turn to see Odell trotting towards us.

"I checked the dates he's been here and looked at the corresponding tapes," he says, standing before us and breathing hard. "It seems that every time he visited he snuck into the pantry when Marvini was in the garden or on a break and put some sort of white powder into the cans of oatmeal."

"What the fuck?" Lydia says.

"Then I checked with the men with erection problems. Remember we were looking for a common denominator? Well, the common denominator is that every one of them has oatmeal for breakfast," Odell finishes triumphantly.

"Well, I'll be damned," Acey says.

"Dick, explain yourself," Muffin commands a decidedly uncomfortable and silent Dick. I can tell by the expressions rapidly crossing his face that he's trying to think up a good lie, fast. "Oh, my God . . ." Muffin whispers, her eyes widening. "It's all about getting revenge on Griff-Margetson, isn't it?"

"I think he's invented a drug that makes men impotent and he's testing it out on our employees," Odell says.

"Why? I can't see men rushing out to buy that," I say.

"They won't have to," Muffin moans. "Don't you see? Dick owns Amanda Foods, they make everything: breakfast cereals, desserts, juices, meat products, snack foods, whatever you can think of. Need I go on?"

"No, no need," I say. "If men eat, they're playing limp dick roulette."

"Right," says Odell, "and I guarantee that the only way to bring those Johnsons back to life puts money in Dick's pocket . . ."

" . . . because as we've seen here, ViriMax is ineffective against whatever he's cooked up, and I would bet that the only antidote is patented by Dixmoor International," Acey says, figuring it all out.

"And probably expensive as hell. Even if it's covered by HMOs and other insurance plans, I guarantee Medicaid and Medicare won't pay for it, and what about the millions of people with no health insurance at all? It's brilliant. Think of how many black men, those 'superpredators' he's so worked up about, won't be able to afford the antidote," Odell says. "I guess you were right about 1-800-HEP-BROS, Lydia," he adds, turning to me. Dick Dixmoor doesn't say anything, just stands there looking simultaneously angry, guilty, and defiant. Muffin glares at him.

"They're right. Aren't they, Dick?" she finally says. "How could you exploit my friendship with Wanda this way, so you could use these poor men here as guinea pigs? Invent a drug that makes men impotent so they have to buy your antidote, so you can get revenge on Griff-Margetson? That's insane!" No longer daddy's good little girl, she towers over him, wagging her finger in his face and admonishing him like a bad little boy. "Most of all, how could you lie to me? You've broken your promise."

"Muffin honey, I'm a compassionate capitalist, not an altruist.

Haven't I done more good than harm? My money funded this place, made it possible for potential superpredators to find gainful employment and get off the streets. Isn't the next step testing out my impotence drug here? Don't you see, once it's in the foods I manufacture, the only men capable of having sex and producing babies will be those who can afford my antidote. Don't you realize what a step forward for mankind this is? Only those who can afford to take care of them can make babies. This is the moment, the beginning of the end of rampant fornication, unwanted pregnancy, and the world of the black superpredator as we know it," he declares rhapsodically.

"Genocide for the new millennium," Odell says.

"Damn, your husband's evil, but he's a smart bastard," Wanda mutters. Muffin nods, looking miserable.

"Cut the crap, Dick. I want the antidote, now," Muffin says, her voice icy. "Then I want you to close down the 1-800-HEP-BROS foundation."

"And let the grantees keep the money, no strings attached," Wanda chimes in.

"And this crazy drug research project has got to go," Muffin concludes.

"Why would I do that? I've got millions invested in this project. Come to your senses, Muffin," Dick sputters.

"Because if you don't, I'll send those videotapes to every news organization in the world, and I'm sure Barbaralee here will be happy to reveal your whole nefarious scheme in the pages of *Girlfriend!* And as we've seen from her attack on the spa, she's unscrupulous, unrelenting, and looking to get paid," Acey says. Barbaralee grins as if she's just received an NAACP Image Award. In her palm, the "on" button of her tape recorder glows red.

"That's right, and I don't come cheap."

"You and Dick can work that out on the way home," Muffin shrugs, turning away. "When you get there, Dick, I suggest you call your attorneys and tell them to start working out the details of a separation agreement. And I don't come cheap, either." She turns on her heels and starts toward the house. But before she takes more than a few steps, Lorene comes flying out of the back door waving a newspaper in one hand and yelling, "You have gotta read Jacques Westin's article in today's paper! You are not going to believe this shit!"

SUPERPREDATOR KILLED BY DIXMOOR WAS AUTOGRAPH HOUND
By Jacques Westin,
Amarillo, Texas

Sources in the office of the Texas Attorney General confirmed today that they are interested in questioning corporate mogul Dick Dixmoor about the circumstances surrounding the fatal shooting of a black man at an Amarillo, Texas, Dairy Queen earlier this year.

According to several sources, the attorney general's office, with the assistance of the FBI, recently succeeded in deciphering the words in the small book Dixmoor's alleged assailant brandished just before he was shot and killed. At the time, Dixmoor described the man's mannerisms as "menacing" and said he believed he had a gun. When told it was a notebook, he contended that the book contained plans to attack not only him but also other corporate leaders, an angle that law enforcement authorities had been pursuing while linguists worked to translate the writing in the book.

"It was an autograph book," said a highly placed source. "The scribblings weren't evidence of a conspiracy, but the signatures, often accompanied by good wishes, of Ronald Reagan, Rush Limbaugh, George H.W. Bush, George W. Bush, William F. Buckley, Trent Lott, George Will, and numerous other conservative Republicans. We think all this guy wanted from Dixmoor was an autograph."

In addition, FBI sources confirmed that they had finally identified the alleged assailant as Howard W. Collins, a black conservative who gained notoriety in the early 1980s when he ran for a Harlem congressional seat against socialite and activist Evangeline Worthington, who won a landslide victory. Collins charged the Republican Party with failing to support his candidacy, and was hospitalized for a year. He subsequently disappeared from the public arena.

Sources said they were making every effort to contact Dixmoor and are confident that he will surrender for questioning at his earliest convenience. The attorney general's office refused to confirm or deny that charges against Dixmoor are being considered.

37

A FEW WEEKS LATER, AFTER ALL THE DRAMA AT A SISTER'S SPA HAS subsided, Acey and I decide to go to Mombasa, Kenya and chill. I'd never been to Africa, but I'd read somewhere that the beaches in Mombasa are among the most beautiful in the world, and Acey said she didn't care where we went as long as it's hot and far, far away.

We asked Odell to accompany us, but he insisted on staying at the spa and took a rain check. All the publicity and controversy has been great for business, and he wanted to hire twenty more sex workers and have them trained and pleasuring women by the time we got back. I guess Odell's role helping us build a successful business worked out great for him. No one could call him a sex object now, though he *was* a fabulous lover. I'm hoping to coax him out of semi-retirement to play Tea Cake to my Janie Starks when we get back.

We invited LaShaWanda to join us, too, but she declined, pointing out in that way only Wanda can that, "I know you sisters are tired, but now that you've beat back the devil, someone still has to make sure our piece of heaven doesn't go to shit." Besides, Claudia Powell had given her a bunch of documents and she'd hired an attorney to pursue Julius Powell and the $2 million McGruder Forbes had taken from her, so there was no way she was gonna leave the USA.

Jacques Westin, whose work we thought had been so honest and fair, asked if he could spend some time at the spa to work on a series of articles about changing sexual mores and black women entrepreneurs. Of course we said okay, and asked Wanda to help him in any way she could. The last we saw of the two of them, she was leading Jacques toward her room and saying, "In order to really understand the unique service to women we supply here, pleasure on women's terms, I'm going to take you through the training all our employees receive." Jacques, an enormous grin on his face, was trotting along behind her. For once, he didn't have a reporter's notebook in his hand.

Muffin stayed at A Sister's Spa to help Odell and Wanda keep things rolling and figure out what her life sans Dick might become. He was begging her for forgiveness and sending gorgeous bouquets of exotic flowers on a daily basis, in between trying to explain to law enforcement exactly why he'd shot Howard Collins. But Muffin's time at the spa wasn't all work and difficult decisions. The last we saw, Sequoia was striding down the road toward one of the new cottage structures we've built, looking like John Henry or some such, carrying a fabulous arrangement of birds of paradise sent by Dick, and she was standing in the doorway waiting for him, grinning to beat the band.

Once their suspension was over, DeJuan, DeQuan, and DeMon decided to go back to UNLV, but resigned from the basketball team in order to focus on their studies. Even though they were juniors, they'd never declared a major, and because they were basketball players, no one ever asked them to. Inspired by their time working at A Sister's Spa, DeMon and DeQuan became business majors, while DeJuan chose film. They'd become so popular with our clients that we asked them to work at the spa on weekends, and they agreed. That way Odell could continue to keep an eye on them.

As for Exultia Wallace and the F.U. troops, after much negotiation we decided to designate one three-day weekend a month at A Sister's Spa for white women only. We weren't persuaded by Exultia's arguments that integration now was the way to go, but making a space for white women did make economic, political, and feminist sense. All women can use a little sexual healing, and the Feminists United sisters did have our backs at high noon.

One morning we woke Chef Marvini early, and the three of us piled the forty-four remaining cans of McGinley's Oatmeal in the pick-up truck, drove it all out to the desert, and buried it. Afterward, Marvini insisted that we smoke the peace pipe, so we shared a joint and got stoned, just like we used to in college. Then we told Marvini never to cook oatmeal again in this life, and asked him to keep an eye on Lorene and keep everyone well fed while we were gone. Of course he agreed, still apologizing about allowing Dixmoor into his kitchen and being tricked by him. We assured him it wasn't his fault, and by the time we'd sobered up, I think he believed us.

Then we threw a few things in our bags, called a limo, and got on the plane for Nairobi. The next thing we knew the flight attendant was waking us up for landing.

In the taxi from the airport, I babble excitedly and try to distract Acey as we pass Fort Jesus, a pentagon-shaped fortress built in the sixteenth century by the Portuguese, surrounded by a forty-foot-deep moat. She ignores me and stares out the window impassively as we pass by while I hold my breath. All she says is, "Fort Jesus, now that's a misnomer. More violence done in the name of organized religion," and rolls her window down to catch the sea breeze.

The Serenity Beach Hotel is on Shanzu Beach, on Mombasa's north coast. I chose it because in the guide book it was rated five elephants, the Kenyan equivalent of stars, and had everything: ocean, pool, five restaurants, full spa, masseuse, golf course, even a beauty salon in case Acey wanted to change her hairstyle after a few days. As tired as we are, I wanted a place we'd have no need to leave for anything.

"I'm going to put on my suit, find a cold drink, a chaise, and an empty spot on that gorgeous beach, and not move until I'm starving," Acey says, standing on the terrace outside our suite and looking at the ocean's deep azure water and white sand.

"I'm there. Let me go take a shower, change, and I'll find you on the beach," I say, turning toward the bathroom door. That's when Acey grabs my arm.

"Lyds, we did it, huh? We built our business, fought for it, and won, didn't we?"

"We sure as hell did, Ace. I couldn't have done it without you, either."

"You won't have to. That's why we're best friends, right?" she says, and gives me a long hug.

I take a slow shower, put on my bathing suit, and walk along the beach barefoot, the fine ivory sand like a cushion beneath my feet, admiring the brilliant red, orange, and yellow tropical flowers on my right, the flawless blue water on my left. I must have traveled over a mile before I finally reach Acey, who's managed to conjure up two lounge chairs and a thermos of a delicious fruity, frosty drink. Our own private oasis, with no other humans in sight.

I drop my beach bag and towel, slather myself with sunscreen, and lie down. We're in that companionable silence between best friends, that place where we communicate without words. It feels so familiar we could be on Acey's deck in Oakland except for the smell of salt and spice in the ocean air. The only sound is the seductive swoosh as waves break gently against the beach and the rustling of palm fronds in the wind. The sun is hot, the breeze is cool, and, at long last, all's right with our world.

"Excuse me, sisters," a deep, melodious voice punctures the silence. I open my eyes, but all I can see is the outline of a male form, since the light behind him is blinding. I put a hand over my brow as he moves away from the sun so that I can see him without squinting. Simultaneously, both Acey and I gasp. Standing before us is the most beautiful man I have ever laid eyes on. He is a deep blue-black, with that flawless skin that refracts color, high sculpted cheekbones, sparkling eyes, perfect white teeth, full lips. His hair is cut close to his beautifully shaped head. Broad shoulders taper to a slim waist, narrow hips, and a pair of long, muscled legs, between which is a bulge that demands, no, commands, respect. If I'd known Africa's called the Motherland because it's the source from which all fine men spring, I would have visited sooner. Acey and I stare up at this African Adonis who's materialized in front of us. I know my mouth's open and hell, I may be drooling. He's beyond fine.

"May I help you?" Acey finally manages to say.

"I don't mean to intrude, but I thought you ladies might like a guide to Mombasa's nightlife." When he says nightlife I can feel the muscles of Miss Kitty contract. From the look on Acey's face, I bet she can, too.

Acey glances at me and chuckles. I giggle, and soon we're both laughing so hard our titties shake, thighs jiggle, and tears run down our cheeks.

"Is something humorous?" Afrodonis asks politely.

"No, sorry. We don't mean to be rude," Acey chokes out when she stops laughing.

"It's just that we're on vacation," I say.

"And not interested in any 'nightlife,'" Acey finishes.

"Ahh. I understand. Sorry to have disturbed you. Enjoy your stay in Mombasa," he says, turning to walk away. That's when we catch sight of his high, tight, perfect ass. Do Jesus.

"Wait!" I command, then reach into my bag, pull out a photocopied sheet, and hand it to him. "If you're interested, leave it at the front desk at the Serenity," I say as he walks slowly away.

"What'd you give him?" Acey asks, sinking back in her chair and slipping on her shades.

"An application to work at A Sister's Spa," I say. Acey laughs.

"Well, if he ever gets to Nevada, I'll definitely give him a job. And a try-out," she giggles.

"He may not have to travel all that way." That's when Acey sits straight up, reaches over and, not for the first time, digs those perfect nails into my forearm.

"Lydia, what's on your mind? I know you've got some damn idea in your head. Give it up."

"Ouch." I gently pry her fingers from my arm. "I was just thinking. Once you have a successful product, a customer base, and an established brand name, the next thing you want to do is franchise . . ."

THE END

ACKNOWLEDGMENTS

Thanks to the staff of the MacDowell Colony for solitude, support, and great food, and to Stanford Calderwood for endowing the perfect studio. Also to the Perry family and the posse at the Renaissance Room in Peterborough, New Hampshire, who shared their friendship, fantasies, and much good cheer. Giddy up, ladies.

I appreciate the support of the Humanities Division and the Department of Media and Communication Arts of The City College of New York, especially Professors Linda Prout and Margaret Bates.

Also thanks to Janet Hill, my editor at Doubleday, for her patience and understanding. And to my online editors, Joan Connell at MSNBC.com and Teresa Ridley at NiaOnline.com.

To my editor, publisher, and friend Doug Seibold of Agate, whose courage, commitment, and brilliant editing made this book not only possible but also immeasurably better, thanks, once again, for getting it.

I am grateful to my family of women friends: each of you defines what friendship and faith really mean. Finally, eternal gratitude to my mother, A'Lelia Ransom Nelson, a true queen among women, whose grand sense of humor and frankness made this book possible.

Jill Nelson is also the author of the bestselling *Volunteer Slavery*, which won an American Book Award, and *Straight, No Chaser*, and the editor of the anthology *Police Brutality*. She lives in Harlem.

SUGGESTED READER'S GROUP QUESTIONS FOR *SEXUAL HEALING*

1. *Sexual Healing* is Jill Nelson's first novel. She is best known for her book *Volunteer Slavery*, in which she writes about her experience as a journalist. In what ways do you think her background as a journalist and social commentator influenced her writing as a novelist?

2. When Earl appears for the first time in Chapter 2, he vaguely describes some differences between Acey's Christian understanding of God and the reality of the spiritual world. What is Acey's reaction? Why is this dialogue important to the context of the novel as a whole?

3. Chapter by chapter, the novel's point of view shifts, primarily between the first-person perspectives of Lydia and Acey, but also to a close third-person point of view centered on other characters. How do you think this affected your perception of the story and the characters? If the novel had been written from one fixed point of view, how do you think it would have changed the story?

4. What do you think of the novel's sex scenes? Do they, in your opinion, have literary significance (for example, do they tie into the plot or play upon any themes), or are they more or less intended titillate?

5. Some reviewers suggested that Jill Nelson created T. Terry Tiger by combining characteristics of real-life people. What famous Americans do you think he is intended to parody? Which of their characteristics are the focus of Nelson's satire, and what is your reaction to them?

6. Do you think that A Sister's Spa could work in reality? What kinds of problems would arise with its creation? What if it were available to all women?

7. Nelson describes many obstacles that African-American women face in today's society. What do you think of her commentary on the competition between black men and women?

8. Chapter 12 is the employment application for A Sister's Spa. Do you think that it covers all the attributes desirable for a competent sex worker? What parts, if any, would you change? What questions would you add?

9. What purposes does the character of Dick Dixmoor serve within the novel's plot? What themes regarding contemporary America does his character introduce or expand?

10. A large number of minor characters make brief appearances throughout the book. Which ones did you enjoy the most and why?

11. Would you agree with Lydia and Acey's justification of the exclusivity of A Sister's Spa, or do you think it seems more like reverse discrimination?

12. If you are female, would you frequent A Sister's Spa? If you are male, would you work there? Why or why not?